# Any Wicked Thing

# Any Wicked Thing

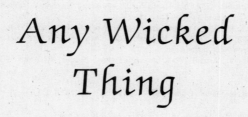

MARGARET ROWE

HEAT / NEW YORK

THE BERKLEY PUBLISHING GROUP
Published by the Penguin Group
Penguin Group (USA) Inc.
375 Hudson Street, New York, New York 10014, USA
Penguin Group (Canada), 90 Eglinton Avenue East, Suite 700, Toronto, Ontario M4P 2Y3, Canada
(a division of Pearson Penguin Canada Inc.)
Penguin Books Ltd., 80 Strand, London WC2R 0RL, England
Penguin Group Ireland, 25 St. Stephen's Green, Dublin 2, Ireland (a division of Penguin Books Ltd.)
Penguin Group (Australia), 250 Camberwell Road, Camberwell, Victoria 3124, Australia
(a division of Pearson Australia Group Pty. Ltd.)
Penguin Books India Pvt. Ltd., 11 Community Centre, Panchsheel Park, New Delhi—110 017, India
Penguin Group (NZ), 67 Apollo Drive, Rosedale, North Shore 0632, New Zealand
(a division of Pearson New Zealand Ltd.)
Penguin Books (South Africa) (Pty.) Ltd., 24 Sturdee Avenue, Rosebank, Johannesburg 2196,
South Africa

Penguin Books Ltd., Registered Offices: 80 Strand, London WC2R 0RL, England

This book is an original publication of The Berkley Publishing Group.

This is a work of fiction. Names, characters, places, and incidents either are the product of the author's imagination or are used fictitiously, and any resemblance to actual persons, living or dead, business establishments, events, or locales is entirely coincidental. The publisher does not have any control over and does not assume any responsibility for author or third-party websites or their content.

PRINTING HISTORY
Heat trade paperback edition / March 2011

Library of Congress Cataloging-in-Publication Data

Rowe, Margaret.
    Any wicked thing / Margaret Rowe. — Heat trade paperback ed.
        p. cm.
    ISBN 978-0-425-23864-6
    1. Family secrets—Fiction. 2. England—Fiction. I. Title.
PS3618.O8729A84 2011
813'.6—dc22
                            2010042110

PRINTED IN THE UNITED STATES OF AMERICA

10  9  8  7  6  5  4  3  2  1

*For my girls:*
*Sarah, Jessie, Abby, Ely, Kris and Tiff*

# Any Wicked Thing

# Chapter 1

*He has not changed a bit. Except to become more handsome. ~~I hate him.~~*

—FROM THE DIARY OF FREDERICA WELLS

"What is the point?" Sebastian Goddard, reluctant heir to the duchy of Roxbury, looked around the long gallery with disfavor after a particularly adept *attacque du fer*. Grim and grimy portraits of gentlemen who thankfully were not his ancestors glared down from the castle walls. Motes of dust swirled in weak shafts of light, stirred up as he fenced with his oldest friend, who seemed to be wearing a patched pair of pants that he'd cast off after a growth spurt at Eton. He spared his opponent nothing, and it took a bit for her to catch a breath to answer.

"I rather think it's at the end of your sword, Sebastian. That sharp thing."

"I didn't say where; I said what, Freddie. Why would he buy this dump when there's a reasonably good house at Roxbury Park?" He executed a perfect flying parry. Freddie overcompensated, slipped and landed on her well-padded bottom on the hard stone floor with a thump.

He was a cur to engage her, but she had insisted on swordplay to start the day. An insistent Frederica Wells was, in his long-suffering experience, impossible to ignore. He was more than a foot taller and several stones heavier, a visitor to the finest *salle d'armes* in Great Britain and the continent, fit and fresh from his lengthy grand tour after a lackluster year at university. His father had sent him off with a private tutor in the hopes of civilizing him, but Sebastian had become crafty ditching the old bird. In fact, for the last four months Sebastian had been wholly on his own. Mr. Tetley had thrust a purse at him at the acropolis in Athens and washed his hands of him, preferring the duke's wrath to one more day with his scapegrace son.

Freddie had been stuck at home as all girls were, no doubt singing and painting and doing other useless things. Her fencing skills had improved some from the last time they went at it, but poor Freddie looked like she'd had two too many lemon tarts thrice daily. He recalled they were her favorite. Even at eighteen, she had not lost her baby fat. Her freckled face was red from exertion, but she grinned up at him like a cheerful pixie as he pulled her to her feet.

She pushed a sweat-soaked brown braid behind her ear. "You know your father's love of all things medieval. How could he resist? Didn't he tell you all about it yesterday?"

"If he did, I was not paying attention. You know how he bores me." The pater had rambled on yesterday about some of the structure dating to the eleventh century, not that Sebastian cared. Gray rock was gray rock, and his mind had drifted to visions of boiling oil or molten lead being poured down through the machicolations on the old man. At twenty-one, Sebastian saw nothing but the duke's disinterest in anything contemporary, including himself. His father had preferred to spend his time with his secretary and their dusty tomes and broken relics rather than his only son. The men traveled all over Europe outrunning Boney himself in their quest for medieval miscellany.

"Well, the story of Goddard Castle is not boring in the least," Freddie said, her eyes lighting.

*Blast.* It seemed she had been bitten by the history bug as well. *Goddard Castle* indeed. The Archibald family crest and motto was stamped on virtually every flat surface. The castle was originally home to the Earls of Archibald, and had been called Archibald Castle until his father had the hubris to rename it after himself. "I suppose you're going to give me a lecture now, aren't you, brat?"

"Your tutor gave a thorough report. I know you care nothing for history, so I won't waste my time trying to enlighten you if he couldn't," Freddie said, taking no trouble to mask her superiority. "But we are at war with the French, so even a blockhead like you might see the fascination in this tale. But never mind. I'm sure you have plans for the morning. Seducing housemaids and whatnot."

She stomped off in the direction of the armory to return her foil. He followed, amused by the sway of her backside. His old breeches looked fairly good on her.

"I know you're dying to tell me," he called after her. "You never could keep your mouth shut for any length of time."

She turned like a clockwork gear, as he knew she would. "Go to the devil, Sebastian Goddard!"

"Already there, Freddie." He smiled at her, hoping she wouldn't decide to raise her weapon and run him through. He leaned against a leaded window, praying it would hold his weight.

Her blue-gray eyes narrowed. "You have not changed one bit."

"Au contraire. The past two years abroad have been very educational."

"I'll bet. Not that I would ever know. You never wrote."

"I'm sure I did a time or two." But most of the things he'd seen and done could not be divulged to a young lady in a letter. He supposed Freddie qualified as a young lady. From the way her chest heaved, it seemed she had grown breasts. "But you're right about the war. It was difficult to find accommodations that Corsican upstart hadn't mucked with."

"Your father was worried."

Sebastian rather doubted that, but held his tongue. He really was too old to be rebelling and railing against the pater. He'd turn into a cliché if he wasn't careful.

"Yet here I am, not a hair on my head harmed." Sebastian fluffed some up. He was rather proud of his hair. It was dark, thick and curly. Women loved to run their fingers through it, and he loved letting them.

"He's very glad you're home."

"This isn't home, Freddie, and never will be." Sebastian thought the castle, whatever it was called, was the gloomiest place he'd ever seen. Parts of Yorkshire were indeed beautiful, but no one could ever claim Goddard Castle was. It rose on its motte from a bare landscape like a set of blind giant's blocks. Even in its prime, Sebastian was sure it had been ugly. There was no sense of symmetry, and more than half the structure lay in ruins, even after more than a year of his father's occupation.

Sebastian wiped his brow with the back of his sleeve and gazed out. He counted two twisted trees and three oozy black patches in the brutal sweep of land beyond the fallen curtain wall from this vantage point alone. Thank heavens his father had filled in the moat, or he'd be tempted to drown himself. He did not know how he was going to survive this visit with his father without resorting to drink, drugs or murder. Fortunately, he'd come prepared.

He sighed. "Go on. I know you're salivating to tell me about the castle. You're bristling like a terrier after a rat."

"Hello, rat," she said, suddenly sunny again. She slid to the floor opposite, propping the blade up against the stone wall, and crossed her ankles. No, she was not a young lady yet.

"I'll skip ahead through the centuries, although the Archibalds played a large role in the Pilgrimage of Grace in 1536."

Sebastian looked at her blankly. He was no pilgrim.

"You know, the uprising over Henry the Eighth dissolving the monasteries. No? No matter. Anyway, the Archibalds have always been a prominent Catholic family in this part of the world. Some say that's why the last Earl of Archibald sided with the French, but I think he was just in it for the money. He ran the largest spy ring in Britain!"

Sebastian perked up. Money was always of interest to him. There was never enough of it, especially when his father kept spending his on ruined castles.

"What did he do with his blood money? He obviously didn't use it to repair this place."

"No one knows. But for years, all sorts of traitors walked these halls making their evil plans," Freddie said with enthusiasm.

"And dodged the falling timbers," Sebastian replied. "Bloody dangerous work, spying for the Earl of Archibald."

Freddie laughed. "We've found no bodies. But people do say the castle is haunted."

"Utter rubbish. What became of the treasonous earl?"

"He was stripped of his title and lands for colluding with the French, and threw himself off the roof, plummeting to his death into the slimy water surrounding the keep to avoid the hangman's noose," she said with a dramatic flourish.

"Bloodthirsty wench." While Sebastian had been traveling, his father had paid the Crown what Sebastian considered to be a fortune for the property and renamed it. Who had been madder—old King

George, the Earl of Archibald or Phillip Goddard, seventh Duke of Roxbury? It was a near thing, one Sebastian was glad he wouldn't have to judge. He was not particularly impartial.

"So that's the recent history of Goddard Castle. And now your family has a chance to add to it."

"I won't be here long enough. As soon as this damned house party is over, I'm leaving." His father was in alt about refurbishing the castle, but as far as Sebastian was concerned, the place was still a death trap.

"Your father is tremendously excited, you know," Freddie said, interrupting his brooding. "He and my father have been closeted in the library for weeks making plans. There's to be a fancy dress ball tonight. What will you wear, Sebastian?"

"Evening clothes, I expect. Dressing in disguise is for children on All Hallows' Eve."

Freddie's brows knit. "Spoilsport. I bet you a shilling you will not recognize me."

"I haven't a shilling to spare, brat. Travel is ruinously expensive, you know."

Freddie scrambled up and joined him at the window. The view did not seem to trouble her, but she must be used to it after living here for a while. "Was it very wonderful?"

Sebastian noted the wistfulness in her voice. He wasn't about to tell her all the "wonderful" things he'd seen and done—her definition of wonderful would doubtless differ from his.

"It was all right. A pity I had to miss Paris and Parisian ladies, but I made do. You know I thought about enlisting so I could conquer France sooner."

Freddie nodded. "Uncle Phillip was quite upset when he received that letter."

"So upset he dictated *his* letter to your father to write for him. I don't believe I'd even recognize His Grace's handwriting." Poor Wells must have had fits translating his father's rage to paper.

"An heir to a dukedom can't risk getting shot at."

"Why ever not? It's not as though the Dukes of Roxbury have ever amounted to much. I daresay the Archibalds on the wall over there are more useful, except for the last one."

"You have obligations. Responsibilities."

Sebastian snorted. "Like my father? If he turned up in the House of Lords, not a soul would recognize him. He hasn't been to Roxbury Park in ages. The place is going to rack and ruin. I stopped there before I came north." And discovered his father had bought himself a castle.

"Oh, dear. I didn't know."

He and Freddie had run wild at Roxbury Park, at least until his mother died. After that, he was mostly farmed out to relatives, or spent holidays at school with masters who were paid extra to watch him. He'd had a lonely childhood, but then, so had Freddie. She had no mother at all to remember, and a father who jumped at the sound of his father's command and left her behind when he carried the duke's valises from one antiquarian auction to the next.

"So don't lecture me. You haven't the first idea of what's what in this world."

Freddie punched his arm with a fist. "Next you will tell me I'm 'just' a girl. You are the same insufferable, conceited ass you always were."

"And you love me for it, brat." Sebastian stepped backward, expecting another blow, but Freddie was still as a stone, her fists clenched, her face crimson. "Steady. You know I'm only teasing you. Come, let's put our weapons away, swords and tongues both. I believe I have housemaids to corrupt, do I not? Do you have any recommendations amongst the staff?"

This time she aimed higher, but Sebastian pivoted and protected his jaw. "Have pity, Freddie. My face is my fortune. How am I to marry an heiress if you maim me? She'll have to be filthy rich to cover all my debts and the pater's besides."

"I feel sorry for the poor wretch already. You'll make a miserable husband."

"I agree, and have no intention of becoming one anytime soon. Good Lord, you don't suppose the old boy's invited prospective brides here for me, do you? Perhaps I will have to wear a disguise after all. I can go as a hunchback. A leper."

Freddie walked across the gallery to pick up her foil. "I can tell them you're disgusting, if that will help keep them at bay."

"Capital! Mention all my vices. Make some up when you run out."

She looked at him with scorn, then set off down the hall. "I won't need to dissemble. You've given me plenty to work with."

"Freddie, Freddie. Such a shrew you are. And I thank you for it."

They entered the armory, a vast space newly filled with deadly and deteriorating weaponry. Standing on tiptoe, she tried unsuccessfully to return the sword to its bracket.

"Here, brat, I'll do it. I take it you've stopped growing."

"Only vertically. There seems to be no limit to the horizontal," she muttered.

"You'll find some man who likes you as you are. As long as you don't talk." And with that parting shot, he found it prudent to jog away from her and run through the warren of corridors and stairwells to his room. There was not a thing to do up here but wait for the masquerade party to commence tonight. Sebastian had met some of the guests over breakfast—not a soul was younger than fifty. A few more were arriving today, but no doubt they would be equally ancient. The duke had the clever idea of housing most of them in the dungeons.

Sebastian really couldn't distinguish the dungeons' condition from the bedchambers'——everything was primitive. Sebastian's own room was as spare as a monk's cell, although he had noted his father's to be filled with all the trappings of comfort. A massive gilt bed. Tapestries hanging on the walls. Carpets. And chairs whose upholstery was not fraying. Quite a difference from the rest of the dwelling.

But Sebastian would never spend a minute in the duke's room. Once the pater popped off, this castle and all its contents would be sold to the highest bidder.

Sebastian rummaged through his traveling trunk and found what he needed to pass the day. He filled his pipe with hashish, saving the opium for later, once the festivities began. His grand tour had been, as he told Freddie, very educational. He'd picked up a few bad habits and was glad of it. A mellowing of his senses came in handy when he had to encounter his father for any length of time.

Not that he often had. The duke was much too busy with other things. He was very good at ordering Sebastian about from a distance, but, when confronted with him in person, tended to retreat into his library or abscond on a trip. He'd given Sebastian a quick tour of the castle yesterday, more to spout off knowledge than welcome his only son home after two years.

No matter. Sebastian would make his own fun. There might be a wayward wife to seduce, or Freddie to torment. The evenings ahead were likely to be a dead bore, but he could endure it for a few days.

He took a deep draft of his pipe, felt the lassitude creep into his limbs. Yes, he could endure it. Especially knowing that in two days' time, he'd never see Goddard Castle again if he could help it.

# Chapter 2

*The worst night of my life.*
—FROM THE DIARY OF SEBASTIAN GODDARD,
MARQUESS OF DEANE

*The worst night of my life.*
—FROM THE DIARY OF FREDERICA WELLS

The castle was ablaze with candles. Sebastian wondered how much of his patrimony was tied up in tallow. People had taken his father's intentions to heart, and were arrayed in a variety of absurd costumes. The duke's authentic mail vest and spurs clinked every time he moved about the banquet hall, which had had been set up as in days of yore, its usual dining table dismantled and a dais built at one end of the room. Plain wooden benches and tables were set in rows; plain wooden trenchers served as plates; plain wooden goblets held mead and ale. His father had commissioned local carpenters to make all this useless stuff, at what cost Sebastian could only imagine and cringe.

"What do you think? Isn't it marvelous?" Freddie was at his elbow at one of the lower tables, wearing an unfortunate pink velvet dress that looked very much like a discarded curtain. With one hand, she balanced a pointed hat on her head, its veil falling over half her face.

The other half was obscured by a pink silk mask, but Sebastian would know her anywhere.

"I think it's ridiculous." He grabbed a whiskey from a passing footman. At least he was not forced to drink the medieval swill. "What's your pleasure, Freddie?"

She squinted through her veil at the tray. Impatiently, Sebastian snatched the hat from her head, so that she was now merely covered by what looked like a linen bandage wrapped around her hair and chin. The waiting footman averted his eyes in pity.

"Sebastian!"

"Freddie, you haven't moved from this spot in hours. You haven't even been able to cut your meat one-handed. The hat is a disaster. Admit it."

"You have no idea how long it took me to make it," she said crossly. "A woman was not permitted to wear her hair uncovered. It was considered a sin."

"It's a sin in this day and age to adhere to such silly rules. Take the rest of that stuff off."

Muttering, Freddie unwrapped the linen to reveal a rumpled coronet of braids.

"There! Much better. Now. Champagne or ratafia?"

Freddie rubbed her hands in nervousness. "I don't know. I've never had either."

"What! Impossible. You really have led a sheltered life. Hm." He tapped his chin. "Champagne is apt to go straight to your head on an empty stomach. I'd advise the ratafia." He took two glasses and set them in front of her.

Freddie took a suspicious sniff. "Apricots."

"Yes, fruit. Good for you. How can one abstain? Drink up. I can't believe you're still sober. I know I'm not."

"As does everyone else. You've been quite rude tonight."

"Oh, don't go all governessy on me, brat. Bad enough the old man is giving me the eye. What's next on the agenda now that we've eaten the wild boar?"

"It was only Farmer Easton's pig. Two of them, actually."

"You never touched your bream and eel pasty."

Freddie shuddered. "I have more enthusiasm for the wardrobe of the Middle Ages than the menu. The frumenty wasn't bad. You can't go wrong with honey and raisins."

"Porridge by any other name. And impossible to eat with a knife. Just like my father to forgo the bloody forks for us peasants." Sebastian set his elbows on the table. "I'm afraid I've had enough, Freddie. Of the food and the company. Oh, not you," he said quickly, seeing her hurt expression. "You've been an amusing dinner companion, for all you didn't eat your dinner. But I'm for bed. Care to join me?"

Freddie blushed as brightly as her hideous dress. "Not if you were the last man on earth. And there's to be a scavenger hunt. You won't want to miss that."

"How old are we? Eleven?"

Just then his father tapped his crystal goblet at the dais and the room fell still. No wooden drinking vessel for the Duke of Roxbury. Sebastian leaned back as the duke rambled on about Goddard Castle through the centuries. He was so long-winded Freddie drank both her glasses during the speech, so Sebastian flagged down another footman for her. Her cheeks were rosy and her eyes gleamed in the candlelight. The poor little thing was getting drunk for the very first time.

He stumbled up when the talk got around to the scavenger hunt and its rules. Sebastian always broke rules when he could, and the quest for a mock unicorn held no interest for him. He whispered to

Freddie that he was leaving, and she waved him away. She sat transfixed at his father's nonsense, an odd smile on her face.

When faced with the four stone walls of his little room, he had a desire to escape. He changed into an elegant striped robe, a souvenir from a grateful Italian widow, stashing his comforting brandy flask in a pocket. He made his way through the Byzantine halls of the castle by flickering candlelight, carrying a tooled leather case with his smoking utensils inside. Precious balls of poppy resin mixed with headache powder rattled around between the implements, promising peace.

His father had warned the guests about the north tower. It was unsafe, therefore off-limits for the foolish revelers. There was a rope with threatening signage blocking the steps, which Sebastian cleared easily even though he was more than a bit drunk himself. Soon he would be entirely at one with the universe. A universe where his father was in a different galaxy altogether.

He gave up counting the steps, but there were many. They were worn and slippery beneath his bare feet. Once he reached the top, he found himself in an odd-shaped room with half its ceiling gone. The black Yorkshire sky was sprinkled with stars winking down on him, cementing his idea he was rather insignificant in the grand scheme of things. He swept away some rubble and settled in the window alcove, or what would have been a window if it was still intact. A pleasant summer breeze swept through the space, nearly clearing his muzzy head. That would not do.

With the sort of patience his father would apply to reconstructing a medieval document from fragments, Sebastian opened his case and heated his metal needle, turning a pea-sized lump of opium into a cone. Holding his pipe over the flame, he warmed it, then placed the cone into the bowl. Some of his friends skipped all these laborious steps and simply wrapped the opium in rice paper and inserted it into their rectums, but Sebastian respected the traditional way. The ritual was nearly as compelling as the smoke. He inhaled deeply.

Heaven. Or hell. Opium was highly addictive. He felt the need for it more urgently every day, especially since he was now subject to his father's disapproval. His supply was limited, and not apt to be replenished in Yorkshire. He could fob himself off with drink or hashish for a time, but this was his greatest, most sinful pleasure.

He took the flask from his pocket and drank, feeling the heat of the brandy dance with the cool detachment of the drug. Sebastian no longer felt insignificant but invincible now, like a prototype of mankind. He removed his robe, rolling it up under his head, and stared at the night sky. So many stars, so far away. How many men had seen the same grouping of constellations since the world began? Perhaps as many as the stars themselves. He sipped and puffed until the stars spun.

His cock called to him. It had been some weeks since he'd had a woman, an unnatural state for a man of one and twenty in full possession of his wild oats. He wrapped his hand around his shaft and set his imagination free. There was no shame to it. He was halfway to stroking himself to completion when the masked milkmaid tiptoed in.

At first he thought she was part of his opium dream. She was a fetching piece, her hair covered by a ruffly mobcap, her skirts hiked up to reveal her garters. Her girdle was laced so tightly that her breasts burst over the trim on her low-cut blouse. But she was not his usual fantasy. If she blushed, it was hard to tell for her powder and rouge under the black mask. Her lush mouth opened. She had a naughty beauty patch at the corner of her reddened lips. Sebastian had an urge to kiss it off.

He didn't miss a stroke. "Hello, darling. You must be my reward for bad behavior. Do you want to help me finish this properly?"

Her eyes widened and she gave a strangled gasp, not at all the sound he preferred from his ladies. No doubt she was shocked. One of his father's dull guests was bound to be. This one looked a bit younger than most of the women downstairs. He hadn't noticed her at dinner, but then, he hadn't been looking hard.

"Come closer. You are much too far away."

She took a step forward and coughed.

"Don't mind the smoke. I'll share if you like."

The milkmaid shook her head so violently that her little cap fluttered.

"Very well, then. I trust you have no objection to a bit of brandy." He unfisted his cock and extended the flask, his arm moving in slow motion.

She kept her hands in the pockets of her apron. "You are wicked," she whispered.

"Very. Let me show you how much."

"I—I was looking for you."

Sebastian grinned. That was more like it. At least someone had taken note of him downstairs through the boring banquet. "Well, you've found me. What are you going to do with me?"

She was silent. Sebastian thought he might drift off to sleep before she finally spoke again. "H-have my way with you."

"Capital! As you see, I'm ready. Lift your skirts, love, and ride me."

She glided across the floor and blew out the candle. They were enveloped in the mystery and safety of darkness. When she kneeled over him, her breasts were close enough to lick, so he did. He didn't need light to know they were perfect in every way. To aid him, she untied her cotton blouse, and his hands filled with warm woman.

"Lovely," he sighed. "What does your husband think?"

She shrugged. "No one appreciates m-me."

She sounded so sad. "That's a pity. I promise, I shall appreciate every inch of you, as you will appreciate me."

She smelled of roses and ratafia. He grasped her corseted waist and planted her on top of him, smoothing all the ruffles away between them. He was nearly giddy—she was not wearing drawers, and he could felt the wet of her cunt on his skin. The hardness of her nipples under his thumbs lured him to kiss one, and then the other, suckling until she shook. One hand slid under her skirts and he slipped a finger through her curls into her passage. She was tight but soaked.

He could not wait. Well, he could, but why bother? She was a gift to him, one he deserved after being trapped here without his usual indulgences. He didn't need illumination to guide himself to her entrance, thrusting in as she bucked above him. For an instant, doubt crossed his mind, but then he imagined her rouged lips open with the slyest of smiles.

Somehow he'd seen that imagined smile before, and recently. He shook the doubt away as he buried himself in her warmth.

"You're like a cat at the cream, love. Do you like it?" He gasped.

"Oh, yes." Her voice was little more than a breath. Gripping her hips, he raised her up and down in a languid motion until she found her rhythm, and then she did all the work. Her cunt clenched his rod as if he'd been made for her. For a fleeting moment, he wondered who this skillful little lass was, and then she robbed him of thought altogether. There was nothing but the sound of their bodies gliding and slapping against each other, their breaths harsh, the stars twinkling above.

Some considered opium an aphrodisiac, but Sebastian knew better. It didn't so much heighten the performance as prolong it, although he was very much afraid he was about to embarrass himself. The milkmaid was relentless in milking him in record time. He surged up help-lessly and spilled into her.

Too soon. Too fast. Couldn't be helped. Perhaps he'd stay an extra day and give his father's naughty guest another go. Show her what he could really do when he was sober. He'd learned a lot when he was away. Wanted to learn more.

Oh, but she was hot around his cock. So sweet. She hovered over him uncertainly, as if she didn't know they were done. He pulled her down to kiss her, thank her, when the door opened and a shaft of lantern light beamed onto the bare stone floor. There was a shuffling of feet. The door closed, the bar sliding across with a snap, the sound echoing in the chamber.

She froze in his arms. Her heart thudded wildly, not simply in sat-isfaction, but terror. But they were in the alcove. Perhaps they wouldn't be discovered. He put a finger to her lips and felt her nod. Pray God it wasn't her husband.

And then his heart stopped.

"It's a grand success, Phillip. They'll be talking about this party for decades."

"Thanks to you. What would I do without you?"

There was a chuckle. "I hope you never find out. I wish to serve you the rest of your days. You need someone like me to keep you organized."

"Why don't I show you how much I appreciate you for a change? I do love you, you know. Always have."

There was a rustle of fabric, the clink of spurs, a hiss of pleasure. And then Sebastian fought to block the grunts and sighs from his mind. He lay like a dead thing, and almost wished he was.

They would have been fine, safe and still behind the corner, if the milkmaid hadn't lurched up and vomited all over him.

The sound of her helpless, seemingly endless retching brought the attention of the two lovers, and spared Sebastian from listening to his father suck another man's cock.

"What the devil? Who's there?"

In seconds, his father was standing over him with the lantern, his chain-mail vest glimmering. Freddie's father, dressed in a belted velvet and fur-trimmed robe, was a step behind him.

No one said anything for a long moment.

Sebastian would be hard-pressed to determine who was more upset, but then the milkmaid burst into tears and settled the issue.

"Frederica!" her father rasped.

*Freddie?* His lusty little milkmaid was Freddie?

Simply. Not. Possible.

The girl was scrambling to cover her breasts, a look of sheer mortification on her face. Her mask was askew, and a strand of golden brown hair had escaped from her ruffled mobcap. Sebastian reached up and ripped the black silk from her face.

It was difficult to keep one's composure, naked and covered in vomit, realizing one's life as one knew it was definitively over. He hadn't even kissed her mouth. The scent of apricot ratafia was nearly overwhelming, explaining so much. He and Freddie were foxed and would be forced to marry, but there was no excuse for his father and his secretary.

"I—I'm s-so s-sorry, Sebastian."

He ignored her. There were years ahead when he'd have to listen to her, but tonight was not one of them. He squinted up into his father's pale face.

"You could be hanged for your perversion."

"Do not threaten me, boy." His father's tone was icy. He was every inch the Duke of Roxbury, even if he had been on his knees a few minutes ago.

"Wells was in your employ long before my mother died. Did she know?"

His father stiffened. "She understood. She was a duchess. She had you, and was content."

Sebastian didn't believe that for a minute. "She was unhappy. Fool that I was, I blamed that on your preoccupation with this medieval shite. Now I know why you ignored us. Were you afraid I'd find out? Is that why you went away on one of your 'buying trips' every time I was home, sent me away every chance you could?"

"Don't whine, Sebastian. I've given you every educational advantage, not that you've been worth the blunt. Getting into one scrape after another. Cavorting with the lower classes." The duke flicked a dark eye on Freddie. "I see you have not changed."

"Don't worry. I'll marry her! I didn't even know who I was fucking."

The duke's lips thinned. "Charming. But you certainly will *not* marry her. The next Duchess of Roxbury must be one of the Upper Ten Thousand, with sufficient dowry to replenish the Roxbury coffers. Frederica is—is unsuitable, for all that she is a very nice girl." He laid a hand on his companion's arm. "I'm sorry, Joseph, but there it is. You of all people know how we are fixed. I can scrape together some money for Frederica's future, but she cannot be my daughter-in-law."

Sebastian felt an unaccountable rage. He'd just been spared a bullet—he would not be trapped into marriage as Freddie had no doubt intended—but he was not the least grateful. "So the father is good enough for you to fuck, but the daughter is *unsuitable* for me?"

"Don't be crude, Sebastian. Frederica, my dear, you are unwell. Do something about your bodice and go to your room. I'll speak to you in the morning about my arrangement for you."

Freddie tripped to her feet, clutching her gaping blouse. She gave

Sebastian an imploring look, her eyes filled with tears. He'd never seen her so miserable, not even when she had fallen out of a tree and broken her ankle when she was a child. He had carried her all the way home, watching her chin quiver trying to be brave. Now her tears flowed freely, leaving tracks in the paint on her face. Five minutes ago he'd thought she was a beauty. Now she was just Freddie.

"Is this what you want, Freddie? Money for your silence about his indiscretion and mine instead of an honorable offer of marriage?"

Her eyes dropped. "Your father is right. I—I cannot marry you."

*Adding insult to injury.* "Will you really sell yourself so cheap? After all your deception, it hardly seems worth your maidenhead. Unless I wasn't the first to begin with."

This proved too much for Joseph Wells. Sebastian's head snapped back against the stone floor from a surprisingly strong blow. He lay dazed as, one by one, his enemies left him alone in his puddle of vomit and semen.

His father was the last to leave. "I'll speak to you in the morning as well. We have numerous things to settle between us."

Sebastian counted the metallic rattle of the spurs to the door. He had wanted to see the stars. There were plenty now, whirling around the insides of his eyelids. If he could pull himself up from his ignominy, he would leave Goddard Castle tonight, even if he wound up falling off his horse into a ditch. He could not get much lower than he was already.

* * *

Frederica locked her bedroom door. After five minutes, her father ceased his pounding and pleading and went away. If he remained, he'd call attention to himself, as the guests were still scurrying through the hallways on their search for the blasted unicorn. She had crafted it herself out of papier-mâché, when the duke had teased she was the only virgin in the castle.

She was a virgin no longer, but she hadn't even been kissed well. She tipped the pitcher of water into her bowl and scrubbed between her legs, rubbing hard enough to flay off her skin. There was very little blood. She deserved more—enough to punish her for her folly and ruination.

It had not been Sebastian's fault. As she sat in the banquet hall, she did not think of hunting for the unicorn, but of hunting for Sebastian. He would be her virgin's prize. She'd gone upstairs and changed out of her princess finery into her second, rejected costume. The slutty milkmaid outfit was so very shocking she did not know what she had been thinking to sew it up. It was hellishly revealing and uncomfortable, as if she had had a bad fairy sitting on her shoulder urging her to use less fabric than was decent. She had laced herself so she could barely breathe and searched the castle until she found Sebastian in his stupor. Once she discovered he was not in his room, it had not been hard to locate him. He was in the one place everyone had been forbidden to go.

He was naked, doing the most salacious, unimaginable thing she had ever seen. She could have walked out when she came upon him in the north tower, but she had been unable to take her eyes away from his hand and his penis, even blinded by the smoke. He hadn't recognized her, masked and half-naked as she was. In the flickering candlelight with blinking stars overhead, she had become a different person. When she extinguished the candle, it had been so easy to whisper and flirt, climb atop him and take him into her body, ride him in the dark.

It had not quite been everything she'd dreamed of. Two illusions shattered in one night. Next she'd discover she was a changeling—some fairy's prank had placed her in the bosom of Sebastian's family to torment her. Maybe she was about to be snatched back from whence she came.

It might be better to disappear. How could she face anyone when they could not possibly understand? She had loved Sebastian most of her life, for all he went out of his way to bedevil her. But whatever she had dreamed of, she could not marry him now under such circumstances. He would hate her for trapping him, curdling whatever she felt until she'd be more alone in a marriage than she was now. Every time he looked at her, he would remember this night and its consequences, the knowledge that their fathers had a secret life their children had been too stupid to see.

Freddie loved her father. He was gentle and patient with her when he was home. But, of course, the duke—she had always called him "Uncle Phillip," as he claimed her as part of his household, and probably to annoy Sebastian—had always come first for him. Now she knew why. It wasn't only because they shared a passion for antiquities.

At first, she had not understood what she was hearing as Sebastian held her so tight she thought her ribs would snap. Then everything collided—the liquor, the risk, the knowledge. The ragged words her father uttered across the room, dropping like stones down a deep well. She had been dizzy, then shamefully sick all over Sebastian's exquisite body.

She had seen his disgust in the dim light. His hatred. They could never be friends again.

But she wouldn't take his father's bribe. Despite what Sebastian thought of her, money and consequence had never entered her mind as she slipped into the tower room. She did not think "marchioness, future duchess." She thought "lover," and, if the gods smiled on her, "wife." She hadn't meant to trap him, but to make him see her with fresh eyes. He'd seen too much.

Frederica wiped her face of the powder and rouge, rubbed the color from her lips. She would apologize to her father and the duke tomorrow. Make them understand that Sebastian had not been responsible. If Sebastian would listen, she would beg his forgiveness, too.

She dropped her soiled costume on the floor and went to the mirror. Bright red lines from the corseting streaked her lumpy body. She was a woman now, but looked no different than she had this morning.

She pulled a night rail from a drawer and climbed into bed. Against all odds, she fell asleep at once, the wine and the misery twinning to shut her eyes.

When she woke late the next morning, the guests had left. Including Sebastian.

# Chapter 3

*If he thinks he can come here and lord and master it over*
*me, he has another think coming.*
—FROM THE DIARY OF FREDERICA WELLS

"No and no and no."

"Frederica, you know you can't refuse to see him forever.
This is his house, after all." Mrs. Carroll spoke calmly, but Frederica
was not one bit fooled. Her companion preened in front of the pier
glass, retying the strings to her widow's cap for the third time, getting the bow angled just so. Sebastian Goddard, the new Duke of
Roxbury, was apt to make the most devout of widows toss up their
black petticoats for a blissful tumble with the ton's most revered, most
thoroughly unrepentant rake. Mrs. Carroll was devout only when considering her own pleasure, and Sebastian its possible provider.

"I can do anything I like. And this is hardly his home. I doubt he
knows an inch of Goddard Castle—he's only been here the once, and
that was ten years ago. I imagine he'll get lost and fall down the garderobe." Frederica pictured Sebastian, stained and stinking. Some brave
souls had once stormed Château-Gaillard through a latrine drain in

1204, if she remembered her history correctly. But mentally it was much more satisfactory to push Sebastian down than to picture him climbing up, conquest on his mind.

"He *is* your guardian."

"I don't need a guardian! I'm a grown woman, for heaven's sake." The terms of his father's will had been explicit, however, and Frederica was stuck with him. She had dreaded the day he would come here again. Even after ten years, she had not been able to imagine what she would say to him. The fireplace in her chamber was filled with ashes that had once been saucy scribbled words, all of which seemed like wretched dialogue in a bad French farce.

"You may be long in the tooth, but not," Mrs. Carroll said shrewdly, "in possession of your fortune just yet."

"It's hardly a fortune," Frederica said with disparagement. Well, she supposed it was, really. She could live quite independently until her hair was silver and she didn't have a long tooth in her head. The old duke had made surprisingly wise investments on her behalf. It was a shame he'd been unable to do the same for himself. The financial climate at the castle was chilly at best.

Frederica stabbed at the fabric in her embroidery hoop with a vicious stitch. "Duke or not, I won't have Sebastian Goddard bully me for the next two years. Whatever was his father thinking?"

"If only you had married when you had the chance, you wouldn't find yourself in this predicament."

Frederica tossed her sewing aside. "Oh, stop! Not that again." Living with her eccentric ducal guardian Uncle Phillip had been no picnic, but it had not been bad enough to marry the lisping, lecherous Earl of Warfield, one of several suitors who had come here at the duke's invitation to court her like she was a Yorkshire Rapunzel in her tower. The ensuing attentions had been most unpleasant, Warfield leaving in high dudgeon to blacken her name after she brandished a fourteenth-century sword at him in defense of the virtue she had already parted with. No one wanted to marry a martial shrew, even if well dowered. Frederica was content to be left alone, although lately she had begun to wonder if independence was all that it was cracked up to be.

Sometimes Frederica thought that the old duke had invited the least suitable men on the planet to Goddard Castle to meet her. She suspected in his heart he hoped she was still carrying a sputtering torch for Sebastian. If she was, she planned on dousing herself in very cold water before she saw him again.

Mrs. Carroll adjusted a suspiciously bright red curl and turned from the spotted glass. "Very well. All my nagging doesn't seem to matter a whit to you anyway. But now, my girl, you are about to pay for your stubbornness. I shall enjoy watching the new Duke of Roxbury torment you."

Frederica stayed her impulse to stab the woman with her sewing scissors. "You really are the most odious companion."

The woman gave her a nasty smile. "I am a necessary evil. You wouldn't want to be left all alone here with him, now, would you?"

Frederica shuddered. Trapped between a bitch and a bastard. Her late guardian had been oblivious to Mrs. Carroll's waspish nature, but then, women were not his specialty. With him, she had always been a model of false rectitude. Uncle Phillip would not hear a word against her, which had made Frederica wonder what she might be holding over his head. But he was dead now, and Frederica had suffered long enough. Why not do precisely what she wished right this very minute?

"All right. I will see him. And the first thing I shall ask him to do is to dismiss you."

Mrs. Carroll blanched, revealing suspiciously bright red circles of rouge as well. "You wouldn't dare!"

"Why, I believe I would. When he discovers you helped yourself to some of his mother's jewels after Uncle Phillip died, I think he'll see reason."

"How did you——" Mrs. Carroll bit her tongue and her face mottled to match her paint most unbecomingly.

It had been a guess—an educated one, as Frederica had no absolute proof. Mrs. Carroll was a wily woman, always locking her rooms behind her. But why be so secretive when one had nothing to hide? And Uncle Phillip had no interest in and was careless with valuables that were less than three hundred years old. "I'm as good a snoop as you are. I'll write you a reference if you go away today—I can lie as well as you can, too. But leave the duchess's things behind."

"*Today!* You little bitch! I will go, and good riddance to you. Sebastian Goddard will have you in his bed before the week is out, not that you deserve him. But I hear he fucks anything, so even an antidote like you stands a chance."

"Get. Out. Now."

Frederica picked up her embroidery, not flinching when the heavy door slammed. She was *not* an antidote.

And she'd been in Sebastian's bed before, with disastrous results.

Well, she had not been precisely in his *bed*. But the consequences were the same, and she was ruined. He'd been much the worse for drink and drugs, and she had been in disguise and tipsy herself, so eager and enthusiastic to take advantage of him that she had no one to blame but that footman who passed her those extra glasses of apricot ratafia. And what happened afterward made the night unforgettable for all the wrong reasons.

Frederica had been a remarkably stupid girl the night she'd taken advantage of that fancy dress ball so Sebastian could take advantage of her. Or vice versa. She wasn't sure she was all that much smarter now, for just the thought of Sebastian's long dark body anywhere near hers gave her palpitations. But he couldn't stay up here forever in his father's castle folly. A few days of it would bore a man like him senseless.

The late duke had purchased the near ruin on a whim almost a dozen years ago. It had sucked up a vast proportion of the Roxbury treasury and was still a drafty, dangerous place, the moors beyond it even worse with their sinkholes and fierce winds. Sebastian would soon go back to London or Paris or wherever there was sufficient amusement to be had and leave her alone.

Frederica removed her spectacles and rubbed the bridge of her nose. She didn't want to see her embroidery anyway—she was making a dog's dinner of the vines and flowers on the pointless pillowcase. Why embellish something that was to be drooled on? It was not as though she'd ever have a man in her bed to impress with her neat French knots and chain stitches. And if that was all he'd be looking at—

A perfectly wicked thought crossed her mind. True, she had pledged to herself to never marry. She planned on hiring a much nicer companion than Mrs. Carroll in two years when she came into her funds, and living modestly on her inheritance, with perhaps a faithful dog or a few cats. Perhaps both. Men were, on the whole, disappointing creatures who cared for nothing but their own comforts, and often had fleas besides. Sebastian was the very model of such a man—selfish, careless, reckless. The play upon the family name—he was known as the God of Sin by the chin-wags—was surely deserved.

Frederica's paltry attempt at sexual experience a decade ago should probably not even be counted as such. While she had undoubtedly lost her virginity, she'd never been transported to heaven as was rumored possible. Over the years, she had achieved it for herself with considerable effort without going insane or blind, but how lovely it would be to be brought to abandon by a skillful lover.

A Sebastian who was not dead drunk or full of poppy smoke. A Sebastian who had had ten years to hone his skills and earn his disreputable reputation. Of course, he might have picked up something far less desirable than knowledge—gentlemen were dying off left and right from debauchery. But if Sebastian didn't have the pox or nasty little insects nesting in his nether hair, he just might do again.

How very shocking. She was considering making a second mistake with Sebastian. In a real bed this time, with embroidered pillowcases and clean linens and candles scattered about the room illuminating his masculine perfection.

Of course, there was a considerable impediment to her plan. Sebastian Goddard hated her.

She *would* see him. But not like this, not in a worn-out dress with her hair every which way. She would bathe and ask for apple cider vinegar to bring out the shine in her light brown hair. She would powder her face and chest to conceal her unfortunate freckles, perfume herself from top to toe, find a dress that revealed just enough of her skin. And then, if she could figure out a way, she would seduce Sebastian all over again and see if the God of Sin was a misnomer or the God's honest truth.

# Chapter 4

*She is nothing like I remembered.*
—FROM THE DIARY OF SEBASTIAN GODDARD,
DUKE OF ROXBURY

Unaware of the nefarious plans that were presently in train, Sebastian Goddard, eighth Duke of Roxbury—with a long string of other honorifics to his name—entered the inner ward to find his father's elderly butler clucking over a haphazard pile of trunks.

"What's all this, Warren? Miss Frederica hooking it?"

The butler blinked owlishly at him. "I beg your pardon, Your Grace?"

"Is she running off? Have I scared her senseless before she's even set eyes on me?" He hoped so. It was his ardent wish to rid himself of the duplicitous Frederica Wells for life.

"No, sir. It's her companion, Mrs. Carroll. It seems she's been dismissed."

"Indeed? Did I tell her to hop the twig? I confess I have no memory of it." Sebastian had dined with the woman last night—a saucy redheaded piece who all but wrote him an invitation on her dinner napkin to join her later in her bedroom. He was not averse to fucking older women, but did not want to complicate matters. Fucking anyone else in Goddard Castle was bound to bring him bad luck. Fucking Freddie had caused him no end of trouble and discomfort. He'd learned all about karma on his travels, and didn't wish to put himself in further jeopardy.

"Not you, Your Grace. Miss Frederica did so herself."

"Did she, now? Without her companion to stand in the way, I suppose she expects me to fall into her vile clutches so my virtue can be compromised."

Warren opened his mouth like a dying carp but said nothing. He seemed flustered by most everything Sebastian said. The duke would have to watch it so the old man didn't have an apoplexy—good help was hard to come by in this blasted, bleak Yorkshire hell.

What had his father been thinking of, buying this wreck of a castle? He'd asked the same question of Freddie ten years ago, and it made as little sense to him now as it did then. The Duchy of Roxbury had a perfectly respectable if dilapidated ancestral estate in Dorset. But his father had buried himself in all this rubble, neglecting his duties for years. Sebastian had been left with crushing debt and was now forced to sell every foot of unentailed land and every spare candlestick and chamber pot. It would be a pleasure to dispose of the castle, if he could find someone mad enough to buy it. He'd run out of assets, putting off evicting his unwanted ward as long as he possibly could. He'd always hated the castle, though his hatred of Freddie and his father had dissipated somewhat over the years. But no matter what he felt, the terms of his father's will were clear.

He passed by the armory, Warren following him like a spaniel. Dull battle-axes and battered shields and stringless longbows hung on all four walls, prompting Sebastian to contemplate taking down something to help him vent his frustration. The restocking of the armory had occasioned that house party a decade ago. His father had thought it more important to acquire maces than proper mattresses, and Sebastian had been profoundly uncomfortable the few nights he'd spent here. The night of the fancy dress ball, the pater had clomped around in tarnished mail organizing a scavenger hunt for a papier-mâché unicorn, just a pretext to allow for dalliances in the castle's cobwebby corners, specifically his own. Utter nonsense. The evening had been a dead bore, and Sebastian had planned to leave the very next day. At that point, he'd thought his father was only dicked in the nob.

To be fair, ultimately the night had not been boring. He hadn't waited around for breakfast the next morning to see a telltale blush on Freddie's cheek or listen to his hypocritical father.

He needed to get Freddie settled and out of his hair. He needed to find a wife of his own. One with pots of money who could turn a blind eye to his particular peccadilloes. Or participate in them.

He'd been a duke for eighteen months, although most of that time he hadn't even known it, cavorting in exotic places in blissful, necessary indulgence until he was finally found and informed of his father's demise. He'd missed the funeral, not that it mattered. And now he was saddled with an ape leader until he could marry her off or she turned thirty, two whole years from now.

It seemed cruel to bear the title and responsibility but have none of the benefits of a dukedom. There was precious little money and absolutely no fun, what with the dusty ledgers and disgruntled tenants and rapacious creditors to be dealt with. There were constant threats of debtors' prison, so this trip to Yorkshire came at a very convenient time. No one would think to look for him up here, since his uninterest in his father's interests was widely known. Sebastian Goddard conceal himself in a creaky suit of armor or pore over inscrutable manuscripts? Not bloody likely.

The butler cleared his throat. "Your Grace?"

"Sorry, Warren. I was woolgathering."

"Miss Frederica would like you to take tea with her in the solar if it would be convenient."

"Would she, now." Tea? He'd rather swallow glass. But he might as well get this over with. Freddie had avoided him the two long days he'd been up here, as well she should. After their last meeting, he had little to say to her now and even less desire to see her. But it had to be done.

He had known Frederica Wells since she was in leading strings, a motherless girl brought to Roxbury Park when his own father hired hers. Sebastian had been sent off to school at the earliest opportunity, but his best childhood memories involved Freddie. As he recalled, she'd trailed after him like a stubborn puppy and he'd tormented her as little boys from time immemorial tormented little girls. There had been the requisite spiders. Mud pies. He hoped none was on the menu today.

His father had had great academic hopes for him, all dashed. Not that Sebastian was stupid—despite his rigorous resistance, his head was loaded with useless facts and figures—but he had not shared his father's passion for medieval antiquity. The pater had fancied himself a great scholar, hence the castle and the unicorn. When one was a duke, almost all manner of caprices were overlooked, even buggering one's secretary.

Freddie, the daughter of that secretary, was probably Phillip Goddard's idea of a virgin princess sent to help him lure the unicorn out of the woods. As there wasn't a forest for miles, unicorns did not exist and Freddie was no virgin, she must have felt somewhat useless living in the middle of this wasteland all these years.

No wonder she'd once plotted to ensnare him. But evidently seduction and forced marriage were no longer on her mind. The *on
dit* around town was that she'd refused several proposals, had even
gone crazy and attacked Warfield with a broadsword to make her
point. Sebastian reflected Warfield was probably in need of attacking.
The man was an unprincipled letch, almost as wicked as Sebastian
himself.

He admired the Archibald crest on the keystone and knocked at
the solar's massive oak door. He thought he heard "Come," though
through the thickness of the door and stone walls it was impossible
to tell. But when he pushed open the polished wood, he stopped listening altogether. All his other senses went on alert, however. Who
needed ears when the sight of Frederica Wells was enough to drive any
man quite as mad as the king or his father or the frog-loving Earl of
Archibald?

Where was the chubby chit he remembered? The girl who fenced
and fished with him? Or even the girl crying crocodile tears? In her
place was a curvaceous creature with gilt-streaked hair, her tongue licking a lucky wayward crumb from plump, pink lips. Whose plumper
white breasts nearly spilled from a flimsy dress that was surely too
low-cut for tea. And damn it, where was her flirtatious companion
Mrs. Carroll when he had most need of her? He'd been without a
woman too long if just the sight of his old enemy caused him such
stimulation. This was Freddie, whose pigtails he'd pulled, whose feet
he'd tripped, who'd bedeviled him like a little leech until he went away
to school.

And when he had come home, she'd tried to trick and trap him,
until her head was turned by the promise of a few pounds.

"Hallo, Freddie. I see you started without me." He swiped a
minuscule biscuit and swallowed it whole.

She wrinkled her perfect little powdered nose. No doubt she found the childhood nickname abhorrent. He'd have to continue calling her that to keep her at arm's length, make sure she knew she held no sway over him. Damn her father for dying ten years ago; damn his father for dying more recently; damn Freddie for not finding some other man to bother with her hair and her breasts and her rosy mouth.

She inclined her head, as if she were a queen greeting a vexatious subject. "Sebastian. Or should I say Your Grace, although that seems very odd. How was your trip north?"

By God, she had nerve. The last time he'd seen her, she had been half-naked and white-faced, every freckle on her body like a spatter of mud, their worlds smashed to pieces. One would never know from her sangfroid that they were anything to each other but passing acquaintances. He threw himself down into a chair that looked like some deposed king's throne, devilishly uncomfortable as were all the authentic furnishings in the castle. No wonder the knights in days of old were always riding off to do battle—sitting down at home was as good as getting a jousting stick up one's arse.

"Beastly. I've remembered why I never came back to visit. Every single minute is a fresh reminder." He gave her a pointed look, and was pleased to see her blush of discomfort.

"Your father missed you."

"I doubt it. He was far too engaged with his moldy old books and rusty battle-axes and fucking your father. How have you managed to survive all these years? I've only been here two days and already my mind is going." Lusting after Freddie was a sure sign of it. But sitting in a shaft of late-afternoon sunlight, she showed to exceptional advantage. Her faintly freckled skin was dappled additionally with the jeweled tones of the stained glass window. On it was the Archibald motto, *Fortuna Favet Audaci*, and crest, a stag's head and three sheaves of wheat. The yellow glass of the wheat set her light brown hair to copper and amber.

Fortune favors the brave. He wondered if her position was deliberately brave, meant to dazzle him in her own sunbeam. When she bent to pour him a cup of tea, looking up at him through gold-tipped lashes to see if he noticed her scantily covered assets, he was sure of it. People might conclude from his deliberate demeanor that he was a charming lackwit, but never let it be said he was too witless to miss the signs of seduction, or an opportunity to seize upon them.

*Good God.* Freddie meant to entice him again. Trap him. The dismissal of Mrs. Carroll. That scrumptious, scandalous dress. He'd run away from her ten years ago, cutting her and his father and Goddard-damned Castle out of his life. He'd managed to keep body and soul together—well, the soul part was debatable, but there was no question his body had reaped the benefits of all manner of sin.

Perhaps he wouldn't keep her at arm's length after all, but let her seduce him, if that was what she planned. It might make his immurement in Yorkshire somewhat amusing. And wouldn't the pater frown down on him from heaven—if that was where he was—when his scheme was foiled? Sebastian knew the conditions placed on Freddie's money. Though Sebastian had burned them, he remembered his father's letters always implored him to come back and marry Freddie after all; apparently she hadn't taken the money he'd offered her. Which was absurd, because how did she come upon the thousands of pounds she now possessed? Counting tree stumps and stones? Her fortune was tempting enough for any man, and certainly for a man in Sebastian's situation.

But he wouldn't marry Freddie—he'd rather die of the pox. But he could fuck her, properly—or improperly—this time. He sat back, watching her strain and pour his tea from a dented silver service, calculating what it would sell for. It wouldn't fetch much, but something was better than nothing.

A bird in the hand...

All his problems might be solved by his old playmate, if he could teach her some new games to play. But he'd offered marriage once, and she'd refused.

"I've survived very nicely, Sebastian. After my father died, I assisted your father with his book. Now that he's gone, I've taken it upon myself to complete his work. How do you take your tea? I can't remember."

Rubbish. Of course she knew. They'd drunk tea together in the nursery for years through a series of ill-paid governesses. Sebastian frowned. "Just milk. And what do you mean, his book?"

She passed him a fragile cup. "I suppose I ought to say *books*. He was halfway through volume four when he died."

Sebastian choked on the foul liquid. "*Four* books? What on earth could he write four books about?"

"Why, the Middle Ages, of course. Salic law. Charles the Fat. Otho the Great. I'm almost done with volume five now, and there are to be six altogether. There are any number of fascinating primary sources in the library. Some lovely illustrated manuscripts."

"That no doubt cost him a pretty penny." He couldn't repress the bitterness from his voice.

"He thought the money well spent," she said primly.

"They will all go up on the auction block, although I don't think I'll find as big a fool as my father to recoup my losses."

It was Freddie's turn to frown. To his regret, she had abandoned the flirtatious sideways glances and was suddenly tugging her dress up.

"The history was his life's work, Sebastian. Your Grace. His and my father's both. I don't suppose a person like you has the first idea of what it is like to have intellectual interests."

*Ouch.* So she thought him a dunce, did she? It was only what he deserved after working so hard all those years ago to attain such spectacularly low marks. "We can't help it if our parents were loose screws. Whatever my father collected has to be sold, hand-colored by dead monks or not. You must know that he left me near penniless. It's a wonder he didn't take back your money."

"He would never have done such a thing! But—" She stopped, her cheeks turning crimson.

"But *I* might. That's what you're thinking, isn't it? Now that I'm your trustee, there's no telling how I might exercise my authority over you."

"No man—especially *you*—will ever exercise authority over me!" She bit into a biscuit with a ferocious snap.

Such passion could be put to much better use, although he wouldn't want his private parts anywhere near her teeth right now. He wondered how he could have ever thought her plain. Of course, when they had last met ten years ago she had been like a little sister to him until she made her daring, deceitful move. Freddie had seemed like a brown wren in a muster of peacocks. He'd been such an ass, quite full of himself as only a youth of one-and-twenty could be, never once connecting her with the saucy milkmaid until the lantern light revealed her shocked face.

That hideous house party. There was nothing so repellent as a bunch of middle-aged peers and peeresses trying to recapture their salad days, running about with lances and wimples. He'd slipped off to have a pipe and dreamed of a milkmaid, who'd been full of delicious, sweet cream. The dream had turned into a nightmare, and he'd not willingly taken opium since.

"Your independence does you credit, Freddie, but I'm afraid I've come to uproot you. I can't afford to keep this archaic dump. I've got several potential buyers coming over the next few weeks to look it over. If one of them likes it, I'll accept whatever he offers me. I can't be too choosy."

Her flowered teacup slid off its saucer, splashing her skirts and tumbling to the faded rug under her feet. "You can't sell Goddard Castle!" She bent to retrieve the cup, and Sebastian was treated to the sight of breasts he hadn't seen or tasted in a decade.

"Oh, but I can. I must. You can make your home at Roxbury Park. It's all that's left. Everything else is sold, I'm afraid. It will take years to get the estate to rights."

Freddie stood up unsteadily and walked to a mullioned window. "I cannot live with you. After—after everything between us. You—you and your exploits are infamous. It would be most improper."

How hypocritical to hear her lecture him on morals when she had bared her breasts and more to him like a common harlot. "I've always found impropriety to be most delightful. Almost essential to my well-being." He pictured Freddie sitting across from him at the breakfast table at Roxbury Park after a night of vigorous bed sport. Her lips would be swollen from kisses, her throat pink with love bites. Her wrists and ankles would be only slightly chafed from the restraints he'd place upon each white limb. His cock twitched in anticipation beneath the linen napkin.

She turned, her hair lit by the afternoon sunlight. "Let *me* buy the castle."

No, no. That did not jibe with his new plan for her at all. "You? Don't be daft!"

"I have the money. Well, technically *you* have control of it, as you've just pointed out to me. But I must have enough. The castle cannot be worth much. It's falling down daily."

Sebastian sat back, crossing his arms over his chest. "Then why would you want it?"

She shrugged, causing her luscious bosom to thrust upward. "It's been my home for almost twelve years. I'm used to it."

"Freddie, my girl, as a responsible guardian, I could not permit you to make so foolish an investment with your capital." He did need her money—quite desperately—but right now there was absolutely nothing he wanted more than to take history-mad Frederica Wells up against the ancient moth-eaten tapestry that she was so nervously fingering and kiss her everywhere until she forgot what year *this* was.

He cleared his head. He'd always been a bit impulsive. Just twenty minutes ago he'd been dreading this meeting, and now he was contemplating fucking the one woman who was responsible for the second-worst time in his life.

"Cancel the buyers' visits."

Entreating, her voice was honey, with a dogged edge. He could be stubborn, too. "Why ever should I do that, Freddie? I've just said you can't buy this wreck."

She stared up at the coffered ceiling. "I'll—I'll be your mistress for a month. I'll do any wicked thing you want if you let me buy the castle after. With everything in it, mind you. Your father's manuscripts and artifacts. Just think, Sebastian. Thirty days and thirty nights."

Sebastian felt the breath leave him, taking half his wits along. Was she a witch? A mind reader? He still had the napkin across his lap to cover his erection, so she couldn't have noticed, could she? If she had an inkling that he'd settle for a week—hell, a night—with her, he'd lose his bargaining power.

Time with this version of Freddie would never be boring, especially if he had a month to train her to his tastes. He was sure he could bind her to him beyond silken ropes and blindfolds. After a month in his care, she would do anything he asked and be grateful. Beg him for more.

"Thirty-one."

"Pardon?"

"The month of May has thirty-one days, Freddie. Tomorrow is May Day. I hope you're much more amusing than you were last time. I'm seeing you now, a crown of flowers in your hair. The rest of you—" He lowered his voice. "The rest of you is quite unadorned. And I know just where the maypole is."

# Chapter 5

*I had thought I was entirely immune to surprises. Jaded, if you will. It seems not.*

—FROM THE DIARY OF SEBASTIAN GODDARD,
DUKE OF ROXBURY

She truly hadn't expected him to agree to her outrageous proposition with such alacrity. And insult her in the bargain. *Much more amusing!* She hadn't even planned to make such an offer, but out the words tumbled and here she stood, the recipient of his salacious smile. A smile, blindingly white for a miscreant who probably smoked cigarillos and swilled red wine and brandy for breakfast. A smile that creased his left cheek with a delightful dimple. A smile from curving, full, sensual lips that had once suckled her nipples like a greedy infant.

Merciful heavens, what had she gotten herself into? She was no longer a moony girl with a hopeless crush. She had meant to have a lighthearted fling just to see what all the fuss was about, and now she was to be in his servitude for an entire month, *plus* pay him for the privilege of buying this disintegrating dwelling. She must be mad. Possessed by the devil. Hell, Sebastian Goddard, Duke of Roxbury, *was* the devil who had somehow made her abandon every precept and principle of her twenty-eight years that she'd fought so hard to reacquire.

But he meant to take her home away from her. Her occupation. She'd spent almost a decade being Uncle Phillip's amanuensis, taking down his every word and adding many of her own. Replacing her father as best she could, though certainly not in every way. She had centuries more to cover. Too many King Edwards to count. How could she let Sebastian throw it all away?

It wasn't as though she was a virgin—he'd already seen to that. And he was as handsome as ever. More so, actually. He might live a dissipated life, but one would never know it from his lean, predatory body and his bright dark eyes. Not black, but a green so dark they might as well be, the color of a shadowed forest at dusk. He was looking at her with particular acuity, as though he had already unbuttoned her out of her ill-advised dress. Frederica felt her nipples stiffen to points and warmth spread in her lower belly. He was only *looking* at her. What would happen when he touched her? She was in over her head already.

"You did say *anything.*" The gravelly rumble of his voice made her toes curl.

She cleared her throat. "Within reason. I'm not anxious to have anyone else join us in bed." She tried to sound flippant, but a man like Sebastian Goddard could probably service several women at a time without a qualm.

"You need not worry. I wouldn't want to complicate matters just *yet.*"

"Well, then, we're in agreement," Frederica said briskly, ignoring his deliberate emphasis on "yet." The kitchen maid was twelve and had dreadful buckteeth, the cook, Mrs. Holloway, was nearing seventy, and Frederica's own maid had run off with the last remaining footman three months ago. Thank heavens Mrs. Carroll and her abigail were gone, so there were no other females in the vicinity of Goddard Castle for the duke to lure to sin. Frederica did all the dusting and sweeping herself. Fortunately, most of the rooms were closed because the ceilings could fall down at any moment. Perhaps Sebastian could be stationed strategically beneath a crumbling corbel and she'd be free of him and this ghastly bargain she'd just made. "I'll want the details of our arrangement written down. I'll not have you renege once you've had your way with me."

Once the month was up, *she* might be the one who was so besotted with him again the castle could go to pieces around her and she wouldn't even notice. If his reputation was at all accurate, he'd make sure of that, and she'd spend the rest of her life with the memory of his touch burned upon her skin.

Just as she had spent the past decade.

"You wound me, Freddie. I'm a man of my word."

She wondered. Uncle Phillip had despaired of his only child for years, telling Frederica far more than she should know about Sebastian's habits and haunts. Suddenly she had a perfectly dreadful thought. But Uncle Phillip would have mentioned bastard grandchildren, wouldn't he?

She felt herself blushing. "About—about the possibility that I might become—you know."

Sebastian's dark eyes gleamed. "Become what, Freddie? A slave to me? Totally debauched? As perfectly wicked as I am? I can make no guarantees, but I do hope so."

Oh! He was as impossible as he'd ever been. "Please be serious! I have no wish to have—have a child with you."

The teasing light left his eyes. He gazed down at his hands as he considered her blunt words. His long fingers were, she saw, spotlessly clean, his nails buffed. Soon they would be smoothing over her body and likely driving her wild and witless. She usually hid her own rough hands in the folds of her skirts, but now she was so nervous she was unraveling the fifteenth-century wall hanging with complete disrespect for its survival into the nineteenth.

"Ah. Yes, that would be entirely inconvenient at present. Children cost so much. I'm sure my father complained long and loud about my expense, but it seems he had the last word there, leaving me without sufficient funds and putting us both in this very intriguing situation. I might even come to appreciate the old molly after our month is over." He gave her a smoldering look.

She pulled a twisted gold thread from the tapestry and wound it so tight around her thumb it hurt. "Uncle Phillip was a good man, if not particularly practical. He would much rather have purchased an ancient text than a comfortable bed."

Sebastian filled a plate with an alarming amount of food from Mrs. Holloway's tray. The cook-housekeeper had gone overboard trying to impress the duke, and Frederica wondered if they'd have enough in the larder to last the week, never mind an entire month. If all his appetites were like this—

"So, you're saying we'll do it in my room."

"Wh-what?"

"I take it your mattress has seen better days, like the rest of this place? I remember mine was filled with rocks the last time I was here. But the duke's chambers are more than adequate. My bed is in fact quite ostentatious with all that gold leaf and hangings, big enough for that crowd you were worried about."

Freddie pulled the thread clear of the fabric. "I am not worried about a crowd! Only worried about a b-baby."

"Freddie, my dear, there are many, many ways we can enjoy ourselves without fear of you becoming enceinte. I will tutor you in every one. We might even make up a few new ones of our own. We have thirty-one days."

Really, he was going too far, and enjoying himself enormously, tucking into his tea and sandwiches now as though they were talking about the weather. It was time she set the tone. This was to be a business arrangement only. She would not let herself fall victim to him, no matter what he did to her with his clean fingers or lush lips. Gliding back across to the sofa, she pulled her spectacles out of her pocket and reached into her sewing basket.

"You wear eyeglasses now," he said through a mouthful of muffin.

"Only for close work."

"Rummaging about those old papers and writing books must be a trial for you, then." He reached for a tart. How could he stuff himself and be so calm?

"I manage." She pulled a bit of moss green thread—rather like his eyes—through the linen, trying to keep her hands from trembling.

"You look rather fetching. Like a naughty schoolmistress. Or a nun."

Frederica raised her eyebrow but said nothing. She wouldn't let him get under her skin, just under her skirts. Apparently the vexing man was a satyr who was stimulated by virtually any woman. She hoped he wasn't equally interested in men, like his father—like hers—though she didn't have the nerve to bring such a subject up. But the thought of two prime male specimens in her bed somehow cheered her up far more than the addition of another female. She mentally slapped herself. A few minutes in Sebastian Goddard's company and she'd tossed her moral compass down the garderobe.

Sebastian lifted his napkin and wiped his mouth, apparently done with his raid. It was a good thing she wasn't hungry, for there was very little left.

He leaned back, replete. "I expect you'll want to put me on some sort of schedule. So you can carry on with your history project and whatnot."

Frederica concealed her surprise. She had been ready to defer to him, putting off her writing for a month. Once Sebastian left, she'd have all the time in the world. "That is very considerate of you."

"I didn't say I would do it. In fact, I won't. That's not my style. You will be entirely at my disposal for the next thirty-one days. In every way."

Frederica couldn't help the frisson she felt work down her spine. She watched as he folded his napkin into a remarkably neat square. His hands caressed the linen in a way that made her want to flee the room. She made a crooked stitch instead.

"Poor Warren," he said, after a moment. "He's apt to be shocked."

She looked up in alarm, Sebastian blurring about the edges through her thick lenses. "You won't embarrass me in front of the servants!" Not that there were many of them to scandalize.

"I'll be sufficiently discreet. Providing you don't argue with me like a fishwife as I drag you up—or down—stairs to ravish you, I believe we will rub along well together. There is a dungeon, is there not? And a wine cellar, if I remember correctly. How handy to take you on a brandy cask and have a bottle of wine to hand for after. I promise I'll remove any splinters on your pretty arse you might acquire. I want you to be ready to bed me at any hour of the day or night, Freddie, with or without beds."

He thought she had a pretty arse? The green thread was in a hopeless tangle. "You can't be serious."

"You said *anything*. I think the exact quote was 'any wicked thing.' I am very wicked, my dear, and I find wickedness does not flourish on a set schedule. In fact it pains me to put my wickedness off until tomorrow. I would so like to suck on your tits, with or without this strawberry jam."

"Sebastian!" She knew she was scarlet with mortification, as red as the contents of the little crystal dish he waved tauntingly in her direction.

"Having second thoughts already?"

"No." She poked the needle in her finger and drew blood. It was all she could do to keep her mind steady, but really, she had to be practical about this whole affair. "I want the castle appraised by an independent agent. I'll not pay you a penny more than what he recommends."

"Very well. That seems reasonable." He put the jam down gently on the tea table, then scooped a blob out with his forefinger. Frederica licked her lips nervously as he stuck his finger in his mouth and closed his eyes. "Mmm. Delicious. But not, I daresay, as delicious as you."

She shoved the pillowcase back into the basket, removed her glasses and stood up. "I will take dinner in my room again this evening."

"If you insist. Remember, tomorrow starts at the stroke of midnight. Be ready."

"Not until you've put our bargain in writing."

"You're the writer, Freddie. I'll leave that up to you."

She heard him chuckling as she flounced out of the solar. If she had a brain in her head, she'd throw herself off the battlements like the treasonous Earl of Archibald before the sun set.

# Chapter 6

*Things are worse than I imagined.*
> —FROM THE DIARY OF SEBASTIAN GODDARD,
> DUKE OF ROXBURY

W ell. That was unexpected. Suddenly the prospect of a few weeks on the moors wasn't so onerous. And after that month, he'd have some of Freddie's money, which she never deserved to start with. He would write to Cam and Lord Sanderson to delay their arrival. Just in case Freddie had a return of scruples, he didn't want to cancel their visits altogether.

Sebastian pushed himself away from the tea table. It was time to set the stage for tonight. It was always best to begin as you meant to go on.

He took the worn stone steps two at a time to the south tower. His father had of course picked the best set of rooms. The view was as good as it got of the lumps of grass and rock fields and distant mountains. Three stunted trees and one enormous muck hole were visible from this window. The sun was dipping in the sky, the clouds tipped with pink and orange. This far north, it would be light for some hours yet. Goddard Castle was no place to wander around in the dark, either outside or in.

Sebastian had thought the purchase of this castle folly enough, but to discover that his father was rewriting one thousand years of history confounded him. Who cared about the Domesday Book or the Crusades or the Conqueror? Everyone was long dead, and Sebastian was very much alive, about to make some history of his own.

He opened his trunk, congratulating himself that he never traveled now without the tricks of his trade. He'd not expected to put them to good use here, but it was imperative he have Freddie keep her promise to do whatever he wanted. What he needed. Soon she would need it, too—and if she didn't, it wouldn't be for his lack of skill or practice.

He unscrewed a porcelain jar and breathed deeply, inhaling the scents of oranges and lemons. Tonight he would cover Freddie's body with the cream, from the curves under her breasts to the pink of her cunny to the cleft of her arse to the spaces between her toes. He arranged his implements of sensual torture just so, found a set of tools, set to desecrating the massive Elizabethan gilt bed. Once he had everything to his satisfaction, he ordered a bath after dinner. He would come to Freddie clean as a whistle, if not pure of heart. He pulled out a tawdry novel from his trunk, trying to distract himself until suppertime. He'd overdone it at tea, but Freddie had caused him to feel somewhat unsettled. It had been simpler to fondle the sandwich on his plate than reach for her.

His mind preoccupied, he made no sense whatever of his book as the shadows lengthened in his tower suite. Since he was to eat alone, he did not change but wandered downstairs at the appointed time. The banquet hall was vast and empty, its vaulted ceiling hung with stained and tattered banners of bygone days. The dais he remembered had been removed, and a smallish dining table looked adrift in the center of the room.

Warren served Sebastian himself from an ancient sideboard, as the only footman had decamped recently, according to the old butler's explanation. Sebastian couldn't blame the man. If it were not for the prospect of fucking Freddie for the next month, he'd saddle up and leave, too.

Considering his intake at tea, he made surprising inroads on his dinner. Once he was done, he leaned back in digestive satisfaction. "Have a seat, Warren."

The butler paled, nearly dropping a platter in his gloved hands. "I could not possibly do that, Your Grace."

"Yes, you can. It's an order. Do I not seem ducal enough to you?" Sebastian leveled his most harmless smile at the man.

"C-certainly, Your Grace."

"Well, then. Do as I say. Drag one of those monstrosities up to the table." He watched the old man struggle to push a blackened chair away from the stone wall, its ripped velvet upholstery a sad testament to the castle's general condition. Sebastian sprang up himself and seated Warren before the butler could muster any objection. "Tell me about the servants, Warren. We didn't have much opportunity yesterday, except for your news of the footman." Sebastian had seen very little evidence of any of his father's employees all day. He had left his own valet behind at Roxbury Park, not wanting to subject the man to the indignities that were sure to await, and he'd been correct. Drummond would not have tolerated Goddard Castle more than half an hour before he would have joined the feckless footman.

Sebastian reached for the trifle bowl. "Care for some pudding?"

The butler looked even more dismayed. "No, thank you, Your Grace." He folded his hands tightly in his lap, as though stopping himself from stacking up the spoons. "I believe you met the grooms yesterday when you arrived."

Sebastian nodded. A toothless man and his toothless son. But they were happy to have his horse in the stable, a part of the castle outbuildings that was in better repair than the living quarters.

"Mrs. Carroll and her maid left earlier in your father's—your carriage with John Coachman and young Kenny."

An ancient coach and ancient nags. The ancient driver still had some teeth but a Yorkshire accent so thick Sebastian had been unable to understand one word yesterday. Young Kenny was not especially young, and appeared to be a half-wit, staring at Sebastian as though he were the devil himself. Perhaps the fellow was prescient after all.

"I'm afraid we're rather short-staffed at the moment. There is, of course, the cook-housekeeper, Mrs. Holloway, and the girl Alice in the kitchen."

"Please give her my compliments." Dinner, and in fact all the meals he'd eaten here so far, were more than adequate.

Warren rubbed his wrinkled hands nervously.

"And?"

"That's it, Your Grace. Your father didn't trust anyone near his things except Miss Frederica. And the castle's reputation has discouraged the local people from seeking jobs here. Even if I was able to secure their employment, they never stayed long."

Sebastian had heard the nonsense about the Archibald Walkers. The suicidal Earl of Archibald was just the latest ghost who supposedly haunted the castle, joining centuries of unhappy Archibalds who didn't have the sense to stay in either heaven or hell. He frowned. "My father has been dead for a year and a half, Warren. Who cleans this pile? Lights the fires?" Not that the castle was remotely clean or warm. "Empties the chamber pots?"

"I do what I can, Your Grace. When Mrs. Holloway can spare Alice, she helps, too. The men tend the gardens and animals and see to any repairs and do any sort of heavy lifting. Miss Frederica takes care of most everything inside herself."

"Good God."

"She does the best she can, Your Grace! We all do."

"I'm not casting aspersions, Warren. I'm just—surprised." Shocked, more like it.

The old man drew himself up in his seat. "If I may be blunt, Your Grace. When you couldn't be found after your father died, the funds to operate Goddard Castle were in rather short supply. What money there was froze in probate. Miss Frederica wrote to the late duke's man of business and solicitors many times, but their hands were tied until they heard from you. You should know that before she left, Mrs. Carroll told me that she intends to sue you for her back wages. The rest of us are willing to wait until you get yourself settled."

Sebastian had been home several months. No one had troubled to mention the dire situation in the north, but perhaps that was because Sebastian had found a dire situation in the south, the east and the west. He was beginning to think he had been very ill-served by those his father trusted.

"What have you all lived on?"

Warren swallowed. "I've always run the household with prudence. Your father—I shouldn't like to speak ill of the dead, but he was always dashing off to buy some book or relic, and often forgot to think of our expenses. We—Miss Frederica and the staff and I—got used to being creative. Pinching pennies. There was a little put by to start for a rainy day. Since then, Miss Frederica has been judicious in selling off some of your father's collection. Nothing at all conventionally valuable, mind you. Nothing you'd ever be interested in," he added hastily. "A few old books to collectors, that sort of thing. Items she'd already made use of in her research, or found to be inaccurate. Rubbish, really."

So, technically Freddie had robbed him, although a poor sort of guardian he was keeping an heiress penniless and entombed in this godforsaken place without a pot to piss in. And if there was a pot, she'd probably be emptying it herself.

Now he planned to enslave her to his every need when she had already been subjected to his father's profligacy and his own indifference. It was almost enough to make him release her from their bargain. Almost.

"I appreciate your candor and your service, Warren."

The old man startled. "Am—am I to be dismissed, Your Grace? I assure you that nothing Miss Frederica sold—"

"Just from the table," Sebastian interrupted, pasting on another harmless smile to calm the butler down. Sebastian had spent years perfecting that particular smile. It had never been known to fail, although gentlemen were somewhat less susceptible to it. "I'll be staying at Goddard Castle for the next month, but I don't expect any more extraordinary sacrifices from anybody."

"We don't mind, Your Grace."

"I do." His father really had a lot to answer for, leaving him with debilitating debt and Freddie to boot. "Miss Frederica is not going to do any more housekeeping. Make other arrangements, please."

The butler fixed his eyes on a molting stag's head. Clearly his loyalty was conflicted. If Miss Frederica wanted to scour pots, who was he to stop her? Freddie had always been stubborn, a mulish, puggish little brat that Sebastian thought he knew. Until she donned a mask and ruined his life. He'd spent the first six months away waiting to hear he was to be a father. But then, no doubt the pater would have taken care of that with more money, he thought bitterly.

"Yes, Your Grace," Warren said at last. "Miss Frederica is a lovely young woman. A man would be a fool not to appreciate her virtue."

It was not her virtue he was interested in. She had once tried to compromise him in her clumsy, schoolgirl way. He was anxious to turn the tables and show her how it was really done. It would give Sebastian great satisfaction to bring Freddie to vice, corrupt her so completely she'd walk around wet for him all day. He felt the surge of power to his fingertips. How he was to kill the time until a minute past midnight he had no idea.

He left Warren to clearing the remnants of his dinner, wondering if Freddie was chewing nervously in her room, or if she had abandoned food altogether. Perhaps an après-sex snack would be advisable to tide them both over till breakfast. Sexual activity was hungry work.

After several wrong turns down dim and dank passageways, he found himself in the sooty kitchen, interrupting the cook, her helper and the two toothless grooms as they sat down to their own dinner. A place had been set for Warren, and Sebastian felt a stab of guilt that he'd delayed the old gent from his meal.

Once Mrs. Holloway got over the shock of seeing a duke in her realm, she promised to make up a tray for later in the evening and deliver it. The little crew around the long table was most unprepossessing, but they had been loyal to Freddie for the past year and a half under wretched living conditions, apparently with little or no pay. Sebastian felt obliged to pull out a few precious coins from his pocket and ensure them that one day—one day soon—they'd receive pay beyond their room and board. When he had satisfied himself that poor Warren—or worse yet, Freddie—was not going to haul up the requested bathwater personally, Sebastian excused himself. He'd lived in primitive conditions a time or two before—most noticeably when he was incarcerated for eight very long months—and thought he could manage to adapt here for a mere month. There was, after all, the enticing benefit of Frederica Wells's lush body in his bed.

With nothing left to arrange for the night's festivities but his own ablutions, Sebastian returned to his room and dashed off two letters to his friend Cameron Ryder and Lord Sanderson and sealed them with his father's ring. He was still not used to the weight of it on his hand, its etched sapphire reminding him of Freddie's smoky blue eyes. He closed his own eyes and pictured her as he'd last seen her, looking as if she wished him to Jericho.

Her hair, when it came down to it, was brown. Her blue-gray eyes were surrounded by half-and-half eyelashes, dark at the base but pale at the tips. She was still short, but her bosom was even more spectacular than he remembered. The rest of her was more voluptuous than was in fashion—she was no sylph. But she had a fine mouth, pink and sweet when it wasn't tossing out barbs against his lack of morals. He could see that mouth around his cock now. He *would* see it there in just a few hours.

The two grooms huffed and puffed into his room with a folding wooden tub. After several more trips up the winding stairs, Sebastian had a few inches of tepid water to wash some of his sins away. He was just drying himself with a threadbare towel when he heard a bloodcurdling shriek echoing against the castle walls. *Freddie.* He didn't bother with his robe. There was a demoiselle in distress.

# Chapter 7

*It was nothing—nothing—like the last time. It was worse.*

—FROM THE DIARY OF FREDERICA WELLS

Freddie's room was a floor below his, the door standing conveniently open so he wouldn't need a battering ram. She, however, was nowhere to be seen. He called her name, but there was no reply. Feeling somewhat foolish and extremely naked, he looked behind curtains and under the untouched bed for her. A candle flickered on her desk, revealing that she had been laboring over their contract. Her handwriting was scrupulously legible, fitting for the daughter of a secretary. He noted June the first as the date Goddard Castle was to be transferred to her.

"Devil take it," he muttered. Was she playing a trick on him again? Did she think she'd somehow avoid his embrace by frightening him to death and running away? He was about to pick up the candle and expand his search when he heard a little gasp.

"Sebastian! What are you doing here? It's not yet midnight."

Freddie stood on the threshold, arms folded over her chest, her long hair in the two neat schoolgirl braids he remembered. She wore a night rail with a thousand tiny buttons that marched right up to her chin. He couldn't remember when he'd seen a more welcome or seductive sight.

"Damn it, Freddie! I thought something happened to you. Why did you scream? I believe you must have taken a few years off my life." He covered his heart, but Freddie's eyes were elsewhere.

"Oh, that. *I* didn't scream. You are not dressed," she said as an afterthought.

"I thought your life was in danger. It hardly seemed worthwhile to don my breeches if I was required to save you in a timely fashion."

"How gallant. But I am perfectly fine. You really should . . . put some clothes on." She stared at him for just another moment, causing his spine to straighten and his chest to swell slightly. He knew he was fit. Riding, fencing and long bouts of daytime and nocturnal sex kept him in excellent shape. He was somewhat disappointed when she raised her eyes and resolutely focused on the top of his head. She might be shy when it came to his body, but that bloodcurdling noise didn't seem to disturb her at all.

"What was that ghastly racket, then?"

She flicked a braid over her shoulder and smiled. "You mean *ghostly* racket. Just one of the Archibald Walkers, I expect."

"*What?*"

"You know we have ghosts. Your father was rather proud of them."

"Rubbish and rot." Warren had alluded to the same thing, but Sebastian paid no attention. He didn't believe people wouldn't come to work here because of ghosts, but rather because of the likely chance they'd perish under falling debris. Sebastian certainly did not believe in ghosts himself. The only white drifty thing he wanted to see was Freddie's night rail dropping to the floor.

"I quite agree. I think if the wind kicks up a certain way through the arrow loops, the resulting sound is the noise you heard. It's rather chilling, isn't it? No wonder we can't get the locals to work here—they're a superstitious lot. They say the last earl is still wandering about the castle searching for his germinal francs. Or gold bars or jewels—whatever Napoleon paid him to betray his country."

Sebastian snorted. "If there's any treasure to be found here, I'm the King of England."

She wagged a schoolmistressy finger. "More treason."

"Where were you?"

Freddie lowered her eyes. "The garderobe."

He looked at her blankly.

"You know, the privy, Your Grace. With regular applications of lime, they're still perfectly functional. We've upgraded from hay to rags, however."

*How barbaric.* The sooner he got away from this heap, the better. His father may have preferred to live like a feudal lord, but Sebastian was a thoroughly modern man, although his droit du seigneur was stirring—the right of the landed lord to sleep with the bride before the groom, or indeed any of his vassals at any time he chose. Sebastian knew that was more medieval nonsense, though. The custom was unproven, word of it likely spread about so the peasants would revolt against the casual cruelty of their lords. More often than not, the lord was probably paid a tax in lieu of sexual congress, but Sebastian didn't think any amount of money would stop him from wanting to fuck Freddie.

Sebastian considered himself an expert on obscure sexual practices, and knew of several other methods for a bride to lose her virginity—one, for example, by her publicly mounting a fertility statue's phallus. It was even, God help the poor girl, part of the marriage ceremony, her blood or lack thereof witnessed by the wedding guests. But he wouldn't have to worry about that with Freddie. He'd already relieved her of her virginal barrier.

Freddie raised her chin. Her nightgown had been washed many times, rendering it almost transparent in just the right places, but she might as well have been wearing a queen's robe. Her innocent braids begged for unraveling, but she held herself like the virtuous chatelaine of the castle. She stepped away from the doorway, her velvet slippers soundless on the cold stone floor.

"I still have over an hour until midnight, Your Grace, and I've not quite finished the wording on the bill of sale. Of course, a solicitor will draw up the actual document, but this is between us. If you would be so kind as to leave—" Her voice was cool and dismissive.

She had bottom, he'd give her that. It was not every spinster who could converse with a nude man with such aplomb, but perhaps she'd taken other lovers after him and was used to the sight of a man's cock. Apart from the first few seconds of their encounter, she had not inspected his manly parts, which were rising to the occasion with alarming insistence despite the chilly temperature in the room. Her eyes had risen to his and were watchful. Soon they would be half-lidded in rapture.

His blood was still hot from his earlier sense that Freddie was in danger. An hour seemed like an eternity to wait, and he didn't want to. He would not be bound by an arbitrary time. It was a minute after midnight somewhere.

"No.

"Oh, I'll leave your room, but you will come with me. There's a fire in mine. Wine." He held out a hand. "Come, Freddie. It's pointless to delay."

She clenched the fabric of her night rail. Her hands were reddened and ink-stained, a pity when the rest of her was so perfect.

"I—I'm not ready."

"We can iron out the details of the castle business in daylight, my dear. Let's not waste any more of our first night together."

She made no effort to take his outstretched hand. If she could not come to him willingly, whether out of fear or aversion or pride, he would make her decision for her.

A minute ticked by, and his arm grew weary. Just as he determined to sweep her up and carry her up to his beast's lair, she took one shaky step toward him.

"I do not plan to enjoy myself," she said.

Sebastian had always enjoyed a challenge. The more she fought him, the better he'd like it—and so would she. He knew every button to push, every lace to knot, every kiss to corrupt. She'd be screaming for him within a quarter of an hour, or he wasn't the God of Sin.

# Chapter 8

*Kissing the back of one's hand is a poor substitute for the real thing.*

—FROM THE DIARY OF FREDERICA WELLS

Frederica marveled at her composure. She had barely batted an eye when she found Sebastian poking about her room. Poking was the operative word—his member looked like a dowsing rod that had located a vast underground river. She had fixed her eyes on his damp midnight hair, but the rest of him was all too visible. To think he had come naked and gleaming to her rescue, when all he would do in the end was bring her to grief.

She was used to the peculiar noises of Goddard Castle but had not thought to warn the new duke. Maybe she should have claimed an army of ghosts resided here to drive him south. But he didn't strike her as a man who feared much of anything. He was certainly fierce enough now, looking at her as though he wanted to gobble her up.

Frederica was acutely aware of her threadbare nightgown and her childish hair. She had wanted to deter him with her appearance, but it seemed she'd have to be covered in sackcloth and ashes to repel

Sebastian Goddard. He was hard for her standing half a room away. She ought to be flattered, but as evil Mrs. Carroll had said, he fucked anything.

She'd been a naïve child the last time she'd seen him naked, and had been hopelessly impressed with every decadent scrap of him then. If the planes and angles of his face caused her heart to stir now, his body had more than lived up to its early promise. He was broad and well muscled, without an ounce of fat. He looked as though he *could* defend her from ghosts or dragons or anything inconvenient. Except for himself.

Oh, she was naïve *now*, entering into this ridiculous agreement with him. And for what? The uncertain roof over her head? But it was too late. She took another step forward. And then another.

He pressed his thumbs to her cheeks, his fingers resting lightly on her temples. His pupils were huge, black as his soul—if he still had one—ringed in dark, fathomless green. She longed to touch the bump on the bridge of his nose, the only imperfection she could detect in his shadowed face. He was whispering something scandalous, but she couldn't listen for watching his lips move. Then he smiled and slanted them over hers, the soft strength of them warm and insistent. Her mouth opened in protest and his tongue traced the seam of her top lip slowly, as if he were measuring by touch, calculating the inches of pink. He did the same to her bottom lip, shocking her with his gentleness.

When they'd last kissed, he'd tasted of too much brandy and smelled of sweet smoke. Tonight there was the merest hint of wine. His clean skin was scented with the rose petal soap she had made herself from the overgrown canes that tumbled over the outer wall. What should have been feminine had been converted into something else altogether—he'd captured the briar as well as the bud. She hoped to steady herself with a deep breath, but instead was swept away to the wild roses and the heat of last summer. Her skin beneath the pressure of his fingertips tingled as he drew her closer, his mouth skimming effortlessly over hers, brushing, savoring. There was nothing to do but meet his tongue and shiver as he tore her defenses down lick by wicked lick.

She felt herself sway, and reached for something to hold on to, although she was still sweetly trapped between his hands. She should touch him, if only to feel his smooth brown chest or span his narrow hips or tousle his curling dark hair. But there was no safe place to touch that wouldn't scorch her as he brought her to him, his velvet mouth angled expertly so that even the corners of her lips received attention.

Frederica had dreamed of kisses like this, though doubted their existence. How odd that her oldest friend and newest enemy was the man to prove her wrong. He lulled her into discomfiting comfort, banishing all thoughts with the steady skills of his tongue and teeth. His fingers slipped through her hair, loosening the braids. Her scalp tickled as he massaged her head, and she felt a wash of heat down her neck. Her nightgown was suddenly too heavy, too warm, her arms useless at her sides, her knees weak. Sebastian seemed to know the exact moment of her capitulation, broke the kiss and lifted her from the floor.

"I'm going to carry you upstairs now and take you to bed. Fuck you."

His voice was rough, barely above a whisper. Frederica nodded. She could not have whispered herself if her life depended upon it. Her hand went to her swollen lips, still so sensitive that her own fingers sent shots of longing through her. He held her as if she weighed nothing and climbed the circular stairs. His room blazed with light—too much light. The scent of her rose soap was strong. The tub was still centered in front of a roaring fire, the dropped towel on the carpet. The least he could have done before he came downstairs to slay her was wrap up in it. No mortal woman could withstand his male beauty for long. It had taken just one kiss—one consummate, carnal kiss—for Frederica to lose every shred of sanity.

He set her down on the edge of the bed and wordlessly began the arduous process of unbuttoning her. Frederica raised her arms and he pulled the garment over her head. Despite the blaze from the fireplace, her nipples pebbled to aching peaks. Sebastian flicked a thumb across one, his face shuttered.

Was he disappointed with what he saw? She was not powdered now—she'd had her own anticipatory bath—and tiny freckles spangled her torso and beyond. He cupped both her heavy breasts in the welcome heat of his palms, then dropped to his knees. He peeled her slippers off her feet and now she was as bare as he.

His black curls were drying in riotous disorder. She reached briefly for the silk of his hair, wishing hers was not such a prosaic brown. Wishing she were not so afraid. Wishing she hadn't wished for this night for years. If wishes were horses, she'd be riding away from here right now. But there was nowhere for her to go, and nothing for her to do but sit, waiting for Sebastian's next move.

It didn't take him long to make it. He parted her legs so that the brown of her nether hair was completely visible. His face was so close, his stare so hard, she wanted to snap her legs back together in embarrassment. His hands gripped her hips and he brought her to the very edge of the mattress. Her bottom slid easily on the ruby satin of the bedcovers and she almost tumbled headlong to the stone floor. But he stopped her in the nick of time, his fingers splaying deep into her flesh. She might see the fingerprints of his ownership on her tomorrow, as she bruised easily. The thought was somehow wickedly appealing, the secret of their night visible on her skin.

"Very, very pretty," he said.

She supposed he would know from his current vantage point. Frederica licked her suddenly dry lips, feeling as if she were under a magnifying glass, his eyes as hot as the sun's refracted light. His breath was moist and warm against her thighs as his hands continued to steady her. She willed herself to be still to his thorough inspection. But she lost her control when he parted her folds and buried his mouth in her slit.

"Sebastian!"

He glanced up at her, his lips never leaving her center, his tongue teasing and torturing, watching her reaction, his nose buried wickedly in her curls. She should tell him to stop. This wasn't right, wasn't natural. She opened her mouth but no sound emerged. She could tell he was smiling by the faint crinkles near his eyes and the feeling of his upturned lips on her most private of places. Blood rushed from her throat to her core, her skin flushing pink.

He increased the delicious pressure, his mouth fully covering the center of her pleasure. With one hand on her belly, he pushed her backward on the bed, spreading her legs farther with the other as he licked and stroked and swirled. His hand held her down, as if she would ever want to escape now. She could no longer see what he did to her, but felt every graze, every imprint of his fingers and tongue. The scarlet canopy and curtains above her and around her made her think of the flames of Hell, for surely Sebastian was a devil. A divine one, who seemed to know what pleased her even if she could not tell him herself. She was capable only of gasps and quivers as she fisted the coverlet in sensual agony. She reminded herself she was probably but one of hundreds whom he'd tortured thus with his tongue, but the thought did not lessen his effect in any way. She'd willingly veil herself in his harem to experience this again, idiot that she was.

And she would. Thirty more days of this and she'd be a hopeless wreck. This was nothing like their coupling before, when Frederica had done most of the work. Not that she had known what she was doing then. Not that she knew what she was doing now but lying on her back, her legs stretched wide, her body glazed with sweat and her core weeping into Sebastian's mouth.

His fingers traced a pattern up her thigh and then two were gloved within her, bluntly slipping through her wetness and his saliva with a sucking sound. She clenched around them, too wild to care about the unladylike noises that seemed to be coming from her orifices. She wanted more and told him so, no longer a lady, no longer coherent, her breath ragged. But he understood her jumbled words and obliged, inserting a third finger, rubbing and stroking as his mouth worked in concert with his hand.

And then the waves hit, and she couldn't speak at all. Her scream was as bloodcurdling as any wind through a castle window, enough to raise all the dead for miles around. She felt him chuckle against her as he pushed her further, ignoring her pleas to stop.

Not that she meant them.

His fingers pumped inside her. She wished it was his cock, helpless against the onslaught of her own desires let loose after a decade of chastity. The hand that cupped her belly relaxed, one finger dipping into her navel, and somehow that was every bit as sinful as his tongue laving her core. She was pinned to the bed, body pulsing, heart pounding. Oh, best to leave her heart out of it. This night was nothing but a means to an end. She'd gain her experience and keep her home. Only thirty more nights like this. That would have to be enough.

# Chapter 9

He has picked up peculiar ideas in his travels.
——FROM THE DIARY OF FREDERICA WELLS

But of course he was not done with her tonight, unless he'd received all his pleasure by tasting her in such a forbidden spot. He couldn't possibly be satisfied. She felt the scrape of the dark bristles on his jaw against her thigh as he pulled back. She was still open, too languid and liquid to arrange herself in a more seemly position, but now Sebastian moved her limbs for her. She closed her eyes as he swung her legs onto the bed, turning her so that she was centered on the satin. The mattress pitched as he joined her on the bed, and she expected him to plunge inside her without further ado. She was drenched, still pulsing with the aftershocks of his delicious assault. But suddenly he gripped her right wrist and swiftly wrapped something around it. Her eyes flew open.

"What are you doing?"

"Exactly what I want, Freddie. I gave you what you wanted, did I not? It's my turn now."

He was knotting the length of cording to a ring set into the bed-post. Surely his father could not have placed such a thing there! She tugged on the tie, only to tighten it. She fumbled at it with her free hand but Sebastian snatched it away and fastened her arm to the other bedpost. The braided ropes had been there all along, all through the most amazing moment of her life, waiting like silent snakes to im-prison her. She gave a futile kick but soon he was encircling her ankles, binding them to the bed as well.

"This is not necessary, Sebastian," she said in irritation. "I won't run off. We have an agreement. This—this is uncivilized. Almost cruel."

He said nothing, but disappeared into the shadows, returning with two long strips of silk.

"I suppose it's too much to hope that you're going to tie yourself up as well," she said tartly.

The expression on his saturnine face told her it was useless to argue, but she tried anyway, only to have him cover her mouth with the soft fabric. Frederica gave him a vile look before her eyes met the same fate.

She was bound, mute and blind, not to mention furious. If this was how Sebastian garnered his reputation—taking advantage of help-less women—he was very much deluded if he thought such methods would work on her. Although it was clear from her last glimpse of his rigid cock that he was in an excited if not euphoric state.

What sort of man was he? She'd thought him merely convention-ally wicked. This went far beyond regular rakish behavior, or so she imagined. She really had little to compare him with.

"Perfect. I have a little project in mind, Freddie. Something that should please us both."

She groaned. He could do *anything* to her and she had no recourse.

Water splashed. At least he'd not put cotton batting in her ears. The sounds in the room became her universe. The ticking of the clock. Sebastian's footfalls as he moved something across the room. His breathing. His sinful chuckle as he examined her in this indecent state.

"You told me earlier you would not let any man have authority over you, Freddie."

She remembered. It was why she would never marry. Why give a man power over her body and her money when she could take care of her needs herself? Not that Sebastian hadn't given her enough orgasms just now to cherish for a lifetime. But she would not cherish this degradation. This violation. He had spoiled their night with his peculiar need to see her humiliated.

"I'm afraid you underestimated my wickedness, my dear."

She heard the clink of metal against porcelain, the slide of something on a tray. She had been too drugged from his kiss to notice much about the room when they entered. Was he going to carve her up like some mad butcher?

"I want you to understand what this next month will entail for you, Freddie, if you want to get your hands on my castle as well as my cock. And you do want my cock, don't you? You're soaked for me, even though you wish me to the devil right now. You're going to change your mind."

Never! When he untied her, she'd hit him on the head with the nearest chamber pot. Their deal was at an end. She'd rather burn Goddard Castle to the ground than submit herself to another minute of this—this— She had no words for what he had done. She thrashed on the coverlet as much as she was able.

"You have spirit. I like that. But relax now. I'm not going to hurt you. Unless, of course, you want me to. I'm quite skilled at causing pleasurable pain. But," he said, sounding thoughtful, "it's a bit too soon for that."

He was mad. When she was free—

If she could have, she would have jumped a mile as he covered her mons veneris with a warm, wet cloth. She smelled her soap, then felt the foam as he lathered up the area. Perhaps he had found her feminine scent offensive earlier, and she felt a blush deepen on her cheeks.

If he meant to kiss her there again, she supposed she could endure being washed like a baby. Tethered like a dog. But then she twitched as a cold blade smoothed over her skin. He was shaving her! She cried in protest beneath the stifling silk, but his strokes didn't falter. For all she knew, he was about to slit her throat. She bucked her hips.

"This is traditional for your sisters in the East. Be still. I wouldn't want to cut you." His voice betrayed no emotion, as if he spent his days barbering one woman after another. Frederica had never felt more vulnerable.

This was her own fault. She had placed herself in this inconceivable position, all because of an odd mixture of sexual curiosity and the desire to grow old in the castle library, hunched over papers that made her sneeze and itch. Who was more ridiculous, the madman who tied her up or the bookish demivirgin? She was afraid she knew the answer.

There was nothing for her to do but feel every slip and slide of the razor and his hands as he stretched her folds. Her world was reduced to his careful, warm touch, the snick of the blade as it lightly scraped her skin, the sound and feel of his breaths as he labored over her. Time passed in slow motion, measured by deft, invisible lines. Her blood pooled low in her belly and she felt a gush of moisture that had nothing to do with the cloth or soap.

"Even more perfect."

He said it almost reverently. She could only imagine the display she made, lashed to the gilt bedposts, every inch, every freckle exposed. This was absolutely unnatural. Absolutely wicked. Absolutely . . . interesting. My God, what was he doing to her?

She knew when he finished. He swiped her thoroughly with the wet cloth. The mattress shifted and the cool air prickled her core. He padded away, silent. How long would he keep her in this state? Aroused, yet unable to articulate her desire? Best that he didn't know how much she wanted him right now. It shamed her that she had fallen so easily under his spell, but she knew she was just one of many. Who traveled with silken blindfolds and gags and rope? A man who was used to getting a woman just where he wanted her.

God of Sin. If she had ever doubted, he had convinced her.

He returned to plop something cool on her belly. A scented cream. Lemons and oranges, a slice of Mediterranean summer in the cold Yorkshire spring.

"I'm going to explore you again now, Freddie. You are mine for a while, and I mean to know you. Everywhere." He coated her with the fragrant salve, massaging every curve and indentation, tracing the veins from her wrists to her elbows, circling her nipples, brushing across her bare mons. He lifted her, kneading the globes of her bottom, teasing the cleft of her arse with more of the cold cream that was soon warmed by the friction of his gentle rubbing. She was boneless beneath his clever hands, her head filled with citrus and sin.

Thoughts of escape were fading. He stopped for a long moment, fiddling with something on his tray. She wanted more. And then she got it. Shockingly, he slipped a creamy slender object into her anus with slow, exquisite care, then brought her to orgasm again with a few fingers and more of the slick unguent. She shattered quickly, desperate for him to take her. Cover her. Make her complete.

So this was what he meant by making her a slave to him. She cried into her silk, almost grateful he had deprived her of speech, for she could not make sense of the barrage to her body and her mind. When he cupped her cheek and slipped the fabric from her mouth, she kissed him with thirsty fervor, not wasting her tongue with words. His hands glided to her breasts, thumbing her peaks, and then his lips followed. This she remembered from ten years ago, the tender suckling and fondling, only now she was not shocked and half giggling from her boldness. She'd been so ignorant then, but in the short time she'd spent in Sebastian's room she felt as wise as Sophia, wisdom incarnate.

When he raised himself over her, she braced for the pain that never came. He entered in one long stroke, the cream and her own honey easing his way. And then he took his own ruthless pleasure, guaranteeing hers, deep and deeper as she shuddered around him, each brush of him against her skin a dart of fire. She was filled to completion, the little object in her back passage making his every thrust more scandalously thrilling. She imagined him, his head thrown back in the candlelight, his body glistening with balm and sweat, his dark eyes closed in bliss. One day she might see for herself. Tonight it was enough to dream of the perfection that truth might reveal as something less.

He swept down to kiss her again, his mouth more demanding, devouring, as he crested toward his climax. She matched him, equally close. And then suddenly, he withdrew, spurting his hot seed on her belly and wrapping her tightly to him. Sebastian rocked against her until spent, his heart thudding so hard she could feel it.

"Christ," he muttered.

It was far too late to pray, Frederica thought. "Please untie me."

The silken gag was tight at her throat, the ropes chafing when she'd struggled to hold him.

"I shouldn't. I like you this way." He didn't move except to sweep the blindfold up to her damp forehead. The firelight was dying, the candles guttered. He was still beautiful in the shadows, like a golden statue. She felt wrecked, wet and foolish.

"Please, Sebastian."

"I did not hurt you?"

"Of course not. I imagine you have all this down to a science, knowing precisely how long one can be tied without getting pins and needles, don't you? It would be inconvenient to kill any of your victims."

He snorted. "I see a good fuck has not sweetened your tongue."

Good? How very inadequate a word. But she was determined not to praise the man who'd made her a captive to his lust. Let him see how he liked it when she turned the tables on him. Which she would. She had thirty days to do so.

# Chapter 10

*Things are going almost too perfectly.*
—FROM THE DIARY OF SEBASTIAN GODDARD,
DUKE OF ROXBURY

Freddie had the audacity to stick her tongue out at him. And what a tongue it was. Pink. Plump. Perfect.

"Baggage." Sebastian refrained from leaning in to nip it, struggling instead with his expert knots. For some reason his hands trembled a little as he tried to untangle the skein of braided silken rope. He'd had the rope made to order in Italy—an indulgence he currently couldn't afford—and he was down to his last few pounds of it. How pathetic it was that he couldn't simply slice it with a knife, since he needed to reuse it. And often. Freddie looked so spectacular spread upon the crimson coverlet that just standing over her made him hard again. His seed glistened white on her belly, the rest of her flushed pink with temper and orgasm.

Perhaps it was too soon to release her. He had half an idea she'd rise from the bed like a Valkyrie and point her finger at him, choosing him for death. But death in battle with Frederica Wells would be well worth a trip to Valhalla. Sebastian could not recall a more fulfilling evening.

Speaking of which . . . He abandoned the ropes and went instead to her beautiful bare mound. "Lift up for me."

"What now? I can barely move, Sebastian."

She had been more than ready for his entry. He'd seen to that. She'd been so wet and hot and tight, so very fuckable. But she seemed to have forgotten her part in their play and now looked daggers at him.

"Are you comfortable, then?"

"Oh, certainly. I love being tied up like a rabid animal."

"I'm not talking about the bonds, Freddie, but the dildo."

"The what?" Her color darkened with realization.

"You don't mind it, do you? I know for a fact that it feels rather good. Perhaps we'll leave it in, then."

"No! T-take it out. It's horrid." Her hips canted as she lifted her bottom an inch off the bed. The base of the thin marble cylinder was visible and he turned it ever so gently.

"Ah! Sebastian, stop! You are—you are despicable to use me this way."

He raised an eyebrow. "You'd best get used to it, Freddie. I plan to put my cock there when you're ready."

Her eyes widened in shock. "I'll never be ready for such a thing! Never!"

"No?" He pulled the dildo out a little way, watching the tension on her face fade, then embedded it back slowly. He repeated this several times while Freddie cursed him to Hell. Yes, she was a Valkyrie, minus the helmet and wings. Her full breasts rose and fell, her nipples dark and hard. His hands may have been unsteady before, but they were sure now, sliding the toy back and forth until Freddie became silent and pale, her blue eyes clouded, her breaths coming in short gasps.

He touched the tender flesh above her swollen bud with seven hard strokes, pressing his fingertips into her pubic bones as he drove the object languidly in and out of her lovely arse. On the eighth, she cried out, straining her bonds as she rocketed off the bed.

"See? I was right." He was as hard as he'd ever been in his life. The night was proving too much for both of them, but he wanted to see it all, do it all. He was botching her initiation, but he couldn't hold himself back. He turned from her weeping for the razor, then cut the cords. Damn the expense. He had to have her again, right now.

She scrambled off the bed, tripping on the dangling ropes, the blindfold and gag still tangled in her hair. She rushed to the tub, fished the sponge out of the scummy water and scrubbed her belly of his seed.

"Freddie."

"Don't you touch me. Don't you talk to me. Our bargain is at an end."

"Freddie."

She turned angrily toward him, her eyes blazing.

"Do you know why you're upset, Freddie?"

"Why?" Her voice pitched into a shriek. "Because you are a perverted degenerate—that's why!" She aimed the sponge at him in fury. He caught it in one hand and casually wiped his erect shaft and balls.

"And you loved it," he said quietly.

"In your dreams! I hate you, Sebastian Goddard. I've never hated anyone so much in my life."

"Then why did you call out my name over and over? Beg me to fuck you? By my count, you've just come four times. Maybe five. You are delightfully responsive when you are helpless, you know."

Her cheeks were flushed with color. The evidence of his

domination—the frayed ropes, the silken strips, the love marks on her magnificent little body—stirred his rod.

"And a woman must be helpless—and an idiot to boot—for you to perform, isn't that right, Sebastian?"

It was his turn to flush in anger. For a short while, that had been true. He had needed to ensure that he was in control at all times. That his plans took precedence. That women were at *his* mercy, not he at theirs. "Don't be ridiculous. We all have preferences. I assure you I'm perfectly capable in any situation."

"Well, I'll never know, will I? Keep the bloody castle. I'll begin my search for some long-lost relative I can live with until I turn thirty. And then I'll have my fortune and you won't be able to touch me or it."

"I'll make a new bargain with you, Freddie." He really had to. The thought of being deprived of her body now that he'd begun to explore it was almost painful. There was a way he could appease her independence and her volatile temper. It might be diverting to see what his little mistress was capable of.

And to test himself to see how far he would let her go.

She shook her head stubbornly and pulled at the fabric around her neck as though it choked her.

He took three long strides across the stone floor. "Here. Let me. Hold still."

"Get away from me!"

"I'm only going to untie it."

She held herself in rigid control, her back straight, her lovely bottom curving. He concentrated on the knot instead of the tempting creamy globes. He'd gotten too proficient in his knots, but managed to relieve her of the gag. The blindfold was simpler to pull over her golden brown hair, although he snagged a strand.

"Ow!"

"Sorry. There. You're almost back to rights. Sit down and I'll work on the ropes. Then we'll have our late supper and talk."

"I am not hungry." Her own right hand worked furiously on her left wrist and he stilled it.

"Freddie, I said I'd take care of it."

"I don't want any help from you."

"But you're going to get it." He scooped her up in his arms and carried her to a plush velvet chair by the fireplace, one of the few seats in the castle that didn't have stuffing spilling out of it. A tray with covered dishes had been placed on the table beside it. He settled her onto his lap, his stiff cock seeking the slippery crease of her arse. She tried to pull away, elbowing him in the process.

"I'm only going to talk to you now, although I admit you distract me." She flinched as he picked up the tiny silver fruit knife from the tray, but quieted when he began to patiently saw through the give on the rope.

"Here's our new plan, Freddie. As you pointed out, I do enjoy dominating women in bed. But I'm never cruel, and it's always mutual. It has nothing to do with my ability to fuck you senseless. I believe I could do that even if you tied *me* up."

"That might be diverting," she grumbled.

"Indeed it might, and should you choose to do that, I will cooperate in every way." He was fairly sure he would respond to her. His cock twitched at the mental image of Freddie riding him to oblivion. She jerked against him as his words sunk in, the honey from her cunt dripping down.

"You are truly insane."

"I beg to differ. It's not insane to want to experience every sexual pleasure imaginable, Freddie. You might say I've devoted my life to it."

"God of Sin." She snorted. She was full of scorn and snorts and sniffs. That didn't say much for his earlier performance, but he knew down to his toes she was putting up a front. The shrew that Warfield had complained of had returned. No longer was she liquid in his lap, but stiff and prideful. No doubt she was embarrassed by her behavior in the throes of passion. And she *had* been passionate. Wild. Wanton. If she hadn't been tethered to the bed, he was sure she would have bitten and scratched him like a little hellcat in heat. It would be delicious to tame her and introduce her to every wicked thing he could think of.

"Indeed. I understand that's what some call me. I find it a bit blasphemous, don't you? I'm in enough trouble with the Lord without adding to it."

"You are a devil!"

He bent her leg and held her heel in the palm of his hand. "Such a dainty foot. You're a lovely little package, Freddie."

"Stop trying to cozen me! Your words mean nothing. You've probably got the usual lines of dialogue folded in your back pocket."

"Has it escaped your notice that I'm not wearing breeches?" He managed to slip the rope from its knot and massaged her foot, tracing the faint pink line that now graced her ankle. Beautiful to see his marks upon her. The scents of citrus cream and sex invaded his senses. He breathed deeply.

"Stop sniffing me like a dog. Although you are one. A cur."

"A devil. A dog. And despicable. 'Who often, but without success, have prayed for apt Alliteration's artful aid.' "

"Never tell me you were paying attention in poetry class."

"They didn't teach Charles Churchill where I went to school. I read him on my own."

Freddie turned to him, her profile visible. Her nose was straight and freckled and utterly delightful. "You are not stupid."

"Of course I am. Hasn't my father always said so? 'With various

readings stored his empty skull, / Learn'd without sense, and vener-
ably dull,'" Sebastian said, quoting Churchill again. Really, why was he
trying to impress her? He attacked her other ankle.

"Your father *did* love you."

"He had a peculiar way of showing it. I don't wish to talk about
the pater. It's simply too banal to have had an uncaring father whose
secret life caused me to hide my pain by drinking and drugging and
fucking everything in sight. Until, of course, I come under the influence of a good woman, who reforms the rake right out of me. I suppose you think that could be you." He laughed at her look of loathing.
"Why, I understand it all now! You were only trying to save me from
myself all those years ago, isn't that right? My God, our lives are worthy of a bad gothic romance novel. Here we are, in a crumbling castle,
the wind whipping outside. There are ghosts. Goblins. The fair damsel
is about to save my spotted soul for the second time. Horrors."

He gave a mock shudder. He'd made partial peace with his father's
indifference and sexuality long ago, seeing and doing a great many
things since he stormed off in the middle of the night as a hurt young
cub. Nothing could shock him anymore. The truth was, it felt damned
good to be bad, and he saw no earthly reason to change his ways for
the foreseeable future.

"Stop speaking nonsense. We are done." She made no effort to hop
off his lap, though. He took the opportunity to brush his fingertips
against her nipples. Her breasts were full, more than a handful, and he
had big hands, as he supposed he was big all over. Certainly he gave
ladies no cause to complain about the size and thickness of his cock
or the breadth of his shoulders or the length of his talented—if he
did say so himself—fingers. He'd not feasted on her breasts enough
tonight and would make up for it later. They were not done by a long
shot.

She was as tempting as Eve. He held a slice of apple to her lips in a role reversal, but she shook her head. He ate it himself, savoring last fall's harvest, and supplemented it with a piece of sharp cheese. Had Freddie made it? Picked the apples as well and stored them in a barrel in a cool dark place? She was a model chatelaine.

"Now," he said mildly, "hear me out. Remember, I said I had a proposal for you. You want this wretched castle, although I cannot see why. You agreed to let me use you in any way I wished for a month. But you seem to have some objection to my methods now, although it did seem to me that you were enjoying yourself very recently." His hand inched down the velvet of her belly.

She slapped him away. "You are insufferable."

"What if we take turns, Freddie? You follow my orders one day; I follow yours the next? That way there will be parity. Equality. You will obey me tomorrow. Without question or objection. But," he said, squinting across the room at the clock on the bedside table, "for the rest of today, I am yours to command."

Freddie was very still in his arms. He could almost hear the wheels whirring in her head.

"You can't mean that."

"Oh, but I do." He took another bite of apple. Why not? He had confidence he'd get his way in the end. She had been a revelation, all heat and silk and artless innocence, with a touch of tigress thrown in for good measure. He could not remember the last time he'd enjoyed himself so thoroughly. He could not with honesty admit that his current vices bored him, for what red-blooded man could spurn the kind of life he'd led? He was the envy of his peers and the scourge of the peerage. Wives, daughters, Cyprians and milkmaids fell to his feet with alarming abandon, provoking his friends' admiration, unless said ladies were their relations.

Ah, milkmaids. The last time he'd seen so many freckles was that hellish night with her.

Sebastian swallowed back his inexplicable panic, nearly choking on a bit of apple that had lodged in his throat. He washed it down with a slug of red wine. Would she want revenge? Why should she, when *she* had seduced *him*? He'd been her ticket out of Goddard Castle, and he'd ruined her in the ruins, then abandoned her. When he had tried to do the honorable thing, he had been rebuffed. Totally, completely, repletely rebuffed. "So you agree?"

Frederica stood, dusting off her pert backside. "Yes. Why should I not? I believe our agreement was for 'any wicked thing.' I presume you'll honor that on *my* days."

He'd just given her a perfect opportunity to carry out the most diabolical depredations on his person. She probably had devoted the past ten years of her life to waiting to weasel him into this corner, thinking if she got her claws into him this time, he'd ask her to marry him again. That was not about to happen.

Had she expected sex to end in marriage all those years ago when she came to him in the dark? Why, yes, she probably had. Her head was likely filled with all sorts of romantic drivel. She had been what—seventeen? Eighteen? But then the pater had hypocritically talked of duty to the dukedom, bloodline, dowry. After that little lecture, Sebastian had wanted to stuff his ears with cotton and fuck everything in sight, and had done so. For years he'd thought Freddie had opened her palm and waited to be bought off. Whatever she had felt for him disappeared like the smoke from his opium pipe. He'd flown the coop in the dark, shutting out the hellion who bucked over him in the milkmaid's costume. He pictured Freddie waiting patiently for him at the breakfast table, to talk, to explain. She might have collected dust by the time she realized he was long gone.

Frederica was busy braiding her hair back, snatching up her night-gown, whirling around the room like a dervish. "I am going to sleep now. In my own bed. I trust I have your permission? Or do I even need it? This is now my day."

Sebastian was unaccountably tired. He would fuck her again just as well in the daytime later, her day or no. "All right. Sweet dreams."

With one last snort of disgust, Freddie left him in the firelight, slamming the heavy door behind her. The wine glowed ruby in its glass, but Sebastian was loath to drink any more. Managing Freddie's conversion to perversion would take every ounce of his skill. He was just about to take his rest when his door reopened and her freckled face popped in.

"Meet me in the long gallery at ten."

"In the morning? I never rise at such an hour if I can help it."

"A day has only twenty-four hours, Your Grace. While I recognize the need for you to sleep to maintain your"—she flicked her dark blue eyes at his cock, which was still somewhat rampant—"stamina, if we meet at ten and my power over you exchanges at midnight, that gives me only fourteen hours to have my wicked way with you."

Sebastian nodded. "Just remember the code."

"What code?"

"When one engages in games of domination and submission, one is cruel only if the other partner agrees to be treated cruelly."

"Why would anyone agree to such a thing?" she asked, her brows crinkling.

He shrugged. "Sometimes a touch of pain is pleasurable. You'll discover that when I spank you."

"You wouldn't dare!"

"You may tell me to stop at any time. I suppose we'll have to come up with a word that lets me know when."

Frederica looked grim. "What's wrong with 'stop'?"

Sebastian grinned. "You might say that, but not really mean it. Kind of like when you cried, 'Oh God, I'm coming,' earlier. It really would have been most inconvenient to summon the Old Gentleman to bring you to heaven just then."

Frederica looked ready to fly at him. "Well, then, what's it to be? Bastard? Troll? Toadstool?"

"Rutabaga." He doubted very much he'd ever hear the absurd word pass Frederica's lips.

Her dismay was comical. "I can't possibly scream out the name of a vegetable."

"A fruit, then? Kumquat? Pomegranate? Pineapple?"

"You are being ridiculous."

"Rutabaga it is, then. Good night, Freddie. Sleep well."

"My name is Frederica, Your Grace. You shall call me that today and every day when it's my turn. *Miss* Frederica. Actually, Miss Wells is even better."

He tugged an imaginary forelock. "Very good, Miss Wells. Is there anything I might do to you—I might do *for* you tonight?"

"Not a thing. I believe you've done quite enough."

The door closed again with a thud. Sebastian picked up her slippers from the side of the bed. His own Cinderella, but he was hardly Prince Charming. He was a despoiler of innocent virgins and wasp-tongued spinsters, and often they were one and the same. He threw his head back and laughed.

# Chapter 11

*I really didn't mean to, but I cannot say that I am sorry.*
—FROM THE DIARY OF FREDERICA WELLS

Frederica paced nervously in the long gallery. Generations of Archibalds hung on the wood-paneled walls that covered the damp stone beneath. She knew them all, and every contribution they'd made to Archibald Castle and the world beyond. They glowered down upon her in disapproval, possibly because she was wearing young Kenny's rolled-up breeches. Once, she had worn Sebastian's, but they had fallen apart even after her careful tending. Proper young women did not wear trousers, but she was no longer young, and certainly far from proper, if her behavior last night was any example.

Frederica had never been successful with the old duke in persuading him to get rid of the paintings of the previous inhabitants of the castle. To her, the haughty Archibalds were unlucky and resentful. The Duke of Roxbury might outrank them, but he was an interloper, as was she, and after her acrobatic activities last night, they were probably in the highest ghostly dudgeon.

No, she took that back. Nothing about her had been flexible or acrobatic, as she had been harnessed to the bed like a madwoman in Bedlam. And she had screamed like a madwoman in Bedlam. Sebastian Goddard was sin incarnate. He had done the most perversely pleasurable things to her body, things she had never even imagined existed. That object—his tongue— She shuddered.

It almost made her sorry that such amusements were to be limited to every other day. Frederica had been very surprised when he made his offer to take turns with her, nearly as surprised as she was when she made her original offer to him. He had an unsettling influence on her—an hour in his company and she'd promised to be his mistress for a month. Now she was his mistress for half a month. That was an improvement. Wasn't it?

She had stopped in the adjacent armory for the blades before entering the gallery. If she'd had more time, she would have polished some of the rust off,.but they would do. Sebastian was a keen fencer and all-around athlete. She would test his mettle and hers in a few minutes. He'd be shouting rutabaga well before luncheon.

"My, my. What have we here?"

A lean and predatory Sebastian stood at the end of the wide corridor in a shaft of May Day sunlight. Wearing only a linen shirt, boots and dark gray pantaloons, he had dispensed with his neckcloth, waistcoat and jacket, which would make it all too easy for what she had in mind. His overlong hair was still damp, and she could smell her rose soap and his sandalwood cologne that had clouded her senses when they had tea together yesterday afternoon. A pity he'd wasted his time in the bath. She'd have him sweaty and panting soon.

"Good morning, Your Grace."

He bowed. "Good morning, Miss Wells. May I say how very

lovely your ar—ah, you look in those breeches? Most unexpected. And tailor-made for you."

"I borrowed them. You needn't throw out compliments on my days, you know." Though she did know just how fetching she looked in pants—even old Warren's eyes lit up a bit before he collected himself to give her a stern talking-to. He seemed very agitated about something, giving her warnings against succumbing to Sebastian's charms. If he had seen her last night and lived through the apoplexy, he'd know his reproof had come a little late.

"Forgive me, Miss Wells. I shall endeavor to do exactly as directed from here on in." He leaned back against the smudgy window. "What's on the program?"

"You are aware that when the Germanic tribes defeated Rome, swordplay became the prevailing way to settle one's differences. Dueling grew out of that and spread throughout the Christian nations, right into the Middle Ages and the Age of Chivalry."

Sebastian looked amused. "A history lesson and a challenge. You plan to duel with me, I take it? Hopefully not to the death. And you do know duels are illegal, Miss Wells. You seem to be remarkably well-informed and intelligent."

She ignored him. "Dueling evolved into the art of fencing eventually. You have a copy of the very first book on fencing in your library, Your Grace. Diego de Valera's *Treatise on Arms*, written in the middle of the fifteenth century. It is most edifying. A translation, of course, from the Spanish to the French."

"I do not wish to read it in either language, Miss Wells."

He sounded bored now. She walked up to him, pulling a faded curtain aside to reveal the weapons. "Your father has some fine examples of medieval swords. These are Italian foils, indicated by the crossbar grip, although they're somewhat more modern. The seller threw them in as a gift when your father made some major purchases from him."

"Delightful. At least the old boy got a bonus for a change. Do you plan on giving me a tour of the armory again to see all the fascinating acquisitions, Miss Wells? The last time I visited, I nearly fell asleep."

"No, Duke, I thought we might spar a bit like we used to. There's plenty of room in the gallery, as you remember, and if we get lucky, we might stab some of the Archibalds in the process."

Sebastian's mouth dropped open. "You're not serious. You're not a hoydenish tomboy anymore, Freddie. And remember, I always beat the pants off you. But wait," he said with a wicked gleam. "That might be amusing after all."

"*Miss Wells*. We do seem to disbelieve each other on a regular basis, don't we?"

"By God, you mean it! I can't fence with you now! You're a grown woman, although you're still on the short side. I wouldn't want to take advantage of my superior reach or harm a hair on your head."

Frederica's hand went up involuntarily to her viciously braided bun. She'd scraped back every bit of hair, for there was nothing so annoying as having one's vision obscured as a pointed blade came toward one.

"That never used to bother you. And I've found a way for our match to be on a more equal footing. Speaking of beating the pants off, please remove your clothing."

Frederica glimpsed a fleeting—a very fleeting—moment of Sebastian's shock before he regained his cool composure. "Pardon me?"

"You're worried about hurting me, and I'm worried about hurting *you*. Don't worry; if you're naked, I'll be so aware of your dangly bits that I'll make sure to stay within the lines of attack."

Sebastian now struggled to appear aloof, but it was clear to her she had flummoxed him for a change. Good. She watched him toy with an ivory button.

"Is this some sort of a dare? Remember what happened the last time you dared me."

Yes, she did. She had been eight, he almost twelve, and her ankle still ached when the weather was damp.

"I see no trees here today, Your Grace."

"You must have fallen on your head as well as broken your ankle all those years ago."

"Crying rutabaga already? We haven't yet begun."

"And we're not going to. Not without proper fencing attire and masks."

"It's *my* day, Sebastian. My rules," she said sweetly. "When we fence tomorrow, you may set the rules."

"We will not be fencing tomorrow. We will not be fencing *today*." He turned from her to leave.

"Afraid I'll best you?" she taunted.

"Afraid you'll slice my balls off. There are no buttons on those foils. I don't trust you an inch, Freddie."

"Oh, very well. You may keep your clothes on. But for every touch, I'll require you to remove something. A shame that you're dressed so casually. You will be naked in no time."

# Chapter 12

*I'll be damned. No pun intended.*
—FROM THE DIARY OF SEBASTIAN GODDARD,
DUKE OF ROXBURY

Sebastian's shirt was the first to go, and his other garments followed suit in rapid succession. He cursed himself for coming downstairs to meet her in such a hurry that he had not dressed properly, for she had dispatched him with brevity, even pinking his chest with the tip of her foil. She was an amazingly efficient swordswoman, light on her feet, not wasting a motion. Vastly, horrendously improved from the time he first taught her. What she lacked in height, she made up in quickness, lunging, thrusting, cutting over with a deftness that would have made him speechless even if he was not winded and bleeding the tiniest bit.

He had decided early on that he would not try to actually win the match. Getting naked with her could lead to starting his morning off as it should be started. But it hadn't taken him long to realize he might have difficulty even if he put his heart and dubious soul into the effort. He had studied with French, Spanish and Italian masters during his self-exile from England, familiarizing himself with each distinctive school's methods and philosophy. Fencing was not a sport for just those with the necessary brawn. One must have intelligence and strategy. And nerve. Frederica Wells had an overabundance of all of that, and once Sebastian let her get him naked, he wondered what she would do with him. To his disappointment, when his breeches were at last flung onto the pile in the dim corner, Freddie wiped her sweaty brow with an incongruous lace handkerchief and tossed her foil aside.

"Thank you, Your Grace. That was very diverting. You may dress again."

Strands of golden brown hair had fallen from the spinster-neat bun. He should not want to, but he itched to unwind her braid, loosen the waves and bury his face in it.

"How on earth did you ever learn to fence like that?" Somehow he couldn't see the pater running up and down the gallery with his ward.

"I told you. De Valera's book."

Sebastian stumbled as he stepped into his pants. "You learned all that from a *book*?" he asked, incredulous.

"It is remarkable what one can learn from books. You really ought to try it sometime."

"I told you last night I am not the dunce you seem to think I am. But the skill you display—you put most of my former opponents to shame. Very impressive."

Her cheeks were already pink from exertion, but he thought he saw additional color. "Even helping your father, I had plenty of time on my hands. Some of his guests condescended to indulge me. Your friend Warfield was one of them."

"Yes, and you stuck him with a sword. He never told me that you were fencing. I was under the impression you tried to run him through for his lechery."

"That, too, but he's a very poor swordsman. No doubt he was ashamed at his defeat at the hands of a woman and told a great many lies about me." Freddie tucked an errant curl behind her ear, and Sebastian's fingers itched to help her.

"I gather you let him keep his breeches on."

Freddie shivered in disgust. "Believe me, he was forever trying to unbutton his falls. Odious man. But handy for the exercise while he was a visitor here. There is not, as you have noted, much to do here, but I've managed to teach myself any number of useful things from the ancient books in the library. Making medicine and soap from old receipts, for example."

"Freddie," he said, remembering, "is it true that you are obliged to clean most of the rooms in the castle?"

"You're to call me Miss Wells today. I've simply done my share. We've all worked hard up here, Your Grace, while you were off gallivanting across Europe and Africa."

"If I disliked my father before, I detest him now for making you his drudge," Sebastian said, wiping the perspiration from his face with his shirt before he pulled it over his head. "I won't have it, Freddie. You're to cease with the housekeeping immediately."

"Miss Wells."

"For God's sake," he said in frustration, "I've known you since you were a puling brat. *Miss Wells*, then."

"Thank you. Sebastian. You must have realized by now that we're short on servants. There isn't anybody to turn the housekeeping over to. And *you're* short on funds, so we can't hire anyone even if they were willing to come here and work. There's no way to fix that unless you release my funds and sell me the castle, and then of course it won't matter to you. So I shall continue to do what I've been doing for the next month. Unless"—she brightened—"you wish to forgo our arrangement and I buy the property sooner. You'll have some money and can stop worrying over how clean or dirty this place is. Go back and do whatever it is you do and leave me in peace."

Aha. Clever girl. "You won't escape me so easily, Fr—Miss Wells. We made a deal, and I plan to live up to my end of it."

"Speaking of which, follow me into the library. I completed the terms of our arrangement in writing. You may sign the contract now."

Sebastian felt the slightest misgiving. Of course, this paper of hers wasn't worth a damn thing, really. But it was a promise on his part, and he did try not to break promises. Which was why he never, ever made them. He didn't want anyone to depend upon him, as he preferred not to depend upon anyone. Not anymore. He'd made his own way and expected others to do the same.

Blast. Just last night, he'd promised the servants he'd pay them. Now he was promising Freddie he'd give her the deed to Goddard Castle.

"All right." He looked down at his father's signet ring, a ring he hadn't wanted. A responsibility he hadn't wanted. He supposed she'd want to melt some wax so he could stamp the crest on the document.

They left the gallery and stepped down into another corridor that twisted abruptly to a set of stairs, not the way he had come. Sebastian wondered if there was a floor plan available for him to study. He had not been here long enough before to ever orient himself. Although the collection of buildings looked reasonably large from the outside, most of the rooms were uninhabitable. He wanted to make sure he didn't wander into an area where he would be buried alive in rubble, too far for his shouts to be heard and trapped under rock until his heart gave out. He had altogether different plans for the circumstances of his death—preferably many years from now in some saucy wench's bed.

After descending a circular flight of stairs, Freddie gestured him into her sanctum. The library's windows were tall and narrow, but there were a great many of them, all sparkling. Sebastian pictured her up on a ladder with a bucket, her backside swaying with each scrub. She went to the long desk and opened a drawer. Sebastian studied her as she put her spectacles on and reread what she had written. The lenses caught the sunlight and made him blink. She really was a dazzling little creature for all she tried to hide it. At length, she nodded in satisfaction and passed the papers to him.

"There are two copies—one for each of us. I realize," she said in a brisk voice, "this is not a binding document. I'm not a fool. But you said yesterday you were a man of your word."

Sebastian would have felt shame if he were capable. He gave a cursory glance at the words, knowing he would be abandoning her to this wretched castle and a lonely life. A good guardian would never agree to such a thing, but he was not a good guardian.

He scrawled his name at the bottom of each page as Freddie melted a bit of sealing wax. He plunged his ring into the dark red blob, making the agreement look most official.

"There," he said, folding the parchment and smiling at her. "What have you organized for me next, Miss Wells? I don't require being held at sword point to get out of my breeches again."

"If you're truly upset about me playing maid, you can help me clean."

Sebastian sighed. He had walked into that one. Freddie was nothing if not practical—she'd gotten her exercise partner and now an assistant in her household tasks. A few blisters on his hands might prove efficacious in increasing sensation to Freddie's dappled skin later, though.

What fresh hell would she put him through? He'd have his chance tomorrow to rest and relax with her, although sex was as vigorous as

any parry, deceive and feint. In his mind he equated the fencing termi-
nology with sexual positions, and was thoroughly preoccupied when
Freddie snapped her fingers in his face.

"We'll start with your bedroom, as you are lord of the castle for
the time being. Do not even think of getting me back in your bed
today. I will show you how to change your bedding and dust properly
and I expect you to pay attention. You'll have to take care of your
room yourself while you're here if you want it to be ordered. I will
meet you up there in fifteen minutes." She disappeared out the library
door, taking their agreement with her.

Sebastian took in the floor-to-ceiling shelves, groaning with battered books and stacks of papers. One taper dropped into the lot and
they'd be smoke and ash in no time. The surface of the desk was neatly
arranged, a sheaf of virgin paper and quills and inkpots lined up. A
basket of thin white cotton gloves sat beside an ancient book that was
propped open on a stand with ribbons marking whatever had caught
Freddie's interest. Idly he thumbed through the pages—without pro-
tective gloves; Oh! The historical horror!—his eyes glazing over at the
mention of the Golden Bull and the Diet of Worms and the Imperial
Chamber. He remembered his reaction first coming across the words
Diet of Worms as a boy as he snooped about his father's papers in
their estate in Dorset, thinking even if he were starving, he'd not eat
such things. When he'd innocently told his father of his resolve, his
father had mocked him for an idiot and made him do a report on
the general assemblies of the Holy Roman Empire that took place
in Worms, Germany in 1521. Sebastian had pushed every fact he'd
learned then out of his mind, and he was not about to familiarize
himself again with such useless information.

His father's three fat published volumes stood at proud attention on a corner of the desk, bracketed by intricate marble bookends of weary-faced Knights Templar. The pater hadn't bothered to send copies to Sebastian, or even tell him he was engaged in such a ridiculous venture. The covers were a deep blue leather, almost black, quite handsome in their way. Sebastian left them where they were without examination. He poked around some more, finding nothing but the signs of efficiency and organization. Freddie must have been a godsend to the late duke, who was known more for his enthusiasm than his methodical mind. When Joseph Wells, that inimitable secretary and sodomite, dropped dead, it must have hurt his father doubly, but Freddie had evidently stepped into the breach. In fact, he wouldn't be a bit surprised if Freddie had written most of the content in those blue books.

On his way to change sheets, he bumped into Warren in a hallway. The butler was covered with a capacious apron and wielded a feather duster as though it were a lance.

"A word with you, Your Grace."

"Make it quick, Warren. Miss Frederica is awaiting me upstairs in my bedchamber."

The butler turned brick red. "Aye, that's just what I wished to discuss with you. It—it is not proper to spend time with Miss Frederica alone in your bedchamber."

"I am not a conventional man, Warren, and you're skating on awfully thin ice. Make your point."

The man's Adam's apple bobbed, belying his next words. "I'm not afraid to speak up. You won't find anybody to replace me, so if you sack me, the only person harmed will be you. I've put a tidy little sum by to see me into my old age and I have nothing to lose."

Warren looked determined. As far as Sebastian was concerned, the man was pretty well in the throes of old age right now and probably should be pensioned off. The butler had been ancient when Sebastian was born thirty-one years ago. But as Sebastian didn't have the ready to shut the man up, he leaned back against a bumpy stone wall. "Go on."

Warren looked around, as if the cold walls had ears, and lowered his voice. "I heard you last night, making Miss Frederica suffer. Worse than the Archibald Walkers, you were. She's a good girl, Your Grace. She shouldn't have to assuage your devilish appetites just so she can keep her home and occupation."

"Ah, I see. So she's confided in you her plans to purchase the castle from me? They were *her* conditions, you know. I had no intention of ever fucking her again."

Warren was now as pale as a walking corpse.

"Thank you for your concern, Warren," Sebastian replied coolly. "I know serving my father, you were privy to a great many odd occurrences. I thank you for your past discretions. But heed this. Continue to mind your own business. If you don't, you might not live long enough to enjoy that tidy little sum you've saved. Are we clear?"

Warren straightened. "Perfectly, Your Grace."

"Very well, then. Carry on."

Before he turned away, Warren looked at him with something like pity in his eyes, and Sebastian felt ten again. *Damn and blast.* What had possessed Sebastian to threaten the old butler? Not that he would ever try to snuff the old boy out. Warren was a sort of father figure to Freddie, and God knew she needed one after how disappointing her young womanhood must have been. Now Freddie had confessed their sins and had gained a knight-errant armed with a feather duster and indignation.

They had both needed sensible fathers, but at least Freddie got a loyal butler. Joseph Wells had died not long after Sebastian decamped. Sebastian wondered if his father's brutal words about Wells's daughter had contributed to the man's death. How ironic that Phillip Goddard, Duke of Roxbury, permitted himself to engage in a criminal affair with his male secretary, but forbade his son to honorably marry the man's daughter. Low birth was not an impediment for love, for Sebastian knew that his father's affection for Joseph was real. He'd heard the declaration himself, Freddie still as a stone in his arms.

# Chapter 13

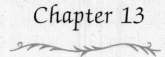

*I must needs watch my wits around him.*
—FROM THE DIARY OF FREDERICA WELLS

He whistled up the stairs, disappointed when he got to his bed-chamber to find that Freddie had shucked her tight breeches. She was now wearing a sack-like gray dress and a pristine pinafore over it. Her hair had been tamed, all the charming little tendrils trapped behind an ugly head scarf. Though the tub had been removed, lingering scents of citrus and rose soap and sex permeated the room, and Sebastian took a deep breath. Freddie went to a window immediately and threw it open to the fitful moor winds.

The bed was a rumpled mess, the ruby satin coverlet half on the floor. Sebastian's clothes from yesterday were on a chair where he'd left them. But the snips of rope and lengths of silk had been stored back in his open trunk, the jar of citrus cream capped, his naughty book shut and angled neatly on the bedside table. Evidently she hadn't been entirely able to wait for him to get started.

"I expect you're used to a valet to trail after you. You may choose to live like a pig while you're here, but I hope out of some negligible respect for me you will not expect me to rut in a pigsty."

"You wound me, Freddie. Again." To illustrate his point, he placed a hand over the splotch of blood on his shirt. If they were to fence another day, he'd need to find some *points d'arret* for the tips of their swords to prevent her from stabbing him again. She was a bloodthirsty little wench.

She narrowed her eyes at him. They were an odd slate blue, bringing to mind the Yorkshire sky before a major storm. From a distance the color was indeterminate, but he had seen their depths up close last evening, and recalled when they had peered at him from beneath a black velvet mask. He should have known who his milkmaid was back then, but he'd been too deep in his opiate dream and drunkenness to question the gift of her warm body rising over his. He was fully alert now.

"Miss Wells," he corrected. "Where do we begin?"

She thrust a bucket, scoop and brush at him. She pointed to a folded pile of rags on their erstwhile dining table. "Clear out the ashes from the hearth first. You'll want to dust after, then sweep. In that order, or all your effort will be pointless. I'm going to take the coverlet outside to be aired—by rights it should be laundered, but I don't think I'll be able to get the sta-stains out of it."

So Freddie was shy about the cream and bodily fluids that had flowed so freely. She bunched up the satin and fled the room. Sebastian got on his knees, swirling up a cloud of ash with overly vigorous applications of the little shovel. After coughing up half a lung, he fell into a rhythm until the bucket was full and his hands were black. He gave a cursory swipe of a cloth to the wooden surfaces of the room, then brandished the broom. Freddie was taking her sweet time hanging up their dirty laundry, so he straightened up the rest of the room as best he could. While he might like his own linen in order, room décor had never been his forte, and it all looked clean enough to him on this bright May morning.

Surely it was too nice a day to stay indoors. He and Freddie should be picking apple blossoms or trilling along with songbirds, picnicking on one of the walls that crisscrossed the moors, pretending that they were normal. He could crown her with dandelions and make slow, thorough love to her beneath the open sky.

But it was not to be. She entered the room with a stack of sheets and pillowcases up to her gilt eyelashes and placed them on the bed.

"I daresay you're used to changing your bedding every day, though I beg you not to. We've enough to do here without daily washing. But I've brought extras from the linen press, so you may decide the appropriate schedule. Have you ever made a bed?"

Sebastian thought of the vast number of disarrayed beds he'd been in, but could not recall ever setting one to rights. Even in the meanest of Continental inns, there had been someone to turn down the blankets and fluff up the pillows. Sometimes even several someones. He wouldn't allow himself to think of the time when he'd slept chained on a mud-packed floor, insects the size of rats scuttling across his sweat-soaked body. No, that dark place was firmly in the past. He supposed in a way he had Freddie to thank for that memory, too.

"You are a veritable who-sis," he mocked, taking in her naïve, domestic perfection. "Whatever is her name? That Greek goddess of hearth and home."

"Hestia. You look like a chimney sweep. I don't think I should let you touch the sheets after all. You are filthy."

It was true his hands were black and his body sheened with sweat from fencing and sweeping. He needed a bath. Perhaps with Freddie in it to make up for all that he had suffered. That would be tomorrow's domestic task.

"What a pity." Sebastian pushed his dirty clothes to the floor and sat down on the chair. "I will simply have to watch you, then. Perhaps I should take notes."

She shot him a scowl. "You'll have to pick those up. I will not." With considerable vehemence, she started stripping the sheets off, throwing them on top of his clothes. She bustled around the bed, presenting a lovely view of her rounded backside. She could not have played into his weakness more if she were reading the script.

"Pay attention, Your Grace. If you fold the ends over just so, the sheet will not come loose as you sleep."

"Freddie, I doubt anything you can do short of stitching the ends together with wire will be strong enough for what I have planned for you in that bed. We'll make it a point to examine your method tomorrow to see if it holds up. Are you sure we must wait until then?"

Her lips thinned and her pert nose rose in the air. "Perfectly. While you're here, I plan to take advantage of your brawn. I will give you a detailed list of things I expect you to do on your slave days. That way I won't even have to spend any time in your company."

She seemed altogether too happy about that idea. Sebastian felt the muscle in his cheek jump. This was not exactly what he had envisioned when he'd altered their original agreement. Somehow he thought she might tie him up and tickle him with turkey feathers—always amusing—but he had not foreseen domestic drudgery. He let his mind wander to other pleasant things his submission could entail, but the insistent snap of her fingers interrupted his daydreams once again. She really was the most managing sort of female. The plain, stubborn little girl had grown up to be a pretty shrew.

"You've seen for yourself the condition of the castle. In a month, when I am its mistress, it will be much more tolerable thanks to you." Sebastian's head spun as she stood in front of him, rambling on about all the chores she had planned for him. He caught snatches of "lye" and "lemon wax" but couldn't be troubled to pay attention. Even in her gray gloom and apron she radiated a winsome sensuality.

He really couldn't help it when his darkened hand fastened around her wrist to draw her to him, or when he smudged her cheek with the other as he covered her lips with his to shut her up, or when he carried her to the freshly made bed and sank down into it with her. After some obligatory—and very minor, to his way of thinking— resistance, her hands became just as busy freeing his cock from his breeches as his were pushing up her skirts. There was no need of citrus cream or blindfolded seduction as he slid deep and true into her deliciously wet passage, her body arching beneath his, her legs wrapped tight around him. Their coupling was uncomplicated, per- haps even ordinary, as though she were the maid of all work caught in a stolen moment by the footman. There was no need for finesse or gamesmanship.

Sebastian performed in the most basic, time-tested way, withdraw- ing and entering as Freddie begged for both beneath him, her nails digging into the linen of his shirt. He watched her, her face strangely wise, though he doubted she had ever enjoyed another man. Sebastian would bet that the first man to ever plow her was also the second, do- ing it now, this very instant. The thought of his ownership over her innocence was exhilarating. He rode her until she broke apart, then flooded her with his seed. There was a freshness to lying with her, even in their clothed state. Her stupid little scarf had not even come loose. He pushed it back so he could enjoy the tangled gilt and old gold and copper strands. Her eyes were still shut, her brow creased, as if she didn't want to acknowledge what had just happened between them. On *her* day. The sheet now looked as if it had been used as a cleaning rag, and one corner had very definitely come undone.

"I told you so," he whispered into her ear, before he gave it a lick and a nibble.

# Chapter 14

_He is the most vile creature imaginable._
—FROM THE DIARY OF FREDERICA WELLS

_Ye gods._ What was wrong with her? She had been in perfect possession of her faculties earlier, even when Sebastian had presented
his exquisite manly form in all its naked glory. She had kept her eye
trained to the valid areas of target, faltering only when she accidentally
scratched him at the high line. She hadn't meant to draw blood, but
he'd seemed more amused than injured. She was also quite sure he
hadn't put all of his effort into defending himself, either, which had
made her all the more determined to prove to him she knew what she
was about.

And now—all her advantages lost. Even her own domination day
had turned on its head. Or should she say on its back, as she lay beneath a perspiring, dirty, _gloating_ Sebastian, who with one wicked kiss
had ruined her resolve. Again.

This resolve-ruining was becoming habitual. She should have
noted that martial gleam in his eye before he dragged her to him and

kissed her speechless. From now on she would stay yards—no, *miles* away from him when she spoke to him. If she ever spoke to him again. Words seemed pointless when she only wound up in his bed.

He didn't like her. She knew it. While he played the charmer, was almost like his old self—the boy she had loved since she moved into Roxbury Park with her father—she caught a glimpse of dark displeasure every now and again as he looked at her. He had not forgiven her, and who could blame him? He couldn't guess that when she refused him, she had simply tried to save him from an even worse mistake than they had already made. Than *she* had already made, really. Sebastian did not have much say when she found him sprawled on the floor and climbed on him like a whore. He'd had no idea it was she. A pity he hadn't taken her up on the bet—he would have owed her that shilling.

She didn't know what had been worse—the look on Sebastian's face when he discovered their fathers were intent on stealing a moment together, or when he realized moments later that the woman who'd ridden him to oblivion was little Freddie Wells.

At least he hadn't tied her up this time. She supposed she could say their tussle had been entirely conventional, save for the way his hand was now between them, causing her to continue to peak. Each wave made her clench helplessly around his cock, which still felt stiff despite his obvious orgasm. Surely he meant to withdraw. It was all too much, and she told him so until he thrust his tongue in her mouth and then her ear and she simply gave up.

Never in her life had she wanted a man as she wanted Sebastian. This was far worse than when she had her girlhood crush on him. Then she'd had no real idea of what transpired between a man and a woman. Now she thought she knew only too well. How would she do without him when he left?

"Get off me, you bloody oaf."

"Such language, my dear Freddie." In one swift move he tumbled her over to lie upon him. Her corset—or something—left her breathless. Before she knew it, he had unbuttoned her gown and freed her breasts, kissing and caressing them with a devotion that Frederica could only marvel at as she watched his dark head burrow into her bodice. They were doing this all backward. He should have divested her of her clothes first, done the kissing and the touching before he impaled her. But it was really much too late to complain.

"If I had known," he said, coming up for air, "that housekeeping was so very delightful, I should have apprenticed myself out as an upstairs maid years ago."

"Stop this at once, Sebastian!"

The pressure of his lips on her nipple ceased abruptly. He looked up and smiled at her. "I've forgotten myself, haven't I? This is your day, after all, and your wish is my command. Forgive me for losing my head. Both of them."

The arm that banded her to him relaxed, and she rolled off his body onto the crumpled sheet. "You will not," she gasped, "take such advantage of me again."

He sat up. "Absolutely not, Freddie. Perhaps it was the allure of your apron. I've always been attracted to the servant class—housemaids, milkmaids. The odd governess. All forbidden to me as a duke's son, and all the more tempting."

Frederica hoped he didn't see her flinch. Milkmaids? Then her choice of costume all those years ago had been unfortunately apt. "Look what you have done to this bed." There were actual handprints from where he'd hovered over her, plunging into her again and again. And again.

"I don't mind a bit of dirt, but I'll make sure it's fresh for you tomorrow. I don't suppose us taking a bath together is on your agenda for me today?"

Frederica scrambled up, pulling her skirts down and apron up. Somewhere beneath it, her corset was corkscrewed sideways. Yes, a bath was on order—for her, so she could wash the evidence of this sin away. Whatever else she had planned for the dreadful duke could wait until the day after tomorrow. She needed to clear her head.

"You—you are dismissed for the day. In fact, I don't want to set eyes on you again for the duration of it. So, stay out of my way, Sebastian."

"As you wish, my lady. Are you quite sure I cannot scrub your back?"

"Quite. Good day, Sebastian."

"Yes, it is rather, isn't it?"

She slammed the door and ran downstairs to her room, locking herself in on the chance that Sebastian would disobey her. He seemed the disobeying sort. When she caught sight of herself in the mirror she yelped and turned away. Cinderella come to life, all because of her oh-so-clever plot to occupy Sebastian in dangerous and demeaning tasks. Turning him into her drudge had not subdued his appeal one iota. Best if she had absolutely nothing whatsoever to do with him on her days. What had seemed like an unusually generous gesture on Sebastian's part had been revealed to be anything but. She was putty in his hands, no matter what day it was. There was something about him—

Damn it, there was something about her, too. She'd grown to prickly independence here at Goddard Castle. She could withstand Sebastian's charm, and anything else he pulled out of his vile trunk. She opened up her diary and put her resolve in writing. It might help her to recite it every day, like the Ten Commandments when one had forgotten that number six was forbidden. Murder was too good for Sebastian anyway. And apt to be messy.

Frederica straightened herself up as best she could, then went downstairs to use the bathing chamber off the kitchen. Mrs. Holloway was already grumbling, heating water for the duke instead of making luncheon, Alice and Young Kenny trucking the water up in pails. Thank goodness Sebastian was unaware of the bathing chamber, else she'd be tripping over him here in her sanctuary. She sank down in a padded chair near the fire.

"'Tis his second bath of the day, Miss Frederica. Does the man think we've got nothing better to do than see to his abnormal needs? What kind of a man washes his whole self twice a day?"

"One who was beaten in combat and turned into a maid of all work," Frederica confided. "I had him cleaning up cobwebs this morning after we fenced in the long gallery."

"You never!"

"I confess I did. We have an odd little bet going concerning the disposition of the castle. Expect him to be down here the day after tomorrow peeling vegetables for you."

Mrs. Holloway gasped. "Oh, miss, I couldn't have that! He's the duke!"

Frederica shrugged. "He's just a man." A rather perfect specimen of mankind, but she wouldn't tell Mrs. Holloway that.

"You must have been right into the filthy corners with him. You're a sight, Miss Frederica."

Filthy corners indeed. "I know. I came down for a bath, too. Once *he's* seen to, of course."

"You sit right there and I'll fetch you a cup of tea."

"That would be lovely." Frederica sat back and watched the to-and-fro of the servants, for once feeling no inclination to help them attend the duke. Her tea was hot and sweet just as she liked it, and eventually accompanied by a simple sandwich. The duke's lunch was far grander, but he would be eating it alone, far from the comfort of Mrs. Holloway's kitchen.

Once she was finished, Frederica shut herself in the little storage room that had been converted into a bathing chamber. It had seemed a practical solution to slopping buckets of water up the twisting stone stairs. The servants made use of it themselves, and a slate schedule hung on the door. No one was chalked in until next Wednesday, so Frederica relaxed back into what had been a long wooden trough. She'd had Eric, the head groom, drill a hole in the bottom so that the water would flow out into a pipe that drained into the yard, thus making the bathing experience easier on all concerned. But she would not tell Sebastian of this room and ruin the privacy for the rest of them. The servants might share the tub with her, but she knew they'd never plunk their arses down where the duke had plunked his. It would not be proper. The standards at Goddard Castle were not high, but there were at least some.

She smoothed her body with a fresh cake of rose-scented soap. Soon it would be time to make more, to gather fruit and berries from the carefully tended, walled lady's garden, to snip and dry herbs. The worn brick paths in the largish garden proved that this part of castle life had gone on for centuries. The castle buildings themselves might be in shambles, but the garden was a jewel, producing even in the foulest weather. The high brick walls trapped the sun and protected the plants from wind. It was as if a measure of Yorkshire magic had seeped into the soil.

Sebastian could be turned loose in the more prosaic kitchen garden where he couldn't do any harm. It would do him good to dig in the dirt, pull up weeds and pinch off garden pests between his elegant fingers. She was just picturing him on his knees, his bare torso shiny with sweat, when the door behind her opened.

"Ah! Here you are."

It was too late to scream or reach for the towel or lather up or pull her hair down from its knot to cover her breasts. Sebastian made himself at home on the little bench, sitting atop her towel with finality. Frederica tried to keep her poise, covering herself and wishing she had at least one more arm. "What are you doing here, Your Grace?"

"I'm giving myself a tour of the castle, as no one was available to show me around. You keep everyone busy as bees here, Freddie. Orienting myself, as it were. See?" He held up a little leather diary. "I'm making a map, taking notes. Trying to discern what rooms need my attention. Anticipating your every need."

His voice was smooth as caramel. He was not talking about cleaning, the wretch.

"As *you* can see, I'm bathing, Your Grace. It does not suit me at all to have company as I do so. I expressly forbade you to seek me out earlier. Did you forget?"

"I was hardly expecting to discover this charming little room, or you in it in so charming a fashion." He gazed around, taking stock of the neatly stacked cakes of soap, the oils and unguents on the shelves. A mixture of floral and herbal scents hung in the steamy air. His citrus cream would be right at home with the remedies Frederica had concocted for the household with Mrs. Holloway and Alice. "You're a kind of apothecary, aren't you? Scholarship, athleticism and now science. What a wonder you are, Freddie. It doesn't surprise me that a schemer like you can conquer any task you put your mind to."

"Sebastian, I am naked," she ground out.

He smiled wolfishly at her. "Yes, I do see that, and I thank heaven for it. Makes me wonder what I've done to deserve such a treat." He may not like her, but Frederica could tell he had no complaints about her body from the leer on his face. But again she remembered the horrible Mrs. Carroll's words. Sebastian fucked anything.

"I'm certain heaven is not involved in any way. Really, Mrs. Holloway will keel over if she finds you in here."

"If she does, I imagine a Renaissance woman like you can cook as well."

"There you would be wrong," Frederica lied. She was not about to let Sebastian order her around the kitchen at three in the morning. She was relatively competent at the stove, but the temptation to poison the duke might overtake her. "Really, you must leave. I still have a dozen hours free of you."

"Only ten, my dear. It's after two and midnight cannot come soon enough. I suppose I'll have to find something else with which to amuse myself in the meantime." He rose, never taking his dark green gaze from her body. "I promise to be careful as I continue to explore the castle. I'm not sure adequate precautions have been taken to secure the unsafe areas."

Frederica imagined his inert body trapped beneath a fallen pillar. It did not please her as much as she might like. "We're all rather used to the vagaries of Goddard Castle. Of course, any improvements you choose to make will be appreciated once the castle is mine."

"I'm off, then. May I help you get dry before I leave?"

"No, you may not!"

He left as quietly as he entered. The water was cold by now, but she waited in it until she was sure Sebastian was far from catching her rise out of the tub. How foolish—he'd seen more of her body than she'd ever seen herself. He'd *shaved* her, for heaven's sake, and put his tongue where no one ought without being struck by lightning. What could he possibly do to her next? She didn't have to wait long to find out.

# Chapter 15

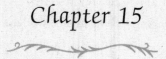

*The only way to shut her up is to kiss her. Not unpleasant.*
—FROM THE DIARY OF SEBASTIAN GODDARD,
DUKE OF ROXBURY

Somewhere below, a modern clock struck midnight. Sebastian had been dozing fitfully in a chair, waiting for the official start of his day. He'd dined alone again, which was becoming a dead bore. Warren resembled a rabid hedgehog as he served him in the echoing banquet hall, the butler's bristly disapproval palpable. Frederica had champions in all the male—and female—staff, not that they were large in number. But after inspecting the castle and its grounds today, he had even greater misgivings. Even though he didn't like her, the thought of leaving her here to molder into spinsterhood was dismaying, not to mention dangerous. He'd spoken with all five of the male servants this afternoon to bar entry to most of the interior, which meant in some instances one actually had to step outside into the elements before one could pass into another section of the castle. Sebastian had half a mind to tie Freddie up and kidnap her as far away from Goddard Castle as possible. Kidnapping was prosecutable, but the tying up was certainly within his realm.

After lighting a branch of candles and tossing another log on the fire, he straightened the fresh sheets on the bed. The restraints were at the ready, because after caving in so easily today, Freddie might feel the need to prove she was not cooperative. Her independent streak was long and wide, and Sebastian had no wish to find himself scored by fingernails or beaten to a bloody pulp. Freddie seemed capable of just about anything. Her competence was frightening.

Wearing a silk banyan this time, he trod carefully on the worn stairs to her room below. She was sitting at a little desk, her spectacles slipping down her nose as she read a thick tome by candlelight. Her beautiful hair was in pigtails, and her voluminous white night rail had not transformed into a saucy negligee. Despite her every effort—and his, too, he thought ruefully—she still had appeal to his jaded palate, and he said so.

She snapped the book shut, and a cloud of dust erupted. "Rubbish."

"Seriously, Freddie. You could turn up at the Hellfire Club just as you are and they'd be mad for you." He began to unravel a braid as she sat stiff in her chair. His fingers worked through the silk, and he thought he saw a lessening of tension in her shoulders.

"I suppose you would know."

"I would, rather. I've made it my business to know such things."

"Why?"

"Why what?"

"Why have you done all the things you've done?"

Sebastian shrugged. It was not an issue he'd spent much debate on, especially since Egypt. What man of his acquaintance did not envy him and the life he led?

"Why not? Life is short, Freddie, and pleasure a fleeting thing. I'm not one to wear a hair shirt and deny myself anything. What's the point? We all have our little indulgences to get us through life. You have your books, don't you?" He gently removed her spectacles and folded them on top of her book.

"You can hardly equate my interest in history with your unnatural desires."

He began on the other braid. "Ah, Freddie. Who's to say what is natural? Man is imperfect. Surely your studies confirm that. Our fathers were living proof. We've all got the seven deadly sins to deal with." His fingers slipped into her silk. "Tell me, which is your favorite?"

She sputtered. "My favorite? What do you mean?"

"*Superbia, avarita, luxuria, invidia, gula, ira, acedia,*" he replied, stroking her unbound hair.

"You know Latin."

"I keep telling you, Freddie, I am not as stupid as you think." He stepped back to judge the cascade of hair down her back. "I'll just go fetch your hairbrush."

He was back from the dressing table in seconds. "Now, then, since you will not dine with me, I have no opinion on your gluttony. *Gula.* However, seeing you deliciously naked, I think you may have the slightest sweet tooth. Am I right?"

She wrestled the hairbrush from his hand. "Are you saying I'm fat, you odious man?"

"No, no, just delightfully rounded. Just as you should be. Rather perfect. You are showing your wrath right now, but I don't believe that's your worst sin. And we know it's not sloth—you run this place like a little general. If I had to guess, I'd say it's a toss-up between *superbia* and *luxuria.*"

Oh, her *ira* was on full display now. She threw the hairbrush against the stone wall. "You think me prideful and lustful? How dare you? I'll admit to the pride—I've plenty to be proud about—but as to the lust, I have never in my life—" She broke off, as if realizing her lie.

Oh, yes, she had been lusty. Ten years ago when she tricked him into taking her virginity. Last night, when she writhed and moaned and came around his cock with abandon. This morning, when she was too overcome to protest tupping a chimney sweep. This afternoon, when her nipples were diamond-hard in her bath, her hand beneath the water betraying her.

"Don't be ashamed of desire, Freddie. You're not dead yet. In fact, you're very much alive, with a thirst for the carnal knowledge you can't find in all your books that I'm more than happy to teach you."

"Ugh. It is you who is prideful, as though you're the only man in Yorkshire with a cock!"

He chuckled. "I should hope I'm the only man present who interests you. It wouldn't say much for your taste if you would prefer the grooms or the coachman or young Kenny. And you'd kill old Warren with just one of your kisses."

"You are ridiculous," she said crossly.

Her face was flushed, her chest heaving from their argument. Her blood was coursing as hot as his, and it would take all his effort not to fuck her right here, right now. But the stage was set in his room, and there they would play.

He held out a hand. "Come. We're wasting my day talking about sin when we can be doing it."

She ignored his outstretched arm and rose from the chair. "What if I've changed my mind about the castle, Sebastian? I'm beginning to think this is all too much trouble."

"Too late, my lady. You've put it in writing."

# Chapter 16

*I simply can't write about it.*

—FROM THE DIARY OF FREDERICA WELLS

She felt his eyes on her as she climbed the stairs to her doom. She'd been in his power not much more than twenty-four hours, although technically the day had belonged to her. She had botched that badly, thinking she could keep him at arm's length or sword point. She'd made an insincere effort to repel him this morning and could still feel traces of his kisses and cock no matter how hard she tried to scrub them away in the bath.

He was too handsome. But depraved. She should not like him so well—it went against all her better sense. He was a libertine with a wicked, teasing tongue who took nothing in life seriously. He would always answer "Why?" with "Why not?" Nothing seemed forbidden, and he seemed to have no shame or conscience. Not once did he question her proposal, or remind her that she would be forever ruined over real estate. He had accepted the offer of her body as his due, and had treated her as the most wicked harlot imaginable last night.

The shocking kisses to her core, the restraints, the opulent cream, the curious toy—all of it designed to subjugate her into his honeyed trap. She'd been defenseless. Witless. Wanton.

She paused on the last step to the tower room and turned to him. With one hearty shove, he could fall and crack his empty skull. "Don't you ever get tired of your form of amusement, Sebastian?"

"You've read too many temperance tracts, Freddie, and listened to too many zealots who espouse abstinence because they cannot get it up. Why should anyone get tired of pleasure in all its variety? I don't believe we were put on this earth to suffer if we can help it. Don't lie to me and tell me you found my cock in your cunt distasteful. Given time, you'll want it everywhere. Your mouth. Your arse." He reached to cup her bottom, his eyes glittering.

She slumped against the wall. Why did she waste her breath? His evil habits were ingrained, and were unlikely to change unless he got the pox and his nose fell off. He was not meant to be steady and dependable, or a husband and a father.

Which was just as well, as she had no need of him or any other man.

This affair was just a means to an end, to secure her future. She would do what he asked, because it meant nothing to either of them. Perhaps he was right. The pleasures of the flesh were basic. Animals did not pause in their rutting to question sin or proper positions. She'd heard the old ribald joke: "Why does the dog lick its balls? Because it can." Sex was nothing more than animal instinct, no matter how intellectual she fancied herself to be or how many books she read or wrote. There was probably no better man in all of England than Sebastian Goddard, Duke of Roxbury, to awaken her baser nature. Once he was gone, she would get back to normal and pray for forgiveness of her sins. Apparently, there were a great many of them ahead.

His room was warm, the only light cast from a tarnished candelabra and the firelight. Dim was good, the better to hide the evidence of her sweet tooth and lack of exercise. She'd had no one to fence with for months. The late duke's scholarly friends had stopped turning up once it was clear Frederica would not part with any valuable resources, and in any event, most of the friends were old and somewhat infirm, hardly a worthy challenge to her hard-won skills.

The duke had lived to a great age himself. He had married late in life, finally giving in for the need of an heir. And when he had, her father married, too. Their experiments with the opposite sex did not last long, and when Freddie's mother died in childbed, it was only natural for Joseph Wells to reunite with his longtime friend. Freddie remembered Sebastian's mother as a kindly, ladylike woman who loved to create beautiful interiors at Roxbury Park, filled with flowers and fluffy pillows. She would have been miserable in Goddard Castle, and horrified to know her little ward had grown up to fence with gentlemen.

It had been exhilarating this morning sparring with Sebastian, and tomorrow she would order him to the long gallery again. But tonight—the bed was turned down, the ropes coiled and ready. Her heart hitched and her hand trembled at the ribbon on her yoke.

"Let me." He stood over her, so close she could smell the mint and wine on his breath. His lean face was all shadow and edge, his eyes dark with evident desire. So she must not be so terribly fat after all.

Although, she reminded herself once again, he fucked everything.

He pulled the ribbon loose, slipping his hand inside the linen to cup a breast, still staring at her to gauge her response. When she didn't flinch, he pebbled her nipple between his fingertips, rolling it to a jewel-like peak. She felt the heat of his touch skitter down her belly to her bare mons. Yet he went no further than to massage her breast, gliding and flicking until she wanted so much more. As if he intuited her unspoken need, he bent to her fabric-covered nipple and suckled, his tongue swirling over the thin cloth until the friction was unbearable. She wished he'd rip her nightgown from her and tie her to the bed, giving her no choice but to allow him everything.

Anything.

Any wicked thing.

He caught her as she swayed, his mouth never leaving her body, tugging on her breast so she felt the pull to her womb. She held tight to him, unable to tell him to stop. Unwilling to lie, ashamed of her quick capitulation. He eased her onto the bed, his hands busy relieving her of the nightgown and smoothing down her skin. She closed her eyes to his triumphant expression, lay perfectly still as he wrapped her wrists and ankles in his ropes. Despite the fire, gooseflesh crept down her neck as she waited for what was to come.

"Ah, Frederica. You are exquisite." His voice was rough, coming from a distance away from the bed. It pleased her that he'd not called her by that silly childhood nickname. "Open your eyes."

She complied, only to see him still in his dark robe, a slender tasseled crop in his hand. Her tongue froze in shock, and then she cried out.

"Oh, God, no, Sebastian!"

"I will not harm you. Do you trust me?"

"No."

"I'll change your mind." He laid the whip across her lips, then trailed the tassels down her throat. The soft leather tickled more than anything. She watched as he brushed her nipples, circling the tips gently. The sensation was rather like tiny warm fingers playing across her skin. Sebastian's face was a study in concentration, as though he were memorizing each freckle and indentation. He inserted an end of the whip into her navel and held it still for a few seconds, pressing just hard enough for her to gasp, then continued to sweep down her body. Parting her labia, he stroked her clitoris, the fronds of leather a mere whisper against her swollen flesh.

"Sebastian!"

He lifted a wicked black eyebrow. "Yes?"

"You—I—"

He stopped the dreadful teasing. "Does it hurt?"

"No. It's—it's not enough." She would kill him tomorrow if he laughed at her tonight.

"What do you want, Frederica?"

"I don't know."

He slipped the length of the crop vertically within her folds. The tasseled tip rested over her belly. "Do you like this? Or would you prefer this?" His hand replaced the crop, plucking her bud between his fingers. She bit her lip to keep from crying out. "Or do you want my mouth there again, Frederica? Tell me."

She wouldn't beg. "I don't care."

"Little liar. I'll tell you what." He pulled the banyan over his head. Beneath it he was naked and marble-hard. Frederica felt an embarrassing gush of liquid between her open legs. "I'll kiss your cunt, Frederica. You tasted so sweet last night, I thought about you all day. But you'll taste me, too. I'm going to come in your mouth, and you'll come in mine."

"What?" His words made her dizzy. He was untying her wrists, and this time whatever knots he'd set didn't require cutting the bonds. He pulled her up to a sitting position, her legs still splayed wantonly.

"I'm going to be greedy now. *Avarita.* Me first. Another day we'll come in concert."

On his knees now, he straddled her body, his cock jutting toward her breasts. "Cup my stones."

She reached out gingerly. She saw the vein in his cock pulse as she touched him, its tip pearled with fluid. He fisted her hair and drew her closer.

"Bend to me and take me in your mouth."

"I don't—"

"Anything, Frederica. You promised. In writing."

She looked up at him, helpless. "I—I don't know what to do."

"You're a smart girl. Just don't bite me, or I *will* use the whip on you."

Frederica shuddered. She licked her lips, her mouth suddenly dry. He shoved some pillows behind her and pushed her head down, stroking the curve in her back until she opened to him and began to suckle. Sebastian muttered something encouraging, and her tongue and lips became bolder, licking from root to tip until he plunged himself deeper. One hand snaked down between them to circle her center as the hot velvet of him filled her mouth.

She knew at once when the power shifted. His breathing was ragged, his hold on her clumsy now, his touches more desperate. She didn't care whether she reached her climax—there was nothing more important than finding a rhythm to bring him to his, to taste the salty jet of semen that coated her tongue and dripped down her throat. She pumped her cheeks and milked his every drop, glancing up at him as he came. He stared back, his eyes black, his mouth twisted in what looked like agony. She knew better.

"Did you read this in a book, too?" he gasped, withdrawing and taking her face in his hands. He kissed her forehead and she suddenly felt like a child being rewarded for good behavior. But she had been very, very bad. The wonder of it was shocking. Thrilling.

She sat still while Sebastian took a corner of the sheet and wiped her mouth. His touch was tender, careful, a change from how rough he'd been earlier. But she hadn't minded his loss of control.

She shook her head. "There cannot be books about such things."

He laughed. "Oh, Freddie, you'd be surprised. We'll go exploring in my trunk another time."

"What else do you have in there?"

"One day at a time, love. I wouldn't want you to get bored before the month is out."

Frederica did not think boredom would ever be associated with this Duke of Roxbury. She slipped from his arms and lay back down on the bed. "I believe it's my turn now."

"It is. You've more than earned it." He eyed the restraints hanging slack from the rings at the head of the bed and raised a dark eyebrow.

She pulled the silk ropes closer, sliding her hands into the loops. Let him tighten them and tie her so she wouldn't fly off as he took her to heaven. Tonight, she was willing to be subject to his every whim. She'd find her conscience later.

# Chapter 17

*She may kill me yet.*

—FROM THE DIARY OF SEBASTIAN GODDARD,
DUKE OF ROXBURY

A shaft of bright sunlight penetrated the gap in the dusty red velvet curtains. He and Freddie had slept the morning away after a night filled with one surprise after another. Sebastian had thought himself incapable of surprise, but Freddie had proven him wrong again and again as she took him in her sweet mouth once more and submitted to him completely until dawn. She lay curled up against him now, her lovely bottom cushioning his hip, her streaky hair tangling down her back.

He wished he could see her face, count her freckles in the morning light, see how red her lips remained from his kisses. He had taken her from behind with ruthlessness and she hadn't objected, teased her from head to toe with the crop, tasted her honey as his tongue laved her cunt. He could not remember a time when one woman had satisfied him so completely or with such devastating innocence. It was as if the night banished the tart, grasping spinster Frederica Wells and left Delilah in her place.

Sebastian slipped out of bed and stretched. There would be no naked fencing today, but an alfresco picnic in the walled garden beneath the apple blossoms. Perhaps a walk on the moor if they didn't sink. Find a little stream where they could wade and splash and have sex. He would give Freddie a few hours of recovery time before he fucked her again. He'd chat her up, charm her, because that was what he did with women. He'd gotten good over the years at sensing what they wanted so he could get what he wanted. What he needed.

"What time is it?"

Freddie sat up, sweeping her tawny hair off her sleep-pink face. She clutched the sheet over her breasts, a rather futile effort since they were pink, too, from his love bites.

"Nearly noon. Did you sleep well?" Remarkably, he had. He rarely spent the entire night beside whichever woman he fucked, choosing instead to claim his own space once he'd taken his pleasure. It had not been much of a trial to have Freddie's soft little body near, however.

"Noon! I never sleep so late."

"Well, my dear, we didn't get to sleep until well after dawn. Don't castigate yourself for a slugabed."

She reached for her discarded night rail. "I have things I should see to."

"No." His voice brooked no disagreement. "You are mine for the day. Did you forget?"

"I thought after last night—"

"That I'd had my fill of you? Ah, no, Freddie. My days are precious to me. You'll not cheat me out of them."

"You cheated me out of yesterday," she muttered.

"For a mere half hour. Alas, perhaps I was even quicker. And as I recall, you were perfectly willing."

She glared at him. "Wipe that smug smile off your face! You are not God's gift to womankind."

"Have you complaints, Freddie?"

She flushed brick red and said nothing.

"I thought not. But do tell me where there's room for improvement. I do aim to please."

She threw the night rail over her head and disappeared for a moment. Sebastian was fairly certain she cursed him underneath the cotton wrinkles. Her face popped out, looking less love-struck by the minute.

"How would I know what you should do? I've never even dreamed of most of the horrible things you've done."

"*We've* done, Freddie. I was hardly alone. And what exactly has been so horrible?"

"Everything!" she cried.

Sebastian smiled and opened his trunk. He heard a hiss from the bed, but he merely pulled a clean pair of breeches from his belongings. "I'm going downstairs to get Mrs. Holloway to pack us a picnic lunch in the lady's garden. It will serve double duty as our breakfast. Say in half an hour? Shall I have coffee or tea sent up to you while you dress?"

"No. The staff has better things to do than climb the stairs for me."

"Don't be absurd, Freddie. That's their job."

"You forget they haven't been paid in eons."

That brought Sebastian up short. Damn it, it would take him months to settle his entanglements and obligations, even with some of Freddie's fortune in his back pocket. She was welcome to the rest—he wouldn't make her wait until she was thirty. He'd release all her funds to her—it was up to the guardian's discretion. She'd have her assets,

but at the moment her tongue was not one of them. He left her grumbling in his bed and wound his way into the kitchens. Alice skittered
to a corner, but Mrs. Holloway seemed to be getting used to seeing
a duke in her domain and barely looked up from rolling out dough.

"I was wondering if we would see you this morning, Your Grace. I
can get breakfast up to the dining hall in a jiffy."

"No need. From last year's harvest?" Sebastian picked up a shriveled apple from a wooden bowl and took a bite.

She waved a floury finger at him. "Oh, Your Grace, you shouldn't
be taking that! I was going to make applesauce. Those there have gone
by for eating. The good ones are in a barrel in the cellars."

His mouth was filled with a combination of mush and wood.
Once he swallowed, he asked, "Is the little orchard productive, then?"

Mrs. Holloway nodded. "It is, sir. Miss Frederica and the men
have tended the trees faithfully. The yield's enough for the household.
The castle grows all its own vegetables, too. What we don't grow, we
barter for. Miss Frederica and Alice and I make fine soaps and lotions
to sell locally. Much nicer than you'd get in any store."

Sebastian recalled the neatly lined shelves in the bathing room,
bottles glistening. Good—when his jar of cream ran out, Frederica
could supply her own. He pictured her rubbing some concoction on
his cock before she eased herself down upon it.

"Could you get together a simple basket lunch for us, Mrs. Holloway? I'm going to inspect the walled garden with Miss Frederica when
she wakes up."

The cook gave him a knowing look. The castle was large, but
sounds echoed against the cold stone walls. He and Freddie had given
the Archibald Walkers a run for their money what with the screaming
and the moaning all through the night, but maybe their voices had
blended with the usual castle caterwauling.

"I'll be happy to. Alice, fetch some pasties from the larder for the duke. A nice wedge of my cheese."

"Some wine," murmured Sebastian.

"For breakfast? Oh! Pardon my rudeness, Your Grace. I don't believe Miss Frederica enjoys spirits that much. Go right to her head, they do. I'll just pack a bottle of lemonade for her."

Sebastian filed away that interesting tidbit. If Freddie was so uninhibited without wine, what would she be willing to do when she was tipsy? He was determined to find out.

But perhaps he already had found out exactly what she was capable of. She'd come to him ten years ago, smelling of roses and apricot ratafia. He'd pressed the drinks on her himself. She was filled with Dutch courage so she could ruin his life while he ruined her.

When he returned to his room with a pitcher of wash water, all traces of Freddie had disappeared. Good little housekeeper that she was, she'd straightened the bed and plumped up the pillows. The window was open to the breeze, his robe folded over the trunk. If he had a farthing, he'd bet Freddie had taken advantage of his absence to snoop inside. He hoped she wasn't too shocked by what she found.

He stripped again and gave himself a rather thorough sponge bath, cleaned his teeth and brushed his longish hair into some semblance of order. Sebastian wondered if Freddie was as skilled in barbering as everything else, although if she truly were his Delilah, he'd not trust her an inch with a pair of scissors. He pulled a fresh lawn shirt over his head and donned his nankeens but skipped all the other constricting layers a gentleman wore. He was no gentleman.

Opening his trunk, he fished through his stockings until he found the slender leather-bound diary. A foolish affectation to be sure—he was no Boswell, either, but it amused him to keep track of his conquests. He had a drawerful of diaries at Roxbury Park dating back to his school days.

There was another diary he buried at the bottom of his trunk. He carried it with him at all times, written not as the events depicted within were happening, but after. The days covered by this diary's notations had not afforded him paper, or pens, or even the will or strength to write about them at the time. But once Sebastian was free of this particular past, he needed to write about it. He was still trying to make sense of the months he spent in Egypt, but wondered if he ever would.

Now was not the time to dwell on unpleasantness. He penned a few lines in his current journal praising Freddie's surprising effect upon him and left the page open to the air to dry, anchoring it on his father's desk with the chipped inkpot.

She was waiting for him on the round stone bench in the center of the garden. It was sheltered by some sort of flowering tree—he was no horticulturist—but she'd clapped on an absurdly outdated straw hat against the sun. She'd already unpacked the basket and was eating a hard-boiled egg with wolfish abandon.

"Starving, are you? A good tupping always makes me hungry, too."

Freddie looked as if a bit of egg lodged in her throat. Sebastian patted her back with some force, then untied her bonnet and tossed it to the clipped grass.

"Ouch! I'm perfectly fine. And that's my best hat!"

"I don't believe it. When was the last time you went shopping?"

Freddie scrunched up her face. "A year or two before your father passed. He was very ill, you know—I couldn't leave him long enough to go to York to bother with shopping."

"I almost wish you'd written." Would he have come home? Possibly not. But his animus toward his father had abated over the years. As Sebastian himself experimented, he had realized just how trapped a man like his father had been in society, being forbidden from acknowledging what he was, being forced to live a lie. Sebastian could well forgive the sex, but the obsession with scholarship was still a thorn. Sebastian wondered how Phillip Goddard had torn himself away long enough from his books to fuck his unwanted wife and plant his seed thirty-one years and nine months ago. Sebastian's mother had died when Sebastian was ten, and Sebastian might as well have. The old duke was too preoccupied living in the distant past to notice that his only child existed in the present.

"The duke forbade me to write to you. And what good would it have done? You couldn't be found for almost a year as it was."

Sebastian uncorked the wine and poured some into a goblet. He took a sip. Vinegar. His father had kept a very good cellar, but this was not a prime example. "I was in Egypt for several years. Signed on for an archaeological dig. There was a bit of a problem, so no mail reached me for months."

"An historical venture? You did not!"

"I did indeed. Of course, they hired me more for my brawn than my brain. Did you think I was simply enjoying myself in a brothel in Budapest? I confess I did that, too."

"Oh, you're impossible!"

He grinned at her. "Undoubtedly. But the pater would have been proud of me poking around *real* antiquities. I had to keep myself in blunt, Freddie, so I made myself useful where I could. There were benefits. The Egyptian dancing girls, for example. All those veils. The dusky skin, the liquid eyes—"

"That's quite enough," Freddie snapped. She sliced a morsel of cheese from the wedge but did not put it to her lips. He took the knife from her and divided a warm beef pasty in half.

"For you," he said pushing it toward her. "There seems to be only the one."

"I ate mine already," Freddie said, her eyes downcast. So she *was* a woman of uncontrollable appetites. He liked the idea of an undisciplined Freddie, who might eat dessert first or shake the Christmas present in impatience.

"Shall I tell you about Egypt?" He had many tales, though a few would remain his secret, only for the diary buried at the bottom of his trunk.

She gave an exaggerated sigh. "If you must."

"I thought a scholar like you would appreciate expanding your knowledge of the world."

"Only if you stick to decency. With that caveat, I expect your stories will be brief."

Sebastian threw his head back and laughed. "I see my father did a thorough job convincing you of my sins, and what I tell you this afternoon will only confirm your opinion. I was factotum for a few months to the notorious Henry Kipp. You've heard of him?"

"The man who steals Egypt's treasures? Oh, Sebastian!" she said with dismay.

"The very same. And beds every female he meets, willing or unwilling. A friend of a friend of a friend got me the position, but between Kipp's dishonesty and his penchant for schoolgirls, I resigned as soon as I was able. But I should have stuck with him. He at least passed around enough baksheesh to keep us all safe. I threw my lot in with another company, and wound up spending a bit of time in prison. Filthy place."

Freddie's mouth hung open. "You were in gaol?"

"My friend Cameron Ryder and I both. I told you there was a mix-up. One Englishman is much the same as another in that part of the world, and I believe we were arrested to pay for Kipp's sins, although we were hardly on his level. I used my courtesy marquessate to no effect whatsoever. My captor did not care that I was heir to a dukedom. Once I extricated myself, I was anxious to see if all my parts were in working order. I'm afraid, Freddie, that I embraced debauchery for a few months after my release with a fervor that would make you blush. I was not checking my poste restante on a daily basis."

There. That sounded sufficiently vague and devil-may-care. His voice did not betray him in the slightest fraction.

"Ooh. Was it very awful?"

"Don't sound so pleased, Freddie. Yes, it was. Made me almost glad to come back to England and the mountain of debt that awaited me. I count myself lucky I was able to escape."

"How did you?"

"Cam's very clever. A self-made man who's done quite well in the antiquities business. Not a crook like Kipp, and handsome to boot, although not as handsome as I." She rolled her eyes at his outrageousness. It was such fun to tease her, and it turned his mind away from the darkness. "Cam has a unique interest in this castle. He is one of the gentlemen I've invited to look it over for purchase."

Freddie glared at him. It was an expression he was getting used to. "You said you'd tell them not to come."

He licked the crumbs from his fingers and tucked into the second half of his lunch. "And so I did. Sent someone off to mail the letters yesterday. We shall be quite alone for the remainder of May."

She didn't look as relieved as she might, probably counting all the nights—and days—ahead that belonged to him. But after all, this arrangement was her idea.

"How did you and this Mr. Ryder get out?"

Sebastian wiped his lips with a linen napkin. "That's a story for another day. I propose—if you're finished crushing that piece of cheese between your fingers—that we go for a walk while the weather's so fine. With any luck, you might be able to push me into a bog and I'll sink into oblivion. I'm not certain who's next in line to the succession, but I doubt they'll be as demanding as I. I want to fuck you under the open sky, Freddie, so we'll need to get away from the prying eyes of the servants. I expect I'll see nose prints on the windows when I go in. Go into the castle like a good girl and fetch a quilt for us. I wouldn't want you to get a thistle up your arse."

Freddie responded by throwing everything back into a heap in the basket and stomping off under the archway. Sebastian was left with the gentle breeze and the birdsong. It really was a lovely day, certainly a better view than that from his prison cell. And it would be even lovelier with Freddie beneath him. Or above him.

# Chapter 18

*When will it ever end?*

—FROM THE DIARY OF FREDERICA WELLS

The nerve of him! She could barely walk as it was. Would he never relent in his wicked seduction? She wished he were still in an African prison, giant beetles crawling into his every orifice. Certainly up *his* arse.

Phillip Goddard, her late guardian, had never said one word about Sebastian's employment in Egypt, if he ever knew of it. Sebastian was an extremely poor correspondent—even before the estrangement it had been too burdensome for him to write letters. Sometimes years would go by without Uncle Phillip ever receiving anything in his son's handwriting, and then they were the barest bones. He never asked for money, which was a lucky thing, because there wasn't any. Uncle Phillip had outspent himself on his collections, and several investments had failed rather spectacularly. But he wouldn't hear of dipping into Freddie's trust.

She had inherited bits and pieces from her family. They had not been rich or elevated high in society, but were respectable enough. Unlike his own luck with money, Uncle Phillip had managed to invest hers with better results. And he turned over every penny of royalties to her from the books. His guilt money. She knew he regretted all those things he said that night about her. And what he'd done, telling Sebastian she'd been paid off not to make a fuss.

It might have softened the old duke's opinion to know that Sebastian was off on a dig, although probably not. Henry Kipp was not the sort of man whom proper scholars respected. He was a thief and worse. In any event, Uncle Phillip had no interest in any historical time period save the Middle Ages.

Frederica set the remains of their picnic down on the kitchen worktable, avoiding Mrs. Holloway's eyes. "Thank you for the lunch. It was delicious."

"I don't reckon his lordship liked the wine, though."

Freddie bit a lip. It had been very bad of her to put the most sour of the old duke's bottles in the basket. "One should not be drinking so early in the day," she said, falsely virtuous. This at least was one form of corruption she could resist. She knew all too well what happened to her when she drank. She became brazen enough to seduce handsome young marquesses in tumbledown towers. "His Grace wishes to take a walk and examine the property. We shall be gone for some time."

"Very well, Miss Frederica. You two enjoy yourselves."

Freddie pulled an old moth-eaten cloak off a hook. "Just in case the wind comes up. You know how undependable the weather can be."

"Mm-hmm. And don't forget to pick up your bonnet. You don't want to give those freckles any more encouragement."

Lord, Sebastian had been right. The whole household was probably watching them as they ate. They'd seen Sebastian toss her hat aside and give her those wicked, smoldering looks. At least he hadn't kissed her, even though much of the time he seemed focused on her mouth.

"Will you be dining with the duke tonight, my dear? I'm roasting a joint."

Oh, yes. Sebastian would probably insist on her presence, all the better to stare down the long table at her, undressing her with his eyes.

"That sounds delicious, Mrs. Holloway. I look forward to it. Tell Warren to set two places tonight, but tomorrow, the duke will definitely be dining alone."

Happy to exert her authority in this one small thing, she returned to the serpent in the lady's garden. She bent to pick up her hat, knowing that Sebastian was inspecting her muslin-covered bottom.

"I'm ready. Let's get this over with."

Sebastian quirked an eyebrow, but said nothing, simply extended his arm. With the utmost reluctance, she took it, and they passed through the garden gate.

The grassy track was uneven, as was her heartbeat. Forced to cling to Sebastian's arm so she wouldn't lose her footing, Frederica climbed up the rise to the highest point on Roxbury land. Odd that Goddard Castle wasn't on it for defensive purposes. It loomed behind them, a picturesque ruin that would soon be hers. The rolling hills and moors framed it, the variegated colors of green and gold and gray deceptively bucolic. There wasn't anything else to be seen for miles save sky and earth and crumbling castle.

She planned to hire masons who could repair what was repairable. The rest she would have torn down. She didn't plan to spend her old age worrying about collapsing walls and crushing debt. She would limit the amount of money she invested. As it was, her expenditures were sure to alter her future. No longer was she absolutely sure she could live comfortably for decades with a hired companion. She and

Sebastian had not agreed on a price as yet, but she wouldn't let him steal her blind. Bad enough he'd stolen her senses.

He had taken the black cloak from her and twirled it now and again, like some villain in a bad melodrama. He'd made her unfasten her bonnet ribbons, so the hat bounced on her back with every step she took. Frederica's hair was loosening from its pins, and her cheeks were warm from keeping up with Sebastian's brisk pace. His strides were ever so much longer than hers and she had lost her breath a mile back, which suited her. If she could talk, she'd only be wasting her words on Sebastian. He had a singular purpose in mind and was not about to be deterred.

How fortunate they'd encountered no one, not even a stray sheep, on this excursion. Frederica prayed that their luck would continue. The thought of being found in flagrante delicto under the York-shire sky was too mortifying. Sebastian would go back to Budapest or Egypt, but she would be stuck here for the rest of her life with a ruined reputation.

What must it be like to travel the world? She envied Sebastian a little, although she didn't yearn to be imprisoned. She'd known only two homes—Roxbury Park and Goddard Castle. She'd come to the Dorset estate with her father when she was just a baby. When her father and Uncle Phillip traveled, she'd been left safe at the park, the pet of Warren and the other staff. After her father died, Uncle Phillip had traveled alone in his quest for medieval grails and she remained at Goddard Castle, doing research and organizing the duke's notes. She'd had no debut, of course—she was not from a high ton fam-ily, and her virginity was definitely disposed of. She'd given it to Sebastian, tossing it away as heedlessly as he'd tossed her bonnet in the lady's garden.

Uncle Phillip never spoke of that night directly, but she knew he was filled with deep regret. His pride had proven his downfall. His *superbia*. He had been a distractedly affectionate second father to her, but she'd had no idea he thought her so very unfit for his precious only son. His words had been ruthless, hurting her father far more than they hurt her. She knew Uncle Phillip had changed his mind over the years, in hopes that Sebastian would come back. But it was too late to soften the blow to Joseph Wells—he'd died of a broken heart.

But she had her money. And now she had a month of such sexual splendor that it terrified her.

Sebastian stopped at last, surveying the vista. The moorland stretched out below, broken here and there by crumbling limestone walls and stunted trees. With a flourish, he spread the cloak on the ground and pulled her down beside him.

"Tolerable view," he said, looking at her rather than the distant castle. His hand clasped hers, his thumb idly circling in her palm. Even this light touch felt wicked. She tried to ignore it and him, gazing out at the spring green grass and sedges.

"It is pretty. I don't come up here often enough."

"You've got your nose buried too deep in books."

She sniffed with it. "I have an obligation to your father's publisher to complete the set. I'm lucky he agreed to let me continue."

"Why bother? Your name isn't even on them."

Nor was she mentioned in a dedication or appreciation—that went to her father—but the work was more important than the recognition. And Phillip Goddard had put every penny of his royalties into a trust for her, when he could have used the money himself. Schools used the texts, and libraries throughout Europe—and even America— stocked the series. It had netted quite a bit, and was the source of all her riches. "I do it to honor the memory of Uncle Phillip. And my father, too. They spent their lives gathering information and artifacts."

Sebastian gave a disgusted snort. "They were mad, the both of them. And I don't mean because they fucked each other."

She flinched. "You know as well as I do they were in love, Sebastian. You heard them."

He said nothing. The subject was obviously still too raw for him, so she switched tacks. "You should at least understand their interest in history after you yourself went on archaeological searches."

"To *sell* things, not buy them, Freddie. That's a big difference."

"Well, at least you'll get the proceeds when I complete the last volume of *Roxbury's Middle Ages*. The publisher will honor the contract settlement to your father's devisal."

He stopped teasing her hand, dropping it into her lap. "*I'm* to be paid for your work? That's preposterous! Even a devil such as I has some integrity. I'll not touch a penny of it." Sebastian's face had darkened in anger. If he wasn't really upset at the prospect of ill-gotten gains, he gave a very good performance, now the hero of the melodrama rather than the villain.

"But I thought you needed money."

"I do, but I've got some standards. I won't harness a woman to my plow." He ripped up a tuft of grass, scattering it in the breeze.

"But you'd marry an heiress, wouldn't you? What's the difference?"

His face was truly an alarming color now. "I'm not marrying an heiress! I'm not marrying anyone! Damn it, Freddie, I may be ramshackle, but not even in the same league with my father. He enslaved you in his project and bankrupted the duchy. The man deserves to roast in hell for what he's done to the both of us."

"I assure you I was perfectly willing to help him. There was no enslavement. He hired me in my father's stead. It is *you* who relishes being my master."

"That's completely different."

"How so? You tie me. You—you tell me to do shocking things."

"And you do them. And enjoy them."

That was only too true. For a woman who'd considered herself independent for as long as she could remember, she was shamefully drawn in to Sebastian's sensual sport.

"What if I said no? Would you force me?" She searched his face for a trace of cruelty.

Sebastian caught a strand of hair and tucked it behind her ear, looking at her as earnestly as she looked at him. "You misunderstand all of this, Freddie. It's not a question of me having all the power. Forcing you. I could not do what I do to you without you wanting it. You need to remember that when it comes to your days. There's no pleasure in humiliation. Or housework. This is all about pleasure, Freddie. Living your fantasies. Don't lose sight of that in your attempts to one-up me."

Frederica swallowed. "I'm not used to such pleasures."

"I know. The corruption of innocents is always a favorite fantasy of mine. Although you're not precisely innocent, are you? How are things going in the dairy barn, little milkmaid?"

She batted him away. "Are you never serious? Everything is a game to you." She would not try to make excuses. She had been every bit the deceiver he thought she was, foolish enough to think if she gave him her body, he would somehow fall in love with her, make him see that she was not just little Freddie, his semisister.

"Yes, I'm an idle, rutting bastard. Don't try to make me feel guilty. I don't, and I won't."

"You say you won't marry. What happens when you grow too old to indulge yourself?"

His eyes slid away. "Contrary to what you hear, old people still have sex. Perhaps not with such vigor as we've experienced the past few days. Perhaps with more moderation. I have every hope that I'll go to my grave with a smile on my face after expiring under the lips and hands of my lover."

"Eww! How revolting for the woman, to have a man die in her bed!"

"Don't worry," he said, his lips curving. "I still have a few good years left. But fewer hours in this day than I'd like." He pulled her bonnet string and her hat rolled down the hill. "Leave it. It's ghastly. I'll buy you a nicer hat."

"With what money?"

"Mere details. You're so full of questions, Freddie. Before you ask, let me tell you what we're going to do right here, right now."

He bent to her ear, whispering words both so alarming and so alluring she felt the blush to the toes in her slippers. His fingers were nimble, unhooking her dress, unlacing her corset, unpinning her hair. She was down to her shift in seconds, and after the dark look Sebastian gave her, she pulled it over her head.

"Help me with my boots, Freddie."

She got down awkwardly on her knees, too aware that Sebastian appreciated the picture she made. After a few tugs, the leather boots slipped from his stockinged feet. He stood up and took care of the rest of his clothes himself, then returned to the spread-out cloak.

It was the first time she had a clear understanding of him naked. There were no shadows from candles at night or the dim light from the long gallery, nothing but bright sunshine to reveal every plane and muscle. He sat perfectly still, as though he expected her to inspect him. His cock was already at the ready. Frederica put a hand to his chest, and he covered it with his own.

"Do you like what you see?"

"You are vain. And arrogant."

"Yes. I have no false modesty, I'm afraid. I like what I see, Freddie. You are luscious."

"I bet you say that to everyone."

"Not always. Sometimes I tell them they're incomparable. Delicious. Divine."

"Just empty words, Sebastian. Show me."

He lifted an eyebrow in surprise. "So bold for a woman on her knees. Lie down."

This was not what he'd described with his wicked whispering, but she complied. His hand stroked her body as he kissed her deeply, his touch so deft she trembled. There was something very primal about kissing naked and with such naked abandon under the sky. Her reservations about the wisdom of Sebastian's plan became as wispy as the clouds. She felt as natural as the grass and earth beneath her, as free as the light breeze that gentled over them. Though the sun warmed her body, she shivered.

Sebastian broke the kiss and held her close. "You are not cold?"

"No. I just—feel things. Don't stop."

"Sweet as your mouth is, I want to kiss you somewhere else now. Do as I said, Frederica."

He lay flat on his back. What he asked of her—what he ordered her to do—took her one step further into his web. She felt clumsy, but she turned and positioned herself on her parted knees over his body. No longer could she see the lazy sensuality of his face, but rather his cockstand. It hovered up near her lips, dark and hard. His black nether curls were trimmed, though not as thoroughly as hers. It horrified her to think what he was looking at right now, her bum in the air, her glistening bare folds above his face. She could feel his breath, his hands holding her thighs, his tongue as it swiped and swooped and plundered. He had kissed her there before, and she had taken him in her mouth before, but never from this position, never feeling both so vulnerable and so commanding at the same time. She took a tentative lick, earning his groan against her center.

And then she duplicated what he did to her, hands and lips busy, relishing the heat and hardness. Each movement was an echo of his, until he was buried in her in the most profound ways. They attacked and anticipated each other, all wet mouth and salty taste and slippery sensation, bringing them both to such a dizzying edge that they lost control. The unbearable tension snapped, the invisible knots unraveled, and Frederica was as free as she had ever been, separate yet joined to Sebastian in the sweetest of sin. She crested, tumbled, then rolled over him, collapsing on her back, too stunned to speak.

They lay side by side in satiated quiet. Sebastian reached for her hand and squeezed it. She was too weak to return the gesture, sure she would never move again without a week of sleep. She smiled— perhaps Sebastian could carry her home.

His voice rumbled near her ankle. "What are you thinking?"

"Nothing. My mind is a perfect blank."

"Come, now. No compliments?"

She struggled to sit up. "You are without a doubt the most conceited man I've ever met."

"I don't doubt that is true. You haven't met many. It's been slim pickings for you up here. I should take you to London to meet my friends."

"I have no wish to be fashionable," she said honestly. "And if your friends are anything like you, I shouldn't enjoy their company at all."

Sebastian laughed, clasping his hands behind his head. His body was too long for the cloak, and blades of grass stuck to his dark hair. "My little wasp. Needless to say, I would not allow my friends the liberties I've taken with you. I'd be a bit possessive, I think."

"Is that supposed to make me feel better?"

"I can't tell you how to feel, Freddie. But I hope you trust me some. I didn't come up here to be seduced."

"True. You came to throw me out of my house."

"Let's not quibble over details. The devil's in them."

He seemed perfectly satisfied to lie naked where anyone could come upon them. Distancing herself from his spell, she reached for her shift. He stayed her hand.

"Not yet. I want to look my fill in the daylight."

"Really, Sebastian, you have seen *every inch* of me after today," she said, annoyed.

"Places I bet you haven't seen yourself, Freddie." He grinned. "Candlelight is all very romantic, but nothing beats the sun for a thorough inspection. Your freckles, for example. I knew you had some, but they're everywhere, aren't they? Even here," he said, smoothing his hand where her pubic hair used to be. "I think I see constellations. Is that Virgo right there?"

"I'm hardly a virgin now."

"No," he said, his voice thoughtful. "Tell me the truth, Freddie. I want to know about that night ten years ago. Oh, not about our fathers. About us."

Frederica felt a prickle on her scalp. She straightened her shoulders and looked down her nose at him. It was hard to appear superior when she felt so very exposed. Not only was she undressed, but Sebastian seemed to have the unnerving ability to see straight into her soul. "I was stupid. And more than a little drunk."

"Did you think to trap me into marriage back then?"

*Yes.* No, not really—that would have been too much to hope for. She had just wanted him so. But her tongue refused to say that, saving what pride she had left after becoming his concubine. "Why would I have wanted to marry you? You were already a disgrace," she said, trying to keep her voice light. "I was just curious, and you were handy."

"So you felt nothing?" It was hard to tell what *he* was feeling *now*, so neutral was his tone. She couldn't give him an honest answer to his question anyway. As to why she had thrown herself at Sebastian Goddard ten years ago, she had no idea except she had been a total idiot. And she wasn't much smarter now.

"I know no matter what I say, you'll think I tried to trick you. But you made an offer of marriage, and I refused. It was not the most romantic proposal I've received."

"No," he said dryly, "I imagine not. The circumstances were a touch farcical."

"Not tragic?"

"Not anymore. I admit to being naïve back then. About our fathers, I mean. One doesn't want to see oneself as simply a necessary cog in the Roxbury lineage, just another name to add to the family Bible. I kept hoping—" He broke off, apparently loath to reveal more. "I've been careful not to litter the landscape with by-blows, but I suppose at some point I'll have to secure the succession, just as my father did, only perhaps with more enthusiasm for the gender of the mother." He sighed. "More Dukes of Roxbury for the future—just what the world needs. I think most of them have been cork-brained or criminals so far. Perhaps my son will break the mold."

Her heart squeezed just a little. "So you *do* plan to marry."

"Not anytime soon. And certainly not you."

Frederica was stung. "I wouldn't marry you anyway, even if you begged on bended knee with a raft full of roses and singing bluebirds. When June first comes I shall be free of you and your wicked ways. I loathe you, Sebastian Goddard. You—you bring out the very worst in me. I could easily murder you in your sleep."

"I'll have to sleep with one eye open. You are so passionate, Freddie. It's a pity you seek to hide it. You're eight-and-twenty now, not some starry-eyed schoolgirl. It's past time for you to have a bit of fun."

"I'd hardly call this a bit of fun," Frederica raged, struggling to break Sebastian's hold. Her face grew as hot as her temper. He released her arms, and she rubbed away his touch. Throwing on her clothes, she left him sitting on the cloak, the wind ruffling his dark hair. He looked so handsome she wanted to take a rock to his head. Worse, he made no effort to stop her as she scrambled down the track.

# Chapter 19

*One really must think before one speaks.*
—FROM THE DIARY OF SEBASTIAN GODDARD,
DUKE OF ROXBURY

By all that was holy, and everything that was not, he had bungled in the worst way. It never did to bring up the past. He was no Janus—he wanted only to face the future. And what did it matter if she had been a foolish girl and had loved him a little bit? He was in no danger from her now.

Sebastian watched her march off. He really should go after her in case she fell into a sinkhole and took her ill-gotten dowry with her. He imagined he would not find he was the beneficiary of her will.

He could still taste her essence on his tongue and smell her womanly musk. He would be hard-pressed to find another demivirgin who took to sin as well as Frederica Wells. He fished his pocket watch out of his trousers. Ordinarily he never gave a damn about time. He came and went as he pleased. But now that his hours with Freddie were fixed, he checked to see how many more of them he would have before she tossed him into the dungeon at midnight.

Not enough. Dinner would take up precious minutes, but maybe he could persuade her to spread herself out like a banquet on the trestle table. He chuckled. Not likely. She would be prim and proper for old Warren, mincing up her food and ingesting tiny morsels. Whereas Sebastian would want to gobble up everything in sight, particularly Freddie, the sooner he could get them both behind closed doors.

The more he fucked her, the more he wanted to. There were several methods of lovemaking as yet unexplored. She'd been an apt pupil so far, not needing to be restrained to obey him. His cock twitched thinking of her blindfolded and spread-eagle on his bed. But then he thought how appealing her legs would be locked around his hips, her nails scoring his back, her hazy blue eyes drugged with lust. Truly, any scenario to his way of thinking was as good as another.

He took a deep breath of Yorkshire air, but it did nothing to clear his head or calm his cock. If he hustled, he could catch up with her, toss her on the ground and fuck her before teatime. The view would not be as compelling below, but it was hardly the scenery he was after.

Having years of experience getting in and out of his clothes in record time, he rolled up the cape and jogged down the path before Freddie had walked too far. She'd forgotten that abomination of a hat, and a fistful of her hairpins was in his pocket. She was battling her hair in the wind, which had picked up as the afternoon waned. Medusa-like strands blew across her face and she was looking even more irritated than she was earlier, if that were possible.

"Freddie! Hold up!"

She gave him a scathing look but didn't stop. He caught a fistful of hair and brought her to heel.

"Ouch! Unhand me, you devil!"

He did as she asked, watching a bronzy wave of hair get stuck in her mouth. "I've come with hats and hairpins, Freddie. Sit down and

I'll make you presentable." Turning away from him, she tripped on a stone on the path and he caught her before she fell to the ground. "There, see? I told you I'd be useful."

He dropped the cloak again. Freddie looked at it with suspicion, as though she divined exactly what his purpose was. They were closer to the castle now, but still far enough away from prying eyes. He was as hard as the stone she tripped on, and she eyed his bulge with suspicion, too.

"I'm going to be *very* useful. Let's make up, Freddie. I'm sorry I quizzed you. It doesn't matter what you were thinking back then."

"I wasn't thinking of anything. I told you I was drunk," she said mulishly.

"I wish you were right now. You'd be a lot easier." But she would do what he told her. She had to. "Lift your skirts first, and then we'll get to the matter of your toilette."

Without a word, she lay back and bunched up the muslin. He noticed as he mounted her that her hooks were fastened incorrectly. He'd see to them later, too. Right now, he was sheathed in her decadently wet passage for a quick, hard fuck, because he was far too impatient for finesse. Even angry at him, Freddie seemed to have no objection, bucking beneath him and moaning. His last coherent thought before he spilled himself in her was that if she got pregnant, he might be forced to marry her after all. He'd have to be more careful in the future. His orgasm ripped like thunder through him, and then he remembered to kiss her. The entire event had taken an embarrassingly short amount of time.

Could he manage the walk home? The lassitude was nearly overwhelming. Sebastian thought he could lie out here forever, teasing Freddie's soft skin with his fingertips. She was smooth everywhere save for her hands, which showed the evidence of her labors. But their roughness felt like welcome fire against him.

He was getting soft in the head, being led around by his cock. Freddie was a surprising diversion, but he must not lose sight of his needs. He'd given too much up to her already. Pleasant as it had been, it was time for him to regain control. His whip had been underused last evening.

Not that he would hurt her with it. Not as he had been hurt.

"Sebastian."

"Mm."

"The clouds."

He flopped over on his back, his eyes still closed. "What of them?"

"Look to the west. It's going to rain."

Reluctantly he stirred and squinted above. "Impossible. The sun is shining."

"Storms come up quickly here. We really should get back."

"And here I was feeling like Adam to your Eve. Except with too many clothes. Sit up and I'll straighten you out."

He saw to himself first, then combed through her tangled hair with his fingers, pinning it up quite credibly with the hairpins he'd salvaged. He hooked her dress and brushed the blades of grass from her back. All the while she was too quiet, as still as a doll on the toy store shelf. He'd expected her to rail at him for the somewhat brutal tumble, but her pink lips stayed buttoned, her eyes downcast.

"There. Good as new."

"I'll never be good again," she said morosely.

"Why should you be, when bad is so much better?" he joked. She didn't smile.

Fine. He'd give her a few hours to herself. She was worn out from sex and sunshine, as was he. Sebastian helped Freddie to her feet and tied the hideous bonnet to her head. A strong gust of wind blew the brim back, revealing every sweet freckle on her face. He took her hand and placed it on his arm.

They walked back in silence, the only sound a distant rumble of thunder and the whistling wind. Gray clouds scudded low across the sky, warring with the sun. Before they reached the outer wall, fat droplets of rain were coming down upon them.

"It's a good thing we're home," Freddie said. "The rain may not last long, but the midges that come out after a storm would bite us without mercy."

"How delightful," Sebastian drawled. "There are no midges in London, you know."

"I am not going to London or anywhere else with you! And a little lavender or lemon oil works quite well to repel them. I wish I could find some oil to repel *you*."

"Tut-tut. Even if you are a bit of a white witch, there is nothing in your jars and bottles which would have the power to turn me away from you, Freddie. We made a deal." That was all it was, a bargain on paper for a castle he didn't want with a woman he didn't trust.

A crack of lightning rent the sky, the accompanying clap of thunder drowning out Freddie's undoubtedly disparaging retort. Feeling a sudden burst of energy, Sebastian picked her up and dashed into the courtyard with her as the rain pounded down and turned the world gray-green. As if he'd been waiting for them all afternoon, Warren opened the massive iron-banded front door.

"Cutting it awfully close, Miss Frederica. I told you it would storm this afternoon."

"So you did, Warren. Sebastian, do set me down." Once her feet were on the flagstones, Freddie took her soggy hat off and studied it with dismay. Good. It was now beyond the pale. Sebastian decided he would buy a new hat for her at the earliest opportunity, perhaps even two or three, expense be damned. There must be some milliner in York who would extend credit to the Duke of Roxbury. A day's drive to the city would be just the thing to enliven his stay, get her out of this gloomy place. They could put up in some historic inn and he could treat her to the sights. He supposed York Minster would be on the tour, medieval monstrosity that it was.

"Warren, see that tea is served for Miss Frederica in the solar in an hour. I'll take a whiskey then if you have it. Push dinner back until nine."

"Nine!" both Freddie and Warren exclaimed at once.

"I know you keep country hours here, but if I'm to have a sandwich in an hour, I won't do Mrs. Holloway's cooking justice. Freddie, I want you to go to your room and rest. Our walk was most invigorating and you must be exhausted. See you in a little while."

She looked as if she wanted to snap something back at him, but she mounted the stairs, her back straight. Sebastian admired the sway of her bottom until Warren cleared his throat.

"Yes, yes," Sebastian said impatiently. "You want to lecture me. This is becoming a daily occurrence. Well, I don't want to listen. Let me guess. It was untoward of me to cart Miss Frederica around in my arms."

The butler was stiff as his starched shirt points. Sebastian wondered if it was Freddie who ironed them. "It's not my place to lecture you, Your Grace. I should hope at my age I know what is proper."

The implication being that Sebastian did not. "Damn propriety, Warren. It and I do not see eye to eye."

"Miss Frederica has always been all that is proper. Except when she was fencing with gentlemen. That, I could not approve of."

"You needn't worry for her safety. She's very accomplished. Had me disarmed before I knew what hit me. But I don't plan on fencing with her again, so rest easy."

"She'll ask you anyway. We can't keep up with her. She tried to teach young Kenny, but the boy was hopeless."

"What's wrong with him, anyway?"

"Your father inherited him when he purchased the castle, the last of the Earl of Archibald's retainers to remain. I suppose he had nowhere else to go. Young Kenny was never 'all there,' as one might say, but several years ago he took a bad fall. He's been worse since, although we do keep hoping. Miss Frederica nursed him herself. He's very devoted to her."

Freddie was a bloody paragon—scholar, housekeeper, nurse. And now a sexual temptress to boot. He clapped a hand on Warren's shoulder.

"I know you're concerned about your mistress. You have nothing to fear."

"I'll not stand idly by and watch her get hurt."

"Good Lord, man! You've made your point. But you know, we all get hurt. There's nothing you or anyone can do to stop the vicissitudes of life."

Warren looked dissatisfied, but nodded. "Very well. But it's becoming impossible for me to stop the tittle-tattle. You were watched on your picnic in the lady's garden. If you are to do this—this *courting* of Miss Frederica, you'll have to do it away from prying eyes."

Sebastian was truly exasperated now. He summoned the most ducal voice he could muster. "This *is* my home, Warren, and I should be able to do as I please without censure from the servants. I am not *courting* Miss Frederica; we are *copulating*. At her insistence and invitation, I might add."

Warren blanched. "Of course, Your Grace. I meant no disrespect. I only worry for Miss Frederica."

"Well, stop. That's an order. And tell everyone else to mind their own business. There's too much for them to do here as it is without concerning themselves over Miss Frederica's virtue." And far too late.

"Very good, sir."

Warren shuffled off. Damn it. This daily castigation was worse than the usual dressing-down at school from the headmaster. Sebastian had stood unrepentant through many of those, but Warren seemed to have a surprising influence on him. To Sebastian's mind, the one positive thing at present was that there were so few servants to alarm. How the castle was even managed as poorly as it was, was a minor miracle.

To a man who'd always had some concern for his comfort, his life was topsy-turvy. He'd had to let a great many people go at Roxbury Park, people his father should have released from service long ago, as he was an absent master. Even so, there were still far too many folks dependent upon the Duchy of Roxbury. The house was not in such dire straits as Goddard Castle, but it needed more than a lick of paint. Sebastian dragged his hand through his hair, silently cursing his father one more time.

But it didn't pay to curse or complain. What was done was done. It was up to Sebastian to turn the situation to his advantage, justice that he would be doing it with Freddie's money. He could keep the wolves at the door without inviting them in to dine upon him.

Speaking of food. He'd have to get out of his damp and dirty clothes for tea with Freddie. He could do with a catnap himself. There were a proscribed number of hours left to his day, and he needed the energy to make the very best use of them.

As he mounted the stairs, he gave some thought to what he wanted to introduce Freddie to next. She'd been an amazingly willing pupil so far, considering she seemed to hold him in aversion. But her body appeared disconnected from her brain when she was with him, and that was just how it should be. Sebastian may have lost his fortune, but he hadn't lost his touch with the fairer sex, thank God. There had been a time when he had worried. At some point he would have to consider holy matrimony. Not that holiness had a thing to do with the God of Sin.

# Chapter 20

*I have been such a fool.*

—FROM THE DIARY OF FREDERICA WELLS

Sleep eluded her. Unless she was ill, she was incapable of napping during the daylight hours, when there was so much to be done. Not that there was a ray of sunshine to be seen right now. The rain lashed against the windows with considerable fury, suiting her melancholy mood perfectly.

This affair with Sebastian had gotten completely out of hand. Apart from that first wicked night, he had not withdrawn as his crisis came to him. Frederica was not entirely stupid—a man's seed caused babies. Mrs. Holloway had given her quite the lecture when she was eighteen, when Frederica had gone to her in a fit of conscience after that horrible night with Sebastian. Even then she had known not to ask Mrs. Carroll anything. Her canny companion would have somehow detected what she had done in the tower, and with whom. The one positive aspect of Frederica's life was that she was now free of Mrs. Carroll, although the lack of chaperone made it so very convenient for Sebastian to corrupt her.

And corrupt her he did. She was awash with lust, and weak with wanting him. *Weak.* In thrall to a depraved duke. Frederica almost giggled, but her predicament was not at all amusing. "Depraved Duke" sounded like the title of one of those dreadful gothic romances Mrs. Carroll read.

She would have to insist that he withdraw the next time they had sex. And they would, probably soon. Over the finger sandwiches. After dinner. Sebastian seemed to want to make the most of his days of domination. He had said there were many ways to satisfy each other, and today had certainly proven that. Frederica felt a squirmy sensation low in her belly thinking of what they had done together on the hill. She could not have imagined that such a position was possible. Or so very tantalizing.

Disgusted with her lecherous thoughts, she rose from the bed and stripped off her wrinkled clothes. Even as she sponged off her body, Sebastian's scent lingered despite the rain and rose soap. She would have to sit across from him twice more today, a victim to his considerable charm. She should—and did—know better, but in the space of just a few days, she had lost her mind again. Sebastian was not quite the feckless wastrel she'd always thought. His travels had been extensive, his adventures—if she could believe the tale of his imprisonment—many. He might make the most of a rainy afternoon bragging of his conquests, although she suspected he'd be doing other things with his mouth than talking.

She fetched a clean shift, front-lacing stays and stockings from her chest, thinking ruefully it would simplify laundering if she just went down to tea in the nude. All the staff must know by now that mischief was afoot. Mrs. Holloway had been fairly sparking with curiosity. Tomorrow Frederica would place Sebastian firmly into some dim corner and carry on with her usual routine, grab some respite from his incessant sway over her morals.

She did have some. And it was hard to do the right thing. It had taken more courage than she expected to refuse him when he proposed ten years ago. There had been fury and confusion on all sides of the tower room, but she could have said yes. She could have doomed them both to a miserable marriage to save her reputation. By now, as Sebastian's duchess, she would have had several babies to add to the Roxbury Bible, if she hadn't died in childbed like her mother. She might have somehow mended his relationship with his father. He would not have disappeared for a decade of sin, proving to himself that he was not like his father at all.

But what was more moral—to force a man into marriage to preserve a fiction, or lie to spare him unhappiness? She had taken her path and had to live with it.

At least her hush money would help him—she still thought of it thus, even though, along with Sebastian's proposal, she had refused his father's bribery. She didn't need any money not to speak of that night. The look on Sebastian's face would always haunt her. Her father's, too. If she hadn't sought Sebastian out, hadn't blown out the candle, the duke and her father would have noticed Sebastian in his doze and found some other trysting spot. Her father might even still be alive. But she *had* accepted the duke's offer of employment, the royalties, and his investment advice, so she could be useful to Sebastian now, for she would be poor as a church mouse. When she bought the castle from him, at least he'd not be thrown in prison again.

She took some trouble with her hair and buttoned herself into a white batiste dress trimmed with jonquil ribbons. She had not worn it in years—trailing about the dusty, drafty castle in thin white fabric was foolish in the extreme. Wrapping herself in a handsome green paisley shawl, she was as close to being a picture of spring as she ever had been. She did not question herself why it was important to be attractive for Sebastian. She already knew the answer.

Sebastian was standing at the casement window, staring through the raindrops, holding a glass of amber liquid. He, too, had changed his clothes. At first glance, he looked the perfect, harmless gentleman, but his slow, crooked grin reminded Frederica there was nothing innocuous about him.

He nodded toward the massive stone fireplace. "It was chilly enough for me to start a fire for us. I say, is it ever warm in Yorkshire?"

"It was warm enough this afternoon for you to remove your clothes outdoors." Frederica slipped into a chair and poured herself some tea. She added extra sugar, as if that would make her feel any sweeter about her situation.

"So it was." He swirled his own drink, then set it on the window ledge. "It's warm enough in here, too."

Frederica rolled her eyes. "Is there ever a moment when you are not thinking about sex?"

"You say I bring out the worst in you, but you seem to bring out the best in me, Freddie. Come here."

"I thought you were hungry. Mrs. Holloway has made enough to feed an army." Frederica reached for a biscuit to delay the inevitable. She had difficulty swallowing with Sebastian's gaze lingering on her mouth. Beneath the batiste, her nipples beaded as if the room were in its usual frigid state. Dear God, she was every bit as bad as he was.

"Now, Freddie."

His tone brooked no denial. For the thousandth time, she wondered if ownership of Goddard Castle was worth it. Setting the biscuit on her saucer, she wrapped her shawl tight and walked to the window. The world beyond the fallen wall was a blur of gray. She traced a rivulet of rain with a fingertip, waiting for Sebastian to touch her.

But he didn't. He was a good three feet away from her, relaxed and perfectly still. Her shoulders tensed in expectation, but the only movement came from the flames in the fireplace and the pinging of rain on the wavery glass.

"Why can't we sit down, Sebastian?"

"We will in a moment." His eyes swept over the length of her, as if he were committing her to memory. She squirmed a little, impatient to get back to her tea. "You look tired."

"I am tired, you devil! I haven't had a moment's rest since you've come here. And there is so much to do that I'm not doing. My housekeeping is falling to rack and ruin."

"Leave the dust be. I'll not charge you extra for it. Think of it as an added amenity to the property." The corner of his lip quirked.

"Are you ever serious?"

"Not if I can help it. I've been giving some thought to how we will spend the rest of my day."

"I suppose you'll want me swinging from a chandelier next. I must beg off. Most of the ceilings won't support my weight."

His discerning eye raked down her form, making her wonder why she'd bothered to put on a pretty dress. "You do have a point. And Warren would notice once the plaster came down. He gave me quite a lecture after you went upstairs."

"Good," she replied tartly. "It's about time someone stood up to you."

"I suppose what I'm saying is a warning to you. Old Warren is suspicious of me. The servants are awfully nosy, aren't they?"

"They care for me, Sebastian. We're our own little family up here. Have been, even before your father died. The hardships the household faced once he was gone have brought us even closer together."

He took a step closer and cupped her cheek. His hand was warm, and she felt her skin flush to match it. "You are lucky, then. I've spent my whole life with no one to give a fig for me."

"Rubbish. You're too old to keep rebelling against your father. You may not have had much in common, but he did care about what happened to you."

Sebastian's hand dropped. "Sorry, Freddie. I saw no signs of that. I was sent to school at age eight, even before my mother died. Farmed out amongst distant relations almost every holiday. But you are right about dwelling in the past. So here is what I plan for the next hour."

With a speed that reeled her senses, he unlooped the tasseled, braided cording from the dusty curtain and bound her hands in front of her. She glared up at him. "And just how am I to drink my tea?"

He bent so that his lips brushed hers when he spoke. "I will feed you."

She snorted, picturing the tea dribbling down her chin. "You are the most ridiculous man."

"Perhaps." He led her back to the sofa instead of her chair, nestling her into the corner. He fetched her teacup, sat down beside her and held it to her lips, angling it perfectly. She took a nervous swallow. To her relief, nothing dripped. Sebastian turned the cup and placed his mouth where hers had been. There was something oddly appealing about that. He took a sip and made a face.

"Too much sugar."

"Drink your whiskey, then," she snapped. She had a dreadful sweet tooth. It would be her undoing.

"An excellent idea." He went to the window for his glass, tipping some of the golden liquid into the tea. "A vast improvement, to be sure."

Oh heavens. She had absolutely no head for spirits, another significant undoing. He knew it, too. She had told him just today. Frederica shook her head.

"Just a taste, Freddie. It will warm you."

He must have noticed the gooseflesh, not from cold but from his warm breath at her throat. She screwed up her face as though tasting medicine and took a tiny sip. He wrapped an arm around her and brought her closer to his body.

"What would you like to eat now? A jam tart? Some seedcake?"

"N-nothing, thank you." She was not going to sit here like some baby bird waiting for a bit of chewed-up worm.

He reached for a butter and cress sandwich and held it in front of her. "You planted this yourself, didn't you? I saw fresh greens in the raised beds this afternoon." He took a bite. "Delicious. The very taste of spring. Are you sure you don't want any?"

She shook her head, stubborn to the end. She sat rigid while he helped himself to the tier of sweets. He ate as he did everything else— with elegance and abandon. Before she knew it, she was licking her lips in envy.

"Ah, I see I'm tempting you." He picked up a frosted square of cake. "Chocolate buttercream. My favorite." His tongue darted out and swirled the frosting. "Here. Taste this."

He didn't push the cake toward her, but toward his own mouth. There at the tip of his tongue was a blob of brown. Chewed-up worms indeed.

"I certainly shall not."

"Chocolate kisses, Freddie. You have not lived unless you've shared one."

His voice itself was chocolate—rich, deep, smooth. She could not help but shiver again.

He sat back, devouring the cube of cake after it was clear to him she was not going to participate in his idea of fun. "All right. We'll play a different sort of game." He unwound his neckcloth. He had changed from their picnic clothes and looked nearly reputable, but now his shirt fell open to reveal the smattering of dark hair on his chest.

"Wh-what are you doing?"

"My scarves aren't handy, but the cravat will do in a pinch." She stifled an oath as he wound the warm linen around her head. She smelled starch, cologne and Sebastian.

He noticed her involuntary sniff. "We shall see how accurate your sense of smell is. Taste, too. I presume there's nothing on the tea tray that you find indigestible?"

"Well, I wouldn't think so. Mrs. Holloway usually knows what I like." And had gone mad fixing all her favorites, hoping to impress His Grace, the Duke of Roxbury, with her considerable culinary skill. Frederica would have to tell the woman to cut back, or they'd run out of household money before this endless month with Sebastian was over.

He made sure the stock was tied securely, his long fingers tracing her cheekbones. "Capital! Now, relax."

"Easy for you to order me about. You're not tied and blindfolded," she grumbled.

"I could be, if you wish for it tomorrow." Although she couldn't see him, she knew he was smirking. "Now, you must promise not to bite my fingers as I feed you. Agreed?"

"I told you I'm not hungry! Honestly, you are the most—the

most—the most vexing man!" Sebastian merely chuckled. Tomorrow she would find a dictionary to expand her choice of criticisms. "Vexing" didn't begin to cover her feelings.

"So they tell me. Here's your first test."

His fingers brushed her upper lip as he held something under her nose. The sharp tang of lemon made her mouth water.

"Lemon curd tart."

"Excellent. Do you want some?"

It was her very favorite, but she would *not* permit him to feed her. "No, thank you."

She heard him chomp into it, could nearly see the shortbread crust crumbling between his lips. "A pity. It really is remarkably good. I thought you liked these."

*He remembered.* If she was not mistaken, he was licking his fingers now, savoring every bit. He was a man of excess appetites in all spheres, and she envied him his artless enjoyment.

"At the rate you are going here, you are going to outweigh Prinny," she said sourly.

"If you're concerned about my waistline, you could help me. I'm only eating all this out of duty. I wouldn't want Mrs. Holloway to think her efforts are not appreciated."

"Balderdash. You just want to torment me with your lip smacking and chewing, which are absolutely revolting."

"Show me how a proper lady eats, then." She felt the sofa shift as he gathered up another morsel.

"Ugh! Fish paste. Put it down this instant!" Mrs. Holloway must be experimenting on the duke with a new recipe. And if he were to eat that, she would not enjoy his kisses at all. And Frederica presumed he would kiss her eventually, after he'd taunted her enough.

"As it happens, I don't care for fish paste, either. Please tell Mrs. Holloway to save such treats for the staff. Now, this one's easy, and much more fragrant."

Frederica took a sniff. "Apricot jam between two almond biscuits." She sounded wistful even to herself.

"Mm, yes." The sound of crunching was practically deafening. She gave a little sigh. "You smelled of apricots the first night I fucked you. Apricots and roses. You're in luck, Freddie. There's one more left."

*He remembered that, too.* She felt the biscuit slip between her lips. Frederica knew just what it looked like—two thin round crisps, apricot jam sandwiched between them. She'd put up the jam herself last summer. Eating the biscuit was like swallowing a burst of sunshine. His finger touched the corner of her mouth. "You have a crumb. Right there."

Her tongue swept out, but his beat her to it. He tasted of apricot, almond, chocolate and lemons, with a trace of whiskey for bite. He kissed her as if he were going to eat her next. She melted into the back of the sofa, all thoughts of escape pushed firmly from her mind.

Each time he kissed her was a variation on perfection. No two kisses seemed the same; like snowflakes, they had their own permutations and eccentricities. This afternoon, he was definitely a warlord out to storm her castle. She was helpless to resist, and not just because her arms were bound and she was blinded by white linen. Every parry of his tongue required retreat and surrender, hardly a hardship when defeat ended in sensual splendor. She felt him free a breast from her bodice, his thumb flicking her nipple to a hard point. He gave a satisfied growl into her mouth, then bent to suckle.

She knew only sound and touch now—the pop of the logs in the fireplace, the spatter of the rain on the window, the wet, sucking sounds of his mouth tugging on her breast, the blood rushing in her ears beneath the blindfold. Her legs parted under the batiste skirts, waiting for his hand to give her pleasure.

He slowly broke away, his breathing labored. "I am getting ahead of myself. We have not finished with your sensory test."

Damn him and the food. There could not be much left on the tray by now except for the nasty fish paste sandwich. He held something else before her. She puzzled over it, trying to remember the small squares and circles and triangles Mrs. Holloway had so painstakingly offered up. He had eaten all the cress sandwiches and most of the sweets before he blindfolded her. She was suddenly ravenous, both for food and for Sebastian. She had a wicked vision of dabbing clotted cream on—

"It's a nut bread and butter sandwich."

"Spot-on." He held it to her mouth and she bit into it delicately. There was a black walnut tree on the way to what passed for a village hereabouts. Once home to the castle serfs, most sensible Yorkshiremen had picked up and moved on from the cluster of buildings more than a century ago. All that remained were a few humble cottages, a vacant pub and a tiny church that was open for worship every third Sunday. An unlucky young clergyman rode the circuit once a month, was in fact due next week. Frederica would loyally troop into the village, as she had even more sins to pray over now that Sebastian was here.

Despite her misgivings, young Kenny had climbed that walnut tree and shaken the branches last fall, and it had rained nuts for Frederica to gather and Mrs. Holloway and Alice to shell. Luckily, he hadn't fallen again, for she did wonder what another accident would do to the poor man. So much of her time this past year had been spent in homely pursuits—gardening, preserving, making do with nature's bounty when her funds dried up. She was uncertain if she could trust Sebastian to straighten out her finances. More than likely once he was paid for Goddard Castle, he'd disappear again and she'd be back to shaking trees and praying to get over his skilled, sinful touch. But she sat still now, not resisting, longing for the oblivion he guided her to.

He touched her, his fingertip circling her wet nipple as she sat dazed against the back of the sofa, her bodice somewhere down around her waist, her hands tied, her face half-masked by his neckcloth, the nut bread forming a lump in her throat. She was completely at his mercy, the gush of liquid between her legs a shameful acknowledgment that she did not find his mastery of her objectionable in the least. He plucked the fabric of her yellow-sprigged skirt up and a shiver ran through her despite the warmth of the fire. It was probably far too late for prayer, and every third Sunday would be inadequate anyhow.

# Chapter 21

*I must not lose sight of my objective.*
—FROM THE DIARY OF SEBASTIAN GODDARD,
DUKE OF ROXBURY

He could scent her arousal over and above the applewood burning and the lingering aroma of the Mrs. Holloway's delicacies. And while he knew she had washed upon retiring upstairs, he could still smell himself, his imprint upon her body from their afternoon. His head spun from the drenching sensual hold she had over him.

It was he who was supposed to be in control, yet her very helplessness was driving him mad, wrapping him in knots tighter than those at her wrists. Of course, her tongue was still as sharp as ever, but she was unusually subdued, splayed open to him on the tattered sofa, her nipples raspberry-dark and hard, the smooth skin of her mons glistening with dew. She was silent as he dipped a finger in and brought it to his lips, the taste far sweeter than anything the tea tray had provided. Slipping from the sofa, he knelt before her and slanted her hips, then feasted. She shattered on the first lick, so ready was she for him.

But he was not done, could not get enough of the flavor of her.

She tensed beneath his hands, struggling to be quiet when any of the staff could enter the room. He should have locked the door—it was careless of him to expose them like this—but somehow the threat of possible discovery made him even harder. Juvenile of him, he knew. He was past the age of deriving enjoyment from flaunting his sins in front of servants. His first night with Freddie had been a cautionary tale—the disaster of being discovered by their fathers still haunted him.

But it had been Freddie who had forgotten to lock the door, creeping in on cat feet as he'd sat drifting in his opium haze, a half-drunk flask of brandy at his side. He'd left his evening clothes in his room and changed into an Italian silk robe, an extravagant memento of his years abroad. He'd climbed the tower with a candle stub to see the stars and get away from all the foolishness downstairs.

He'd seen stars. And luscious skin. Bountiful breasts that burst from a tightly laced stomacher, giving Freddie a waist he didn't know she possessed. How could he have known that naughty creature in short, saucy ruffles and mobcap was Freddie? She hadn't spoken above a dusky whisper, putting her finger to his lips as she fisted his cock. She'd been more enthusiastic than skilled, but he was more than happy to thrust up into her hot, tight cunt.

As he was now.

He studied her as she lolled against the sofa. Freddie would so hate to be seen like this, her naked breasts quivering, her legs loose, her lips forming a secret smile that he was sure he wasn't meant to see. Because her vision was obscured, it was as if she had no idea of the image she presented, so entirely wanton she took his breath away. Her cries drove him to kiss her quiet and lace her up before Warren came in with a blunderbuss.

Her wrinkled forehead told him she was frowning. Perhaps she thought he would sink into her again, spill mindlessly inside her as he'd done earlier. How he wanted to—but delay would make what he planned for tonight all the more delicious. He would take her further with one more step. The more she wanted him, the easier it would be to show her his most needful pleasures.

Sebastian fumbled with the ropes and unwound his cravat from her pinkened face. Her eyelashes were curled up from the confinement, her eyes unfocused. If anyone saw her, even with her skirts down and her hands folded in her lap, they would know what he had done to her. And that she had loved it. He tucked a strand of hair back under its pin. She blinked a bit like a startled fawn, then rubbed her wrists.

"Why did you stop?"

He straightened the ribbon over her bosom. "We have all night."

"Until midnight, you mean," she said, starch creeping into her voice.

"I'll have to throw out the clocks, Freddie. Perhaps I can persuade you to forget it's your day."

She rose unsteadily from the sofa. "There's no chance of that, Your Grace. I shall hold you to your word."

"Even if it means depriving yourself?"

She flushed with pique. "Really, Sebastian, you have an exaggerated sense of your own consequence. I am perfectly able to go without you rooting around my body for a day."

He laughed. "You make me sound like a badger."

"More like a rat. A large one."

"You cannot insult a man as long as you tell him he's large." He watched her walk to the window, her head high, her shoulders thrown back in pride. He knew he could rob her of it and make her moan again within minutes, but it didn't seem sporting. "I have a few business matters to attend to, letters to write and so forth, so I absolve you from my company until dinnertime. I won't be using the library, so if you want to get back to your book for a few hours, I have no objection."

She didn't turn around. "How kind." Her voice was flat, but he wasn't fooled. He picked up the last decent sandwich, ham with a dab of brown mustard, then put it down again. He wanted nothing that would erase the taste of Miss Frederica Wells in his mouth. Nonsense, really, but there it was.

He left her to dwell on the raindrops that coursed down the wavery windows and returned to his tower. He opened the satchel that contained the many threatening missives that his father's man of business, Paulson, had pressed upon him. As Sebastian had told Freddie, he'd been imprisoned once already. Although he was certain that any sojourn in an English gaol was apt to be far more sedate and comfortable than his previous accommodations, he was still unwilling to subject himself to prove it. He wrote to Paulson, inquiring about the disposition of Freddie's funds and the exact direction of the solicitor in York.

In a few days, he'd pack her up in the moldering old travel coach and escape the moldering old castle. They could make a vacation of it—it would be heaven to get out of the gloom of Goddard Castle, although the medieval city of York could be every bit as gloomy. Sebastian thought of the architecture he'd seen on his travels in Greece, simple square houses built into hillsides, blindingly white against the Aegean Sea. He'd trade every decrepit property he owned for one of them.

Roxbury Park required refurbishment. Neglected by his father for more than a decade, the Jacobean wing really needed to be torn down and the drains replumbed. But its productive farmland was Sebastian's one hope. His tenants knew what they were about, so if the weather in the south cooperated, he might escape penury yet.

He wondered if Freddie missed her girlhood home. He could almost see why she had dug in up here, reluctant to make another change. But his father's scholarly madness had leached over to her and she seemed to prefer being hunched over foolscap to anything else. Hunched over himself, he studied his columns for the next few hours, growing increasingly needy and nervous to get his hands on Freddie's money. And on her body, too. It was becoming clear to him that just as he had tempted her to sin, he was equally tempted. If they had married all those years ago, would he still be attracted to her? It would be a novelty to be attracted to one's own wife—the gossips in the ton would never believe it of him. But he'd been unconcerned with rules for ten years. Why should he care now if he broke any?

# Chapter 22

*Unbelievable.*

—FROM THE DIARY OF FREDERICA WELLS

D inner had been disposed of. Sebastian could not even remember what he had eaten, so anxious was he to get Freddie alone in his room. The conversation had flagged long before pudding was brought to the table. Freddie had been less than engaged in his flirtations. She sat on his bed now, fiddling with the yellow ribbon that trimmed the dress she had worn to tea. Her skirts were still crushed from his earlier exploration, her cheeks flushed from the wine he had pressed upon her at dinner. She was nowhere near to being tipsy or relaxed, however. She looked very much like someone who was going to have a tooth drawn, so Sebastian knew he had his work cut out for him.

He poured her a glass of port from the tray at his bedside, but she shook her head.

"I've had enough, thank you."

"You are awfully tense, Freddie. You know everything we have done has brought you pleasure." He took a sip himself and unwound the cravat from his shirt collar, draping it on a chair.

"Don't remind me. I've behaved like a hoyden." She chewed a plump lip, a task Sebastian wished to take over himself.

"And I thank you for it." He grinned. "We've had a lovely day so far, have we not?"

"If you say so."

"Ah, Freddie." He dragged the chair to the side of the bed and sat on it, patting her knee. "You needn't feel shame for enjoying yourself with me. You are made for this."

Her eyes looked a bit bleak. Sebastian wondered if she had been practicing off-putting expressions in her mirror. Right now she looked like an actress in a second-rate tragedy. "Am I? I thought I knew who I was before you came. Now it seems I am nothing but a trollop."

"You'll not get me to give you a reprieve with all this guilty-conscience nonsense. I have two more hours left and I intend to make use of them."

"And use of me."

She meant to make him feel pity, but he would have none of it. "Who have we hurt, Freddie? Old Warren, who puts his nose where it doesn't belong? We are adults. Youngish. Healthy. Before I arrived, you had resigned yourself to a spinster's life, buried in books and counting raindrops out of boredom. You cannot honestly say you would prefer to be untouched, false virtue intact. I wouldn't believe you if you claimed it to be so."

"I suppose not. I showed you my colors ten years ago, didn't I? What have you planned for me tonight?" She gave a little sigh and shifted away. Sebastian was determined not to fall victim to her attempt to deter him, leaning forward to get closer to her. They were now knee to knee. He could smell her rose soap and the vanilla sponge pudding she'd eaten.

"That's my secret. But I assure you, you will be ready for it." He reached for her hands and held them still, gently thumbing the skin over her delicate bones. She'd nearly ruined her hands with drudgery. "But first, we're going to get you out of this dress."

There were tiny yellow buttons at the bodice, made to look like flowers. Sebastian freed them from their yellow-stitched loops, then untied the grosgrain ribbons over and under Freddie's breasts. He pulled her puffy little sleeves down to her elbows. She made no effort to help him, focusing her eyes on the fire he'd stirred up when they first came upstairs. It was still storming much harder than any spring shower had a right to, and he could feel the damp seeping into his bones. The sooner he got warm with Freddie, the better.

"Stand up."

If he had been doing this with any other woman, he might have said, "Stand up, love." He would have tossed off endearments without a thought. But this was Freddie, the girl who had plotted to bring him to his knees at the tender age of twenty-one and claim him for her husband. For life. Dukes did not get divorced.

No man was fit to be married at twenty-one—Sebastian had not even begun to sow all his wild oats during his grand tour, though he'd made an excellent beginning. He wasn't fit to be married now, although if some rich cit's daughter stumbled in his path, he'd better snap her up for the benefit of his creditors.

At least he hadn't fallen prey to his father's desire for a wellborn wife. Some simpering society ninny who embroidered and played the pianoforte and was so inbred she was cross-eyed. A woman who would close her eyes like a dead person and think only of the ducal succession every time Sebastian entered her. Who really would die if he told her what he'd done in Egypt.

The conversation with Freddie had picked at that scab today, and the oozy pus of it was contaminating his thoughts. He'd gone months without reliving it, but Freddie would help relieve him. He pulled her off the bed and let the dress drop at her feet. She stepped out of it, tripping on the flounces. Her freckled skin, rosy from their time out-doors, puckered with goose pimples. Carefully, he unlaced her short corset, his reward being the sight of her erect nipples beneath her white shift.

There was a tentative knock at the door. Freddie looked wild-eyed, and dashed behind a faded jacquard screen.

"A moment."

Sebastian went to the door, opened it and stepped out into the hallway, shutting the door firmly behind him. Young Kenny was hold-ing a flickering candle and a large tin can of hot water, the steam rising invitingly. Sebastian took it from him. "Thank you. That will be all. Tell the rest of the household to go on to bed. I won't need anything until morning."

"Aye, sir. Yer Grace." The man shifted from side to side, as though he hadn't heard his dismissal.

"Good night, Kenny. Sleep well." He waited long seconds until Kenny collected himself and loped off down the corridor. Sebastian slipped back in the room, hoping that the man made it all the way downstairs. He didn't like to think of anyone eavesdropping over the next two hours.

When he came in, Freddie was seated again out in the open, un-rolling a pale stocking. The strap of her chemise dipped down her shoulder. Her clothing had been neatly folded on the chair with Se-bastian's neckcloth. She seemed resigned, but Sebastian wanted more from her than that. No lying like a lump and thinking of England for her, not that she would have any part of the Roxbury succession. He set the pail before the fire, took the stocking and garter from her hand, then unpinned her hair. It tumbled to her waist, a torrent of gold and bronze. He remembered how it teased his body as she moved over him this afternoon, when she was untroubled by reservations of any kind. But her mood had changed during the course of the day just like the fast-moving clouds over the moors. Sebastian knew he'd made a mistake bringing up the milkmaid business. What difference did it make if she wanted to keep her secrets? It was too late to change anything.

From the crease on her brow, he could tell Freddie was thinking, and thinking too much. Too hard. Her inhibitions were gathering like bees to her garden, buzzing warning notes to him. He had wanted her ultimate submission tonight, but it was becoming clear to him he might have to be satisfied with less.

She stood without his asking and pulled the chemise over her head. Her body glowed in the lamplight, each tiny freckle a flake of gold dust upon her fair skin. "Well, where do you want me?" she asked, her martyrdom layered fast in her words.

"Lie down on your stomach."

She cast him an odd look, then complied. She raised her arms above her head as if waiting for him to bind them together, but that was not his current intention. Lifting the waves of hair from her back, he twisted them aside. Uncapping a jar of fragrant citrus unguent, he set it on the sheets, warming a dollop of the cream between his hands, then began to rub her shoulders.

"What are you doing?" she mumbled into the mattress.

"As I said, you are tense. We've had a busy day." He worked at the knotted muscles and moved up to her neck, putting pressure on each rigid bit of spine. More cream, more smooth territory to cover, more friction between his palms and her skin. He traced her angel wings and she quivered at the tickling sensation. With every sure stroke, her body grew looser, her breaths almost purrs of satisfaction. He made his way down her back to the beautiful cheeks of her arse, circling and kneading until he determined she was melting into the bedclothes. His fingers skimmed down one leg to her toes, downy fuzz glimmering along her calf. The firelight was her friend, bathing her in golden glow.

Sebastian could look at her for hours, as long as he could touch, too. He bent her leg, rotating her foot at the ankle, tugging gently on each toe until she felt boneless. Her small foot, so pink and pretty, deserved a kiss. She startled as he pressed his lips to her arch, then methodically kissed his way up her white thigh. He felt her stir restlessly beneath him, as if she wanted to participate again. Good. He had broken through her reserve, at least for now. Which was fortuitous, as he was hard as granite. He had delayed his pleasure for hours, but could not wait much longer.

He dipped into the pot again, parted the crease of her bottom and painted a line of cream from one orifice to the other. Her sex was already wet, easily accommodating a probing finger. She wiggled to give him greater access, and he fondled her until she was close to breaking for him. But that would come later. Tonight was his, what he had been waiting for since he saw her in that shaft of sunlight the first day.

In general, he worshipped women, all their soft, uncomplicated curves. His intent to bring them to the forbidden was no perversion on his part—he knew the benefit of every avenue explored, every door opened. He'd spent his life immersed in sexual indulgence and was the better for it. Even his Egyptian prison had taught him something unexpected, at first unwelcome, ultimately the thread that kept him alive. There was nothing he had not done in the art of amusement, for his own and others'. He would bring Freddie to capitulation tonight without bonds or blindfolds—she would be a willing captive to his sin, once he initiated her.

He coated his cock, stroking himself until every bit of him was covered with citrus cream. To his regret, he'd learned one could never have too much lubrication.

Freddie turned her head so she could make eye contact with him. "I—I must talk to you before we proceed."

He didn't want to talk. He wanted to fuck. Sebastian could feel Freddie's tension creep back in and spread to him. He continued to glide his hand over his cock, not letting her words dampen his erection.

"What is it?"

"You have not—you have not withdrawn as you promised. We agreed I was not to fall pregnant."

Sebastian almost laughed. There could be no better motivation for her than what he planned tonight.

"You know, people do things differently in parts of the world where a woman's virginity is prized even more than it is in England. Young girls who wish to save themselves for their husbands can still take lovers without breaking their hymen."

"How can a man tell, anyway?" she muttered into the pillow.

A very good question. He'd had no idea when the milkmaid came to him ten years ago that she was no one's wife, but virginal Frederica Wells. He hated to think of words such as "unspoiled" and "ruined"—people placed far too much consequence on a bit of tissue that could be ruptured so naturally. "The truth is, often we can't, unless there's a great deal of blood. But I told you the other day there were ways to have sex without fear of conception. What we did today, for example. Mutually exquisite, was it not?"

The back of her neck turned rosy, but she said nothing.

"Some married couples regularly enjoy each other in the way we are about to, without fear of adding any more mouths to feed." He flattened his hand on her bottom in ownership.

"Wh-what you did with that toy."

"Yes, Freddie." He waited for her to object. Maybe it was all too much for her to deal with today—he had certainly put her through most of the paces in a remarkably short period of time.

"Will it hurt?"

His heart jumped. "No. Not if I'm careful. And I will be."

"Why would you want to?"

*Because it is forbidden. Taboo. Because I acquired a taste for it in Egypt.* "You'll be tighter there. And you won't have to worry about a baby."

"I—I think you'd better tie me up."

He had wanted her voluntary submission, but for her to ask this was possibly even better. She trusted him with her safety, even though she was uncertain of what was to come. But he didn't want her afraid—of herself, or of him.

"Let's try it without the restraints. You know what to say if you're unhappy."

"Rutabaga. Honestly, Sebastian, can't we come up with a better word? It's absurd!"

"I can almost guarantee you will never have to say it, Freddie." And he was anxious to prove it to her by starting to worship her beautiful freckled ass.

She shrugged, and he continued his massage, this time concentrating on her lower back, the tops of her thighs, the soft, tender space between her vagina and anus. His fingers teased each orifice, plying cream and sensation on her sensitive skin. She melted once again under his hands, and he knew it was time.

He settled himself over her, pressing the tip of his cock to her puckered rose. He watched her struggle with herself not to twitch in embarrassment. More cream, more penetration. He stared as he slowly disappeared into her, blood singing in his ears. His awareness was heightened by blissful friction and total dominance. She had given what he needed without constraint, indeed with a sigh that told him her pleasure was as great as his.

If that were even possible. He had never felt like this in all his life.

The dance was delicate, fragile, its subtleties a revelation to him—he, who had experienced everything. He continued to refine each deft thrust until he knew she was as enthralled as he, then lost himself in the heat of the perfumed room. He made no sense of her urgent cries, nor his own. There was nothing but the hardness of his shaft in her welcoming passage, the fire in his balls, the rush of his seed. He waited until the waves subsided, then tumbled off her to lie on his back in the bed.

She lay in profile and was still, her hands still gripped together in sacrifice over her head. One blue eye met his.

"If you turn over, I will finish it for you."

She blushed, was flushed all over. "I'm all right."

"Better than all right, I hope."

"It was—unexpected. Quite different from when you put—that thing there."

How could she still be shy with him after all that they had shared? He decided Freddie couldn't talk about fucking, but could perform like the most skillful whore at Mrs. Brown's Pantheon of Pleasure, the most notorious house in all of London. Fine. He'd prefer fucking to conversation any day.

She rolled as requested, spreading her legs for him. She was becoming intuitive. Shameless, too, as forward in her demands as he was, as long as she didn't have to say them aloud. But her body did the talking as she inched closer to him. He suckled a breast as he found the hard knot of her lust, and he brought her off with a series of short, quick strokes. Her keening nearly ruptured his eardrum.

"Some woman orgasm from anal stimulation. I hope you will eventually."

She swallowed. "I was very close."

God, but she was beautiful, damp and rumpled and breathless. He fingered the crease on her cheek. Could he persuade her to insert his anal toy into herself to play? Into him? He had never asked that of a woman, a niggling fear of rejection always within reach. But he had a few weeks to awake Freddie to his every desire. She'd come far in two days, but he could bring her further.

"It must be midnight by now," she said, throwing cold reality on his fantasies. "I'm going back to my room."

He didn't argue. He preferred to sleep alone, although when Freddie left, he placed his hand on the warm spot she had vacated and closed his eyes. The bedsheet was a poor substitute for the silken skin he craved.

# Chapter 23

*I want to be alone.*

—FROM THE DIARY OF FREDERICA WELLS

Her day. And Frederica didn't dare trust herself to see him. Poor Alice had balanced the breakfast tray all the way up to her room once she'd begged off getting up, claiming to be ill.

And she was, in a fashion. Ill from longing to throw herself on top of Sebastian until she didn't know where she stopped and he began. Ill from realizing she would let him do absolutely anything to her. With her. How many days had it taken for him to break her defenses down? A paltry few, and she was putty to any wicked proposal.

It was another unusually beautiful spring day so far, but Frederica was determined to stay abed. This meant no cleaning, no writing, certainly no naked sword fighting. No sex of any kind, wherever Sebastian's clever cock, tongue or fingers could fit. Last night had taught her the folly of thinking she was simply a detached observer in a sexual experiment. She had seen Sebastian's face afterward, knew that such methods would not be limited to a single incident.

And she did not want them to be.

She had not found the attention to be abhorrent. He had prepared her well and taken great care. She'd felt like a spun-sugar egg, cosseted in yards of satin and cotton batting. She'd belonged to him utterly, even if he was going to leave her without a backward glance.

She sat up against pillows and crunched into some toast spread with blackberry jam. Oh, she could not lie up here all day like a lump. It wasn't in her nature to let her duties slide because she wanted to cower under the covers and hide from Sebastian. There must be a thousand things to do. All of them would require getting out of bed.

Unless she sent for Sebastian.

Which she would not do.

She didn't have to. There was a knock at the door, and he opened it, not waiting for an invitation. Typical. He remained in the doorway, a picture of perfect sin, clean, brushed, his country clothes impeccable.

"Good morning, Freddie. *Miss Wells* today, but somehow I keep forgetting. I heard you were not well."

She swallowed the bite of toast with difficulty. How like him to throw out her formal name now, when they had been so completely, ruinously informal for days. "Mm."

"I was worried. I trust you are suffering no ill effects from last night?"

She felt the heat of her flush tingle across her cheeks. "No."

His relief was unmistakable. "May I come in?"

*No.* She hesitated. Could she suddenly develop some communicable disease that she could frighten him away with? Measles or mumps? She'd had both as a child, and as she recalled, he had given them to her on separate holidays from school. Chicken pox, too. She should have dreaded his rare returns home, but instead she'd lived for them. "If you must. I hope you don't catch what I have."

He crossed the room. Instead of sitting on a chair, he plunked himself on the bed and held his hand to her forehead. "You have no fever. And you don't look sick. You look—luscious."

"Don't be ridiculous!" she retorted, ridiculously flattered. She must look a mess. Her hair hung in a tangled ponytail—her hands had shaken too much last night to braid it.

"Are you going to eat that other piece of toast on the tray?"

Frederica realized she still had one sticky slice in her hand. "No. Go ahead." It was unfair that he could pack away so much food and look so fit. Her every mouthful was visible on her hips and bottom. Just thinking about that area after last night brought a fresh blush to her cheeks.

Sebastian made quick work of the remains of her breakfast and licked his fingers. Odious man.

"I've come for today's instructions. Mrs. Holloway has already apologized to me in advance if you stick to your plan to have me peel vegetables. The old girl tells me she'll lie and say I did them."

"She's a traitor! You've wormed your way into everyone's good graces in no time."

"Except Warren's. And yours, of course. It's my natural charm. I cannot help it."

Frederica itched to throw the butter knife at him. She stuck her tongue out at him instead. He must know how he affected her. His charm was every bit as potent with her as his legion of conquests.

"Tsk tsk. That pink tongue. Don't tempt me again in so provocative a manner. I may forget myself. So, what's it to be, mistress? I am yours to command."

*Go away. Stay and make love to me.* No, it was simply fucking. Love had nothing to do with it. "I—I have nothing for you to do, except keep out of my way. I'm going to get up."

"Freddie, don't push yourself if you're unwell. We can manage somehow without you, vegetables and all."

"I'm not sick, not really. I was just tired. Out of sorts." And a coward. Sebastian was unavoidable—no matter how large the castle was, she could not escape him.

"Well, that's good news. May I help you get dressed?"

"Fat chance of that. Knowing you, you'd throw my clothes out the window."

He grinned. "What an excellent idea. Imagine a life with no stays or stockings or petticoats."

"I'd have to live somewhere considerably warmer than Yorkshire."

"I recommend lodging on the Mediterranean Sea. Greece was lovely. But it's a fine day right here at the moment. Warren's old bones have not predicted anything different yet. Can I interest you in another walk?"

She snorted. Even if it was her day, she didn't trust him to stick to the rules. "I hardly think a walk is what you have in mind. I'd prefer to be alone today, thank you."

"A man can hope." He stood up, brushing crumbs from his inexpressibles. "If you don't require me for anything, I believe I'll ride out and explore the countryside. Visit in the village. Atlas needs a workout, and so do I."

"It's rather a far ride, and not much when you get there. If you blink, you'll pass it right by. And I should warn you, the pub was closed long ago. In fact, not a lot of it is still standing. Someone came for the bricks to build a new house."

"I'll get Mrs. Holloway to pack me a lunch. You're *sure* I can't keep you company?"

"Perfectly."

Sebastian stopped at the doorway. "Will you join me for dinner?"

Could she last the day without falling into his arms? There was only one way to find out. "No."

"See you at midnight, then." He had the audacity to blow her a kiss before he left.

Frederica tossed the covers aside and scrambled out of bed. She would lock herself in the library with the safety of her ink and pens, write until it was too dark to see and she was too tired to think. But she doubted she'd be successful in driving Sebastian from her mind.

*  *  *

The world was verdant and relentlessly rocky from Sebastian's seat on his gelding Atlas. If stones were a crop, he'd be a rich man. He kept to the well-worn track, too grassy to be called a proper road yet the only way to the nearest village without risking his horse's footing. The worst of the sinkholes seemed behind him, but Sebastian was alert to any danger. In the days of serfs there must have been considerable traffic to the castle, but in its present state, Goddard Castle discouraged visitors. The most recent traveler on it—leaving—had been Mrs. Carroll, and Sebastian wondered when the dunning letter would arrive from her.

Atlas had served him well on the journey north. Sebastian had taken his time for his animal's sake and his own, staying in cheap, out-of-the-way hostelries, reluctant to deal with Freddie. Now he was reluctant to leave. Freddie had been a picture this morning, all tousled curls and innocent white night rail. He knew what the curls felt like between his fingers and what the night rail concealed—Freddie's ripe, gold-dappled body, a body he had the privilege to explore and revere. Last night had been unbelievable, more gratifying than he could have ever dreamed.

But this morning, he had sickened her. She'd hidden away from

him in her room, too afraid or disgusted to face him. So he had gone
to her, to face the inevitable. He was now inclined to think she'd just
been embarrassed that she had permitted herself to be used in such a
way. Her reserve had returned, her tart tongue newly sharpened. He'd
have his work cut out for him tonight, as she had adamantly dismissed
him for the day.

Perhaps if he explained—

No. He'd have to face his past, share his soul with her. And that he
could not do, not now, not ever.

A sad cluster of buildings appeared in the distance. A few short
days ago, Sebastian had passed through, giving his surroundings very
little attention. He'd been morose, focused on the four towers of Goddard Castle looming on the hill. Freddie had said the village was all
but deserted, but he would introduce himself to his neighbors and see
if he could induce some female to hire on as chambermaid. And if by
some miracle there was a pretty hat to be found in a store, he would
buy it for Freddie.

As he rode into the village, a small Norman chapel sat at the end
of a narrow lane to his right, its windows shuttered with thick boards.
Sebastian turned Atlas into the churchyard and dismounted, tether-
ing him at the lych-gate. Many of the ancient headstones had broken
and fallen flat on the unmowed grass, but the Archibald plot with its
intact monument was prominent. Sebastian walked between the rows,
reading the lichen-encrusted tablets. A little way from the centerpiece
of the cemetery was his own father's marker, standing out like a debu-
tante in the middle of bent, gray-haired dowagers. The grass here was
trimmed, the simple marble stone clean, its writing clear. Someone had
planted a clump of rosemary, probably Freddie. Her father had been
interred a few yards away, with his own rosemary for remembrance.

The seventh Duke of Roxbury was buried far from the family seat in Dorset, far from his wife, far from generations of Goddards. Sebastian had neglected to ask Freddie about his father's funeral. She must have taken care of everything herself, no doubt following the duke's wishes. Sebastian had definitely been unavailable to attend.

Did Freddie visit regularly, or did she send one of the men from the castle to tend to their fathers' graves? She was loyal, more of a dutiful child to Phillip Goddard than he ever was. She worked to carry on his legacy, had made peace with the man who had once rudely said she was unsuitable to marry his son. Sebastian's father had come to rely on Freddie. In the letters that infrequently caught Sebastian in his travels, his father had urged him to come home and wed her after all.

He stood over his father's mound. Belatedly, he removed his hat and let the wind buffet his hair. If he had the opportunity to speak with his father today, what would he say? In a sense, the duke's disparagement of his only son had been the making of him. Sebastian had been forced to become independent, make his own way in the world. He'd traveled extensively, acquiring knowledge that could not be found in books or museums or ton drawing rooms.

If he'd remained in England, Sebastian probably would have become like so many other aimless men his age, waiting to inherit and securing the succession with a passel of brats so that they could wait, too. Gambling in moderation, hunting in season, growing stout, making the rounds of boring parties, marrying some proper, empty-headed deb—these were all perfectly acceptable activities for a future Duke of Roxbury, or a Lord Anybody. Generation after generation might chafe under the strictures, yet the heirs followed the same narrow, well-trod path. Sebastian had occasion to cut his own trails, several times quite literally with scythes and hatchets. Whatever could be said about his years abroad, they had not been idle or safe.

Even if he hadn't discovered his father's secret life, likely he and his

father would have grown no closer. There had been too many disap-
pointments between them. But now, under the open Yorkshire sky,
Sebastian felt the coil around his heart loosen. Life was too short, and
frequently too brutal, to cling to past resentments. Were he a praying
man, he'd have some handy quotation about redemption and forgiveness memorized, but he made do with scattershot yet sincere thoughts.
He took a breath, then pinched a stem of rosemary and tucked it into
his buttonhole.

Atlas tossed his head in impatience as Sebastian exited the cemetery. The scent of peat burning hung over the tiny village. There were
not more than a half a dozen dwellings intact, and alas, no milliner
for Freddie, no store of any kind. Two dirty little boys were engaged
in a game of jackstraws in front of their cottage, but the pile of sticks
collapsed once they caught sight of Sebastian.

The bolder of the two rose up from his patched knees. "Ain't you
the new duke what lives in the castle?"

"I am. Is your mother at home?"

"She's next door to Gran's. Tom, go fetch her."

The other lad scurried off around the back of the cottage. Sebastian remained at the gate, holding Atlas's reins. The boy said nothing
more, just stared at Sebastian with such curiosity that he began to
feel like a bug under a microscope. There seemed to be no point to
small talk, so Sebastian allowed himself to be inspected, feeding Atlas one of Mrs. Holloway's antique apples from his saddlebag. After
what seemed like an eternity, a round young woman accompanied
by a rounder older woman peered over a bush at the corner of the
house.

Sebastian gave them his practiced smile. "Good morning, ladies. I
am the Duke of Roxbury, and I wonder if you could help me."

The older woman shook her head. "No. We won't do it."

"I beg your pardon?"

"You've come to ask us to work up at Archibald Castle, haven't ye?"

"It's Goddard Castle now, Mum," the younger one said.

"Whatever you call it, the place is evil. We don't need the money that bad, and from what I've heard, you don't have any anyway."

Good Lord, but he was being put in his place. There were no vestiges of feudal fealty here.

"Miss Frederica is a lovely girl, but I wouldn't work there again, even for her." The woman folded her arms across her ample bosom and looked implacable. "Worked up there for the bad earl, I did, years ago. Place was a disaster then. Unsafe. Can't be any better now."

No, Sebastian was sure it had not improved with age. But at least there was no talk of ghosts from these two. "What about you, miss . . . madam?"

"Don't you be letting him turn your head, Cathy. She's not interested."

Cathy gave him a shy smile and a shrug. "My man's in the mines at Rotherham. He sends us enough to get by."

"Do you suppose—"

"No, Duke. Not a one of us would leave our comfortable houses to come work for you. Cathy's the only one in the village young enough to be of any use anyhow, and she has her boys to look after."

Sebastian knew when to give up. "It was a pleasure meeting you, Mrs.—"

"Mariah Godfrey. My daughter, Mrs. Rae."

"You have handsome boys, Mrs. Rae," Sebastian lied. Tom chose that moment to extract a booger from his left nostril.

"Thank you, Your Grace," Cathy said, blushing fiercely.

"Will we see you in church a week from Sunday? Mr. Clement is due."

Sebastian looked over his shoulder at the unwelcoming stone structure. "I take it Miss Frederica attends service?"

Both women nodded.

"Then I shall make every effort to accompany her." And hope God did not smite him as he crossed over the threshold.

"You tell Miss Frederica old Mr. Capstow loved her bramble jelly. The man's got a sweet tooth."

One of the boys snickered. "He ain't got a tooth in his head, Gran."

"Figure of speech, lad," Sebastian said, rewarded by another stare. "There's no school about, is there?"

"For two children? Nay. I teach them at home," Cathy Rae said, shy. "Miss Frederica has given me books from the castle. At Christmas she sent for primers all the way from London. My boys can read, Your Grace. They'll make something of themselves, but I suppose they'll have to leave here to do it."

Looking at the filthy little hellions, that was rather hard to believe at the moment, but Sebastian knew pretty much anything was possible. "How many folks still reside here?"

"Just the nine of us. Mr. Capstow—he's your man of all work, young Kenny's da. His wife was a cook up at the castle, God rest her soul, and he the carpenter until he got crippled falling from the roof. Lucky he didn't end up like Archibald, eh? Then there's Fred and Molly Gardiner, but they're away in the south at the moment at their daughter's, and Mrs. Pearl. Cathy's husband is home when he can be."

"And I gather most of you were once in employ at Goddard Castle?"

"Aye, for the wicked earl or your da, poor man. Had his head in those books, didn't he?"

"Aye," replied Sebastian, mimicking her accent. "I was just visiting him."

"Too late, aren't you? But better late than never. Miss Frederica comes down regular-like to tend to those two graves. She's a good one, she is."

Too good for the likes of him. "See you Sunday next, Mrs. Godfrey, Mrs. Rae. Boys." Their grandmother gave them a stern look and they reluctantly bobbed their shaggy heads.

Sebastian turned his mount toward home. No, Goddard Castle was definitely not home, this dismal little village not his responsibility or priority. There were ten times the number of people who depended upon him in Dorset to drag Roxbury Park into the nineteenth century. He needed new mechanical equipment for his fields, new seed to plant, cottages to repair and roofs to thatch. The sooner he got away from here, the better.

Why should he keep Freddie to her promise? It was cruel to continue to corrupt her, keep her away from her work, make her a disciple to his deviltry. Last night should be enough for him.

But, he thought ruefully, it was not, nor likely to be.

# Chapter 24

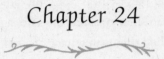

*A first. I am a little ashamed of myself. But she deserved it.*
—FROM THE DIARY OF SEBASTIAN GODDARD,
DUKE OF ROXBURY

After an hour, Frederica wiped the nib and laid her pen carefully in its tray. She stood, brushing the wrinkles from her skirts. She was bored—bored by her own words, blocked from her usual facile attention to detail. She'd had to look up the same facts twice and still had trouble integrating them into her paragraph. Sebastian had made it impossible for her to write, even if he was not hovering over her shoulder, whispering sin into her welcoming ear.

What else could be in his trunk? She had opened it once to hide the evidence of their first lustful night, but did not have the time to peruse it at her leisure. But Sebastian was gone now, so there was plenty of opportunity for her to satisfy her curiosity. She wanted a closer look at his toys, his lengths of braided silk, his books. One could tell a great deal about a person from their taste in literature. Of course, she knew most of the pertinent facts about the Duke of Roxbury—he was an unrepentant satyr who had somehow managed to penetrate her defenses.

*Penetrate.* She chortled. The most apt word of her day. She felt completely open to Sebastian as a lover, when she knew she should snap her lips and legs shut and send him on his way. What would he do if she refused him? Their bargain was not truly binding—she had been deliberately vague when she wrote out the sales agreement for the castle. No, the only binding things were to be found in Sebastian's trunk, and she was anxious to see what else he might have in store for her.

She slipped upstairs to his room, finding it relatively tidy. Sebastian had opened the windows to the sunshine, so the air that greeted her was fresh. While he may not be keeping his sheets as well tucked as she had shown him, there was little dust to be seen and his clothing was not littering the floor. His battered travel trunk sat at the foot of the bed, its brass hinges dull. He'd had this same case as a boy when he went away to school, but Frederica was not expecting to find Latin and Greek texts within.

It was not locked. The items inside were also tidy. His collection of short whips was tied with a black lace ribbon. Upon further inspection, Frederica saw it was a woman's garter. What kind of woman permitted herself to be whipped? Beaten? Sebastian had used one of them to tease her body, but had not struck her. She would never permit such a thing, even if it was his day.

Unscrewing an enamel jar, she inhaled the refreshing citrus cream that was Sebastian's secret ingredient for awakening her body. If she knew what was in it, she could duplicate the aroma and make it herself. Then she'd have something to remember him by when he left. If she could bear to.

Frederica opened a polished wooden box to find an assortment of marble and ivory toys, their design making perfectly plain what they were meant to resemble. She had never seen another man's organ except Sebastian's, but judging from the contents of this box, they came in all shapes and sizes. None of them looked as large—or as luscious—as his.

She shook her head. She was well and truly ruined. How many days had it taken? A handful. She rooted around beneath his stockings and small clothes and felt tooled leather beneath her fingertips. The book she withdrew wasn't thick, some sort of diary, three-quarters full as she riffled through it. The dates written in Sebastian's sprawling hand started many months ago, probably dating to his time in Egypt. He'd told her very little, but if she wanted to know him better, she imagined this volume would make fascinating reading. She reluctantly returned it to the bottom of the trunk, loath to invade his privacy any more than she was already. Besides, his handwriting was impenetrable. There she was, with another "penetrating" word. She really needed to consult a thesaurus.

"What the fuck are you doing?" A hand came from behind her and slammed the lid shut, just missing her fingers.

*Oh dear.* Caught very much in the act. "I—I—I was looking for something to read."

"With all that shit you have in the library? Tell me another! You were spying on me."

His voice was arctic, icicles dripping with every breath. She turned to look up at him, very much at a disadvantage on her knees. The delicacy of her position was not lost on her. "Yes. I was wondering what else you had in that trunk to torture me with."

"I would have gladly shown you, Freddie, had you but asked." He threw open the trunk again and rummaged around, fishing out a small jewel case. He popped it open. "See these?" Nestled in the blue velvet lining were two peculiar silver pins. "They're for your nipples, Freddie, to pinch them so that when I whip your breasts, the pain will be exquisite."

Frederica felt dizzy with disgust. "You—you wouldn't."

"I have, and I would. I admit I hadn't planned to use them on you, but after this—you deserve some sort of punishment."

Her mouth was dry, her tongue thick. "I'm sorry, Sebastian. I was just curious."

"A smart girl like you must know curiosity killed the cat. Never ask a question you don't already know the answer to."

"That makes no sense at all. One would never find out anything." She struggled to her feet, Sebastian refusing to extend a hand to help her. "I admit I was wrong. But really, I wanted to know what kinds of books you read."

Sebastian said nothing, just pointed to his bedside table. There, stacked up neatly, were four volumes. Worse and worse.

"I'll just leave now."

"No. I said you must be punished, and I meant it."

She lifted her chin in false bravado. "What are you going to do? Spank me?"

"An excellent idea. And it is your day, so I shall do as requested."

"That was a question, Sebastian, not an order! You will not lay a hand on me!" She felt her panic mount, but glared at him with what she hoped was a completely quelling expression.

"All right." He reached into the trunk again and came up with a quilted black satin paddle she had somehow missed in her exploration of his trunk. "This should fulfill your terms."

"I have no terms! This is ridiculous!" His hand shot out and caught her at the elbow. "Let me go!"

"I find I am unable to perform all of your instructions today. They are somewhat contradictory. I did my best, you know. Respected your earlier wishes. Left you in bed when I thought you were unwell, and what was my reward? I came back to find you snooping. For shame."

"I—I thought you'd be gone longer." She tried to tug herself away, but he held fast.

"Sorry to disappoint. You were right; there wasn't much to see in the village. And I had a hankering for you, Freddie, fool that I am." He brought her up against him. She felt the hard, angry length of his cock at her belly. "I'm going to spank you, and then I'm going to fuck you."

There was no point reminding him again that it was her day. She could practically taste his fury. But really, his reaction far exceeded her transgression.

She was prevented from telling him so as he tied a length of silk around her mouth and bound her hands in front of her. Before she knew it, she was over his knee, her skirts hiked. He tore her linen drawers down and smacked her with the paddle.

Her father never spanked her, even when she deserved it, not that she often did. She'd been an obedient child, anxious to please him and the duke he worked for. She'd shadowed them in the library, sharpened their pen nibs, organized the stacks of papers that were strewn everywhere. She'd made herself indispensible. But now she was humiliated, unappreciated. She beat her bound fists into Sebastian's calf, but that did not slow the inexorable whump on her bottom.

She lost count of the strokes. She supposed they could be harder. The satin was hot against her, the friction bearable. She screamed into her gag, not so much from pain as from anger.

And then it was over. She heard him toss the paddle aside as it skittered on the rug. The blood rushed to her head, but he wouldn't let her up. His hands were heavy on her back and at the tops of her thighs, pressing her in place onto his lap. Frederica twitched as his lips came down on her, kissing her skin so lightly it was like being tickled by butterfly wings. He blew warm breaths on her warmer cheeks. She lay still as the hand that had cupped her arse slipped between her legs. A mortifying gush of moisture met it.

She heard the sharp intake of his breath, felt him explore her secret places with fingers so gentle she could not help but sigh herself. At least he could not hear her tacit approval of his actions, upside down and bound as she was.

At last, he pulled her up and bent her over the edge of the bed, her arms stretched above her head, her face on the coverlet and her arse embarrassingly on display. In seconds he was buried deep inside her, doing precisely what he said he would do. This was fucking, pure and simple. No pretty words, just near-violent thrusts as he gripped her waist, rocking, rousing her to a fever pitch. As if he knew the precise moment she was about to splinter apart, he withdrew and spattered her bottom with his seed, punishing her further. It was the first time he had not seen to her need, and she groaned in frustration.

He pulled her dress down roughly, not bothering to wipe her clean. He'd never before displayed this cruel side in all their previous games, and she hated him for it. But perhaps she ought to thank him for showing her his true colors. It would be easier to see the back of him at the end of the month.

Frederica pushed herself off the bed and stood on wobbly legs. Her drawers were down around her ankles, and she could do nothing until he untied her. She flashed him her darkest look, but he paid no attention, taking a key from his pocket and locking the trunk with a snap. One would think she had been trying to rob him—but he had nothing she wanted, she reminded herself. Certainly she no longer had any interest in his sexual aides. A man who needed such things was beneath contempt.

And she was worse, succumbing to his blandishments. Well, no more. Never again. She couldn't wait to tell him so, but first he needed to remove the muzzle from her mouth. But to her horror, he walked out of the room, slamming the door behind him, leaving her at a dreadful disadvantage. She couldn't seek anyone's help—no one could see her like this, could know what Sebastian Goddard had done to her. What she had done to herself. Her muffled shriek was useless.

Kicking off the undergarment at her feet, she clawed at the silk wrapped around her mouth until it fell below her chin. Instead of screaming after him, she muttered a string of creative invectives that appeased her anger but would not alarm the servants. She needed to free her wrists from their braided confinement. Sebastian's razor lay on his shaving stand, but whether she could use it without slicing herself to ribbons in the process was anyone's guess. So she set about chewing the knot at her pounding pulse with her teeth, like some frenzied animal. That was all she was, her civility and humanity stripped from her by a madman.

Who turned her to liquid even as he paddled her bottom. There was something wrong with her now. She'd better find a way to get herself under control, shut the lid on her Pandora's box of chaotic feelings just as Sebastian had locked his travel trunk.

But Frederica was afraid it was already too late.

*    *    *

Had she read either of the diaries? Probably not, else she would have wasted no time telling him so. A prideful girl like Freddie wouldn't much care to be listed amongst his other sexual affairs, although he'd been less descriptive about theirs out of some misplaced honorable impulse.

But his Egyptian journal—

He imagined the revulsion that would mar her beautiful face, but there had been only embarrassment at being caught going through his things. If she had known its content, she would have run screaming from his room.

He had spanked her, as she deserved for nosing about, but perhaps he'd let his anger—his fear—get the best of him. His dominance over her had not given him the usual thrill, nor had his climax been the release he craved. He was as tense as a man awaiting the hangman.

He should have ridden around the countryside as he'd intended. Atlas had expected it, but Sebastian had been unable to get the vision of Freddie in bed out of his mind. A lick of blackberry jam at the corner of her mouth. Her white night rail for once unbuttoned, revealing the swell of her plump, freckled breasts. Her golden brown hair escaping from its plait. He'd wanted to devour her instead of her toast this morning.

Sebastian was losing his structured control, the rigid walls he'd constructed around himself turning to gossamer. He was falling for Freddie—he'd almost forgotten it was she who betrayed him all those years ago. Of course she would want to pry into his past, search for clues to see how she could best manipulate him again. She'd gotten him back into her bed, hadn't she, with this ridiculous castle scheme. It had not been *his* idea to sleep with her.

He would put a stop to it. There was no reason he could not release the trust to her in its entirety right now. In fact, it was the only sensible thing to do so he could wash his hands of her. According to the diabolical guardianship the pater devised, he didn't have to wait until she turned thirty or married—he was free at any time to give her the money. *His* money, but there was no point crying over spilled milk. He'd see enough of it back when she paid him for Goddard Castle, and he would never have to deal with her again.

Sebastian smiled grimly. Yes, it was an excellent plan, one he would put in train as soon as he could. A few days, perhaps, just enough time to get Frederica Wells completely out of his system. To finish what they started, although really, he had little left to teach her. But tomorrow was *his* day, perhaps the last. He'd make use of her every single minute of it.

He returned to the stable, confusing the two grooms and probably Atlas as well. Sebastian had hours to kill before he ate his solitary supper. His saddlebag still contained the lunch Mrs. Holloway had given him, which Sebastian suspected the grooms had looked forward to eating themselves. He would go on a blasted picnic on the blasted moors, although May was improving the landscape with greening sphagnum moss, cotton grass and bilberry plants. With any luck, he wouldn't tumble into a peat bog and would live to fuck Freddie one last time.

# Chapter 25

*I will end it today.*

—FROM THE DIARY OF SEBASTIAN GODDARD,
DUKE OF ROXBURY

Frederica had spent a restless night, her sex still aching from Sebastian's selfish retribution. She awoke to gray skies and Alice's anxious face.

"His Grace said to bring you your breakfast in bed, Miss Frederica."

Frederica sat up. "Oh, did he? How kind of him." More than likely it was not kindness but guilt that accompanied her poached eggs this morning. She dipped a toast point in her bowl, watching the bread absorb the dark golden yolk.

"He also told me to tell you to meet him in the library in thirty minutes. *Or else.* Those were his exact words, miss. He seems awful grumpy today."

Suddenly she lost her appetite. If he planned to beat her again out of anger, she had no intention of setting foot downstairs.

To be fair, he had not exactly beaten her. The satin paddle had been thickly padded and his strokes somewhat tame. And then there were all those confusing kisses afterward. But he had taken her roughly without a word of apology, and left her alone to extricate herself from his knots. She'd been very tempted once she had two free hands to toss his belongings all over the room, but *someone* had to show some restraint over one's temper.

Frederica had rarely seen Sebastian truly angry, not even when they were children. He generally handled any setbacks with resignation and some wit. Even his feeling toward his father had been more often exasperation than animosity. But that night ten years ago, Sebastian had been very angry indeed.

Yesterday she had incited him again. One would think he had a body buried in his trunk the way he'd reacted. Let him keep and protect his secrets. Whatever he did, whoever he was, was no concern of hers.

Frederica forced herself to eat half her eggs and toast and drink her tea. She took the time to sponge-bathe and perfume her body, braid and pin up her hair. She found a dress as colorless as the day, which suited her mood perfectly. Confident that she presented a clean yet indifferent appearance, she entered the library with five minutes to spare before she discovered what "or else" entailed. Sebastian was standing at one of the narrow leaded windows, what little light there was setting a gleam to his jet hair. He radiated a restless energy she could feel from the threshold of the room.

"Good morning, Sebastian," she said briskly, as if nothing untoward had happened between them yesterday. Or the day before.

"We're going for a walk. Get the cloak from the kitchen."

She knew the cloak was not for protection from the weather, but to cover the heather so he could lie with her. "But—surely it's going to rain again."

He raised a black brow. "Your point?"

She could see he did not plan to make today easy. Two could play that game. "I believe Mrs. Holloway instructed Alice to wash it."

"Then find another. Take a blanket off your bed. I don't care."

"You needn't be so rude just because it is your day. If anyone has the right to be rude, it is I."

"How do you figure that?"

"You—you hit me."

Sebastian gave a derisive chuckle. "Believe me, if I had wanted to hurt you, you would not be standing here arguing with me. But I have some honor. I've never in my life hurt a woman—unless requested to."

Frederica's anger bubbled up. "I don't want to hear another word about your other women and all the horrible things you've done to them."

"I've just said I haven't done anything horrible to them."

"You could be lying."

"I never lie." His lips thinned. "Or invade someone's privacy. Or pretend to be someone I'm not."

*Ah.* So they were still fighting his ten-year-old grievance. She had hoped they'd made some progress away from that. Not that she wanted him now the way she did then. Then she had been a hopeful, heedless child. Today her feelings were somewhat more complicated. Damn him.

"We all wear masks, Your Grace. Some of them are just more transparent than others."

"And what mask am I wearing, Freddie?"

She cocked her head to really look at him. There was something harder about him today. More ducal, but she wasn't going to say that. "I don't know you anymore. Something happened to you when you left."

"Something happens to everyone unless they're locked away in a tower."

"I suppose you mean me. While you were off having your adventures, my life was more mundane; that much is true. I wasn't contemplating tying up lovers. I never even knew——" She blushed, unable to repeat some of the things she'd done with Sebastian.

"You know now."

She nodded. She did, God help her, only she didn't expect His intervention on this subject.

"Go, Freddie. I haven't got all day."

She stayed stubbornly rooted to the spot. "But you do. All of it, according to our deal."

"I want to talk to you about that. But not here. Run along and get something so we can sit down outdoors."

"You mean lie down."

"That, too. As you pointed out, it is my day."

There was no trace of playfulness in his voice. Sebastian had reverted to the man who had come to Goddard Castle a few days ago, distant and chilly. His demeanor would make it easier for her to untangle herself from their affair.

She climbed back up the stairs in search of an old quilt and a proper cloak for the damp of the day. Out of spite, she tied on her battered straw hat, whose brim had not improved since Sebastian tossed it in the lady's garden. She left off her gloves. Wearing cotton ones so often working with old papers and artifacts, she preferred to actually touch things, feel things, when she had a chance.

She wondered if Sebastian would take her hand in his as they crossed the moors. His hands were long and elegant, yet not so smooth they were dainty. He must have done rough work in his time abroad, and seemed prepared to work at Roxbury Park in order to set the estate to rights. This bargain of theirs was holding him up. Perhaps he could be persuaded to simply sell her the castle and leave to get on with his life. Surely he must be tired of her by now.

He was waiting for her at the bottom of the staircase. "It won't work."

"What?"

"The hat. The dress. I'll have you anyway, as is my right."

"Why do you even want to?" she blurted. "It's obvious you're still angry."

He was silent for a long moment. "I don't know. Perhaps I've lost my mind."

"There is no 'perhaps' about it," Frederica said, loud enough for him to hear.

The effect of her words was not what she expected. Sebastian laughed, the echo in the great hall amplifying the low rumble. "It must bore you to be so consistently right, Freddie. I have not been myself ever since I came to this accursed place. Well, it won't be too much longer and I'll be off."

"I shall look forward to that day."

"I as well." He extended an elbow. "Shall we?"

He struggled a bit with the heavy door, and then they were outside in the grassy courtyard. A gust of wind nearly took Frederica's hat.

"Are you sure—?"

"Yes. All your damn servants keep giving me the evil eye. Even the child. What's her name?"

"Alice." They crossed the lawn to the ruined gatehouse and went through the arch. When they came out, Frederica was certain she'd felt a drop of rain on the back of her neck, but said nothing. A bit of spring rain wouldn't hurt her—she wasn't some silly gothic heroine who'd dance with death just because the hero lured her out in a storm. Sebastian led her from the road over a tussock of grass. "Where are we going?"

"I rode out this way yesterday. After I discovered you going through my things like a ragpicker."

She was not going to apologize again. "Is it safe? I generally stick to the cart tracks."

"Safe enough. I promise to try to save you if you get sucked into a bog."

"How comforting." Patches of wild daffodils, their bright yellow petals shriveled to translucent beige parchment, sprung up through the rough blades of the field. There was nothing of interest to see but a few stunted trees and a vast assortment of rocks. The mountains were misted over with gray clouds, the sun a pale disk overhead. The bleakness of the landscape was not lost on her, and for the thousandth time she wondered why she was trading the lush, rolling green downs of Dorset for this.

Frederica could have managed for two years at Roxbury Park under Sebastian's guardianship. When Sebastian had arrived at Goddard Castle, he certainly had harbored no desire for her. If she hadn't proposed this mistress business, she doubted he would have thought of it on his own and would have left her at peace in her childhood room. It was her own fault that she had stirred things up between them.

She hadn't been to Roxbury Park once in more than a decade, although Uncle Phillip had made a very limited number of trips south. But his heart was here in his adopted home. As hers must be. It was pointless to imagine life as it might have been.

She was out of breath trying to match Sebastian's long strides. "How much farther?"

He stopped, glancing back at the castle. "Hard to tell."

"Do you actually have a spot in mind, or are we on a forced march to nowhere, General Wellington?"

"Do you think this little walk compares with what our brave troops went through?"

Her worn half boot slid on the damp grass. "Of course not," she snapped. "But look at the sky. It doesn't take a genius to know we're in for another deluge."

"You won't melt in the rain. You'd have to be made of sugar."

She was not feeling very sweet at the moment. What did it matter where he decided to fuck her? Here was as good a spot as any. She threw the quilt on the ground.

"No. Pick it up."

"Come on, Sebastian! Whatever you're going to do to me, you can do here as well as one hundred yards ahead."

"No." He bent himself to retrieve the blanket and rolled it up under his arm. She watched him walk faster still, his broad shoulders filling out his hacking jacket. He was once again dressed in country attire, but today wore a neckcloth. She was afraid she knew what that meant.

She could not keep up the killing pace. If he wanted her, he'd have to settle for whenever she arrived at their unknown destination. So she trailed after him. Never once did he look behind him to see if she was following.

Sebastian disappeared down a hill. Frederica wondered that his horse had managed the uneven terrain without a stumble. But at least the ground seemed dry, no blanket bog in sight. As she crested the rise, she saw a thin glittering stream twisting below. The slightest of waterfalls splashed musically between the howls of the wind. Had this been a nice day, the sight could almost be called romantic.

Sebastian had spread the blanket near the jumble of rock and lay on his back, his jacket a makeshift pillow under his head. The sky he stared at was leaden and forbidding. Frederica took careful steps down the bank, too nervous to appreciate the unfamiliar scenery. She hovered over him, casting no shadow.

"There you are."

"My legs are not as long as yours."

"No, they're not. But they have their uses."

Frederica stifled the urge to kick him with one of her useful legs. Instead, she sat on the quilt, tucking them beneath her. "This is pretty. I've never walked this way before."

"I'm not surprised. It's off the beaten path. It would make a nice bathing spot, if one were so inclined."

Frederica could see herself sitting on the rocks at the center of the stream, the cold water sluicing over her bottom as it fell to the river-bed. There would be no danger—she thought her legs would touch bottom. But today was too cloudy and cool. She'd get wet for sure, but only when the heavens opened, as they were sure to.

"Let's get this over with."

She startled. She was about to say the very same thing. Coming from him, the words seemed even more cutting.

"Very well. How do you want me today? Naked? Clothed? Face-down? On top?"

Something passed across his face, but was too fleeting for her to analyze it.

"Naked and on top will do very nicely." He tore off what remained of his clothing, as if a fiend were after him. Her fastenings gave her more trouble, but he was there to help her in the end.

He was erect already, without a kiss, without a touch. Men were such odd creatures. But she was wet, too—had been almost from the moment she saw him this morning. He gripped her hips and centered her over his cock, inching her down slowly. Frederica felt exposed, his eyes everywhere, taking in each roll of skin, each blemish. Sebastian thrust up, and they developed a rhythm that suited them both. She felt a little wild, her hair blowing across her face in the wind, her full breasts bouncing with every move as she straddled his body. Confident that she knew what to do, his hands left her hips and caressed her breasts and belly, sending darts of desire through her body, increasing her tempo.

The first needle of rain fell as she shuddered to orgasm, but Sebastian was not finished. He held her fast as the rain pounded them, oblivious. Her pleasure was quickly eclipsed by the violence of the storm, but it brought him ever closer to his crisis. The rumble of distant thunder caused her to jump, and that was all he needed to tear her off him and spurt his seed into his hand.

He wiped his hand with his cravat. Frederica realized she'd been unbound the entire time and was able to see Sebastian's face as he moved beneath her, his dark brows a slash of concentration, his moss-colored eyes meeting hers. She hadn't looked away, touching his flat copper nipples and crisp dark chest hair as he stroked her breasts. There had been no kisses, but connection nonetheless.

He said nothing as she struggled into her wet clothes and dashed up the hill toward home. Let him stay outside like a madman. Let him get struck by lightning. Fried to a crisp. She'd be rid of him then forever, never see his painfully beautiful face again.

\* \* \*

He let her go. He couldn't move anyhow. Couldn't find the voice to speak. Sebastian lay like a dead man as the rain skittered across his skin. He should rouse himself and see that she got home safely, but his legs felt like lead weights.

This was to be their last time. But somehow he'd omitted to mention that their bargain was at an end. That she was free of him, and he of her. That the castle in all its dilapidated glory was hers—and his heart was not.

But the storm had prevented this exchange, had given him a reprieve of a sort. For he was not quite ready to give her up. He'd miss the warm weight of her breasts in his hands, her slick seduction of his cock, her lush mouth open with release. He'd watched her every minute this morning, thinking to have a memory to file away, but he could not end it. Not yet. In a day or two or three.

And then he'd ride away without a backward glance. He was almost sure he could.

# Chapter 26

*No host can be hospitable enough to prevent a friend who has descended on him from becoming tiresome after three days. Plautus, I believe, but my classical education is sadly deficient.*

—FROM THE DIARY OF SEBASTIAN GODDARD,
DUKE OF ROXBURY

Warren practically pounced upon him when he came through the door. Unfortunately, he was not bearing towels or a fresh set of clothing.

"You have a visitor, Your Grace. I took the liberty of putting him in the library, and am readying the ivory chamber for him. I wish you'd mentioned his arrival," he complained.

Sebastian was getting accustomed to feeling chastened by his butler. His idle fantasies as he walked home concerning Freddie's heavenly arse crashed to earth. "Devil take it! I wasn't expecting anyone, so you can't blame me. Who is it?" Please God, not one of his numerous creditors who'd finally ferreted out his hiding place.

"A Mr. Cameron Ryder, Your Grace. He says he was invited for a fortnight."

Sebastian felt an odd thud in the vicinity of his heart. "Shit. I wrote him not to come. It must not have reached him. Damn it."

"I shall set another place for dinner. At nine." It was obvious the butler still disapproved of the late hour for dining, not to mention his language. Sebastian imagined he was wreaking havoc with the kitchen schedule, but it was at his pleasure to set. Everything at Goddard Castle was at his pleasure. He had suffered enough at the hands of others to ever give up what he wanted now. He was the bloody Duke of Roxbury, for Christ's sweet sake.

Cam could stay one night, and then Sebastian would send him packing. Freddie would have a fit to think he was trying to sell the castle out from under her, and Sebastian needed no friend to distract him from her. Or have his friend distract *her*. Cam could be quite the distraction. Cameron Ryder was tall, darkly blond and very handsome, with eyes as blue as the Aegean Sea. Even if the man had more or less saved his life, he was not at all welcome at Goddard Castle at the moment.

Their friendship had been forged under trying circumstances, made even stranger to discover they shared an odd connection. Cam was the natural son of the late, unlamented Earl of Archibald. Sebastian had once promised to show him Goddard née Archibald Castle if they ever escaped the filthy hovel of their jail cell. When Sebastian discovered he could dispose of the property—*had* to dispose of the property—Cameron was the first person he contacted, even if it meant stirring up the past. Lord Sanderson was merely a backup—the man had more money than he knew what to do with, and collected castles as one might collect snuffboxes. But for Cam, the castle was a key to his birthright, and his enthusiasm for it, sight unseen, had given Sebastian hope for the way out of debt.

And now he was here, uninvited.

Well, not precisely true. But Sebastian had uninvited him, if only Cam had stayed at home to receive the letter.

Sebastian looked down at the state of his attire. But Cam had seen him worse, naked and starved in his Egyptian prison.

Maybe Cam would be interested in purchasing something or other from his father's vast collection of rubbish and the quick visit might be worth the disruption. Sebastian needed money. Cam was a broker of all sorts of antiquities, enabling him to live on the fringes of society quite comfortably. People intuited that he had some connection with the ton. It was true, but not a connection Cam cared to reveal, especially when his father had jumped from the roof of this very castle rather than be hung as a spy. Very few people knew of his Archibald blood. Sebastian had only found out after a drunken night in Cairo when he complained long and loud about his own father's foibles. Cam had been keenly interested in hearing about Goddard Castle, or Archibald Castle, as he preferred to call it.

He found Cam sitting behind Freddie's desk, his hands encased in white cotton gloves, holding a magnifying glass over some decrepit volume. Yes, Warren had put the man in the right spot to wait.

"Sebastian! Did the cat just drag you in?" Cam rose with a grin and extended a gloved hand.

"It's raining cats *and* dogs, in case you haven't noticed." A crash of thunder emphasized Sebastian's words. He'd expected to be hit with God's lightning bolt the whole way home. "But you were probably too busy snooping around to notice." He sank down into a bloody uncomfortable chair on the other side of his father's desk. Cam resumed his position and gingerly closed the book he'd been examining.

"You've got an amazing amount of stuff in this library. I trust you want to sell the contents separately at auction. I can help you with that. You'll make more than I can afford to pay you."

Sebastian grimaced. "Here's the thing, Cam. The sale of Goddard Castle needs to be delayed a little while."

"What? No, no. You know how I'm fixed. And you know how much I want Archibald Castle. You can't shake more money out of me than I've got by teasing me, Sebastian." Cam sat down again, looking every inch like most of the grim portraits in the long gallery.

"It's not that. I owe you, Cam, and I'll never forget what you've done for me. But there's a—problem."

Cam grinned. "What's her name? It's the ward you told me about, isn't it? Doesn't want to leave? Is she pretty? She can stay here with me and warm my bed."

Sebastian struggled not to jump over the desk and throttle his friend. "She cannot! And she is pretty. Just not in the usual way."

"Prim and proper, is she?"

Primness and propriety had very little to do with Freddie lately. He thought of her above him, her breasts swaying as she rode him. Sebastian shrugged. "She wants to buy the castle herself. She's something of an heiress. I think we can deal together and come to some sort of agreement."

"In *your* usual way?" Cam winked.

Sebastian shrugged again. He was acutely uncomfortable talking about Freddie, trying to recall exactly what he'd told Cam about her.

"Good Lord. You're being reticent, almost *too* discreet. Don't tell me you're going to marry the girl! This is the one who tried to trick you into getting leg-shackled years ago, isn't it?"

Blast. Apparently he'd confessed almost everything. He was fairly sure he'd omitted the actual deflowering and the massive quantities of vomit, however.

Sebastian felt a twinge of guilt, but only a twinge. Cameron would see Freddie for himself, and very likely she'd lapse into her starchy self confronted with a man such as Cameron Ryder. "She's a bit long in the tooth to be called a girl—eight-and-twenty, a dreadful bluestocking.

She wears spectacles, and her fingers are black from ink. Not your type at all. And I have absolutely no intention of marrying her. I've known her since she was a little butterball baby."

Cam raised a golden eyebrow. "Not your type, either, then. Just how much money has she got?"

"Rather a lot, and it's rightfully mine to begin with. I've got to get to York and meet with my father's solicitor there. The one in Dorset is as useless as a boil on my arse, and the business manager even worse. The pater was a totally disorganized bastard."

"Now, now. You don't want me to take offense. We bastards want to keep our line pure."

"This is serious, Cam. Things are even worse than I thought when I first wrote to you. I expect my creditors to find me here any day and lay siege. In fact, when my butler told me I had a visitor, I was ready to turn tail and sleep on the moors. I thought you were the bailiff."

"So sell me Archibald Castle. Marry your heiress. Problem solved." Cam snapped his gloved fingers, but there was no accompanying sound.

"I don't want to get married. Freddie doesn't want to get married. She wants to write history books."

"You're joking. By God, you're *not* joking. And all this time I thought you were irresistible."

Irresistible or not, it would be a disaster to marry Freddie. To marry anyone in his current state of upheaval. But he would not bore Cam with his troubles. Instead, Sebastian pointed to the corner of the desk. "Look at those. I'll bet she wrote most every word in them, even though my father took the credit."

Cam removed the gloves and took a volume from the knight bookend guards. "*Roxbury's Middle Ages*. These have an excellent reputation in the trade, you know. They're full of scholarship, yet accessible to the reader. Very popular. Schoolboys all over the country have it shoved down their throats and they don't mind swallowing."

"Perhaps so. Freddie wants to finish the series—here. You know I'm a selfish bastard, no further offense to bastards meant. I may be her so-called guardian, but if she wants to spend the rest of her life watching the walls fall down around her, who am I to stop her? She can pay me from her trust and that's all that counts. Now that you've actually seen the place, would you still really want to throw away good money on it?"

Cam gave his dimpled chin a thoughtful stroke. "I'm not sure. But I am most anxious to meet the rich little bluestocking. I could do with an infusion of cash myself."

Sebastian felt an unaccustomed wave of proprietary interest. "We may have shared women in the past, Cam, but Freddie is not on offer."

"Steady, old man. Although it would be fun to see if I could poach a chit from a duke. As I recall, I beat you a time or two when you were only a marquess."

"She's not my chit to poach. We are just—friends of a sort." They used to be. What was between them now was impossible to describe.

"Well, then. Open season."

"You're welcome to try," Sebastian said, his pride getting the better of him. Surely after what he and Freddie had already shared, she would not be attracted to Cameron Ryder. She had chosen him, Sebastian Goddard, as her first lover, after all.

"Capital! You know how I thrive on competition. That should make my stay in this dreary dump much more amusing."

"I thought you considered this dreary dump to be your ancestral home." Sebastian itched for his whiskey now. He also needed to make himself presentable for tea with Freddie. Cam, despite traveling, looked to be a regular Beau Brummell. "And you can't stay. You'll spoil everything."

Cam turned down his mouth. "Can't stay? You invited me up here for two weeks. I'll have you know I moved heaven and earth to get here. Left a very promising house party in Berkshire with two well-born widows and a vapid viscountess after me just so I could inspect this place."

"Not even you could service them all. If you'd stayed in London, you would have gotten my message eventually. I wrote and told you not to come."

"But I'm here now, and not at all inclined to leave, Sebastian. Surely you don't want to upset my valet and my driver. They're knackered coming all this way. My valet may never forgive me, as a matter of fact. He's not at all impressed with the accommodations."

"I don't give a damn about your servants. I left my man Drummond at Roxbury Park." Sebastian ran a hand through his damp hair. Cameron Ryder was an unexpected complication, but Sebastian supposed he owed him some courtesy. Owed him much more, really. "All right, you may stay a day or two, just long enough for your horses to recover and eat their heads off in my stable. But then I want you gone. I have plans for Freddie, and they don't include you."

"Make it a week."

"Three days. That should give you enough time to rummage around here and listen for the echoes of your ancestors. But you're not to say one word to Freddie about you buying Goddard Castle. Nor are you to lay a hand on her."

Cam laughed. "Not one finger. I won't promise away my other appendages, though."

Sebastian smiled, but his cheeks felt frozen. "You really are a bastard. Don't get in my way, Cam."

Cameron looked as though he wished to continue their banter but thought the better of it. "Say, what does a man have to do around here to get a drink?"

"Tea is being served in the solar in half an hour. Get old Warren to lead you there. As you can see, I've got to go change."

"Been rutting in a field, have you? Who's the lucky girl? Some Yorkshire milkmaid?"

Cam had the uncanny knack of always hitting on the truth, no matter how unpleasant it was. Sebastian attempted a leering smile.

"Will the fabulous Freddie be taking tea with us?"

"That's Miss Wells to you. Don't be charming."

Cam shook his head. "Now you're asking too much of me. Bad enough I'll have to drink tea."

# Chapter 27

*There is now one more mouth to feed.*
—FROM THE DIARY OF FREDERICA WELLS

Frederica had been unable to nap, although she had tried, lying on her bed for half an hour after she dried off, staring at the timbers across her ceiling. Her body was in a state of agitation—the slightest press of fabric against her skin reminded her of Sebastian's tongue. The swipe of the washrag at her nether region brought her nearly to orgasm. Her nose was filled with the smell of him, the starch and sandalwood, the semen, although he'd been thoughtful at least in the end. She blushed to think of all that he had done to her, and she to him, over the past few days. And now according to Alice she was to take tea with him like a proper young lady, as though they had not been rolling around at the waterfall like crazed animals in a rainstorm.

She would swear off him tomorrow—no fencing or cleaning or setting eyes upon him. She needed to retreat into her library world, review her notes, finish a chapter. This afternoon he might take her again up against the wall after his whiskey—and she so hoped he wouldn't, didn't she?—but the next day was hers to command.

She was drowning in sensation, and didn't like it one bit. Sebastian had the power to unsettle her, she who was logical and private with her feelings. Apart from her almost-dead, girlish crush on him, Frederica had spent her whole life submerging herself in scholarly pursuits. There had been no room for anything or anyone else. But he had kissed her everywhere, touched her everywhere—spanked her, for heaven's sake—and she simply wanted more. It was like eating too many cunning marzipan fruits. One day she would be sick from the richness of it, but right now she longed for the taste of almond paste on her tongue.

She dragged herself off the bed to change her dress and do something about the nest in her hair. She did miss her runaway maid, but now that Frederica had experienced lust for herself, she understood why the girl had fled with the footman. Although there were plenty of places in the castle one could go to for a forbidden assignation. She would have to find one on one of her days just to keep Sebastian off balance.

But it was still his day. She would not make it any easier for him. Choosing a deep gray charcoal dress that did nothing whatsoever for her figure and seemed to have a thousand damned difficult buttons, she braided her hair into a coronet and refused to pinch her cheeks or bite her lips for color. She looked as tired as she was, robbed of sleep and still weak at the knees from riding herself into orgasm.

If it weren't raining, the sun would now be low over the distant hills. If Sebastian weren't here, tea would be her last meal of the day, and she would take it in the kitchen with the servants. Now poor Mrs. Holloway was knocking herself out for tea *and* dinner to please the duke even if he had no coin to pay her and the larder was emptying at an alarming rate.

She was not going to spend the next two years pinching pennies and living solely by the kitchen garden. But perhaps she could convince him to release all her funds. He had the power to do so, and they could be quit of each other forever.

She entered the solar, her mind filled with vexing domestic difficulties. When the tall fair man rose to greet her, she was so startled she squeaked.

"Good afternoon, Miss Wells. I am delighted to make your acquaintance. Allow me to introduce myself. I am Cameron Ryder, an old friend of His Grace the Duke of Roxbury."

"Oh!" This was one of the men Sebastian had invited to the castle to buy it. And the same man who helped him get out of gaol. He was quite formidable physically, and almost too beautiful. If Sebastian was a dark angel, Cameron Ryder was all light. But he had the same devilish twinkle in his eye as his friend the duke. Birds of a feather, rakes taking pleasure wherever they landed. She felt her tongue thickening with nervous stupidity.

"I didn't mean to surprise you so. My arrival was unexpected. And apparently unwelcome. I understand you and Sebastian have entered into an agreement for you to purchase Archibald Castle. Or Goddard Castle, as it is called now."

Frederica stiffened. "He *told* you?"

"Why, yes. Is it a secret? I assure you, I can be the most discreet of fellows. And I don't know a soul in Yorkshire, although my family hails from around these parts."

Frederica practically fell down on the sofa. Her hands shook so badly she didn't think she could possibly pour the tea that sat in its dented silver pot. Once again, Mrs. Holloway had outdone herself.

There was even an entire decanter of whiskey for Sebastian and his guest, which Frederica very much wanted to pick up and drink down, even though spirits disagreed with her most profoundly.

"I say, Miss Wells, are you all right? You look as though you've seen a ghost. One of the famous Archibald Walkers. Even I have heard of them. Am I to expect a display at midnight?"

"By midnight I shall be in my own bed, and you are certainly not welcome to see any display!" How could Sebastian betray her like this? It was bad enough that the servants suspected what she had to submit to in order to keep her shelter, but to involve this stranger was beyond belief. Would Sebastian expect her to service this blond giant, too? Frederica felt a wave of dizziness swamp her.

"Well, of course not. I would never intrude. Unless, of course, I was invited."

"Oh! You—you—you are every bit as bad as Sebastian."

He reached for a sandwich, smiling. "Guilty as charged. I think we're getting off on the wrong foot, Miss Wells. You have misunderstood me. I was referring to the ghosts putting on a show for me, not you. Although no man could be averse to your womanly charms. Sebastian seems quite in your thrall. I've never seen him so besotted. He's warned me off, you know, and disinvited me from staying any longer than three days. He wants you all to himself."

Well, she supposed that was a relief. But for Sebastian to be discussing her and what they did with Cameron Ryder—it was disgusting. Men were disgusting. Rutting, rude, abominable pigs, every one of them.

"Uh," she said.

"You are aware of his feelings?"

"Sebastian has no feelings, only appetites," she grumbled.

Mr. Ryder continued his menacing, catlike grin. "Speaking of appetites, would you mind very much if I help myself to a whiskey? I've had a long day of travel, and I'm parched."

"Suit yourself." If he thought she would act as a proper hostess, he was mistaken. She folded her hands tightly in her lap, leaving the tempting morsels on the tea tray untouched.

"Ah, there's my old friend now. Sebastian, you dog! Your description did not do Miss Wells justice. You never told me how lovely she is. I can see why you want me to disappear."

Frederica snorted. Sebastian cast her a guilty look and sat down next to her, much too close. She scrunched into the arm of the sofa, noticing how very worn the velvet was. One good pointed elbow on it and it would shred.

"Cam, I'll have some of that if you're pouring. Freddie, you're not taking tea?"

"I am not hungry. Or thirsty. In fact, I'd like to skip tea and dinner altogether if you will *permit* it." How galling to grovel in front of Mr. Ryder.

"Ah, Miss Wells, I hope you change your mind. I'd like the opportunity to get to know you better before Sebastian throws me out. It doesn't seem fair that he gets to have all the fun."

Frederica leaped up abruptly, her knees rattling the tea table. "Mr. Ryder, if you will excuse us a moment, I'd like a private word with the duke."

"Certainly. I'll just go wander out in the hall with my whiskey, shall I?" He loped off with a smooth grace that Frederica found too provoking.

She turned to Sebastian, who was biting into a jam tart.

"Sebastian," Frederica hissed, "how could you tell him?"

"Tell him what?" he asked, once he'd swallowed.

"About your blackmail. How I'm bedding you so you will sell me the castle."

Sebastian raised both eyebrows and opened his mouth, the perfect picture of surprise. "I never said such a thing! Honestly. Freddie, you must believe me. And anyway, it was your own damn idea! I'm not blackmailing you—you're blackmailing me!"

"He knows. He *smirks*."

"Oh, that's just Cam's smile. He always looks like a tomcat who's gotten into the cream. Now, I did tell him you had offered to buy the castle, but not a word about the strings attached. I'd canceled his visit, Freddie. His and Sanderson's both. Bloody hell, I hope he doesn't turn up, too." Sebastian took a large swig of whiskey. "Freddie, I know you think me an utter cad, and in general you are right, but I most assuredly did *not* tell Cam that we are playing at domination and submission. You can flog me with my best crop tomorrow if you don't believe me, but know you will be beating an innocent man."

"You! The last time you were innocent, you were in your mother's womb." Frederica stumbled away from the couch and went back to unravel more of the tapestry.

He was behind her in an instant, his whiskey breath hot on her neck. How she wished she wore a fichu. "Freddie. I would never compromise your reputation."

"No, just compromise *me*! Just today you f-fucked me outside again where anyone could have come upon us!"

She felt his smile on her skin. "Oh, Freddie, I love it when you talk dirty. And if the damn servants weren't so nosy, I could fuck you inside."

She stomped on his boot to very little effect, since he put his arms around her and cradled her to his chest, his hands going straight to her breasts. He circled her nipples with unerring skill and nibbled on her left earlobe.

"Look," he rasped into her ear, "I'm sorry he's here. So very sorry. He'll be gone in three days."

Frederica felt herself slipping under his spell again. His breaths, his touches, the timbre of his voice all combined to send signals directly to the juncture of her thighs. She would be dripping on her feet in a minute. This would not do. She pushed back against him, recognizing by his erection he was as aroused as she. "At least you'll have to stop bothering me while he's here."

Sebastian turned her around so she was facing him, so close she could count the dark whiskers that were shadowing his jaw. "What do you mean?"

No more talking dirty. He liked it too well. "Well, you can't—we can't—you know."

Sebastian grinned, looking like a tomcat himself. "Of course we can. Fortunate for you that two of those next three days are yours, but the day after tomorrow I expect you to do just as I say, whatever it is, from midnight to midnight."

She shoved him. "Oh! You are horrible."

"And you wouldn't have me any other way. I'm going to kiss you now, Freddie, even if you look like a drab bird at the moment. That is the ugliest dress. But it doesn't matter what you wear, you know. I'll have you anyway."

His lips came down on hers. Despite the warning, she didn't move fast enough and his tongue edged the seam of her lips open. The tea grew cold as she lost herself in his arms, swept away by irritating, undeniable passion. When he released her she knew she was pink and disheveled. And embarrassingly wet yet again.

"Sit down now and have a cup of tea. Some biscuits. I'm going to call Cam in, and you are going to behave just as you ought. But watch out for him. He's a dreadful rake."

"It takes one to know one," she said sourly, arranging herself and her ugly dress on the sofa, wondering if she'd have a damp spot on the back of it when she stood.

"Precisely. You are mine, Freddie, for the rest of the month. Don't forget it."

Frederica felt a shiver down her spine. When he looked at her like that, when he spoke to her like that, she couldn't imagine what June would be like without him.

She heard the masculine rumbling between the two men out in the hallway, but couldn't catch the words. Feeling reckless, she filled her teacup half-full of whiskey, reconsidered, then filled it to the brim. Dutch courage would be required to get through the hours until midnight. She needed to begin anew with this Mr. Ryder, who probably thought she was a madwoman.

Which, she reflected, she was.

# Chapter 28

*Things are stranger here than I expected.*
—FROM THE DIARY OF CAMERON RYDER

Cam was lounging on a long dusty bench. He had used a fingertip to spell his name on it while he was waiting, and his glass was empty. That kiss had gone on awhile, but not quite as long as Sebastian wished. He shifted his cock in his breeches before he sat down. Cam did indeed smirk at him.

"She's rather adorable, like a pixie, but you didn't mention she was more or less cracked, Sebastian. *This* is the girl who caused you all the trouble when you were a pup? I must say, she doesn't look at all like a femme fatale."

Cam knew all his secrets. He had spoken of that night, omitting the most salient details, because it really was too ridiculous to repeat. "She isn't cracked. Just—just under a bit of stress. There was a misunderstanding. We've cleared it up now."

"She specializes in misunderstandings, I gather. What exactly are the terms of your agreement? She shook like a leaf when I mentioned you'd disclosed the sale to me."

"Don't concern yourself. Really. Everything is fine." Sebastian began to trace his own circles on the scarred wood surface, wishing he was touching Freddie's skin. Damn the foul weather for rushing them.

"What's going on between you? She looked like she wanted to rip off your head. I can't say I want to find myself in the middle of some sort of domestic dispute."

Sebastian shrugged. "I told you we've known each other since we were children. There's a lot of history. You know the worst of it."

"So, once, she was like your little sister. Until she cornered you in disguise and tried to fuck your brains out until your fathers interrupted."

Even when he had thought he and Cam would never live to come home, Sebastian had spared Freddie in his story of that night. Protected her by omission. He wasn't about to come clean now, and whatever was happening with Freddie was certainly nothing at all like incest. She was nothing—nothing—like a sister to him.

"Freddie's a stranger to me—you know I haven't seen her in a decade. Not since I was a beardless boy on that awful night. Whatever I felt or feel toward her now is not—filial."

"Does she know what happened?" Cameron asked quietly.

There was no need for him to be specific. Sebastian knew what he referred to. He closed his eyes, blood blooming and rushing to his head. "No, she doesn't. And I'd like to keep it that way, if you don't mind."

"She won't hear it from me. But if you care for her, you should tell her."

"I don't care for her. It's not like that at all." Sebastian's own words were not quite convincing, even to himself. Good God. He was not actually still under Freddie's spell, was he? He'd talked himself out of that yesterday, although he had yet to make good his determination to end their arrangement. Surely he thought of her as just a convenient dalliance now, a way to stave off his creditors. Just a few days more. A week at the longest, now that Cam had interrupted them. He was not falling *in love*. He'd had all the love beaten out of him anyway.

Cam crossed his arms over his chest. "Whatever you say."

Cam knew him too well. Once, they'd been able to read each other's thoughts by a flick of an eyelash. It was clear to Sebastian the man was going to be a thorn in his side, however long he stayed.

"So, we agree to three days. I did save your life, you know," Cam prompted.

"And how long will you dine out on that tale? Yes, yes, I'm grateful, but just at present, you're a complication I don't need." Sebastian sighed, defeated. He did owe a great deal to Cam, but if the man threw a spanner into the works and Freddie backed out of their deal out of embarrassment, their friendship would be at an end. He needed her money.

*He needed her.*

He must not wander down that alley. He would never subject himself to anyone's will again. Freddie's demands upon him were nothing—she was an amateur.

He could be a congenial host to his old friend, could he not? Pretend that all was right in the world, at least for three days? Of course he could. He could pretend a great many things. "Come on. Let's freshen your drink and do justice to the tea tray. My cook Mrs. Holloway is a treasure."

An odd look flitted across Cam's face, but he rose off the bench, dusting off his trousers. "I can help you with the pixie. Sing your praises to earn my supper. Make you out to be a hero of the Nile so that the chit will fall in love with you and you can get your hands on all her money."

Sebastian picked up Cam's empty glass and twirled it between his hands. "I don't want her love. Or anybody's for that matter. I don't believe love even exists in this world, as you well know."

"I doubt you'll find it where you're headed. I hear hate reigns in the hot spot."

Sebastian stood up. "Now, Cam. I don't believe in hate, either. I'm done with all that. It's far too much trouble to hang on to, and is apt to make one spit and sweat. I am regrettably devoid of all those emotions that produce war, dreary ballads and bad poetry. Give me a warm body and a bed, and I won't have to feel anything but lust."

"I remember."

Neither one of them took a step toward the solar. They were quiet for a time with their own thoughts. It was easier not to speak of some things. Eventually Sebastian placed a hand on Cam's shoulder. "Don't worry. I have everything under control."

"So you'd like to think. But be careful. For some reason, Miss Wells strikes me as a danger to you."

Freddie naked. Freddie armed. Yes, she was dangerous. "You have no idea." Sebastian paused at the door. "Meet me in the long gallery tomorrow morning after breakfast. I'll arrange for a tour of your ancestors. And perhaps a fencing match with a surprising adversary."

It was Freddie's day tomorrow, but so far he'd been able to worm his way into her plans to suit himself. Imagining Cam fall victim to Freddie's fencing skill brought a wide smile to his face.

"Uh-oh. I don't like the look of that. But it's not enough to drive me from Archibald Castle. It will take more than a show of your teeth to do it."

"I said three days, and I meant it. I haven't got much more than my word at present."

Cam stared off into a corner where a suit of armor listed precariously on its stand. "If I have to, I could spot you a loan."

"Really, Cam, how much more in your debt can I be? No, that won't be necessary. I'll survive."

"I—I care for you, you know."

"And I you. We're blood brothers of a sort, after all. But I won't take your money, unless you want to buy that suit of armor you're looking at."

"Not my cup of tea. Speaking of which, I suppose we'd best go in so I can be uncharming."

Sebastian laughed. "It will be a trial for you, but nothing to what you've already gone through."

"Amen to that."

The past was a closed book. Long may it stay that way, Sebastian thought, as he followed his friend through the solar door.

# Chapter 29

*I must never drink again. Oh! My head. I cannot write another word.*

—FROM THE DIARY OF FREDERICA WELLS

They were out in the hall a damned long time, Freddie thought as she sipped the vile whiskey. Talking about her. Even if Sebastian hadn't spelled out the exact terms of their agreement, that Mr. Ryder had given her knowing looks, like he could see right through her dress to her stays, which were not laced as tightly as they should be at all. Without a maid, life was hard on Frederica and her bosom ever more bountiful. Her hair was usually a fright and her hands worn down with work.

Tomorrow was Sunday. When she went to church, she would beg Mr. Clement, the young clergyman, to help her find some poor soul on his rounds who didn't believe the ghost rumors and would come to work at Goddard Castle for free.

For an instant, she was tempted to ask Sebastian to accompany her to the service. He would have to if she commanded it—it was her day. It would serve him right. How he would hate sitting still and feigning piety. She really didn't think he was capable of it, as he exuded a restless energy that was not about to be tamed by a sermon or a psalm. But she didn't trust him. Likely his hand would creep up her skirts in the high Archibald pew, thinking no one could see what he was up to. Hell, even if he were exposed to all the prying eyes, he was devil enough to despoil her in church.

How could she sit in prayerful silence after all the things she'd done since Sebastian arrived? She would probably be struck by lightning, fried to a crisp. Maybe she should step outside right now and get it over with.

The solar's windows rattled in the rain, and flashes of sheet lightning brightened the gray sky. The storm could last another few minutes or until tomorrow—there was no telling with Yorkshire weather. Frederica was only just getting the winter chill from her bones. The cold of the winter had dragged on forever into spring. Whether one was indoors or out, the castle had a forbidding climate.

Why did she want to stay? She topped off her teacup with more whiskey, knowing that the answer was not to be found at the bottom of a bottle. The taste of it was not so bad now. She could see why gentlemen were forever in their cups. A comforting warmth spread from her chest to her limbs, nearly as pleasant as Sebastian's kiss.

*Pleasant.* Ha. She needed to come up with a better word than that. She was a writer, wasn't she? Even though she wrote about true occurrences, she tried to make the past come alive, as though she were telling a story to a tousle-haired child at bedtime. Uncle Phillip had gotten rave reviews.

She gulped down more whiskey. She wasn't resentful the duke received all the acclaim. Without his interest and acquisitions, Frederica would have had no purpose to her life. She had to finish the series. Had to. She hiccuped.

The door opened and Sebastian and his handsome friend entered, both looking like the answer to every spinster's prayers. But she was made of sterner stuff. Sebastian might play her body like a master violinist, with those long tapering fingers and his even longer cock, but he was nothing but a selfish rake. Cameron Ryder was surely just the same. She lifted the china cup to her lips and drained it.

"Here we are, Freddie. Sorry to have left you alone for so long. Just catching up on old times." Sebastian eased back down beside her, throwing an arm over the back of the ratty sofa. It was perilously close to her, and she fought the urge to lean her head on it.

"The duke tells me you helped him escape from prison, Mr. Ryder." Oh, dear. Her tongue felt thick, and she was almost sure she said "prishon."

"Yes, Miss Wells. I'm forever getting His Grace out of one scrape or another."

Frederica leaned forward. "Tell me all about them."

Cameron Ryder gave another catlike grin. Or perhaps it was wolfish. Were wolves ever blond? She thought not. Gray was the usual color, perhaps silver. Whatever kind of wolf he was, he had far too many blindingly white teeth to fit in an Englishman's mouth. She must ask for his brand of tooth powder. Discreetly, she loosened the top button on her bodice. It was so very hot in here all of a sudden she thought she might faint.

"I'm only here for three days, Miss Wells. We won't have time to scratch the surface."

Frederica waved a lazy hand. "Begin anywhere. I have not seen Sebastian for ages. Tell me all his shecrets. He musht have been very bad."

Mr. Ryder shot Sebastian a puzzled look. Sebastian picked up her teacup and took a suspicious sniff.

"By God, Freddie, you're under the hatches. How many cups of whiskey did you drink? We were only gone five minutes."

"What dosh it matter? I'm a grown woman. I can do as I pleashe."

"Not today, you can't," Sebastian muttered in her ear. "Excuse us, Cam. I'm going to see Miss Wells upstairs."

Frederica tried to push him away as he bent over her, but she was always unlucky pushing Sebastian away. He had the most unnerving habit of being just where she didn't want him. Except when he was between her thighs. He was quite all right there. And now he was carrying her out of the solar up to her bedroom. He might be between her thighs in minutes. Poor Mr. Ryder would have to eat his sandwiches alone. She settled into Sebastian's arms as he mounted the twisting stairs.

"Fuck me, Sebastian," she whispered.

"You hoyden. I should, just to punish you. You have no head at all for liquor, do you?"

Frederica sighed sadly. "I cannot dr-drink a drop. P'raps a drop is shufficient. Much more that that means bad things happen. Look at ush."

Sebastian's face swam over her. He had the most elegant eyebrows. He must practice lifting one, then the other, in the mirror every morning. The left one was up now, winged, taking flight. Or was it the right? His left, her right, or the other way around. What did it matter? He was beautiful.

"You mean the night of my father's fancy dress ball. You had too much to drink and found me in the tower."

"Yup. Thatsh it. The f-fucking. It washn't what I hoped for. I loved you so much. But you've got better in bed. So. Much. Better."

"Good God."

Sebastian said not another word until he deposited her on her bed. "Go to sleep now, Freddie. I'll have Mrs. Holloway make up a dinner tray for you."

"Only want to eat you." Oh, that was not the proper thing to say. She should say something different, but the room was spinning. It was probably best not to speak anymore. Frederica closed her eyes to stop the unicorn on the tapestry from undulating so freakishly. His horn reminded her of—

\* \* \*

"Just as I said, cracked."

Cam had pillaged the tray and there wasn't much left for Sebastian when he came back downstairs. He poured himself another drink, not knowing whether he should be grateful for Freddie's intolerance to alcohol or damn it. She really had not been herself when she seduced him ten years ago. Or perhaps she *had* been herself, her inhibitions released. In vino veritas.

She said she had loved him.

Puppy love, to be sure. She had barely been out of the schoolroom. He must have seemed a glamorous figure, fresh from his jaunt on the Continent—at least to places that Napoleon had not gotten to first.

It was a crush. Meant nothing then. Nothing now.

"Sebastian! Are you listening?"

Sebastian snapped out of his reverie and cut a slice of seedcake. "Yes, yes. Cracked. As I told you earlier, Freddie has had a tough time up here. Lonely. Isolated. Unused to male company." And what male company there had been had not been precisely run-of-the-mill.

"And obviously a lush. The girl drank half the whiskey while we were out in the hallway." Cam lifted the cut-glass decanter and splashed the last of the amber liquid into his tumbler.

"No, she rarely has spirits. Some wine with dinner, that's all."

"She's an odd little duck, isn't she?"

Sebastian bit the inside of his cheek. "Why do you say that?"

"She doesn't have much polish. Sophistication. Says things she shouldn't. She looks the sort who will expect a man to stay home and read books with her. Not," Cam said hastily, noting the glare that Sebastian aimed toward him, "that she's not attractive in her own way."

"I think she's attractive in anybody's way." He closed his eyes, seeing her lashed to his bed, her white thighs spread wide, her naked pussy wet, her generous breasts tipped to the side. *Damn*. He certainly couldn't relate that image to Cam. The man would be beating a path to Freddie's door before he finished the sentence.

His thoughts must have been revealed on his face, for he heard Cam chuckle. "Look at you! You're hard as a schoolboy. Go to her. She'll never know you're not a dream. I'll entertain myself until dinnertime. I don't suppose there's a frisky parlor maid anywhere about this dump?"

Sebastian got hold of himself. "Freddie's sleeping. And drunk. I may not be much of a gentleman, but I'll not take her when she's unconscious." She'd said she wanted him. But he didn't want a muddled Freddie. He wanted her alert, aware that she was ceding herself to him, capitulating utterly. "Come, I'll take you on a tour of the castle. The weather's perfect for it, all gray gloom and whistling wind."

"Must we save the long gallery for tomorrow? I'm anxious to see centuries of Archibalds before their ruin."

"We'll start there, then. I'd better bring a branch of candles. There won't be much natural light with the storm outside. You've never said—did the old earl ever acknowledge you?" Sebastian led the way up a set of circular steps, their footsteps echoing on the slick stone.

"He paid for my schooling, but I never had the dubious pleasure of meeting him. My mother was a respectable woman before she caught his eye. But he was married."

"And there were no other children."

"No, and he had three wives, the randy old goat. Just as well. Any heir would have had the title stripped, too, and all the holdings. It doesn't pay to do treason."

Sebastian paused to strike his flint and light the candles. Despite them, the long gallery was steeped in shadows. More than a dozen portraits lined the wall, most life-sized or larger. The Archibalds had been a handsome lot, although a few looked as if they smelled something that disagreed with them. Their faces showed excessive pride. Superiority. Hubris bred into the bone to enable the last Earl of Archibald to betray his country and think he could get away with it.

"Fascinating." Cam paced the corridor, standing at a respectful distance from his blood relatives. He turned to Sebastian and struck a pose. "Do you think I fit in with this lot of rogues?"

"You have the eyes, don't you? I'm surprised Freddie didn't notice. She's the expert on the castle and its history."

"Which one is my sainted papa, I wonder?"

"From the clothes, I would venture to guess that one on the end. With the spaniels."

Cam stepped closer to this painting. It showed a young man not long out of school. His fair hair was unpowdered, his face not yet formed with the haughtiness of his ancestors. "I am by far the more handsome."

Sebastian laughed. "And somewhat more principled. Cam, I don't mean to pry, but why would you want anything to do with this place? It's not as if you even knew your father or grew up here."

Cam stuffed his hands in his pocket. "I'm not interested anymore.

Your bluestocking will buy the place and we shall all live happily ever after."

Sebastian knew him well. When Cam lied, his fingers inevitably crossed, a leftover from his fatherless childhood. Sebastian had seen his share of finger-crossing in Egypt, when they both would say anything, do anything, to survive.

Sebastian slapped his hand to his forehead. "Bloody hell! You think there *is* treasure hidden away here, don't you? Did you plan to cheat me out of it?"

Cameron showed no shame. From his perspective, he probably thought he was owed anything he could get to make up for the indignities he'd suffered. "From everything I've learned about my father, money was his sole motivator. He didn't love the French or hate the English. He cared absolutely nothing for his three wives. In fact, my mother told me there were whispers that he did away with at least one of them. The government never found the germinal francs that were used to pay him to set up his spy ring. I've seen the damning paperwork, Sebastian. You know I helped the war effort in my own way as I knocked around, and have access to things that you do not. Allegedly the earl received a substantial amount. Substantial. The rumors are all over the place, but even if a fraction of the amount discussed is accurate, it would take your breath away.

"There was nothing found at his town house in London. Not here. A swarm of His Majesty's agents picked apart every stone of Archibald Castle before your father bought the place."

"Well, then. How did they miss it?"

Cam shook his head. "I don't know. But I've got a feeling. And, fool that I am, I'm telling you this. You and your little bluestocking could live for a couple of centuries on the reputed sum."

"We'd have to find it first." Sebastian leaned back against a rain-splattered window. His heart tripped. What if Cam was right, and there *was* a fortune to be found? He could afford to let Freddie stay right up here scribbling away, and he could go back to traveling the globe. He'd have his life back, with no fear of being clapped in the Fleet. "Does Sanderson know about this?"

"I don't think so. He just wants to add the castle to his collection. Eccentric old bird. If you're thinking to pit me in a bidding war with him, don't bother. My funds are limited."

Sebastian rubbed his jaw, working out the best way to proceed. It was true he probably wouldn't even be standing here, hot candle wax dripping on his thumb, without Cam's friendship. He set the candelabra down on the window embrasure. "I'll give you a week to find the money and we'll split it. I keep the castle, and you have a consolation prize. We're talking about gold and silver coins, yes? Easily melted down? I don't want the government claiming a centime."

Cam gaped at him. "That's bloody generous of you, Sebastian."

"What can I say? You did save my life. But not another word from you about it. If you don't find anything, you'll leave."

Neither one of them was entitled to Napoleon's bribe. For a moment, Sebastian wished his father was alive so he could quiz him on the steps the government had taken over the Archibald estate. The pater could have used the blunt, too, to fritter away on his Middle Ages muck. He and the king's men must have been satisfied there was nothing to the tale of hidden treasure. If Sebastian and Cam did indeed find the missing money, they would have to be the souls of discretion disposing of it. Getting rid of half would prove to be easier than getting rid of it all, and if what Cameron said was true, half would be more than enough to get him off the River Tick for life. "Fair enough. You do know how indolent I am, though. I'm not apt to exert much muscle to tear this place apart."

"You won't have to," Sebastian said dryly. "It looks as though it's tearing itself apart on its own."

"What about your Miss Wells? Shall we engage her in this scavenger hunt?"

"I'm not sure yet. Let me think on it." Law-abiding little Freddie would probably want to box up the francs and send them straight to Whitehall.

"She might notice when we strip down and start digging holes in the dining hall."

"Will it come to that? Don't you have a theory where the money might be?"

"Not really. The Crown looked in all the conventional spots—the well, the wine cellar, the dungeons, etcetera. I'm at a disadvantage not knowing my old man personally. I had to spend a fortune to bribe a fellow in the War Office to get my hands on the diary he left behind. Not the original, mind. The fellow copied out the pages, so for all I know, when he couldn't read my father's writing he made something up. From what I have, it's been difficult to piece together Archibald's thought process. He may look innocent in this portrait, but I assure you he had a twisted mind. The spy ring he ran was the work of a mad genius."

"Freddie can help, I think," Sebastian said thoughtfully. "She's used to poring through old rubbish to figure things out, and she knows the castle inside and out. I'll talk to her tomorrow. When she's sober." He extended a hand. "Partners again, then? You won't unearth the fortune in secret and abscond in the middle of the night?"

"I am not my father. And I owe you, too." Cam gripped his hand, and their eyes truly met for the first time since Sebastian found him in the library. No words were necessary between them.

Sebastian broke away first, wondering what he had gotten himself into. He'd have to creatively juggle his days with Freddie and still scour the castle. If nothing was found in a week, Cam would leave them in peace to their sin. Seven days would be a long time to deprive himself of Freddie's body—too long. Not even the lure of the Archibald treasure was enough to make Sebastian turn celibate. He was not ready to give her up. What had started out as a kind of punishment for her was punishing him instead, stirring up things better left unexplored.

She said she had loved him. Nonsense. Certainly now she used him as he used her. Whoring with him ensured a roof over her head and lined his pockets. That was all it was, all it could be.

Sebastian looked out the window. The rain had ceased while they had plotted, and a rainbow bent over the misty moors. A good omen, to be sure, not that he believed in such things. "Come. We've still got a few hours of light. Let's walk the grounds before supper. Catch up."

"You'll risk your boots in the wet grass?"

Sebastian smiled. "If you are right, I'll have the wherewithal for a dozen pairs."

# Chapter 30

Madness.

—FROM THE DIARY OF FREDERICA WELLS

Freddie woke from her stupor at first light. Her mouth was dry as dust, and a determined band of tiny elves were clog-dancing on her temples. It would be impossible to rise and go to church this morning as she had planned, although the Lord only knew, she needed intercession through prayer in the very worst way. She lay still on her bed, her hands clasped in front of her as though she were a marble effigy. She got directly to the point, promising that at least for today she would not have carnal relations with Sebastian, and for all her tomorrows, she would never, ever drink anything alcoholic again.

Her untouched supper tray did not tempt her. There had been a bowl of broth, now scummy, a roll, a wedge of cheese and a flask of water. The water still had appeal, and she drank it down quickly. Making herself presentable took some effort. Bending over to pick up hairpins that her clumsy fingers dropped was agony. It took her two tries to button her bodice properly, and all the rice powder she possessed to mask the green cast to her face.

Once she was dressed, she refrained from inhaling and carried the tray downstairs to the kitchen. Sebastian and his friend were taking their breakfast at the long table, a most unwelcome assault to her senses. The sight of two beautiful men and the smell of bacon, kippers and eggs caused havoc with her stomach, and she set the tray down hastily as they both rose from their seats.

"Good morning, Freddie."

Sebastian looked as fresh as if he'd just stepped from a fashion plate depicting a country gentleman at his leisure, his friend the same. Injustice, when they had probably drunk brandy late into the night.

"You are up early," she croaked.

"Yes, we have plans. Sit with us. I was just about to send Alice up with my never-fail potion to relieve you of your headache."

Frederica didn't bother denying that she had one. On cue, the kitchen maid stepped out of the pantry holding a small tray with a glass of cloudy liquid and a large cup of coffee. Frederica's stomach continued its rebellion, but she joined the men at the table, taking a deep sniff of the comforting rosewater at her wrist.

Alice dropped a curtsy, an affectation she usually dispensed with when dealing with Frederica. They had worked too often side by side to stand on ceremony. She must be trying to impress the duke and Mr. Ryder, poor child. "Here, miss. His Grace says this'll work wonders."

The entire household must know of her drunken disgrace. Ever since Sebastian's arrival, she had lost all her propriety—fornicating, drinking. Next she would be kissing strangers and dancing naked on the moors.

She eyed the glass warily, stirring the gray concoction with a spoon.

"Thank you, Alice. I do beg your pardon, Mr. Ryder, for my unforgivable behavior yesterday. I am unused to spirits—cannot, in fact, tolerate them at all. I should have learned my lesson by now. I must have made a dreadful first impression."

"Think nothing of it, Miss Wells. We all have our faults, don't we, Sebastian?"

"Speak for yourself. I'm rather perfect." He gave her a slow wink.

Frederica nearly spat her mouthful of Sebastian's drink out at his conceit. She was afraid to ask what was in it, but the taste was not too awful. She took another sip, avoiding looking at Sebastian's egg-smeared plate or his smug face.

"Freddie, after breakfast, we'd like you to join us in the library. There is something we can use your help with."

Sebastian knew as well as she did that today was *her* day. She needn't do a single thing he asked of her. "It's Sunday. I thought I'd go to church."

"What a novel idea! Are you up to it?"

No, she wasn't, but she did not want to spend the morning anywhere near Sebastian and Cameron Ryder. Church was the very last place she expected to find either of them.

"We'll all go," Mr. Ryder offered with a sunny smile. "It will do us good."

The thought of being shut up between the two of them in the Archibald pew was not a happy one. The elves picked up their pace and pounded harder on her head. "Perhaps I spoke too soon. I am feeling rather unwell still."

"Drink up, Freddie. The sooner you finish, the sooner you'll feel better. I guarantee it."

Perversely, Frederica took a swallow of coffee instead. She usually drank tea in the morning, but strong coffee was what she needed. The men watched her, concern on their faces. They had both finished eating, refusing Mrs. Holloway's attempts to replenish their plates. "You two run along. I'll join you once I've had a muffin."

"Take your time, Freddie. We won't go anywhere."

And that was the trouble. Twenty-odd more days of Sebastian, three with Mr. Ryder. Frederica wanted her old life back.

They rose from the table. Frederica had to allow as how they both looked exceptionally fit as they made their exit. There was something about properly tailored breeches—

"Jam, too, Miss Frederica?" Mrs. Holloway fussed over her, buttering a freshly toasted muffin.

"I don't think so." It would be all she could do to choke down the muffin, but she knew she needed something in her stomach. She'd not eaten since yesterday's lunch. "What do you think of the duke's friend?"

"Handsome devil, ain't he? He seems a nice enough gentleman. The two of them were thick as thieves at breakfast, although I couldn't catch everything they said. I think my hearing's going in my old age. But I'll bet my best copper-bottomed saucepan they're up to something."

"I wonder what it is." Frederica closed her eyes and swallowed the entire glass of Sebastian's brew.

"You'll find out soon enough, I reckon. Are you sure you don't want an egg or some stewed fruit?"

"Positive." Frederica set the glass down and slumped over the half-eaten muffin. "Oh, Mrs. Holloway. I made a total fool of myself yesterday. I drank some of Sebastian's whiskey—most of it, I'm afraid."

Mrs. Holloway waggled a finger. "His Grace did mention it. We had a little dustup over whose antidote we were going to send up with Alice. I was overruled, but should His Grace's drink not work, I'll make you my own specialty. Mr. Holloway, God rest his soul, was often in need of it. Alice, child, come and clear up these plates." Now that the men had left, Mrs. Holloway relaxed. She sat down to keep Frederica company, serving herself a cup of coffee and an overlooked pastry from the transferware platter at the center of the table.

"You know I never drink more than half a glass of wine with dinner. Alcohol is like a poison to me. I don't know what possessed me."

Mrs. Holloway looked at her with shrewd brown eyes. "The duke makes you nervous."

If she only knew how much. "How can that be? I've known him since we were children."

"Aye, but you've both changed, my dear. He's a fine figure of a man, and you are a grown woman. It's about time you had a bit of romance in your life."

Frederica coughed out some crumbs. "Romance! Hardly that."

"I see the way he looks at you. He's spending quite a bit of time in your company, isn't he? Good thing that witch Mrs. Carroll's gone. She'd have something to say about that."

Frederica couldn't agree more. The woman would probably want to get in on the action.

"I think you exaggerate the situation, Mrs. Holloway. We're just old childhood friends."

"I'm never wrong about these things. I wouldn't be a bit surprised if I wasn't calling you duchess before long."

Frederica rose unsteadily from her chair. "Rubbish. Sebastian will never ask me to marry him, and I would certainly never say yes if he did! I'm only being agreeable to him so I can get my hands on the castle."

But he *had* asked her to marry him. Ten years ago. A lifetime ago. But he hadn't meant it, hadn't really wanted to.

Frederica felt a sharp stabbing in her head. The elves were armed now, abandoning their wooden shoes for swords. She'd like to join them, skewer Sebastian and Cameron Ryder with a rusty rapier so they would leave her alone. She would make her excuses to them in the library, spend the day in her room or roaming about outside if it didn't rain again. Though if she could dislodge them from the library, she might work on the chapter discussing Phillip, Duke of Burgundy's festival in 1453, where the knights swore before a pheasant on the banquet table that they would go on crusade. She swore before her partly eaten muffin she would undertake a crusade of her own to drive the men away if she could. Her writing deadline loomed.

She left Mrs. Holloway to her breakfast and Alice to her dishes, gingerly stepping through the corridors of the castle. With every step, her entire body ached. This was a hard lesson for her to relearn—clearly, she should never imbibe spirits. They wreaked havoc with everything. Once, they had made her feel invincible—sensual, daring, willing to seduce Sebastian no matter the cost.

Today, she was far from feeling powerful. And it was her day to wield control. The only thing she wanted to control was the covers as she crawled back in bed. Alone.

The men had pulled chairs up to the wide desk, leaving the old duke's chair—her chair now—available. They rose again when she entered the room. Really, this show of gentlemanly courtesy was rather ridiculous. She waved them down and sat, folding her hands tight in her lap to keep them from shaking.

"Perhaps this isn't the most convenient time for this," Mr. Ryder said to Sebastian.

"I won't give you more than a week. It began yesterday."

A week? Frederica remembered that three days was set to be the limit of Mr. Ryder's visit. "What is all this about?"

"I'll get right to the point. Cam here is in possession of the late Earl of Archibald's diary. Not a diary precisely, more like a notebook."

"A copy," Mr. Ryder interjected.

"Whatever. He believes there actually is some sort of treasure here and I've promised to split it with him if we find it."

Frederica smiled at the two nitwits before her. "Really, Sebastian, the king's men inspected the castle more than thoroughly before your father moved in. The rumor of the treasure is like the rumor of the Archibald Walkers. A fairy story."

Mr. Ryder spoke up. "I'm not so sure. My father received payments from the French which have never been accounted for, even though he lived a lavish lifestyle in Town."

"Certainly not here," Sebastian murmured.

Frederica's head pounded. "Your father? I don't understand."

"I'm a bastard, Miss Wells. At least by birth, if not in disposition. I'm ashamed to say the Earl of Archibald was my father. I never knew him, so making sense of his ramblings has not been easy."

For the first time, Frederica really *looked* at Mr. Ryder. Oh, she'd admired him yesterday, for what woman would not? But now she saw the Archibald eyes in his earnest face, straight out of the portraits she'd always found so unnerving in the long gallery.

"Some of the notebook seems to be a history of Archibald Castle, Freddie. With the original layout, garden plans and the like. Notations about ancestors. It may just be family pride, but Cam thinks those pages might be important. We spent hours over it last night."

"Who copied the diary?"

"Someone in the War Office whose pockets I lined rather extravagantly. He assured me it is a complete transcription, right down to squiggles on the page. I told him I was curious about the father I never knew. I don't believe he knew my intent, or Archibald Castle would be crawling with soldiers again, and we might both be awaiting execution."

"This all sounds very unlikely. I've lived in Goddard Castle almost a dozen years, and never once have I taken this rumor seriously. Sebastian, you know if your father had believed there was anything to this story, he would have tried to find the money himself."

"And spent it on more junk. I know. But it may not be gold, although we know that's how Archibald was paid. Germinal francs. You told me that yourself."

Yes, she had teased Sebastian about it, along with the ghosts. But it couldn't possibly be true.

"If you don't find this alleged treasure in a week, what happens?"

"Cam goes home and I sell the castle to you, as we agreed."

"And what happens if I have the garderobes cleaned and the workmen come across the money covered in excrement twenty years from now?"

Sebastian's horror was genuine. "Good Lord, it can't be hidden in the shitter, can it? That would be most inconvenient. Cam, I'll assign that task to you."

"I think from everything I've heard, my father was far too aware of his consequence to go digging about in human muck. No, he would have found a cache that suited his purposes better. Something perhaps even in plain sight. I believe he let the castle go to rack and ruin to discourage anyone from nosing about. Played up the rumors about the ghosts. Kept folks away while he was in Town meeting with his minions."

Frederica considered. "It's been nigh onto impossible to employ local people. Uncle Phillip brought his people from Dorset and hired additional staff from London. Of course, conditions became intolerable and most of them left long ago."

"I think we're hooking her, Cam," Sebastian said with a grin.

"I'd have to see this notebook."

Mr. Ryder pulled a slender leather volume from his inside jacket pocket and slid it toward her. "I've been assured the real thing is very like this. My forger copied it as he found it."

"Forger?"

Mr. Ryder shrugged. "That's what the fellow did during the war. He can duplicate any hand."

Frederica took the book from the desk. "And he copied the earl's?"

Mr. Ryder grimaced. "I didn't ask him to do that, I'm afraid. I thought it was enough to simply get the information, not the curlicues."

Frederica felt a stab of disappointment. One could sense a great deal about a person just examining their handwriting. She knew Sebastian's was nigh onto impossible to read. Pulling her spectacles from a pocket, she flipped quickly through the book. "It seems pretty straightforward. Just a jumble of random things. It's not in any obvious sort of code, is it?"

"I don't know. There are appointments with his tailor and whatnot. I did follow up on those. Some of the tradesmen are dead—it was all long ago—but most were legitimate. I found it odd that there is so much about the castle and his family mixed in with dinner parties and races. Of course, it's not a proper daily diary, and seems to have been written over several years."

"I know you've done this sort of work for my father, Freddie—making sense of other people's scribbling. Will you do it for me, too?"

Frederica looked over her lenses at Sebastian. He looked every bit as earnest as his friend.

"Why should I? If you both go away, I'll be left with everything." The looks on their faces were priceless. Frederica waited a beat to torture them. "Of course I'll do it, you silly man. I only wish I had the primary document, but I'll make do with this. But do go away for the rest of the day. Go shoot something or ride something and leave me in peace. And tomorrow, too. I must do my own work, and do it *unobstructed*."

"That will be three days in a row, Freddie," Sebastian said sotto voce.

"That's correct. If you want my cooperation, those are my terms."

He stood up. "Very well. In the meantime, Cam and I will make an unofficial reconnaissance of the castle. Put ourselves in the old devil's shoes and see what we can kick up."

Frederica breathed a sigh of relief as they exited the library. She shoved her glasses back up and began to read the Earl of Archibald's notes. Page after page seemed to be random lists of activities, interrupted by chunks relating to the castle. It looked as if he had plans for renovations, which had sadly not come to fruition. There was a footprint of the ancient foundation, with simple architectural plans to build upon them. Really, if the man buried anything on the grounds, the three of them could dig for the rest of their lives and never find it.

Her head pounded from reading the cramped transcription. She was still distinctly unwell. Placing the little book aside, she went back to her own notes for *Roxbury's Middle Ages*. She immersed herself in Edward IV's military exploits to destroy the House of Lancaster. For the next hour, she alternated between the recent past and the distant past, making little headway in either. Feeling cloistered in the library and longing for fresh air, she stopped in the solar to pick up her sewing basket, slipped the diary into it and went out into the walled lady's garden.

There was a lengthy list of plantings for the garden in the earl's book, and a detailed diagram of the herbs that were still flourishing years later in the brick-heated sun trap. Really, this sort of information was more likely to be written by a chatelaine of the castle than its lord. Most men couldn't distinguish sage from rosemary, or a daisy from a rose for that matter. Frederica had made her own additions since moving here, but many of the plants had probably been in the garden for centuries. According to the diary, the earl had made a point of planting a thick bed of catmint all along the wall to the garden entry door to "keep rats away from the building." It was an old method of rodent control, and when steeped in water, catmint leaves were useful to spray on plants to discourage insects, too. She'd made use of the leaves herself.

What if he had put something other than catmint in the ground? Her heart beat a little faster. There would be no harm in digging up the plants. The bed was not more than twenty feet in length, and would not be so very difficult for two well-muscled men to remove the herbs and then return them in place.

Frederica went back inside to get her hat and find Sebastian and his friend.

# Chapter 31

*Damn her.*

—FROM THE DIARY OF SEBASTIAN GODDARD,
DUKE OF ROXBURY

She felt somewhat useless sitting on the shady bench, stitching as Sebastian and Cam dug on either side of the castle's garden door. And dry beneath the brim of her old straw hat. Perspiration was rolling off both of them, their linen shirts soaked and clinging to their skin. It was not an unpleasant site, but could be improved upon. The catmint had been uprooted, and they were each making a trench. At each sound of their shovels hitting something solid, there was an expectant pause, but so far they'd overturned only rocks, no coffin filled with livres.

"Why don't you two remove your shirts? You must be dreadfully hot." She herself was hot and bothered at the sight of such prime specimens exerting themselves with such determination.

"I'm fine," Sebastian ground out, flinging a chunk of dirt on the grass.

"We wouldn't wish to offend your maidenly sensibilities, Miss Wells."

"You gentlemen are always deciding what's best for the ladies. I for one should like to see a bit of male flesh this morning."

Sebastian knew it was her day, and the rules were clear. What she wanted, she got. He was honor-bound. The muscle jumped in his cheek, and she stifled her urge to gloat. It would be interesting to compare Sebastian to his friend. Simply in the interest of anatomical research, of course. Science at its finest.

With a grunt, Sebastian threw his shovel down and pulled his shirt over his head. Frederica realized she'd rarely seen him in bright sunlight—most of the time, they were in the dark, she was blindfolded or her eyes were closed in bliss as he lay with her in the grass. Her eyes were open now, and the bliss remained. He was lean yet muscled, just a smattering of dark hair on his chest with a faint trail disappearing under his breeches. They dipped low at his waist and for one moment she wondered what he'd do if she asked him to remove those, too. But that would give the game away to Mr. Ryder.

That gentleman was a bit slower to divest himself of his shirt, but when he did, his back was turned to her. She gave an involuntary gasp.

It was not for admiration, although he was broad and well formed, a little heavier than Sebastian but fit. But his back was striped white, a crisscross of healed-over cane marks. Even if he shared Sebastian's predilections for domination and submission, surely he could not have enjoyed its resulting scars. He had been brutally used.

Sebastian was playful in his discipline. He used his whip to tease her. He spanked her the once, and she supposed she had deserved it for spying into his trunk. But then he'd kissed her bottom in worship, and she had been unbearably moved.

She knew that men were sometimes thrashed at school by cruel masters. In the British navy, too, but to her knowledge, Mr. Ryder had spent his life ashore treasure hunting. How could he have come upon such abuse?

She didn't dare ask, and he didn't seem to notice the sound she made or her look of horror. She went back to her needlework, sorry she had ever pushed the men this far. They dug in concert, bantering with each other like two fellows who didn't have a care in the world, so whatever had transpired, it was long forgotten.

When she looked up again from her pillowcase, the embroidery hoop slid from her hands to the grass.

Sebastian had changed position. The lines on his back were equal to—no, worse than—his friend's. Frederica realized she'd never seen his exposed back. The days they made love outdoors, he'd either been dressed or lying on the ground. He'd been careful to angle himself away so as not to reveal the torture.

For torture it must have been.

He had joked about being in gaol, but always changed the subject. Sebastian and Cameron Ryder had been imprisoned together. It had resulted in their easy friendship, the way they sometimes telegraphed their thoughts to each other when Frederica had no idea what was transpiring. She'd been a little jealous of it. Now she was only grateful she had not shared their hellish experience, for it was obvious from the patterns on their backs they had shared the same fate by the same hand.

No wonder he would not discuss his incarceration. She bent to pick up her sewing, a wave of dizziness overtaking her. In her mind's eye she saw their backs, bloody and festering. She squeezed her eyes shut, but the image only became more vivid. She had thought Sebastian a perfect wastrel, going from bed to bed across most of Europe and northern Africa, presenting his immaculate, charming front to dazzle the unsuspecting. He was insouciance itself, quick with wit and practiced seduction. Chronically lighthearted, even when he was engaging in his dark fantasies.

No man who had survived what he had would be untouched. She didn't know him at all.

She felt bile rise, and took a deep breath. The air was sweet with spring and the scent of damp, overturned earth. The fruit trees were budding, and the clumps of herbs with their blend of scents should have cured her of her urge to be sick. But she smelled fear. Despair. Waste. She saw darkness. She felt the lash on her own back.

"Sebastian."

He didn't hear her, stepping on his shovel and rocking it into the compact earth as a flock of crows wheeled above. Mr. Ryder said something to him and he laughed.

Frederica needed . . . something. She could not sit out here under the bright blue sky and pretend everything was normal.

"Sebastian!"

He turned to her, holding a hand over his eyes. "What is it, Freddie? You're as white as a sheet."

"I— Could you walk inside with me?"

"With the greatest of pleasure. Let Cam do all the work for a change. He's been slacking, you know."

Frederica rose from the bench. For a moment she thought she would be missish and faint, something she had never done in her entire life. Sebastian wiped his face with the sleeve of his shirt and shrugged into it again.

"Mustn't give the servants a show." He strode across the lawn and picked up her basket. "Are you all right? Or are you just so inspired that you must act on a wicked impulse with me in the stairwell?"

"I must talk with you."

"Well, that's disappointing. My hopes are dashed. Do you intend to be respectable the entire day?"

She clutched at his arm. "Don't joke, please."

"That's what I do, Freddie."

"I know. But you needn't right this minute."

They walked through the open door to the cool, dim hallway that led to the kitchens. Frederica immediately sank down on the floor.

"Freddie! Are you sick? Let me get Mrs. Holloway."

She reached up to grasp his hand. "No, I don't need anyone but you."

"I have no objection to fucking you here on the floor, but I must remind you that Cam is right outside and any one of our people can come upon us."

"Please sit with me."

He gave her a crooked grin. "I must do as you command. Today, and tomorrow, too. You drive a hard bargain." He was cross-legged in one smooth movement, never letting her hand go. "Now, tell me, what is troubling you so?"

"Your back. And Mr. Ryder's."

Sebastian's face shuttered. "I am disfigured. I assumed you'd already noticed."

Frederica shook her head. "How?"

He dropped her hand. "I don't talk about it. It's over and done."

"It happened to both of you. While you were in prison?"

"Yes."

He uttered that one syllable with finality, but Frederica could not let it go. "How long were you in that gaol?"

"What difference does it make?"

"I need to know."

His hands clenched in his lap. "No, you don't! Don't go all weepy on me, Freddie. Or, worse yet, vomit on me. Life is full of bloody inconveniences. That was one of them."

"It was more than an inconvenience, Sebastian. You—you were mutilated! You could have died!"

"And wished I could, night after night, but here I am." He sprang back up. "I've got to go outside and finish. Talking to you about this is one thing I will not do, even if you are in charge today. And don't go hounding Cam."

"And if I do?"

"I won't sell you the damned castle, Freddie. I'll sell it to Cam instead. And you'll have wasted a few days on *your* back for nothing." He slammed the garden door behind him.

And it had been only a few days, yet Frederica's entire life had changed. There were three weeks more to go. How could she pretend that everything was the same between them? Sebastian was angrier with her than he had been ten years ago, which was saying something. She should have withered under his glare, but all she wanted to do was cup his face and kiss him.

She picked herself up off the cold floor. She could not sit idly by supervising their dig—she'd probably not made sense of the earl's diary anyway. It was a pity that Mr. Ryder had only a copy—it was always better to read source material in its original form. A person's handwriting could reveal so much. The transcriber could have altered the odd word here and there, completely subverting the earl's intention. She may as well return to the library and start from the beginning.

Anything to keep her mind off Sebastian, and what would happen when he left her again.

# Chapter 32

*Sometimes I wish Cam would just shut up.*
—FROM THE DIARY OF SEBASTIAN GODDARD,
DUKE OF ROXBURY

Cam leaned on his shovel. "I wish I had some work gloves. Is she all right?"

Sebastian shoved his own filthy hands in his pockets and headed for the shaded bench instead of the herb bed. He knew he should just work out his anger by digging, but Cam would pick at him until he had the truth. "No. She's rather shocked at the condition of our backs, if you must know."

"So she's disgusted? She's not the woman for you, then."

"I never said she was the woman for me! Stop playing matchmaker."

Cam dropped his shovel and joined him under the tree. He fished a handkerchief out and wiped the sweat from his neck. "You really need to tell her. You'll feel better."

"Don't go lecturing me! Freddie used to be my friend, but all that ended ten years ago."

"How old was she then? Fifteen? How long will you punish

her for losing her head over you? You must have been an elegant stripling."

Sebastian had never divulged the consummation to Cam, whether out of a foolish sense of chivalry for Freddie or plain revulsion, he did not know. But the entrance of their fathers—that had been gone over in minute detail. Ultimately, he was able to laugh over it, but it still remained one of the most ghastly experiences of his life. "I told you. She's twenty-eight now. At eighteen, most girls are married. Freddie was out to snare me. She knew what she was doing."

Or did she? Alcohol was almost like a poison to her. It fogged the clearest of heads taken to excess, but it seemed Freddie didn't need much for the fog bank to roll in with a vengeance.

"Well, she didn't catch you, did she? Your father was looking out for the succession."

And how hypocritical that he didn't think Freddie was good enough. She was from a respectable gentry family, though they had fallen on times hard enough for her father to seek employment as the duke's secretary. Phillip Goddard and Joseph Wells had met as schoolboys, and had carried on their forbidden love all that time. Sebastian's letters from his father had been impassioned with explanations. By the time Sebastian understood, it was too late.

A stray honeybee buzzed around them. Cam shooed it away with his handkerchief. The garden was quiet until he spoke again. "When are you getting married, anyway?"

Sebastian pictured himself before an altar, a strange young girl at his side. A strange young *rich* girl. He felt the bleak reality of it. "I don't hold out much hope for that."

"Nonsense. Turn up in London for the Little Season in September and you'll be married by the end of it in November. You'll have a bit of blunt from the sale of the castle and can afford to visit your tailor.

A few Wednesdays at Almack's in knee breeches—the parson's mouse-trap is a fait accompli. You're a *duke*, Sebastian."

"A poor one. And I'm not normal anymore."

"What's this? You've never been shy about your predilections. Surely you can convince some sweet young thing to don a gag and endure a light caning for the privilege of becoming the ninth Duke of Roxbury's mother."

"Don't joke. And it hasn't come quite to that. I'm not cruel. I would never be, not after what we went through."

Suddenly the garden seemed alive with sounds—the chirp of birds, the beating of butterfly wings, the rustle of leaves overhead. Sebastian studied the dappled shadows on his breeches, remembering darker play of light, when he longed to close his eyes but was forced to keep them open, the better to concede his subjugation.

Cam understood. "You feel the shame of it still, don't you? You needn't."

Sebastian suppressed his urge to stalk off through the garden gate and get lost on the moors. "I still dream of it. As my father's son, it's a bit ironic, don't you think? I spent half my life trying to prove I was all man, only to find myself—" His throat closed. He could not continue.

"I said last night that I was not my father. Nor are you. You did what you had to to survive."

"And came to enjoy it," Sebastian said, tasting the bitter truth of his words.

"We are naught but animals, no matter how we try to deny it. Should you have killed yourself over something that was really so inconsequential?"

"At first I thought I would go mad," he whispered. But the whip-pings and the balm of opium quickly focused him on the tasks ahead.

There was no time for drama or tearing at his shirt. The shirt was long gone in any event.

Cam patted his shoulder. "But you did not, and we made do. I admit I got the better end of the bargain. Unfair, when I am a bastard and you were a marquess. Too bad you revealed that little tidbit. I believe it gave our captor even more glee to debase you."

Cam and he had been in no ordinary, government-run jail, although that might have been hell as well. As "guests" of an influential relative of Viceroy Muhammad Ali, they had gone to Akhom Ali to have him help broker a business deal with the governor. They wanted permission to excavate a sand-buried settlement and remove what Cam deemed saleable to his network of Egyptian artifact collectors. They'd been foolish enough to think that promising a share of the treasure to the viceroy and his cousin would ease their way. Sebastian and Cam had drunk wine from Akhom Ali's vineyard, ate a feast from his table as his "honored English visitors." The next they knew, they were tied up and beaten until they provided his entertainment.

The man's only daughter had been victimized by the notorious Henry Kipp, and it seemed Sebastian and Cam were substitutes for his revenge. Because Sebastian had the misfortune of previously working with Kipp, he received the brunt of the punishment.

But he had not fared worse than Akhom Ali's daughter. Her father had killed her for bringing shame upon the family. That act had unleashed his every sadistic impulse. Ali was unhinged and unrepentant in the creative torture he devised for his two Englishmen. It was a wonder they emerged with their offensive male equipment still attached.

Of course, that had been a constant threat. What they had been obligated to do with said equipment was bad enough.

"Maybe we'll find your father's stash and I won't need to marry for money after all," Sebastian said, yanking the discussion back to something slightly more palatable.

"Not at the rate we're going. From the composition of the soil, I don't think it's been disturbed to do any more than insert catnip plants into the upper layer. It's packed and solid as iron. Where are the castle's cats, anyway? They'd have a field day with the mess we've made."

"My father never kept animals, save for the odd horse. As a boy, I wanted a dog in the worst way."

"There must have been kennels here once, judging from the old earl's portrait. All those adoring spaniels at his feet."

"If there ever were, they're rubble now. Really, Cam, you know a week won't be long enough to find anything, if there's anything to find. The property's more than a thousand acres. Archibald could have buried the gold on any one of them."

"Why all the notations on the castle and the gardens? No, I've got a hunch. I'm hardly ever wrong."

It was true. Cam seemed to have a knack for turning up valuables in a rubbish tip. He'd earned his reputation as a treasure hunter. Sebastian wondered what they would have found had they been allowed to dig in Egypt, but once they escaped, they didn't wait around to find out.

"Who's that fellow?"

Young Kenny was standing at the castle door, his horror over the destruction they'd wrought around it almost comical.

"It's all right, Kenny. We just wanted to tidy up the garden."

"That's my job."

"You're welcome to help us put the plants back if you like. We got a little carried away."

"Catmint's good for tea. And headaches. I was coming out to get some for Miss Frederica."

"That's thoughtful of you. Is she still feeling poorly?" Sebastian asked, trying to be friendly.

"She has not been herself since—" The man's face screwed up. He'd been nice-looking once, but his usual slack-jawed expression took precedence. "For a while." He still had the wit not to accuse the duke outright for ruining their little castle community.

Kenny must view Sebastian as a bad influence, which he was. And he'd threatened Freddie in the hall in his anger, which must have upset her further.

This whole castle contract should be dissolved. The longer he stayed here, the more complicated his emotions were becoming. Cam was acting like a catalyst, making him see that his gamesmanship with Freddie really served no purpose. It was not her fault he'd been lied to and neglected his whole life. It was not her fault he'd been abused and now sought his pleasure in ways no decent woman would sanction. He had proven his point with Freddie—even a bluestocking spinster was prey to his methods. He was a master at sexual manipulation. But he felt no pride.

The three of them returned the catmint bed to order. Cam whistled to rival the birds, filling the awkward silence. Kenny took an edging tool from the little shed at the bottom of the orchard and expertly marked the grass so no trace of upheaval was evident save for the men's filthy hands and faces.

"You two get cleaned up. I'm going to check on Miss Wells."

And what would he say to her when he found her? His conscience, always so casually rumpled, was becoming as regimented and straight as Kenny's flower beds.

# Chapter 33

*It is done. Finally.*

—FROM THE DIARY OF SEBASTIAN GODDARD,
DUKE OF ROXBURY

Shamefully, Frederica had fallen asleep at her desk, after finding nothing else anomalous in the notebook that leaped to her attention. Perhaps the earl was an avid gardener as well as a traitor. When she felt the hand on her shoulder, she awoke with a start, her headache back with a vengeance.

Sebastian stood over her, covered in dirt. "It's time for some nuncheon, Freddie."

"Did you find anything?"

"Just worms. If we dig any deeper, we'll get to China. Now I know I can find work as a grave digger if need be." He paused. "I'm sorry I was short with you earlier."

"It's all right. None of my business anyway. I feel—awful."

"Perhaps you need a hair of the dog that bit you."

Her stomach lurched. "Oh, God, no. Never, ever again. I don't think I'm up to lunch, Sebastian."

"Cam will be disappointed. He's scrubbing up even as we speak." He picked the leather-bound book up. "Any other bright ideas gleaned from this?"

She shook her head, regretting the movement. If anything, she felt worse now than she had when she had woken up this morning, with the addition of a crick in her neck.

"Here, now, go on back upstairs. I'll clean up and bring you a tray."

"What about Mr. Ryder?"

He tucked a loose curl behind her ear. "He can fend for himself, Freddie."

"Tell him I'm sorry. About the lunch. And all that wasted digging. You both must wish me to the devil."

"Nonsense. We thought it worth a try. You didn't hold us at gunpoint."

She pushed away from the desk. "I'll do better tomorrow. Right now, I can't think."

Each step upstairs rattled her bones. She didn't even bother turning down the coverlet as she stretched out on her bed. She was rarely ill—there wasn't time to be—but right now she wished she could stay in her room for the foreseeable future. But she didn't go back to sleep. Her mind was busy racing through the halls of the castle, imagining where a thorough rogue might stash a French fortune.

Sebastian didn't bother knocking when he pushed into the room three-quarters of an hour later, his hands filled with her luncheon tray. He had washed, but had not bothered with a neckcloth, waistcoat or jacket. The ends of his hair were still damp, curling up at his collar. She made a halfhearted effort to sit up.

"I've brought you another draft of headache powder. Mrs. Holloway's, this time, and some catmint tea. Young Kenny's suggestion. Everyone is most anxious over you." He set a toleware tray on her bedside table. Apart from the liquids, there was a soft-boiled egg in its shell, a small ramekin of custard and a slice of bread spread with apple butter. Simple, comforting nursery food, fragrant with vanilla and cinnamon.

"Thank you. You're being very nice to me."

"I'm meant to. It is your day. Here, drink up."

His arm swept around her and he pulled her to his chest. He smelled of her rose soap, clean and sweet. She should perhaps make something with a more masculine scent for him, but that would be a project for another day. He held the glass tumbler to her lips as if she were a child, and she dutifully swallowed it down.

"Ugh."

"Yes, well, the alternative is worse. Mrs. Holloway thought something sugary might chase the taste away. Do you want me to feed you?"

Frederica blushed, remembering their wicked tea when she was helpless and blindfolded. "I can manage." Though it seemed a sin to waste it, she left the quivering egg alone, but took a sip of tea, sharply redolent of the herb, a few spoonfuls of custard and a bite of bread. Sebastian stationed himself in a chair opposite, studying his hands. He'd not been able to completely eradicate the dirt from under his fingernails. Today was the first time since he'd been home that she had seen him disheveled.

*Home.* No, Goddard Castle was not home to him and never would be.

She set the bread down on its plate. "Where will you go?"

"Pardon?"

"When you leave. Back to Roxbury Park?"

"Yes. I'm missing some spring planting. Now that I've proven myself with a shovel, my tenants might welcome me back with open arms. We Dukes of Roxbury are not very popular, you know."

"Things have been bad there for a long while, haven't they?"

"Yes."

"D-do you blame my father?"

Sebastian looked up, startled. "Of course not. I know I've been crude about our fathers' relationship, but neither one of them could help being who they were. They had more in common than most husbands and wives. All that mad medieval stuff to bind them together. It's just a pity my father roped my mother into his life. He could have been happy with his collections and his lover."

Frederica's smile wobbled. "But then you wouldn't be here to feed me pudding."

"Your wish is my command. At least for today." He made as if to feed her, then put the custard in his own mouth, licking the spoon in a very provocative manner. He was teasing her, turning the conversation to steadier ground for him.

"And tomorrow. And the day after," she reminded him.

"Cheat. Just because Cam is here, you think you have me over a barrel." He picked up the ramekin. "Are you done? Please say yes, because this is quite good."

"I'm done. Didn't you have your own meal?" She watched him spoon in like a greedy schoolboy.

"No. I was a bit worried about you and came right up after I had a wash."

"That was kind."

"Please. You'll ruin my reputation. You make me sound like someone's old aunt."

Frederica pictured Sebastian with a little lace cap on his head and laughed. A mistake. "Do not be amusing. My head still aches."

"I'll leave you, then."

"No! That is, please don't go. I might have something planned you will enjoy."

"Knocking down walls? Mucking the stalls?"

She wanted to lie in his arms, feel his breath on her cheek, his clean skin against hers. "Kiss me, Sebastian."

He dropped the spoon with a clatter. "Right now? Aren't you ill?"

"Only from wanting you. You will kiss me and make it better."

Mrs. Holloway's potion had made her brazen. She would blame it if things went bad. She patted the bed, but he didn't move.

"What game are you playing, Freddie?"

"No game. Take your clothes off."

"And I just put them on. You surprise me every day, Freddie."

She watched as he unfastened each tiny, flat ivory button on the placket of his shirt, grateful there were only two of them. His cuffs were next; then he pulled the linen over his head. She decided she would never get tired of him doing so—he moved with an easy grace she envied.

He deliberately turned his back to her and opened his falls, his trousers dropping to his boot tops. He was close enough to touch, and she did so. He hitched a breath but stood still as she gently fingered the longest raised scar.

"Does it hurt?"

"Not anymore."

"I am so sorry." If not for that horrible night ten years ago, he would not have been driven away. His future might have been very different. He must blame her. Her hand trembled as a wave of nausea swamped her. He twisted about and caught it.

"I know what you're thinking. It's not your fault. Have you looked your fill?"

"Yes."

He sat on the bed and worked at his boots. "Look. We were both young and stupid. You made a mistake. I didn't need to—— Well, I did

what I did. Thought what I did. Left, and on the whole had an envi-
able life, apart from those few months in prison."

"I didn't take the money your father offered," Frederica blurted.

"So he wrote. Again and again. But how did you come by your tidy
little fortune?"

"There was a little when my father died. And my mother's aunt
remembered me in her will. Your father invested the money for me.
And then when the books sold—oh, Sebastian, he gave me *everything*.
When he could have used the money himself."

"That seems only fair. You wrote them, did you not?"

Frederica was stunned at his reaction. "How did you know?"

"I looked them over last night. They were much too interesting to
have been written by my father. He was as dull as ditchwater, Freddie.
Knew a great deal but put one to sleep in the telling of it. Cam said
the series is rather famous in academic circles. Chock-full of facts, yet
accessible for even the layman. Even stupid schoolboys such as I once
was can read them. Cam has a set himself and is anxiously awaiting
the sequel."

Frederica felt her face warm from this secondhand praise. "The
only reason the publisher bought it was because your father's name was
on it. He did all the outlining. I just filled in the details."

Sebastian threw his head back in laughter. He was gloriously naked
now.

"Please don't tell anyone."

"Does this publisher think my father's writing from the grave?"

"No, but he believes I'm just polishing up the last of Uncle Phillip's writings. And he wonders what's taking so long."

His nimble fingers were at the hooks of her dress. "May I?"

She nodded.

"I don't suppose," he said, pushing her bodice down, "that our arrangement is helping you speed up any."

"It's all right."

He looked up at her. "No, it's not. I'll sell you the castle anyway, Freddie. Let's rip up our agreement."

She could hardly find her voice. "You don't—want me for the month?"

"I didn't say that. But my presence here is unnecessary, and I really should get back to Roxbury Park. After Cam's week is up, we'll go and leave you alone. I'll get someone to draw up the proper sale papers."

Her nipples were between his circling fingers now. Then this meant nothing to him. She could be any woman, and he'd be as efficient in his lovemaking. It was what he did.

"Why the change of heart?"

"Something Cam said. I really shouldn't punish you for the past."

So sex with her had been meant to be a punishment. Unfortunate that now she craved it. She supposed the punishment ultimately had been very effective indeed.

She said nothing as he continued to unwrap her from her layers of clothing. She could have told him to stop—it was her day. But knowing there would be few more encounters like this stilled her tongue and swallowed back her tears.

She had begun to hope that he liked her again. He seemed to have reached some accommodation for his father. But it had probably been too much to hope that he would become enthralled with her.

And did she even want that? She had her books to write. Her people to take care of. Her garden to tend. Her independence to maintain and cherish. She didn't need him or any man.

He tipped her back on the bed and kissed her as she had demanded.

His eyes were closed, his thick dark lashes crescents on his sunburned cheeks. His tongue and hands dealt with her in a ruthless, professional manner, so that in the shortest amount of time she ceased to think about the past or the future and concentrated solely on the present. His kiss was flavored with the custard, and as smooth. He coaxed her tongue to his, his fingertips lightly massaging her temple. The dull throbbing in her head vanished and she relaxed beneath him, floating in a sea of surrender. There was no point directing him—he knew just what to do, and did it well. She would be a fool to alter a single sweep of his hands or thrust of his hips.

She was not tied, so could return his strokes, feel the textured scarring on his back, rumple his still-damp hair, see the way his dark eyebrows met as he anchored himself. He entered her with care, as if the clock were winding down and all time was in slow motion. There was none of the wildness of the hill in the storm, none of the precise scene-setting of her usual submission. Frederica felt like a fragile china cup, filled with the most delicious temptation. He eased in and almost out of her with such control that she soon lost hers. Clutching his shoulders, bucking her hips up, digging the heels of her feet against his buttocks, she took charge and forced him to match her abandon.

Their coupling was no longer a delicate, regulated waltz but a vigorous mazurka with no fixed steps. Improvisation was all. She could not be sorry for her lack of finesse—the urge to be closer, to somehow be inside *him*, spiraled into a fierce orgasm for them both. But mindful of their parting, he withdrew and spurted his seed onto her belly. Frederica forced herself to keep her disappointment from showing. What was wrong with her? He was only heeding her lecture, doing exactly as she had asked. But his regard for her wishes did not bring her the satisfaction she expected.

He lay atop her, panting, his heart thudding against hers. His mossy eyes were closed. She had watched him throughout, a privilege she was usually denied. Sebastian's face had been impossible to read, but his body at least had seemed fully engaged. She felt his lips brush a kiss on her shoulder, and then he rolled away.

"Are you all right?"

She managed a smile. "Yes. My headache is quite gone."

"An unusual cure. I don't imagine it will be found in most medical textbooks." He took her folded napkin from the lunch tray and gently wiped her stomach clean.

"You should go to your friend."

"Cam's all right. He's taken the diary and is wandering about. Now that he can see the places described, maybe he'll unearth something beyond catnip and bugs."

"I'm sorry. When I read that the earl put new plants along the foundation, I thought he had an opportunity to conceal something else. Everything is back in place?"

"Good as new."

"I'll have to cut the stems back next month."

"We could have done that today. You don't have to wait until the castle's yours."

Frederica felt a shadow fall across her heart. "No," she said lightly, "June's the month for cutting back catmint. Then the plants grow bushy. And I mustn't let the flowers go to seed, else they won't last through the winter. We have our routine."

Sebastian began to dress. "My father was lucky to have you as chatelaine. I just hope you're happy up here."

"Oh, I will be." She had to be. She had no choice.

# Chapter 34

*She hates me. I should be happy.*

—FROM THE DIARY OF SEBASTIAN GODDARD,
DUKE OF ROXBURY

He had done the gentlemanly thing, releasing her from their bargain. He would leave Goddard Castle with Cam when his time
was up, well before the month was at its end. Dissolve the guardianship. Release her funds in their entirety. Sebastian should take some
comfort in his decision, but instead his gesture struck him as hollow.

He was walking away, leaving Freddie to fend for herself. That
was what she wanted, what she had always wanted. But there had been
something melancholy in their coupling today. Something too tender.
He did not want to think of Freddie actually *missing* him.

Or him missing her.

She needed to get on with her life and he with his. If he dis-
tanced himself now—removed himself from her bed or wherever else
he might take his pleasure with her—it would be easier in the end for
both of them.

Which meant that today was the last time he would ever touch her.

He swallowed back a mouthful of what tasted very much like regret.

There was plenty for him to do here to distract himself from pursuing her. The castle was rambling and ripe with possibilities. Just because nothing had been buried beneath the catmint did not mean that the lady's garden was free of loot. But to uproot Freddie's carefully tended plants would be a shame, and quite frankly, Sebastian's back ached from shoveling.

Sebastian recalled the expression on the Earl of Archibald's portrait. Haughty. Aloof. Even as a young man, he did not look apt to do any sort of manual labor to sully his consequence. No, the digging they had done had been an exercise in futility. Archibald was reputed to be clever—he'd find a hiding place that did not require him to soil his hands. They were already covered in the blood of betrayed British soldiers.

Sebastian and Cam would pore over the diary again. Freddie, too, if he could keep his blistered hands off her and she could spare the time away from her writing. He'd been selfish expecting her to drop everything for his games.

He'd wanted to punish her when he first arrived. Ironic, when it was he who was now feeling the pain.

Just a few more days. And he'd given control over most of them to Freddie. He could fix it so she didn't want him. Be as boorish as the next fellow. Push her away, inch by inch.

He could do it. He had to.

\* \* \*

The next few days tested Sebastian's resolve. He had come no closer to discovering where the mythical Archibald treasure might be despite studying the diary for hours on end. After Freddie's misbegotten garden project, they concentrated on the interior of the castle, dividing up the search between the three of them. Cameron orchestrated their assignments, reducing the likelihood that Sebastian and Freddie would be thrown together. He was scrupulous in avoiding Freddie when he could, going so far as to take all his meals in his room. It killed him to think of Cam flirting with Freddie at the dinner table, but it might do her good to be the object of someone else's interest. She should marry—not Cam, of course, but someone who could keep her company through the long Yorkshire winters. Someone who would treat her with respect. Someone who would appreciate her warm heart and lively mind. Someone who would worship her body as he had come to.

He was feeling smugly successful dodging her, but after several days, his luck ran out. On his way to inspect the stable block one last time, he bumped into Freddie in the courtyard. The sky above was steel, the air heavy with moisture. Wind whipped her skirts, pinked her cheeks. He tried to brush past her, but she reached out to stop him.

"Have I offended you in any way, Sebastian? You've made yourself awfully scarce."

"I thought we agreed we were through, Freddie." He would make sure of it now, if she had any doubts. "You'll get the damn castle without further groveling."

Her hand dropped from his sleeve. "I didn't grovel."

"Whatever you want to call it. There's no need to whore yourself any longer. Cam and I are leaving tomorrow and I'll see to it the necessary arrangements are made to get you the deed and your monies. All of them. I'm not inclined to remain your guardian. I admit it's been somewhat amusing, but it's time to move on." He had practiced every brutish word, had anticipated Freddie's response, and was not surprised to feel her fist jab into at his solar plexus.

"You—you cad!"

"I never told you otherwise. Think about it. What kind of gentleman would accept your harebrained scheme? I took advantage of you, plain and simple. I was curious to know if *you* had gotten better in bed, to quote you. But you probably don't recall, drunk as you were the other day. Poor Freddie. You'd really better lay off the intoxicants before you do something stupid again." He stood still for another punch.

"Something stupid? Something stupid! You are the only mistake I've ever made! You've taught me your lesson, Your Grace. Never will I trust another man!"

"Oh, I don't know, Freddie. There might be some poor fool out there who wants to be managed by you. And I have taught you a thing or two of the bedroom arts. Not every wife comes so trained."

He didn't bother ducking when she slapped him soundly across the face. It gave him perverse pleasure to know he was so efficient in alienating her. She shrieked at him for a good five minutes, competing with the howling wind. He didn't listen to the half of it, content to watch the color creep up from the collar of her housedress to her cheeks and back down again. She was alarmingly plum-hued by the time she gulped for breath. The coup de grace came as she took the Earl of Archibald's diary from her apron pocket and hurled it at him. It landed in a cloud of dust, ultimately useless. He lifted an eyebrow.

"As I said, Freddie, we're definitely done."

"I wouldn't choose to spend another minute with you for all the money in the world!" she raged.

"You won't have to. Didn't you listen? I'm washing my hands of you and all your medieval nonsense. Have a nice life." He walked away, but she hurled herself at his back, knocking him down. They landed in a tangle on the grass, Freddie stuck to him like a barnacle.

"Get off me! Have you no pride? No dignity?" He flipped over despite her nails digging into his neck. Freddie scrambled away, a look of horror on her face. Poor thing. He'd driven her to lose her temper, just as he had when they were children. It had never taken much, but usually she preferred to skewer him with her tongue, not her fingernails. As she claimed, he really was a cad. He sprang up and smoothed his clothing. "Don't expect me to lie still while you strangle me. I didn't count on us to end as friends, but don't you think you're taking this too far?"

She could not meet his eyes. She looked for all the world like she was eight years old again—disheveled, freckled, her dirty apron reminiscent of the pinafores she used to wear. If he were a gentleman, he'd help her up. But he'd just gone to rather elaborate lengths to prove he was not.

Hang the stables. There wasn't anything there but hay and horse manure. What he needed was some exercise. He'd get Cam to fence with him and drive Freddie from his mind. Sebastian glanced up to the open library windows. He'd left Cam packing a few of Freddie's cast-off books that he'd already paid Sebastian for so he'd have enough blunt to get back to Dorset. It was the devil to be beholden to him yet again, but one last favor wouldn't make much difference.

Half an hour later, Sebastian was breathless, wet as the world outside. Freddie must have picked herself up off the ground once the rain began, but she certainly wasn't in the long gallery to witness the violent sparring. He did not plan to run Cam through, but he had to aim his blade at something on this gray, rainy day. His fight with Freddie had made him reckless, but it had done its job. He'd bet she wouldn't come out to the battlements and wave her handkerchief when they left on the morrow.

The long gallery rang with the clash of metal and frustrated oaths, the wall sconces casting macabre shadows as the men parried and deceived up and down the hall. Sweat poured down Sebastian's body, but he didn't stop to wipe his brow, which was why he found himself blearily careening into the late Earl of Archibald at sword point. With a snap of wire, the portrait fell from the wood-paneled walls, and Sebastian fell with it. He was almost glad to have crashed to the stone floor, for he could not have lasted much longer against his friend, who did not have the same demons working to defeat him.

"Mercy! You win. Get your damned father off me."

"Tut, tut. You've ruined the frame. All that gilt."

Sebastian rolled out from underneath the canvas, sat up and picked up a chunk of gold-painted gesso. He was too tired to stand yet, his legs trembling like jelly. "Take it when you go. Take them all. That's if Freddie's agreeable, and I think she will be. She's never liked the paintings."

"What, the last bastard live with centuries of Archibalds? See how they disapprove already."

Sebastian laughed, a bit breathless. "They always look like that. You occasionally show a flash of that expression yourself."

Cameron examined the wall, running his hand on the intricately carved dark wood. "Damn me! I'll have to work on that. Make myself look less sniffy. I say, this is really fine raised paneling, Sebastian. Now, if you'd let me remove *it*, I'd consider taking the ancestors to my attic. Some old Archibald must have installed it to keep the portraits from the damp of the walls. Really fine craftsmanship. See this?" Cam pointed to the geometric design that was for the most part covered by the massive paintings.

"I'll have to take your word for it. I know next to nothing about interior decorating."

"Seriously, this paneling would fetch quite a bit from a rich cit trying to gentrify his new house. It has, what we like to say in the trade, patina. If these walls could talk, eh?"

Sebastian sighed. "You'll have to ask Freddie. Our terms are she buys everything in the castle. We're talking of walls here. I rather think she thinks they're included in the sale."

"You'll not see their like again. Here, touch this. Like satin."

Reluctantly, Sebastian got up from the floor, pocketed the bit of frame and poked a finger at a knot of leaves in the center of a diamond. There was a popping sound, and a wide panel of the wall inched backward.

"What the devil?"

"Damn me again! It's a secret passage. How very gothic." Cam pushed the door in a little ways. The paneled carving was attached to a massive door, equal in thickness to the planks of the castle's main entrance. "Stuck, of course. Let me borrow a shoulder." The two of them shoved against the panel as it creaked open.

"Black as pitch. Grab a light from the sconce, would you, Sebastian? Better take the swords in with us. We may have to beat off bats and spiderwebs."

"You're not planning to murder me in the dark?"

"Oh, no. I could have done that anytime in Egypt, remember?"

Sebastian definitely did. Shivering a bit in the cool of the narrow corridor, he led the way with the flickering taper, slashing through the cobwebs with his foil, feeling very much like a little boy on a treasure hunt. He stopped stock-still, and Cam bumped into him, fortunately not with the business end of his sword. "You don't suppose—"

"I see we're thinking alike. My papa's portrait could have been guarding his stash all these years. Come to think of it, the wall panels were even drawn in his diary, not that I recognized what they were. Carrigan—my forger fellow—can write, but not draw. I thought they were just doodles. Wouldn't it be a miracle if we found the treasure after all?"

"Let's not count chickens." Sebastian sneezed, his exercise-damp clothing covering him like a cloak of snow. "I may not live long enough to enjoy his ill-gotten gains. Damn, how far down does this hall go? It's as crooked as that French whore's teeth we shared in Marseilles. What was her name?"

"I don't think I ever caught it, infamous rake that I am. Patience, Sebastian. Here. Let's switch places. You're missing spots and I'm getting mouthfuls of spider eggs."

Sebastian turned the taper over to Cam. It was only fitting that if there was something, Cameron Ryder should find it. He was the one with the reputation for antiquities. It would be one discovery he could never brag about, however, if they wished to keep clear of the law. Sebastian kept to the stone wall so he wouldn't smack his face into the abrupt turns. He'd lost sight of the gray light of the tunnel entrance almost from the beginning. "This hall must be accessible from another part of the castle, but I see no doors."

"Neither do I. One wouldn't build such a tunnel just to stay stuck inside. There has to be an escape. It's possible that the other exits are faced in stone. You'd have to know just what you were about to find a way out."

Sebastian swallowed back the rising panic that this shadowy space engendered. He was safe; he knew it. Torture and worse did not await at the end. He was not shackled and starving. But every step deeper into the bowels of the castle revived something within him that he hoped he'd never feel again. "Cam, now that we know this place exists, let's go back. Wait until tomorrow. Come in with warm clothes and torches and a picnic lunch in case we wind up at the center of the earth."

"We *are* going down. Feel the pitch of the floor?"

Sebastian could feel nothing but the bite of fear in his belly. "Cam."

Instantly, his friend stilled. "Lord, but I'm a lummox. Yes, let's go back."

Sebastian hoped Cam wouldn't raise the taper too close to his face. But Cam knew what he'd see anyway, and started going on with false cheer about tomb robbing in Egypt and a whole host of other blustery tales. Praise God there were no branches in this hidey-hole to lose one's way, but the walk back continued to be as dark as the walk in.

"The air's fairly fresh at least."

"Yes, but where's the bloody door?"

Cam scuffled up ahead. "It won't be long now, Sebastian." There was a thud, then a pause. "Oh, Jesus."

"What?"

"Well, I'm at the door, but someone's shut it." Cam pounded on it with a fist. "Oi! Oi!"

"They'll never hear us. Did you see how thick the planking was? Strong enough to resist a battering ram."

"Don't be silly. Someone's bound to come looking for us."

"And they won't *hear* us. Or they'll think we're the fucking Archibald Walkers and just roll over in their beds." Sebastian tossed his sword aside and slid down to the floor.

"Come, now. We can't give up. We still have light."

"For how long?"

"Maybe we can saw through the door with our blades."

Sebastian snorted at the ridiculousness of that.

"Then let's go on with the search. Maybe we'll find another way out."

"You go. I'll wait here for you to rescue me."

Cam hesitated. "I won't leave you in the dark."

"Akhom Ali's not here. I'll be fine," Sebastian ground out. He was a coward, as weak and vulnerable as he'd ever been. He deserved to die in this black place.

But Cam didn't. Without Cam, he wouldn't be here to die at all. Surely they could not have endured what they did in Egypt to wind up trapped in a Yorkshire castle.

"Here's what we'll do," Sebastian said with resolve. "I'm going to beat like hell on this door. You take the taper and follow the tunnel and see where it leads. Scream as you go. Maybe someone will hear you. We'll raise as much racket as we can."

"You'll be all right?"

"Yes, Mother. I'll try not to go completely mad."

Cam stood over him, his face shadowed. "I—I love you, Sebastian."

"And I love you, too. Go. And bring back the bloody treasure. And a sandwich."

Cam turned with a chuckle, then proceeded to make a series of bloodcurdling noises as he moved down the corridor. Sebastian picked up his sword and thumped the pommel against the door at regular intervals. It was too dark to check his watch. After this morning, Freddie would never expect him for tea. She had vowed to dine in her bedroom. How long would it be before someone in the household noticed that two rather large gentlemen were missing? If he couldn't smell the fear on his own body, this might be laughable. He supposed they could go centuries without someone discovering the trick to the passage. There would be nothing left but his and Cam's bones.

All right, he was being maudlin. He had not been inside this hell more than ten minutes at most. After enduring eight months in such confinement, what was one night? Or even two? Sebastian had gone days without eating, days without dry clothes, or any clothes at all. If he and Cam were lucky, a plump rat might cross their path—they were armed, after all. If only they'd left their swords outside by the open entrance, someone might have realized they'd vanished inside.

Sebastian stopped his banging and listened for anything beyond Cam's muffled shouts. The castle walls were famously thick. His father had bragged on it. He wondered if the damned diary had the key to getting out of here, but Freddie had flung it over his head. Why would she pick it up from the dirt, look for architectural squiggles and somehow realize he was trapped behind stone? She'd wished him to the devil. But he'd been there all along.

His sweaty hand slipped along the hilt and he felt the kiss of metal. If worse came to worst, he could slit his wrists and die at his own will. With his luck, Freddie would find him just as the last drop of blood leached from his body. No matter. He was damned anyway.

# Chapter 35

*He hates me. And I hate him.*

—FROM THE DIARY OF FREDERICA WELLS

Sebastian's right arm had weakened already, so he switched and was doggedly thumping with the left. The sound of his banging echoed on the walls and inside his head, where a dull headache had taken root. The damp of the passage filled his lungs until he imagined mold and mildew taking life inside him, branching out and spreading like the plague. He barked out a laugh at his fantasy. Really, in his current state he was the perfect hero for a third-rate melodrama.

"Hey! Hey! Stop that blasted noise. My ears are ringing." Cam had snuck up behind him in the dark. He had not been gone that long, but there was no sign of the candle, just a looming form. Sebastian heard him set the foil aside.

"What happened to your light?"

Cam eased himself down on the floor. "Bloody bad luck." His voice was hoarse. "There was actually a gust of wind and rain at the end of the passage from some chink in the wall. Blew the candle right out. But the hole is on an outside wall. At one time there might have been an actual window to slip through as the castle was being stormed, but it's been filled in. When daylight comes, I can go back and do some proper screaming, stick my hand out. There might be someone about to hear me."

"Unless it rains again," Sebastian said, certain that more bloody bad luck would follow.

"Then more water will come in. There's an actual puddle on the floor. I admit I took a drink. Not the best water I've ever tasted, but I won't die of thirst. I would have brought back some for you, but I'm afraid I left my flask upstairs. You'll have to come with me next time. It's not all that far."

*In the dark.* But at least Cam had found his way back, sooner than Sebastian had prayed for.

"Or you can drink your own piss," Cam continued jovially. "You've done that a time or two."

*Sweet Jesus.* "I hope it won't come to that. What did you see before the candle blew out?"

"Stone and more stone. Oh! And this." He tossed a drawstring pouch into the general direction of Sebastian's lap. The heavy bag seemed filled with rocks. Sebastian's heart raced.

"What's in it?"

"Jewels, my son. Lots of them. Every pretty color you can think of and then some. Much more portable than a trunk full of French francs when one might have to leave the country with only the clothes on one's back. I'd say I found my father's fortune. Shoved into a niche in the wall where anyone might have come upon it."

Sebastian shook the bag. "Anyone who knew where to look. My God, Cam, you're rich!"

"*We're* rich. Technically you still own the property, but you did promise to split the loot with me if I found it. Which I have, after considerable struggle with a bat. Let me tell you, to have one of those little demons whizzing past your ear—"

"Shut it, Cam!" Sebastian could understand only too well. He'd heard the distant flutters and squeaking between his pounding for the last twenty minutes. "Do you know what this means? If we ever get out of here, I can *give* Freddie the castle. I won't need her money."

"I rather thought you'd have one of these diamonds set for her wedding band."

"Freddie would never marry me. She hates me and everything I am."

"I know, I heard her. The library windows were open. It's not like I was eavesdropping—anyone with ears could hear her banshee screams. For a little thing, she makes a lot of noise, doesn't she?"

Sebastian pushed his damp curls off his forehead. "I suppose you think I've gotten what I deserve."

"Well, you have ignored all the sensible advice I've given you. For a man with a way with women, you've forgotten your number-one rule."

"I didn't know I had one."

"You are always honest, Sebastian. You tell your lovelies just what to expect. Your steps to domination are clear and defined. I imagine you have even have a sequence to ensure your success."

She had known just what he was. He told Freddie what he planned at every step. She never said no. Well, not after the first night. They'd even had a safe word. He'd nearly forgotten the silly "rutabaga." In any case, it had never been uttered by either of them.

"I never lied to Freddie."

"Ah. But you weren't *entirely* honest, now, were you?"

Sebastian felt his bile rise. "If you mean I didn't tell her what happened between us in Ali's makeshift prison—"

Cam placed a hand on his arm. After so many months in the dark together, they did not need light to know where the other was. "No, no. Although if you unburden yourself to her one day, I believe it would ease your soul."

"I have no soul left! What do you mean, then?"

"You never told her you loved her," Cam said, his voice a rough whisper.

"I don't love her!"

"Honesty, honesty, Sebastian. For a disreputable rake, you are positively stuffed with it and so loath to admit it."

Sebastian leaned back into the wall. "I cannot love her."

"You mean you will not allow yourself to acknowledge it. I've watched you two the week I've been here. How careful you both were to pretend nothing was going on between you to protect her reputation. The noises in this castle are really quite bloodcurdling, but I know the difference between ghosts and wind and the sound of a woman orgasming in the morning, my friend. Is that how she convinced you to sell the castle to her and not to me? Trade her body for her home?"

Sebastian's fist bunched. "You make it sound so—"

"Mercenary? Calculating? I admit Miss Wells does not strike me as the conniving type. She must have wanted a taste of you as well as the deed to this monstrous pile. Did she think your peculiar flavor unpalatable?"

"No." No, she had craved his touch, as he craved hers.

"Then she is perfect for you. You need to settle down."

Sebastian let a desperate laugh escape. "Do you hear the absurdity of your words? We may never get out of here, and you're planning my wedding!"

"You must think positively, Sebastian. We've gotten out of worse scrapes than this."

"Freddie will never marry me if we do. No woman would put up with a lifetime of—"

"Pleasure?"

"You of all people know what I'm capable of."

"You're not likely to find yourself imprisoned and addicted to opium again, Sebastian."

Cam always was the voice of reason, even when Sebastian was too far gone to understand him. "I—I was weak."

"Yes. But not completely foolhardy. You're alive. We both are, thanks to you."

"Rubbish. Don't cozen me with this inspirational chat. It was *you* who saved *me*."

"Can we agree at least we saved each other? If you had not agreed to do what Akhom Ali ordered, we would both be rotting in his cellar. We'd be long dead, Sebastian. You held out as long as you could. Think of your back. It was only when the perverted bastard changed his tactics and whipped me that you gave in."

And found himself dragged up in chains for the amusement of his captor. Placed on his knees, Cam's cock in his mouth. Ali had taken great satisfaction in making a marquess grovel. Sebastian was always the submissive, the supplicant, until he and Cam were left alone in the dark. Then they could do as they pleased to ease each other. And had.

They had had no hope of escape. What did it matter how they spent their final days if they could bring each other some measure of ease? Cam was his other half, had made their time bearable until the lucky day they overpowered their guard and fled.

And then—nights of horror, the tremors from opium withdrawal so violent Cam had to bind him to keep him safe. The man nursed him, then provided him with a sequence of woman to prove to him that everything still worked as it should.

But it didn't. No matter how fetching the women were, Sebastian needed to feel dominant. The ropes and the blindfolds became essential to his release. Freddie had been the only woman Sebastian had taken under him with any semblance of normality, and even then, he knew he would always have her submission on the proper day.

"You need to put the past behind you," Cam continued. "Maybe your Freddie can help you. She makes an unlikely femme fatale, but she seems to be your femme. Do you suppose you've loved her ever since you were children?"

No. He'd had feelings for Freddie, of course, mostly those of annoyance. Yet she was always there. Dependable. The fixed star of his youth that had very few points of light.

"I was always daring her to do things. To get rid of her. But she never backed down. She broke her ankle once because of me. I dared her to fly out of an apple tree at home. She must have been seven or eight. She wasn't very high up—I wasn't a total little shit. I had shown her sketches of angels with wings, you see, and told her she had some, too, but they were invisible." He remembered her round blue eyes, solemn with wonder in her pudgy little face. "She fell to earth like a stone, but never cried."

"You bastard."

Sebastian knew Cam was grinning in the dark. "I was. She was like a burr caught in my breeches."

"And still is, from what I can tell."

True. Freddie rubbed at him in the most uncomfortable ways, prickling his conscience as he dared her to become his darkest fantasy.

It needed to stop. He needed to leave her. Keep her safe.

"It's all over, Cam, whatever we were doing with each other. You heard our argument. Now I can leave her in peace and gamble away my new fortune."

"You never were much of a gambler, Sebastian. But Miss Wells is one risk you really ought to take."

"No more lectures, Cam. I don't want the last words I might ever hear to sound too bloody much like a boring sermon."

"Heaven forefend! Well, what shall we discuss in our last moments?" Cam asked, his voice light.

"Nothing right now. I'd like to go to sleep, if you can believe it."

"Good Lord, Sebastian, it's still daylight and will be for hours yet."

"I don't care. I'm tired. My arms ache. We'll wake up in the middle of the night and start banging away again. The castle will be quiet then, people more likely to hear us."

"They'll just chalk it up to my ancestors and roll over. Damned inconvenient, these ghosts."

"They'll be Freddie's problem soon. Shut up now, Cam." Sebastian tucked an arm under his head and closed his eyes. He would be rich, or at least richer than he was, have a chance to get Roxbury Park to turn a profit and perhaps even make some wise investments. In a year or five, he might find some poor girl to marry him to keep Freddie forever out of reach.

# Chapter 36

*I really don't care where he is.*

—FROM THE DIARY OF FREDERICA WELLS

Perhaps Frederica had been silly taking a supper tray up to her room, but she was a coward, plain and simple. She could not face the men at the table this evening, nor could she do justice to her dinner. Tomorrow Sebastian and Cam would be leaving, and she would never clap eyes on them again. The castle would be hers, for good or ill. Her life would begin again, without Sebastian's insidious demands. His drugging kisses. His hands smoothing over her skin. His cock—

The silverware clattered as she descended the stairs. She needed to put the past weeks firmly behind her. He had shown her his true self this morning, and their affair was over.

She expected to find the kitchen empty at this hour, the fire banked, but instead everything was in an uproar. Mrs. Holloway was shouting, slamming pots and pans about, splashing water on the floor. Poor Alice cowered in the corner out of the way, twisting her apron between roughened fingers. Warren was scraping platters, parceling the leftovers into covered crocks, flinching every time Mrs. Holloway cursed. The other men seemed to have slunk away from the battle zone, leaving their half-finished dinners behind.

"Good riddance, I say! All that work, and for what? Bloody cheek, that's what it is!"

"Now, Betty, dear—"

"Don't 'Betty, dear' me! Do you know the trouble I had getting that leg of lamb? Wanted to give him a nice last meal, and what does he do? Goes off somewhere with that friend of his without a word. I suppose when he comes in at midnight he'll expect supper all over again. Well, he'll not get it! He can have bread and butter and like it!"

Girding herself for Mrs. Holloway's criticism at her own uneaten food, Frederica set her tray on the table. "What's happened?" She stacked up the abandoned plates and brought them to the sink.

"Ice-cold dinner, that's what, but it was hot at nine effing o'clock like he always wants it. Two hours Mr. Warren waited upstairs, getting young Kenny to run back and forth with the food to heat it up. Not fit for the pigs now, it isn't. All of us down here, waiting on His Grace before we could relax and have our own meal. My stomach is in knots. I don't know why I ever liked that boy, truly I don't."

Sebastian was gone, then. She didn't need to hide in her room after all. Frederica reached for an apron. "Here, let me help you clean up. I'm sorry Sebastian was so rude, but he's left now, and we can go back to the way we were."

Warren cleared his throat. "I'm sorry, Miss Frederica, but His Grace has not actually departed as yet. His things are in his room, and Mr. Ryder's servants are still here. As are the horses and coach."

"I'll be glad to see the back of Mr. Ryder's valet, too. All the tales he tells about those heathen lands. It's not right for an English gentleman to travel to such places. They can't be healthy." Mrs. Holloway pointed a soapy finger at Alice. "Go to bed, child. And don't think because you're up past your bedtime that you can sleep in tomorrow. There's work to be done, like always."

Frederica waved good night to Alice, then wiped a dish and set it on a rack. "I don't understand. Where could they be?"

Mrs. Holloway attacked a greasy pan with a scouring brush. "Well, we know the village pub is closed, so that's out. There isn't a gentry neighbor for miles and miles, and anyhow, the horses are still here. When they didn't turn up for dinner, I sent the men to comb through the castle, just in case the roof fell in on them somewhere. There's no sign of them inside."

"And it's too dangerous to send a search party out on the moors at night, Miss Frederica. Not that I think they're out there. It's still raining. Why would they be outdoors on such a filthy night?" Warren asked.

Could they be making one last attempt at finding the treasure? "You checked the cellars? The dungeon?"

"That was the first place I told the men to look. I thought perhaps the duke and Mr. Ryder were packing up some of the old duke's reserves to take with them. There are still some fine vintages down there, and I know you don't care for spirits."

No, she certainly did not, but she could see why people craved something in a crisis. If she had a tot of brandy to hand, she would not object. It was unlike Sebastian to be so thoughtless of the staff. Something was not right.

"You're going to rub the pattern right off that dish, Miss Frederica. Go sit down and I'll fix you a cup of tea. You didn't eat much, either. Why do I waste my time for a pack of ungrateful young people?"

"Where is everyone else?"

"I sent them off to bed," Warren said. "If the duke and Mr. Ryder don't turn up by dawn, they'll be ready to search. It just seemed point-less to have them hang around. And Betty scared them half to death." He winked at her.

At least there were six of them to look, counting Mr. Ryder's peo-ple. Of course, she would help, too, if she had to. "You're quite sure we haven't had some sort of cave-in today?"

"I haven't heard or seen a thing, save for the wind and the driving rain. The castle's been noisy all afternoon and night, Miss Frederica, and that's a fact. The Walkers are out in full force."

"Nonsense, Warren. You know you don't believe in ghosts. It's just the weather."

Mrs. Holloway set a cup of tea in front of her and sat down. "Poor young Kenny. All this has overset his nerves. Said the old earl is out and about looking for his lost gold."

Sebastian and Mr. Ryder had stirred something up here, and now they were paying for it. While Frederica did not believe they were vic-tims of ghostly revenge, it did not bode well that they'd disappeared and skipped dinner. They *always* ate. And ate. One would think they were still schoolboys.

What did she care where Sebastian was or if he was hungry? He was leaving tomorrow. She took a sip of hot, sweet tea. "This is deli-cious, Mrs. Holloway. I certainly appreciate you, even if others do not. And once my funds are released to me, I'll make sure your wages are never late again."

The cook flicked a hand at her. "I'm not going anywhere. As long as there's a roof over my head, a bed to sleep in and food in the pantry, I'm fine."

"About the roof. I know you made a jest about it, but I plan to tear down much of the castle. I won't be able to keep it in repair, and there will be less work for all of us."

"It's a good thing the old duke is dead, then. He wouldn't hear of any alterations like that."

Frederica sighed. "I know. I hope he doesn't join the Archibalds to haunt me. Warren, won't you join us?"

"No, miss, I'm off to bed myself, though I doubt I'll sleep a wink. Good night, Betty."

"Good night, William." Mrs. Holloway rearranged the caster set on the table waiting for Warren to divest himself of his oilcloth apron and leave the kitchen. Once he did, she leaned across the table. "I truly thought the duke would ask you to marry him. I'm sorry he didn't. Only proves he's a young idiot."

"I don't want to marry, Mrs. Holloway. I'm content with my life as it is, really." The lie tripped so easily from her tongue, she almost believed it herself.

"Men are the devil. You don't have to tell me twice. Mr. Holloway, God rest his soul, was a dreadful trial."

Frederica remembered Mr. Holloway well. A friendlier drunk one couldn't find, so Uncle Phillip had endured him for the sake of Mrs. Holloway's excellent cooking. When he was sober, he'd been handy with a hammer and nails, but the castle had proven too much for his limited windows of productivity.

"Thank you for the tea." Frederica rose from the table. "It's almost midnight. We all need some rest. I'm sure Sebastian and Mr. Ryder can fix themselves a sandwich when they get in."

Mrs. Holloway sniffed. "I'll not waste a minute of my sleep worrying about them. Good night, Miss Frederica."

Frederica took her candle back upstairs and changed into her nightgown. Warren was right—the castle creaked and shrieked tonight. Somewhere a shutter was banging in the storm. If the downpour kept to this level, perhaps Sebastian would not leave after all. If he came back from wherever he was to leave. She would take a page out of Betty Holloway's book.

But despite her best intentions, she lay awake in the dark, listening to the Walkers do their worst. It was impossible to sleep through the thunking, so being a practical woman, she got up to make the best use of her sleepless night. There were books to stack and furniture to dust. Curtains to shake against the rain-soaked air. Clothes to brush and hairpins to return to their tin.

After an hour of puttering, she was no closer to feeling Morpheus's beating wings. She picked up a book from her bedside pile, but was unable to concentrate on the words. The argument with Sebastian kept intruding, but he was leaving, so why did she care if he had the last word? He didn't care enough about her to spend any more time here, breaking their monthlong agreement. He had insulted her for the last time, but not before she'd disgraced herself like a petulant child. Sebastian brought out the very worst in her. She shut her eyes, remembering tackling him to the ground like a Shrovetide football player. Where was the fencer with finesse?

It was just as well he had ended it. Any more of Sebastian's insidious instruction, and she would be fit to find residence in the most exclusive whorehouse in England. She'd even heard its name once—Mrs. Brown's. So innocent a name for a place that was undoubtedly so wicked. She gathered the full name was Mrs. Brown's Pantheon of Pleasure, which was surely a mouthful. Some university students had made the pilgrimage to Yorkshire to see the famous scholar the Duke of Roxbury, and Frederica had overheard their conversation about it with the poor duke as they attempted to establish themselves as men of the world. Little did those boys know how little Uncle Phillip cared for London or the women that would be housed by Mrs. Brown.

Frederica could not imagine the life of a courtesan. Keeping one man satisfied was apparently more than she was capable of. She had not a shred of moral dignity left, so eager had she been to allow Sebastian such liberties, and still he had rejected her.

Which was a blessing, was it not? Although she would have preferred to give him his congé. At least she would have control over her own money and a house to live in.

The banging had stopped and the castle was at last quiet. Frederica crawled back into her rumpled bed, still unable to find any peace. But when her hand slid down to her bare mons and she imagined Sebastian's mouth there in place of her fingers, she swirled and circled until she climaxed. It was nearly as good as the real thing—perhaps it was even better, for she wouldn't have to depend upon someone so undependable as Sebastian Goddard.

If he wasn't home by dawn, she supposed they'd have to send out a search party. No doubt he and his friend were drunk in some haystack. With that bitter thought, she rolled over and willed herself to sleep.

# Chapter 37

*It is over.*

—FROM THE DIARY OF SEBASTIAN GODDARD,

DUKE OF ROXBURY

It was still black as pitch, but the shutter had resumed its diaboli-cal drumming. Frederica gave up on sleep and wrapped herself up in her robe in the dark. She opened her own window and stuck out a hand. The rain had stopped, and not a breath of air caressed her palm. It was not the wind that was driving the noise, which meant—

She lit a candle and hurried down the stairs. Pausing at the landing, she listened, then turned right. The noise was coming from the long gallery. She stopped in the armory before venturing any farther to take her usual foil off the wall. Missing were two of its companions.

Why had no one noticed? The men must have fenced yesterday afternoon. But where were they now?

"Sebastian!" she yelled.

The thumping became more urgent. She ran through the long gal-lery, feeling a bit foolish with a sword in her hand. "Sebastian!"

There was more rapping and scuffling at the end of the gallery.

Right behind the portrait of the late Earl of Archibald. Frederica skidded to a stop and held her candle high. Everything looked just as it should, save for a piece of gilt frame missing from the bottom. Looking down on the floor, she saw a smattering of gold dust and tiny chunks of frame. The painting had fallen, and someone had hung it back up.

The tapping was fast and furious now, and she was nearly sure she heard muffled voices. She set the sword and candle down and tried to lift the painting from the wall. She was neither tall enough nor strong enough to do so. "Are you behind this wall, Sebastian? If you are, tap three times," she shouted.

There were three deliberate thumps, and then a whole series of excited tattoos.

"Wait here! Well, of course you're going to wait here; what am I saying? You're trapped, aren't you? I'll get young Kenny to help me. I can't get the old earl down on my own. I've always hated him. My apologies, Mr. Ryder. You're in there, too, I take it?"

Three more raps. And words, but too muted for her to make any sense of what they were.

Frederica flew to the servants' quarters, a long block on the ground level near the kitchens. She knew just where to find young Kenny—she'd nursed him through various illnesses over the years. When she knocked on his door, he opened it within seconds. She was astonished to find him dressed, a hat on his head and a small satchel on the floor.

"Where on earth are you going?"

"I've g-got to go. The earl is back."

Warren had mentioned how upset young Kenny was last night. It was beginning to make more sense to her now.

"No, no. He's not. He's dead, Kenny. And I need your help."

"I saw him yesterday. I shut the door, but he'll get out."

"You were in the long gallery?"

The man nodded.

Frederica realized at once what Kenny had seen. "I think you mis-understood. There's a door behind the painting, isn't there? The duke and his friend Mr. Ryder must have found it, and they are now shut inside the wall. You have to help me get them out."

Kenny shook his head stubbornly. "The earl came down off the wall and went to find his treasure."

"Oh, Kenny." Frederica placed a hand on his sleeve. "The bad man is dead. Truly. I won't let anyone hurt you. You trust me, don't you?"

Young Kenny looked down at his belongings. "I want to go."

"And so you shall, later, if you must. But please, please help me first."

He picked up the canvas bag. "All right. Where are we going?"

Frederica thought it best to get Kenny to the long gallery first without going into detail. "Just follow me. You'll be all right. I have my sword there at the ready."

She pushed him forward through the dark castle, her candle cast-ing ghoulish shadows on the walls. Young Kenny's skittishness was catching. Why did she want to spend the rest of her life in this dismal place?

He balked a bit when they got to the arch of the gallery and he heard the continuous knocking on the wall. "Hold your horses!" she shouted. She turned to Kenny. "It's only Sebastian and his friend. Help me get the painting down, and then you can go."

He was rooted to the spot, worrying his lip, his anxiety acute. "*Please*. They've been in there all night." She slipped her arm in his as if they were going to take a stroll.

Young Kenny took a deep breath and stepped with her to the end of the gallery. They stopped before the portrait of the last Earl of

Archibald. The man's blue-green eyes stared at them, disdainful and distant. Kenny touched the frame, shuddering. Then he set his bag on the floor, took the painting down from its hook in the wood paneling and gingerly angled it into the corner. "There. Safe and sound. I didn't break the frame before, either. I didn't mean no harm, I swear, Miss Frederica. S-saw the wall open and the picture on the floor yesterday. Thought when it fell—it might've been his spirit, see, trying to get free. Come right to life again, the villain."

Good heavens. Young Kenny had known all along something was wrong in the picture gallery, but he hadn't the wit to associate Sebastian's disappearance with the fallen painting. She patted his arm. "Of course you didn't mean any harm. Thank goodness the frame was chipped, else I would not have thought to look behind it." She turned her attention to the intricate wall. "Sebastian, I cannot see any sort of opening. Is there a trick to get in somehow?"

Three quick raps followed her question. Ah, good. He could understand what she said. She smoothed her hands down on the carvings, pressing and twisting the bumps, but nothing happened. "Maybe we need tools. A saw or something."

"Let me try." Kenny slapped the flat of his hand up and down the wall until he hit the center of a raised diamond and the wall cracked open.

Sebastian grinned up at them from the floor, his face smudged and clothes filthy and wrinkled, his foil across his lap. Frederica did not know when she'd seen anything more beautiful.

"Good morning," Sebastian whispered.

"Can't talk," Mr. Ryder wheezed. "Screamed and banged all night."

"I didn't realize. I heard sounds—we all did. I'm so very sorry."

Young Kenny was rolling his cap around in his hands. " 'Tis my fault, Your Gr-grace. H-he clouted me, you know, the earl, when I was just a lad. My mam was cook here then, and I helped her like I help you, Miss Frederica. Saw something I shouldn't, but I can't remember what. He hit me until I saw stars and moons inside my head. I d-didn't want him after me again, so I p-pulled the wood p-panel shut. And tied up the wire nice and tight again with one of my knots and hung the old earl back up." He paused for breath. She had never heard him speak so many words at once. "I've listened to the Walkers all my life here. Didn't want to hear them no more, specially the old earl. I'm going to run away, but I got nowhere to go. And now the duke is mad, and I'm sorry."

"It's all right, Kenny," Frederica said softly. "The duke doesn't hold a grudge. Do you, Your Grace?"

"All's well that ends well. If you can bear to stay on at Goddard Castle, I'm sure you'll be welcome," Sebastian croaked. The speech put him at the limit of his vocal ability. He held a hand to his throat.

"Of course you must stay!" Freddie said warmly, clasping young Kenny's hand. "The duke is leaving anyway. I imagine you all would like some breakfast. I'll rouse Mrs. Holloway so you can be on your way."

It was imperative she get away from Sebastian before she said anything she might regret. Like how she spent much of the night worrying about him. Taking back all the dreadful things she said to him yesterday. Fantasizing he was with her in her room, touching her. Kissing her. Fucking her.

She found Mrs. Holloway already up and lighting the stove. After Frederica explained what had happened, she knew the men would be forgiven for skipping supper. Now all she needed to do was avoid them until they left later. She did hope that their departure would not be delayed by their uncomfortable night.

She was halfway up the staircase when Mr. Ryder called out to her.

She pretended not to hear him, not difficult as his voice was cracked and barely audible. But he chased after her, catching her by the arm. She pulled away, annoyed.

"You'd best watch yourself. After your adventure last night, I shouldn't want to watch you to pitch down and crack your skull."

"Point taken. Is there somewhere we may talk privately?"

"Mr. Ryder, I feel quite done with talking, and you shouldn't strain yourself. Everything that's needed saying has been said. To death. I'm glad you and Sebastian suffered from no permanent ill effects, but I am more than prepared to say good-bye to you both."

"And good riddance." He smiled down from his superior height. It was very hard for her to hold him in aversion. He'd been charm personified while they shared their meals the past few days, relating amusing stories about his adventures with Sebastian. She'd been pathetic, hanging on his every word.

"It's nothing personal. I feel no animosity toward you."

"No, just animosity toward poor Sebastian. Miss Wells, if you would give me a minute of your time—"

She sighed. "Oh, very well. A minute, but no longer. Mrs. Holloway is fixing your breakfast. Perhaps a spoonful of honey will help your throat. Some hot tea, too."

"What I have to say is of the utmost importance," he rasped.

"Good gracious. Well, then, come along to my room."

Her room was extremely tidy, considering she'd cleaned it most of her sleepless night. She took a chair by the window and invited Mr. Ryder to do the same.

"I told Sebastian to declare his feelings for you," he said, coming right to the point.

Her heart skipped a beat. "What feelings?"

"If he is not in love with you, and you with him, I will volunteer to spend another night in that cursed, bat-infested tunnel."

Frederica allowed that precious minute to tick away. Had she heard him correctly? His voice was very weak. "Did he tell you that he loves me?" she asked at last, almost afraid of the answer.

"No, not Sebastian. The word is not in his vocabulary, poor fellow."

The disappointment coated her own throat, making her next words difficult. "Then how can you know?"

"Miss Wells, Sebastian and I were imprisoned together for eight very long months, and were friends before that. One comes to know a man—almost too well—under such circumstances. Sebastian loves you. I am sure of it, by everything he *doesn't* say. He thinks himself unworthy, and will spare you from the lifetime of heartache he's sure he'll bring you. In his own boneheaded way, he's trying to be honorable. To do the right thing."

"He's much too late for that," Frederica murmured.

"Yes. Well. He's not shared what has transpired between you two, and it's none of my affair." He coughed, and Frederica leaped up to pour him a glass of water from the jug on her dresser. "Thank you. I'll give my vocal cords a rest now, but you should know where things stand. If he doesn't come to you, you should go to him."

*Never.* Not again. Frederica needed to put the past behind her once and for all. "Thank you for your concern, Mr. Ryder. Have a safe journey home." She held out her hand, and was surprised when he kissed her on the cheek instead.

"Sebastian may be a fool, but he's your fool, Miss Wells. Give him a chance to explain."

But Sebastian had already said quite enough.

# Chapter 38

*The best day of my life.*
—FROM THE DIARY OF SEBASTIAN GODDARD,
DUKE OF ROXBURY

*The best day of my life!*
—FROM THE DIARY OF FREDERICA WELLS

Sebastian arranged for tea to be served in the solar, and Freddie to be fetched from her room where she'd locked herself away all day. He was feeling almost human, and had been sucking on Mrs. Holloway's horehound drops for hours. His voice was still not strong, but he would use it, even if his words did no good. He could not leave things as they were between them when he left, not after last night. He would shake young Kenny's hand, too, for the poor man had made a difference quite by accident.

This time Sebastian was sitting in the shaft of sunlight when Frederica entered the room. He hoped the sight of him dazzled her as she had dazzled him all those days ago. He tried a wobbly smile.

"Hallo, Freddie."

She was all wrapped up like a gray parcel, edges stiff and neat. No matter how she disguised herself, Sebastian knew what was inside.

"I thought you would have left by now."

"Yes. Well. I haven't yet." He took a breath. "Cam told me I must tell you of our captivity in Egypt."

Frederica shook her head. "There's no need. You are leaving, and it's none of my business anyway."

"I don't want to leave," he blurted.

"Pardon me?"

"Well, I take that back. Yes, I do want to leave. Very much. I'd like to never set foot in Goddard Castle again. But I don't want to go quite yet."

"I don't understand."

Sebastian twisted his father's ring on his finger, the sapphire winking dully. "I don't suppose you do. But after last night——" He patted the sofa. "The time in the hidden passage was remarkably instructive. Young Kenny actually did me a favor, if you can believe it. Come, Freddie, sit down. This conversation need not take long. You can cry rutabaga at any time."

She didn't glide across the room at his invitation, just looked reluctant to come anywhere near him. He supposed he deserved her hesitation.

"But Mr. Ryder is waiting on you to leave."

"Cam's been gone this past hour. He and his carriage are bouncing through the moors. I believe he feels he overstayed his welcome."

"Why didn't you go with him?"

"I've just said. I need to talk to you. Explain."

She sat down, looking as if she landed on tacks. "Explanations are unnecessary. We mean nothing to each other, after all. This was just a business arrangement on my part. I whored myself, as you so succinctly put it. On yours, you sought to punish me for my idiocy all those years ago. Well, I'm suitably chastened. I will never give myself to another man again unless I lose my wits completely."

He reached for her hand. "Hush, Freddie. You're making my head ache."

"You *are* a headache."

"I daresay I've done nothing else these past few days but convince you of that. But perhaps I'm a changed man."

Freddie curled a scornful lip.

"Hear me out. I'm not perfect. Far from it. You don't know how much, but I'd like to tell you."

"If this confession will make you leave all the sooner, I'm all ears, Your Grace."

She was as brittle as bone china. Sebastian had faced many difficult challenges in his short life, but the next few minutes were bound to be its worst. But Cam had seemed to think it was necessary, and he trusted Cam with his life. He took another deep breath.

"You know a little about Egypt, but not the whole of it."

"I know you tried to loot their national treasures," she said primly.

"Not true. Not with Cam, anyway. Ours was a legitimate endeavor. We went hat in hand to a relative of the viceroy, begging for permission to begin a dig in an area which had somehow escaped all the other treasure hunters' attention. Cam has a sixth sense about such things—he knows where the holy grails are in one's attic, so to speak. He was certain we would find enough booty for our share and the government's. Akhom Ali had other ideas. After a night of exceptional food and wine and dancing girls, we found ourselves stripped naked in the man's cellar. He didn't like Englishmen, you see. Thought we were all depraved debauchers of young Egyptian girls."

"And were you?"

"Not on the scale of some of my other compatriots. Henry Kipp, to be specific. We were handy substitutes for Ali's revenge. He was a brilliant bastard. Are you familiar with the writings of the Marquis de Sade?"

Freddie shook her head.

"No matter. Ali wasn't, either, I don't imagine, but he surpassed the marquis in his plans for us anyway. He wanted our total capitulation, and he got it, by various means."

"I—I've seen your back. And Mr. Ryder's."

"That was the least of it. When you last saw me ten years ago, I'd developed a bit of a bad habit. I smoked opium on occasion. But after that night you came to me in my fog, I swore off the stuff. Wanted my wits about me in case I fell prey to the next mysterious milkmaid. I missed it, but made do. There were plenty of other diversions for a young man earning his way across the Continent and northern Africa. But Ali discovered my weakness, and provided me with just enough to get me in its thrall again."

Freddie shifted uncomfortably in her seat. "That's dreadful."

Sebastian smiled at her understatement. "Yes, rather. But useful for his machinations. He wanted to bring me low, Freddie. A heathen duke's son. Teach me my true place in his world. I did what I was told, or I was beaten. Even worse—when I displeased him, Ali withheld my daily dose of opium. I became an addict in his prison, Freddie, not the dabbler I was as a boy. I was enslaved to it. Ali used it to control me and what I would do with Cam. After a while, I did anything he asked. I had to."

"Oh, Sebastian."

Did she know what he meant? If she didn't, he must make it plain. "He thought it great sport to watch us. Sometimes he'd bring us up for the entertainment of his friends. Other times we performed solely for his pleasure. And our own, I'm sorry to say." He dropped her hand before she could withdraw it. "I did everything with Cam my father ever did with yours and more. Even when Ali wasn't watching, Freddie. It was all we had in that filthy black hole. I began to live for it."

The room was quiet as death. Sebastian felt his optimism draining from him with each word. Cam was wrong—this revelation of his past was not healing at all. He'd done nothing but repulse Freddie. Drive her away, forever beyond his reach.

Which was only as it should be. He had nothing to give her or any woman. "So, now you know everything. And I will leave you in peace."

He got as far as the solar door. Her voice was so low, he almost missed it.

"You—you and Cam. You gave each other comfort."

Sebastian leaned up against the stone wall, trembling hands in his pockets. "We never thought we'd get out alive, Freddie, so what did it matter what we did to survive the time we had? But we did get out. And then—"

"You lost yourself. I understand."

She couldn't. The space between them was wider than the length of the room. He didn't dare come closer. "No, you don't. I hardly understand myself. You weren't far wrong when you first accused me of needing my sexual partners to be helpless. In the beginning, I discovered I could not get excited until I restrained a woman as I was once restrained. Tied. Bound in darkness. Oh, I was never cruel, but I needed to be in control then. I need to be in control now. At all times. I wasn't for eight months, you see."

She nodded, so he felt emboldened to continue. "When we escaped, Cam sat with me night after night when the visions were so bad I wished I were still in gaol to get my pipe. Cam brought women to me—to us both—so we could prove to ourselves that what happened between us didn't matter. We may have left our honor behind, but by

God, we were still *men*. I found out I was not quite my old self. My usual sins—and there had been plenty of them—had no allure for me. So the games began."

"But you gave me power over you."

He gave her a half smile. "Admit it, Freddie, I nearly always got my way, even on your days. I'm clever that way. And you never tested me sexually."

Freddie paled. "Did you want me to whip you?"

"Lord, no! At least, I don't think so. I'm so mixed up, but there is one thing I do know." He shut his eyes to the pity in hers. "Last night in the dark, when all the old memories surfaced, I didn't want Cam's comfort. I wanted yours."

He stopped. It should be said—words he'd never uttered to any woman before—but somehow his tongue thickened. He came as close as he could. "I don't deserve you. I don't think I'll ever be natural again."

He heard the rustle of her skirts as she moved toward him, felt her touch his lip with a finger. He was afraid to lift his lids, afraid to hope, but found the strength to meet her cloudy blue eyes with his. If this was his last sight of her, he would drink in every second, preserve the tiny, curling golden hairs on her temple, the spangle of freckles on her cheeks, the rose blush of her mouth in his memory forever. She looked up at him, solemn.

"Someone once said to me, 'Who's to say what is natural? Man is imperfect.'"

"How can you remember that?"

"I remember everything, and somehow still manage to—like you. An old affliction, I suppose. There is nothing we did with each other that disgusted me in any way, Sebastian." She smiled. "Ah! I see I've shocked you. It shocks me, too, but I can say it with complete confidence that just as you said you would, you have corrupted me and taught me to enjoy it. Except—as I once told you, I could never have shared my bed with you. Not with other women." She blushed. "Not with Cam. I would have had to be enough."

She was more than enough. She was everything.

He allowed himself to slip his fingers into the silk of her hair. Just to touch her brought him a measure of peace. "I don't want Cam anymore. I had wondered, you know. Wondered if I could fall back into the old habit. It was always in the back of my mind. He's a handsome devil," he joked, feeling very near tears. "Of course, we only spent one night in confinement. Who knows what might have happened if you hadn't found us? If I got desperate? Turned to him in our last hours—"

She shoved him. "Sebastian, don't borrow trouble! What does it matter who or how you loved before? None of us knows what we're capable of unless we're pressed to our limits. I understand that the bond you forged with Cameron Ryder in Egypt is unbreakable. I respect that, and don't think any less of you. You were brought to your wit's end by a madman. But you are free now. Truly free. A duke. And when you release my funds to me, you'll have money to stave off your creditors and build a life at Roxbury Park for yourself."

He'd almost forgotten—she didn't know. She didn't know he was, for all intents and purposes, rich. She didn't know he loved her. "Our deal is off," he said softly.

She took a step backward. "What?"

"If you want Goddard Castle, it is my gift to you. And I'll release your inheritance as well. No strings attached."

"But—you can't! What will become of you?"

"Don't worry about me. I'll sign whatever needs to be signed."

She looked confused, but happy enough. He was doing the right thing, was he not? Apart from leaving her here in Yorkshire to trip over falling debris. But he couldn't let her think he was being self-sacrificing, not with a fortune of precious stones in his pocket.

"I've told you what didn't happen last night, but haven't told you what did. We found Archibald's treasure in the secret passage, Freddie, all handily converted to diamonds and rubies and emeralds and whatnot. So, Cam and I are set, or we will be when we visit a reputable jeweler. I'm thinking I might have better luck disposing of them on the Continent—I wouldn't want to attract the king's attention to my sudden prosperity."

She blinked, just once. Sebastian wasn't expecting congratulations, but her lack of surprise surprised him. "So you don't need my money."

No, he needed only her, but for once he would do what was right.

"Not at all. Not one penny. And you're to keep the royalties from the books. It is iniquitous that they'd be paid to my father's estate when you are their primary author. I'll see to it."

She straightened her shoulders. "Very well, then. Have a safe trip, Sebastian, wherever you're going." She extended her left hand, as she was wont to do after one of their fencing bouts. He wondered if she wished she had a sword in her right hand to dispatch him.

"Thank you, Freddie."

Her hand was firm and dry, her face expressionless. Her composure was his undoing. Somehow he could not bring himself to lift the latch on the door. "Would it be too much to ask for a good-bye kiss? I swear I won't let it go beyond that."

Her voice was barely above a whisper. "What if *I* do? What if I want to throw you down on that ratty sofa and ride you to oblivion? Make you realize, you stupid man, that I love you and have since I was too young to know better?"

Sebastian felt his jaw go slack.

"Stop gaping at me like a booby! Do you really think you can slink out of here as if nothing ever happened between us? Fob me off with castles and book royalties?"

"It's just the one castle. I haven't any others."

Freddie ignored his lame attempt at a joke. "I suppose you think you're being noble, removing yourself. Pretending that you're doing me a favor. That you're too damaged. Not good enough for me. Do I have it right?"

He felt the beginnings of a smile. "You're pretty close."

"Mr. Ryder told me you would do this."

"What?"

"Oh, he didn't disclose the details of your incarceration, but he told me you loved me too much to fight for me."

That was it, precisely. "I do."

"When did you plan on telling me?"

He shrugged. "Never. There didn't seem to be a point. You were so furious with me, you know. It seemed best to leave you that way."

"Coward!"

"Yes, rather. I've just told you in great detail I'll do anything to save my skin. And you, you stupid woman," he said, throwing her words back at her, "are ignoring all the warnings."

"But I *am* a woman now, Sebastian, not some eighteen-year-old with stars in her eyes."

"No, what you've got now is grit—it's a wonder you can see at all. What if—what if I can't make you happy, Freddie? What if we have children and I fail them as a father?"

"Are you *proposing*? If you are, that is the worst proposal in all of history, and I am considered an expert historian."

Good God. He *had* proposed, after a backhanded fashion. He had only uttered his fears aloud, thoughts that had bruised him for days.

He wanted Freddie, wanted her enough to marry her, money or no money. Sebastian wanted to fence with her, and fuck her senseless, and build some sort of a future. But how, when his needs were so at odds with what a proper husband's should be?

"I don't think marriage will work, Freddie."

She scowled at him. "I never said I'd marry you!"

"No, but if you did, and we married, I'm not sure I'd be any good at it."

"I should make a horrible wife myself."

"Not at all. You already do all sorts of housewifely things. Keep this castle in order, for example, with very little help. Make your lotions and potions. Look after the local people. You're a veritable saint."

She began to unravel another tapestry with an inky finger. "But I shut myself up for days in the library to write. It will take me years to complete the history series, even if I have no distractions. A husband, particularly if he was you, would be a distraction. And children would—would be a major distraction."

"Yes. Unpredictably demanding, too, the little buggers. Wanting to be fed and then puking. And what they do in their nappies." He shuddered. "I wouldn't want to change them. But I suppose with all my newfound wealth, I could hire a fleet of nurses. You could just look in on them at night when they were sleeping."

"That's no way to raise children! And if they were yours, they'd probably never sleep anyway, but just dream up more ways to torment me."

"And if they were yours, they would never hold their tongues but drive me mad with their demands. 'Read me this, Papa. Teach me this, Papa, so I might be as smart as Mama.' I'd be useless. They'd run circles around me."

"We could hire a good governess."

"But if they were like me, they'd chase after her with fencing foils and drive her away."

Freddie smiled. "Poor Miss Davies. I remember her. You were so very wicked, Sebastian."

"I was, wasn't I? I'm not much better now."

"Oh, I don't know. You have your charms."

"Do I, Freddie? Are my charms enough? Could you marry me, even knowing everything?"

Her golden lashes dropped to her cheeks. "I should say no."

He brought her hand to his heart. "Please, please don't. Don't say no."

"Must I obey you? Is this my day or your day? I forget."

"Damn the day! Tell me yes, Freddie."

He watched her mouth form the one simple word and swept her in his arms before she had a chance to change her mind.

# Epilogue

DORSET, JUNE 1823

*I am afraid I am far too busy to write in this diary.*
—FROM THE DIARY OF FREDERICA, DUCHESS OF ROXBURY

It was said throughout England that the Duke of Roxbury was a reformed man, and his stout little bluestocking duchess the inexplicable reason for his transformation. Many ladies and gentlemen of quality were deeply disappointed that the God of Sin had abandoned them for the prosaic life of farmer and father. But Sebastian had not quite lost all his wickedness—he was simply more judicious in applying it.

Sebastian tugged the small teardrop sapphire between his teeth.

"The children—"

"Are asleep." His tongue tangled in the filigree ring holding the jewel that pierced his wife's breast. Her adornments were just one of the uses to which he'd put the Archibald treasure. They gave him far greater pleasure than the new seed drills and iron ploughs, although they, too, had their place at Roxbury Park. "Phillippa has bullied Joe all day. She reminds of someone. You, perhaps?" He evaded her swat.

"Anyway, they went down immediately after their story. They're both exhausted."

"But the baby—"

"Is with his nurse. Hush, and let me love you."

"As if I could stop you."

"You could try, but you wouldn't get very far." To prove his point he slipped the silk around her wrists and ankles, cinching her tight. Tonight was his turn, his way. Who knew what Freddie would devise for his pleasure tomorrow? She was very inventive—three children in five years were living proof.

He settled himself between her legs and feasted, earning every breathless cry, wondering why he was so fortunate in his choice of wife. Surely he didn't deserve her, but he wasn't sending her back to Goddard Castle, not that he could. Freddie had sold that grim pile to Cam, and it was Archibald Castle once more. All its mildewy and moldy books and artifacts were littered about Freddie's study here, where it really was difficult to maneuver. He'd tripped over the battered silver reliquary holding some saint's baby teeth more times than he could count as he attempted to tempt her from her studies.

His children, poor little devils, were having their heads filled with medieval ballads and poems instead of lullabies and nursery rhymes. Likely they would grow up begging to go to the Holy Land on crusade. And if they ever did, he'd accompany them to show them the more diverse and less holy amenities the East had to offer. This fatherhood business was no picnic, but he was surprised how well it suited him.

Satisfied that his wife was ready, he set upon a crusade of his own—to keep her heart, to bind her to him beyond silk. To show her she had cut the knots of his own bondage and set him free to love.

He didn't want to fuck Freddie.

He wanted to make love to her.

In fencing terms, she had made an *enveloppement*—she swept his blade through a full circle and attacked his heart. He was back once again in her arms, right where he belonged.